The Heart of Courage

A Novel of the French and Indian War

Blessings
Lynne

LYNNE BASHAM TAGAWA

Blue Rock Press

The Heart of Courage: A Novel of the French and Indian War

Blue Rock Press

5606 Onyx Way

San Antonio, TX 78222

Scripture quotations from the King James Version, public domain.

The Heart of Courage is a work of historical fiction. Apart from well-known actual people, events, and locales, all names, characters, and incidents are the product of the author's imagination or are used fictitiously. All similarities to actual persons are purely coincidental.

Library of Congress Control Number: 2020912304

Cover art: JD Smith Design

To all the men and women
who risk their lives
to bring the gospel to the
unreached peoples of the world

The Valley

~John and Abigail Russell and their children: Susanna, Jonathan, Nathan, and Hannah

~Robert "Roy" Russell, John's cousin, and his wife Elizabeth "Lizzie" and their children

~Archibald "Arch" May, John Russell's elderly factor and his wife Agnes

~William Russell "Grandda," John Russell's father

~James Paxton, John Craig's student

~Samuel and Maggie McClure, owners of a store in Staunton

~Thomas Kerr, the weaver, and his family

~Robert Houston, landowner (grandfather of General Sam Houston)*

~John Craig, minister, and his wife Isabella*

~Andrew Lewis, son of John Lewis, first settler in the area*

~James Patton, militia colonel, landowner, surveyor, and sheriff of Augusta County*

~William Preston, nephew of James Patton*

*Real historical figures

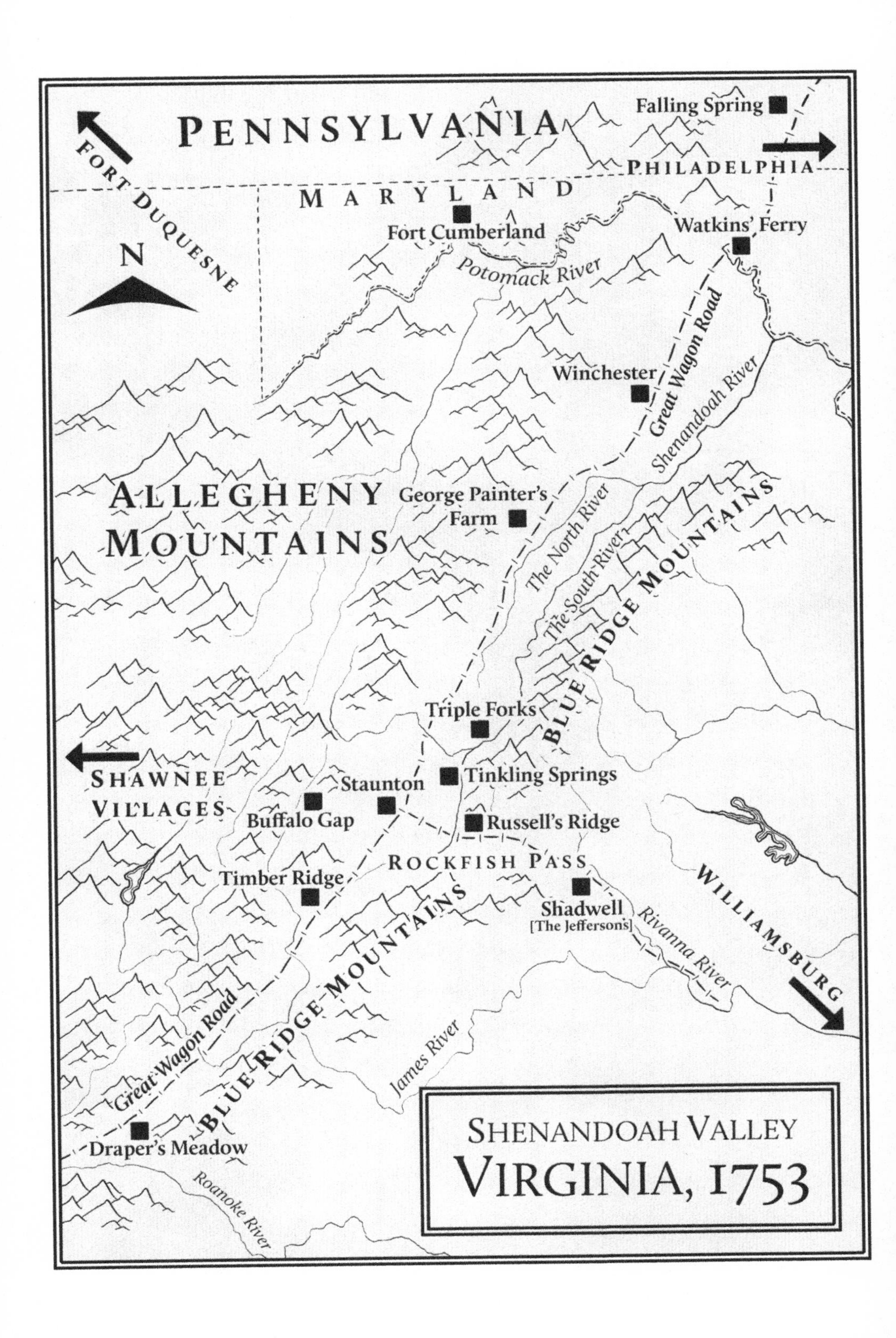
PENNSYLVANIA
Falling Spring
PHILADELPHIA
FORT DUQUESNE
MARYLAND
Fort Cumberland
Watkins' Ferry
N
Potomack River
Great Wagon Road
Winchester
Shenandoah River
ALLEGHENY
MOUNTAINS
George Painter's
Farm
The North River
The South River
BLUE RIDGE MOUNTAINS
Triple Forks
Tinkling Springs
SHAWNEE
VILLAGES
Staunton
Buffalo Gap
Russell's Ridge
ROCKFISH PASS
Timber Ridge
Shadwell
[The Jeffersons]
Rivanna River
WILLIAMSBURG
BLUE RIDGE MOUNTAINS
Great Wagon Road
James River
Draper's Meadow
Roanoke River
SHENANDOAH VALLEY
VIRGINIA, 1753

1

To thee I lift my soul:
O Lord, I trust in thee:
My God, let me not be ashamed
Nor foes triumph o'er me.

—Psalm 25:1-2, *Scottish Psalter*

June 1753

Susanna Russell bounded out the door, grabbed the bait bucket and fishing pole from the shed, and loped down the rutted path. At last she was free.

Free from her baby sister's fussing, free from the admonitions of her father, and from the house itself, whose walls had seemed to close in upon her all morning as she bounced the babe on her hip. Mother was in the garden, and of course her brothers were at their lessons with Grandda, unable to help.

Lessons. She was too old for lessons, and that was another thing.

A sudden gust threatened her hat, and Susanna clapped one hand upon it as she trotted toward her favorite place, descending the slope, past nodding leaves of Indian corn growing thick beyond the split-rail fence and friendly golden ragwort crowding the footpath. Only the ancient stonewall marking the property line seemed properly sober and grim, its mortar crumbling, the structure abandoned by some long-ago inhabitant.

Cheerful foliage cloaked the river ahead, calling to her. She made her way along the bank to the fishing spot marked by willow branches leaning over the water, their long leaves skimming the surface.

Susanna kicked off her moccasins. Her straw hat went sailing underneath the willow. Her hair—she'd leave that up. Wisps of breeze floated past, cool on her neck. She squished her toes in the soft brown clay of the riverbank and inhaled deeply, but even the sweet scent of tulip tree blossoms failed to settle her.

She sighed and fingered her red linsey skirt. There was no way to sit on the riverbank without getting it muddy. *Unless.* She'd slipped on her snug breeches underneath before she left—somehow they'd shrunk drastically over the past year—and decided that if she slipped her skirt up just so, she could sit. Only the hem of her skirt would get soiled, and she could rinse it afterward in the river.

She eased herself down and slipped a grub on the hook. Casting firmly, she managed to land the cedar bob midstream, where the water ran slow and clear, glimmering silver and turquoise in the sun. She breathed deeply, trying to absorb the peacefulness of her favorite place. But her father's words nagged at her.

"Susanna, we need to speak with ye." Her father's voice had cracked strangely. Mother seemed worried. Both pairs of blue eyes were fixed on her. John Russell, tall, strong, a fine shot and the bravest man she knew, was having trouble. "Dinna be alone with a lad."

What did he mean? Mother was studying the table—no help there. "You can't mean my brothers."

Da choked. "No, no."

"You are fourteen, soon to be a woman," Mother said. "And—"

"Young men will come nosing about, like stags in—"

"John."

Her father's mouth opened and closed. "Aye," he said, nodding at Mother then looking at her. "It is too soon for courtship. Until then I want ye safe."

Susanna's face burned. She knew what courtship and marriage were, although those things still seemed far away. Why, only last year she'd wrestled Seth Robinson, who'd shoved a toad down her shift. He wouldn't do that again.

"And no more wrestling the lads."

Da knew?

She sighed. Her world was tightening around her. She stared at the water, its twinkling current mesmerizing her. If only she could be free like the river, free to travel. Mentally she traced the path of the water as it made its way to the northern edge of Augusta County, joining two other tributaries and forming the South Fork of the Shenandoah.

Da had taken her once to a German settlement far down the valley to sell furniture and trinkets. They'd picnicked next to the Shenandoah, watching the birds dive for fish. He had pointed out the great loops of the river, playful rapids alternating with long shady stretches where fish abounded. But she'd never seen the ferry, only fingered the place on the map where the Shenandoah poured itself like an offering into the Potomac River and headed to the sea.

Nor, for that matter, had she seen Williamsburg, the vibrant capital of Virginia. She imagined ladies in silk gowns dancing with men in bright waistcoats. According to the *Gazette,* a theater hosted plays. If only—

The float bobbed, once, then twice. Susanna jumped to her feet. The cedar disappeared, and a moment later, the fishing pole was nearly wrenched from her hands. A trout! And it had to be a big one.

She waded into the river, giving the fish room to run, then pulled up and back. For long minutes she repeated the process, battling the trout —if trout it was—the sun on her head, hands fighting for grip. Susanna shoved the rod into the soft silt of the riverbed and slid her hands higher. She refused to lose it, but her shoulders were beginning to ache. How long could she keep it up?

Suddenly the tension on the line vanished. Susanna lifted the pole out of the bed and retreated, taking in the slack. Was it still there? Had it stolen the bait? Fish were canny as some folks, her father said. She searched the still surface of the water.

Ripples erupted, followed by a splash.

"Caught you!"

Encouraged, she backed out of the water and up the bank a few steps, then braced the pole against the soft mud and waited. A tug—she jerked back with all her might, and a huge fish flopped on the ground in front of her.

She stared at the gasping mouth and gills, scales glistening as the body arched and wriggled, tail slapping the mud with as much force as Auntie Agnes beating a bearskin bedcover. That was no trout. She'd heard Arch May speak of bass, but had never seen one. Whatever it was, the fish was huge. She didn't dare string it in the usual way—it would get loose. No, she'd—

A shadow fell over the fish.

Susanna turned and looked up. Sunlight stabbed her eyes, haloing a tall form. Who was that?

Hard dark eyes and brown cheekbones towered over her.

She gasped. An Indian.

~

JAMES PAXTON ADJUSTED the leather strap holding his satchel against his hip, conscious of his cargo, a borrowed copy of a book the minister wished to return to John Russell: Samuel Rutherford's *Lex, Rex*.

Translated, *The Law and The King*, according to Mr. Craig, the minister and also his tutor. With a lift of his bushy eyebrows, Mr. Craig had asked his students why law came before king. Why not *Rex, Lex?*

James stepped away from the well-beaten track through the knee-high grass, aiming for the cool shade of the trees near the river. Any first-year Latin student could translate that title, but his instructor always pointed out the implications of a statement.

"What does Caesar mean when he says, '*Veni, vidi, vici*'?" Mr. Craig had asked William Preston one winter day, the other student older than James but late to Latin.

"I came; I saw; I conquered?"

Mr. Craig snorted. "Aye, and we ken what he did. He won the battle! Tell me more. What does it reveal about the man?"

William ran his fingers through his thick blond hair. "That he was a good general?"

The minister's piercing gaze fell on James. "Anything else?"

James wasn't afraid to best his friend. The twenty-three-year-old Preston eyed James cheerfully, not jealous of his aptitude for languages. Preston's uncle, an important landowner, had sent his nephew to the minister to learn the mathematics necessary for surveying. History and Latin were less important.

James cleared his throat. "From Plutarch we learn that while Caesar was self-disciplined and fair in many ways, he was ambitious. He had courage, intelligence, and ambition, and at the last, his ambition caused him to overreach, and his friends killed him."

Mr. Craig leaned back in his chair, his gaze returning to William. "A man's words reveal the heart. Is there a connection?"

Young Preston sat straighter, his broad shoulders evident beneath his leather jacket. "It is a singular statement, sir. Definitive. He did not doubt himself, nor give credit to God."

Mr. Craig chuckled. "And yet, he was superstitious. The Romans and Greeks tended to be, ye ken—what with their pantheon of gods and goddesses, as liable to play a trick on ye as help ye. Remember that when ye go to Williamsburg with your uncle. The whole Tidewater is mad for 'the classics,' and they name their slaves and animals after Romans."

William's eyes flickered toward James at that moment. Preston must be thinking about his fine bay colt Marius, named after a Roman general. The previous year the young man and his horse had departed with his uncle for Log's Town, an important expedition, he'd said. Something to do with the Indians. And a treaty.

As for himself, he had no horse, nor mule, only a head crammed full of Latin and history and a smattering of Greek. *En arche en ho Logos ...* He loved Greek; how could he not? Latin was the dusty language of dead emperors, but Greek was the language of the New Testament, and he longed to have more than a casual acquaintance with the sounds and shapes of the strange letters. He wanted to think in the language. Understand the Scriptures better.

James shook his head, focusing on the matter at hand. The Russells' place must be close; he'd been there several times before and knew the landmarks. He fingered the satchel, remembering the man John Russell, who'd helped construct the stone meetinghouse across the valley, though he and his kin attended Tinkling Springs, where Mr. Craig preached every other Sabbath.

James scanned the rolling wooded slope and the Blue Ridge just beyond. He'd already spotted the Tinkling Springs meetinghouse, the dark log structure peeping out behind the foliage on a knoll to his left. To his right was the river, and somewhere ahead was the landmark he was looking for, an old crumbling wall emerging from the grass like the ancient artifact of a long-lost civilization. Perhaps it was, he mused.

Something moved near the river, obscured by foliage. He caught a glimpse of a red skirt, then a man's hunting jacket. Then the naked brown back and black scalp lock of an Indian. A greeting froze in his throat.

James darted to his left, finding shelter behind the wide trunk of a large oak. Male voices carried on the breeze, but he couldn't discern the words. There was a girl—he'd seen a skirt. He felt for his knife, but there were two men; best he run up to the Russell house. He scanned the rolling terrain for the landmark. Yes, a gleam of white shone through the grasses just ahead.

He crouched and scuttled crab-like through the tall grass to his left, aiming for a stand of poplar. He peeked back at the scene from behind a new hiding spot.

Yes, a girl. He could see her clearly now: dark hair, tall. Was that Susanna Russell? She didn't seem to be hurt, but Indians took captives. He'd heard a few stories. Heart hammering in his chest, he made his way up the slope, careless of branches and clutching hawthorn. He had to tell her father.

He circled an apple orchard; there was not enough cover between the young trees. Having a vague sense now of where the house and other buildings were located, James plunged straight through the woods.

Suddenly, the ground gave way beneath his feet. Scrabbling and clawing, he fell into darkness.

2

And this gospel, in the course of providence, I have been called to preach, tho' most unworthy.

—Rev. John Craig, *Sermon*, 1764

"Oh, George, it's you." Susanna slumped in relief. "You startled me." She eyed the fish, still flapping wildly on the bank.

"Here, young'un, lemme help you." The huge man bent and scooped up the fish like a mere bluegill in the great paw of one hand. He grabbed a rock, struck the fish's head, and the bass lay still. George squatted, withdrew a knife, and in moments the fish was gutted.

She smiled her thanks. "Where are your mules?" George Morgan came through the valley at least once a year, exchanging skins and salt for goods he could trade with the Indians. George was an Indian himself, or maybe part Indian. He was dark, but very tall, spoke like a white person, and wore a shapeless hat over his black hair. In her mind, he wasn't really an Indian.

George turned. Behind him a half-naked Indian stood silently, watching her.

Susanna stilled.

Feathers attached to the man's braided forelock danced and eddied in the breeze. Deep lines in his brown face indicated age. A bright copper band circled one bicep, gleaming in the afternoon sunshine. He wore no shirt, only a breechclout and leggings.

Susanna gaped, conscious of her soiled skirt. "George ..." Why she called the trader by his Christian name she couldn't recollect just now. Even William Preston was "Mr. Preston" to all and sundry, especially now that his father had died.

"I have no manners, that be certain." The trader spoke a few words of what sounded like gibberish to the other man, concluding with, "Susanna Russell."

"Russell?" The Indian's chin jerked in acknowledgement. Was he some sort of chief? George seemed to defer to him.

She did her best to curtsey, wrestling with the damp skirt that clung to her breeches. "Pleased to meet you."

George continued the introductions, waving his hat. "Miss Russell, may I introduce" followed by a gabble of sound, "known to the English as Colonel Ayres."

The half-naked man made a proper bow and flourish, and Susanna wondered if she were fevered. The savage had courtly manners.

"He's pleased to meet you as we are looking for John Russell. Your father, if memory serves?"

She pointed. "Just that way. I'll take you." Her moccasins were under the tree near her hat, but her feet were muddy. Embarrassed, Susanna found a patch of dry grass, rubbed off the filth, and scrambled under the willow to try and make herself presentable. Not that she supposed the Indian would care, but his bearing and expression—or lack of it—made her think him an important man.

After stepping away from the riverbank, she saw George's mules, laden with goods, and a lanky man, sandy hair at all angles.

George introduced his assistant, but she only caught the fact that his name was Scottish. The young man nodded, his hands occupied with the animals. He didn't seem inclined to conversation, and neither did she, for that matter.

All Susanna wanted was for Da to take over this strange situation. She scooped up her pole and bucket and hurried toward the house.

JAMES SCRABBLED against the sides of an invisible rocky slope with his hands and feet as he fell, trying to stop his downward motion. Panic clutched at him—he couldn't see and had no idea if he were merely sliding into a small cave or about to fall off a cliff.

With a final bump, he came to a stop. Chest heaving, he tried to figure out where he was.

Darkness enveloped him, but slowly his eyes adapted, and he realized the blackness wasn't absolute. A spot of light high above gave him a reference point, at least. Some sort of underground cave? *Help, Lord,* he breathed.

Then the pain started. He'd wrenched a knee, it was clear. And his side hurt. He became aware of his hands after that, the lesser but irritating protest of scraped palms and fingers. James flexed his limbs and fingers experimentally. No, his injuries weren't serious.

He patted his satchel and fingered the flap. Miraculously, it hadn't been damaged. Opening it, he reached past the book, his fingers meeting the cool steel of his tinderbox. But what could he burn for light?

James explored his immediate surroundings with his fingertips. The smooth outlines of angular rocks felt hard and cold under his hands. But here and there, bits of rubbish—yes, bits of rubbish had fallen in with him.

That Indian—a Shawnee?

A long minute of careful scrounging yielded a small pile of leaves and twigs. He opened his tinderbox, making sure to set it on a flat surface; he couldn't lose that. He had no desire to scale the slope in total darkness. He extracted the flint and steel, cool and solid in his hands.

Strike. A shower of flaming sparks rained down on the leaves, like meteors against the night sky.

Strike. Strike. He fumbled, his hands moist with urgency.

And then, finally, a glowing spot. Carefully James nursed the ember until it burst into full flame. As it fed and grew, the flickering light revealed his immediate surroundings.

James glanced up the way he had fallen. Yes, he could escape. The rocks, so painful to slide upon, formed a staircase of sorts.

He turned and gasped.

Fire glittered from every angle. He had fallen almost to the floor of an immense cavern filled with pillars composed of a strange substance. Great pale projections hung from the ceiling like waterfalls frozen in midair. His tiny fire didn't reveal the back of the cave, only dancing shadows.

The flames faltered and James turned back. He had to get to the Russells'. There would be time to explore this discovery later.

Glancing up, he committed a path to memory, packed his tinderbox, snuffed the feeble fire, and climbed.

MOTHER HADN'T NOTICED the mud on her skirt hem. Having a real Indian at the table was a good distraction, Susanna decided.

Her father hadn't been troubled by the Indian at all. He'd sent her brother Jonathan off to help the young assistant get the mules settled, and they were still at the barn. George had greeted Mother with the fish, including a kind explanation that omitted any unladylike details. And somehow Susanna had managed to tidy her hair a little on the trek up to the house.

As they waited for Uncle Roy and Arch May to join them, Susanna helped her mother fetch ale and cider. Da and the visitors were apparently talking about salt.

"I can give you what I have left. I sold a bag to McClure," George said. "My people down south would supply you, if folks are willing to make the trip."

Susanna pulled pewter tankards off the shelves and set them on the table. The conversation turned.

"Ian has but one year left on his indenture. Would you be needing help right now?"

Apparently, the trader no longer needed the man's labor. Would they be acquiring a servant? This day was becoming even stranger.

Grandda's face appeared at the door, his keen blue eyes shining behind his spectacles. Arch May, Uncle Roy, and the young assistant followed. Jonathan slipped in the door, and soon the men were crowded about the table.

Agnes May hobbled through the doorway and sized up the crowd, her gaze lingering just a moment on the Indian. She was undoubtedly counting heads for supper.

Mother brought her the fish.

"Jonathan caught this?"

"No, ma'am," her brother said from the corner, his voice unusually formal. His gaze flitted back to the Indian. Nathan, his reddish-blond hair mussed, as usual, crouched next to his older brother and goggled at the newcomers.

"Susanna did." Mother handed Auntie Agnes a crock of cream.

"Och, and I ken weel what to do with this. A hearty Boston chowder."

Old Agnes seemed to take great delight in Mother's New England upbringing, receipts and all. Certainly Mother's soap was well thought of, not to mention her skill with herbs, and the factor's wife basked in reflected glory.

Agnes set to work at the hearth, and Mother slipped away to tend Hannah, who had chosen that moment to fuss. Susanna claimed the one remaining stool and found a place at the table.

Da addressed George. "How is trading?"

Susanna would have asked more important questions, but her

father seemed to be content with small talk for what seemed like a long time, finally inquiring into the health of Colonel Ayres's family and tribe.

George managed a running translation.

"The people fare well. Our chief has returned safely from his talk with the Six Nations."

Her father's form straightened. "George, the Catawba chief has been in negotiations with the Iroquois?"

"Yes, and I do know it sounds like the craziest thing," George said. "In fact, I'm escorting Colonel Ayres to Williamsburg, where he will catch a packet north. The treaty is still being finalized."

"But the Catawba have feuded with the Delaware for however long, and dinna care all that much for the Iroquois and vice versa." Her father was clearly surprised. "Now the Delaware have made some kind of agreement with the Six Nations and—"

"The Catawba have a good reason," George explained. The trader spoke to Colonel Ayres in the Indian's tongue and received a long response. The Indian's dark eyes flashed as he spoke.

George interpreted. "The French want the land to the north and west. They use no chains—he means surveying—but they want all the trade."

Susanna frowned. Why did a group of Indians to the south have any care about what went on in the north, or across the ocean, for that matter?

Something blocked the light from the open doorway, and Da tensed, then relaxed.

"Och, it's only you, lad. Care to join us?"

For a moment Susanna didn't recognize him, backlit as he was by the afternoon sun filtering through the trees. The young man's disheveled straw-blond hair brushed the lintel. He was tall and gangly —that wasn't unusual. But the expressive gray-blue eyes were unique. Jamie Paxton. Or should she say *James?* Surely now he deserved a more formal name.

He'd grown. Knobby wrists protruded from too-short homespun

sleeves, and the lines of his face were square and angular, no longer soft and boyish. Several years ago, at a wedding ceilidh, she'd challenged Jamie to a footrace. He'd won, but only just. Today she'd never keep up, not with those shanks.

And his shirt was torn and dirtied. What had happened?

~

JAMES PAXTON SAW the open door and knew he was too late. John Russell's sturdy new house had small windows on the ground floor, and his doors were thick oak with heavy crossbars. Like other homes in the valley, it was built with defense in mind.

But the front door was wide open. He paused at the threshold, terrified at what he might see.

The Indians were there. Well, one Indian, and George Morgan, the trader, whom he'd seen once or twice at McClure's dry goods shop. They were sitting at the table, along with all the men of the area, including redheaded Roy Russell, John Russell's cousin. Tankards were strewn about on the gleaming walnut surface, and the home-like odors of baking bread and sizzling pork filled the room. Shame warmed his face as he realized his mistake.

John Russell welcomed him and motioned to him to sit. Susanna bustled about, helping her mother with a cup and jug. Why, the lass was taller than her mother.

Their gazes met as Susanna passed him a wooden cup. Her eyes were a warm brown the color of strong tea. He already knew that, didn't he?

"Ale or cider?"

He fumbled a response. The men continued their discussion. Listening, James forgot the cavern.

"The Six Nations, especially the Mohawk, are inclined to side with the English. If the Seneca trade with the French, well, that's not necessarily an alliance. The Iroquois chiefs understand the strength of the British forces. And the colonies secure agreements with wagonloads of gifts. The Six Nations merely look out for their own interests, as the Catawba do."

James swallowed his ale. William Preston had gone to Log's Town for some agreement with the Indians. Could it be related?

John Russell signaled his daughter. "Would ye bring Emanuel's *Geography* in here, lass?"

Susanna darted off to another room. Returning with the volume, she handed it to her father. He quickly found the page he wanted and pushed the book in front of George and Colonel Ayres. Craning his neck, James could see a detailed map of the eastern seaboard, all the way from Quebec in the north to the Spanish-dominated land in the south.

George's eyebrows rose in delight, and Colonel Ayres cocked his head as he studied the drawing.

"Here's the Blue Ridge." Russell pointed to a spot on the map. "And here's Williamsburg ... Philadelphia ... Boston." His hand shifted. "Here's Quebec and the French forts and trading posts, all along here to the west and all the way to the wee settlement at the delta of the river." His finger traced a long arc.

James had never considered it. The French had them surrounded. And the French were not their friends.

"Ask Colonel Ayres two questions, if ye please. First, what would happen if the French went to war with us, and second, why is he treating with the Iroquois?"

George relayed the questions, and the other man looked around the table before answering in his strange language.

"The French have few warriors here, he says, and you know that much already. However, many Indians are friendly with the French and would fight on their behalf if asked—and the French will ask. The Indians will become their army."

The room became very still.

"Our chief is wise. He understands what will happen. Every white man's hand will turn against the red man. If we are not clearly in league with the English, we will be viewed as the enemy. Our chief fights for our people and our land, and he has convinced the elders to put away past grievances."

Roy Russell folded his arms across his chest. "What of the Shawnee?"

The Shawnee. The Shawnee lived just over the western ridges. Folks still referred to a man named Sloan who'd been killed by a Shawnee Indian not many years previous. Before that, Susanna's own mother had been killed by an Indian along with about a dozen men in what some called a massacre. Others said it was a misunderstanding turned tragic.

There hadn't been many incidents since, but everyone knew the stone meetinghouse had been built as a fireproof fort against Indian attack. They were on the fringe of civilization, and Williamsburg couldn't do anything to help them.

"The Shawnee have grievances with everybody." This from Russell's aged factor.

George tapped his fingers on the map. "They have been pushed around for many years. First by the Six Nations, and now white surveyors cross the Alleghenies."

His companion spoke, and George translated. "The Shawnee feel betrayed by the Lenni Lenape—the Delaware—because they make agreements with the Iroquois and with whites, and because some of them pray to the white man's god. I am told you are good men, and so we warn you. The Shawnee have been patient. They tend their crops, they hunt the deer. But when they go on the warpath, they are fierce fighters. We know. They have Catawba scalps, and we have theirs."

A baby cried somewhere.

"And ye think there will be war." Russell's statement sliced through the room.

George nodded. "I may not be back very often. At least, not until things settle."

His companion said something in his language. "He says all nations, not only the Catawba, will avoid the great valley. All fear the Shawnee."

James's stomach tightened. Their home had just been proclaimed a battleground. He decided to reveal his discovery. "Mr. Russell?"

Several heads turned.

He swallowed. "I ran up the slope and fell into a cavern."

The factor tapped his empty tankard on the table. "A cavern? A cave?"

"It's very large. A hidey-hole."

John Russell's expression shifted. "Where is it?"

3

Shawnees, your Nation has suffered much by French Devices by which you have been dispers'd. We exhort you that remain, that you keep firm hold of the great Chain of Friendship between us, the six Nations & their allies...

—*Treaty of Logstown,* 1752

Thirty miles west of the Great Valley

Red Hawk crouched under the shelter of a tall oak and studied the ground. The damp leaf litter was disturbed. He lifted himself slowly, breathing deeply, trying to get a sense of wind direction, which sometimes changed at a moment's notice on the higher slopes.

The breeze brushed his cheek like a kiss. *Good.* The buck he followed couldn't smell him. Just yesterday he'd scrubbed himself in the stream to make doubly sure; he had no clue how white men managed to hunt. Everyone said they smelled like skunks.

Red Hawk followed the trail up the slope where oak and maple gave way to pine and hemlock. Ahead he glimpsed a break in the trees near the top of the ridge. Had the animal descended into the next valley?

Sweat trickled down his neck. Yesterday's rain had done little to cut the summer heat, but at least the ground was damp, and he might find more sign.

There. The beautiful double print of a deer in a muddy spot. A good-sized buck, by the size of the depression, and the animal was moving slowly.

Heart quickening, he grasped his bow and removed two arrows from his quiver. The smell of juniper and cedar sharpened his mind as he skirted the clearing and negotiated a rocky outcrop.

The damp ground past the rocks revealed a partial print. Yes, he was on the right path. The buck was descending now, probably looking for the lush foraging available downslope.

He paused and scanned the landscape. The trees, the soil, even the rocks called to him, sang their own song, echoes from the hand of the Creator Himself. Red Hawk loved hunting, even though in the instant when the deer gave its life, its liquid eye dulling in death, he felt remorse and pain. His prayer to the spirit of the animal was always earnest. Laughing Wolf merely mumbled the words when he brought down a deer. Laughing Wolf seemed to enjoy killing for its own sake.

Something moved. Red Hawk tightened his grip on his bow and took a cautious step forward. The breeze had turned, but not enough to betray him.

A black-tipped ear flipped forward, then back, and a great rack of antlers appeared in the midst of the foliage ahead.

There wasn't much cover, just a single red spruce to his left. A laurel thicket rolled away to his right. Head low, he chose his steps carefully as he approached the thicket, his moccasins pressing soundlessly into the moist ground.

Suddenly the buck stiffened, his head in the air. Red Hawk drew and released two arrows, one after another, but even as they left his bow, he knew he'd missed. The deer's flashing rump disappeared up the slope to his left.

The animal hadn't fled from him. He'd made no sound. Had something else alarmed it? He stilled and took a slow breath. The birds began to chirp again, no longer threatened by his presence. Perhaps there was a bear nearby.

He flexed his hand around the bow, loving the feel of the smooth ash; his new weapon had enough draw strength to take down a bear, Father said. He ached for the chance. Would today be the day?

Red Hawk stepped around the thicket and made his way cautiously downslope. The smell of fire stopped him. Peering out from behind a chestnut tree, he saw the thin wisps of smoke above the foliage. There were men in the valley. But who? Shawnee or white men? He didn't know of any from his own village who had come this way today, but you never knew. Could be a trader.

Or not. Stomach prickling, he circled the tree and looked for a place where he might observe in secret. The elders would want to know about white men.

The thick green foliage to his right suggested a stream. He wriggled into the lush wet stillness, stepping on ferns and slick beds of moss until he found the soft narrow trickle at its heart. Hidden from view, he descended until he heard voices and the clank of a metal object. He left the tiny channel and took refuge behind a large beech. Were there dogs? He slid around the tree.

A mule and three horses drank from the stream below. A kettle perched above a campfire. A large silver-bearded man entered Red Hawk's field of view and attended the fire. Red Hawk sidestepped to a place behind a hawthorn patch and found a better view.

There didn't seem to be any dogs. He heard voices again, and now he could see the speakers. Nearest him stood a young man with hair the color of the sun; he held an object with one hand, and with the other he grasped a tiny stick. A vague sense of familiarity brushed Red Hawk's mind as he watched the man turn a leaf-like part of the object. A trader might have the sticks and leaves; perhaps that's where he'd seen them before. Then Hair-Like-The-Sun put the leaves in his bag and motioned to the other men. Silver Beard, a massive man, stood watching as the others busied themselves.

One of the horses, a fine chestnut with a wide blaze, raised its head. Red Hawk shrank within himself. Horses could smell. Then it turned slightly and dipped its head again. He exhaled.

A rope clanked as two men struggled to draw it out.

Chains. So these were the chains he'd heard his father mention. He settled himself to watch and listen.

RED HAWK FOLLOWED his father into Grayfeather's wigwam. The hearth glowed orange in the middle of the stale and smoky house. According to Grandmother, old people felt cold, but at this time of year, he wondered that anyone would desire more than a good jacket. Of course, there was always the need for fire when pipes were passed around; he'd forgotten about that. His own father rarely smoked. But this was an important gathering of the elders, and all the proprieties would be observed.

Feeling conspicuous, Red Hawk attempted to sit behind his father, but with a nudge and motion of his hand, his father directed him to his side. The other village elders murmured greetings to each other, but the tone of the gathering was subdued.

To one side of Grayfeather's seat a lance was propped, decorated by several dark scalps and turkey feathers, emblem of the old sachem's clan. But it had been a long time since the silver-maned man had wielded either bow or tomahawk in battle. The scarred war chief, Elk Tooth, sat at the right hand of the sachem.

"Red Pipe," Grayfeather said. "Tell us all your son saw."

His father used his long pipe to gesture as he told the others about the men and their chains. Elk Tooth narrowed his eyes at the news. In the shadows, Grayfeather's junior wife served something in a cup, stopping behind each man in turn.

The sachem packed his pipe. "How far is this?"

Father described the location, and a slow murmur rose in the dimness. They knew the spot.

Elk Tooth's dark eyes focused on Red Hawk. "Where did they go next?"

His throat felt dry. "They followed the stream north."

"Still, it is much too close." The light from the smoke hole illuminated the long knife scar on the war chief's chest. "I counsel we find their camp and raid them."

Red Hawk ran his palm along his new leggings. His shin itched underneath the deerskin, well tanned but still rather stiff. Dark Water had sewn them just last month.

"You grow like the cane," his aunt had teased. "You will surpass your father at this rate." He pretended to ignore her, but in truth, he'd take up his tomahawk and die to defend her, the only mother he had ever known. He trusted Grayfeather's judgment. He was ready to fight on his say-so.

He tried to ignore the itch as the men continued their deliberations. She-Who-Sings handed him a gourd cup. He took a large mouthful and handed it back to her, the liquid assailing his tongue with a stinging sweetness. He swallowed and his throat burned.

Father puffed on his pipe silently as the others spoke. He was the youngest of Grayfeather's council and even at home tended to be reticent.

The conversation finally died and Grayfeather spoke. "We leave for the Bread Dance soon. I will speak to Big Turtle."

Big Turtle, chief of the village on the Kanawha, kept the medicine bundle. This was proper, to consult with the spirits.

"I will also ask of news from the north. There was much wampum given at Sawkunk, and the Virginia Long Knives were there." He pulled at his pipe. "Peace is better than war."

Elk Tooth stiffened slightly. "The Six Nations have betrayed us. They give away land that is not theirs to give."

That was old news, and the murmur of agreement faded quickly.

"Our village is closer to the rising sun than most," Grayfeather told his war chief. "If war comes, it comes, and I will need every man's strength then. But the Shawnee have survived by adapting. Like the animals, we move to find the best ground, the best hunting. Some conflicts can be avoided."

The old sachem eyed Red Hawk. "The young men do not understand this. They want to boast of their prowess by coming home with scalps or horses."

Underneath Grayfeather's gaze Red Hawk wished to become invisible. He'd love a pony with which to impress Running Deer. The man could read minds.

Father spoke. "You suggest we move?"

"It may come to that. Either way, the women will speak first." The sachem coughed. "Elk Tooth, I want you to send out a couple of scouts. I want to know the location of their camp and their villages. Just in case."

Grandmother would be unhappy if they had to move. The last time, her favorite pot had shattered. And the soil here was good; the fields of the women stretched out fertile beside the river, bringing forth corn, beans, and round orange pumpkins in abundance. Their plum trees were almost full grown, and Dark Water's strawberries were thriving. Children ran about the village merrily, their bellies round. Hunger had not troubled them for years.

Red Hawk did not want to move either. The hills and ridges to the north and east were full of deer and smooth dark chert with which to make arrowheads, and in the winter, many families established camps in the Sacred Hunting Ground toward the setting sun, a place abounding in beaver and buffalo. The Muskogee and Uchee, favorite trading partners, lived not many days away to the south.

If they did move, like as not it would be only half a day's journey away. Perhaps a full day's march. He thought about the men with chains. About Hair-Like-The-Sun. They'd completed their task quickly, eaten, then loaded their animals and marked seven more places before Red Hawk returned to the village. Each chain was almost half the length of a bowshot. How many lengths did they mark each day?

It reminded him of a panther marking his territory. And whatever a panther marked, he would defend against invaders.

No, half a day's journey would not be enough to matter.

4

An Establishment on the River Ohio, is no new or partial Scheme of the French... but a Thing long ago concerted, and but Part of a grand Plan for rendering themselves Masters of North America.

—*The Pennsylvania Gazette,* May 16, 1754

March 1754

James exhaled abruptly as smoke from the tallow candle wafted toward him. In a month they'd be able to throw open the doors for light, but for now, the single winking flame was all that supplemented the daylight from the high, narrow windows in the cabin walls. He squinted at his Bible, open to the Gospel of Mark.

He missed William Preston. The young man had finished his studies and received his surveyor's license. He'd missed several

Sabbath meetings last summer while assisting his uncle surveying who knows where. Meanwhile James continued to work Mr. Craig's fields in exchange for instruction. And during the cold months he'd brought down several deer for the larder.

Across from him, Mr. Craig dipped his quill in their shared inkwell in the middle of the scratched pine table. Only a year ago, his mentor had taught him like a schoolboy, lashing him with questions, but now they spent long hours reading and writing in near silence.

James picked up the Greek New Testament and opened to Mark. The first section of chapter one was littered with every form of the Greek word for baptize he could think of, challenging his mastery of the language. Supposedly Mark was easier than John, but he was beginning to doubt it. He laid his forefinger on the page. Baptism with the Holy Ghost? What was the definition of baptize anyway?

He cracked open the lexicon, but the Greek swam before his eyes. Andrew Lewis had left before dawn this morning to meet with a militia officer appointed by Governor Dinwiddie. They were to build fortifications, Lewis had explained the day before.

"We do not expect battle," he'd said, dismounting at McClure's store. "But you never know." Apparently the delivery of a message from Dinwiddie to the French reminding them of Britain's rights to the Ohio lands had been met with indifference, if not outright laughter.

James had momentarily forgotten his own errand as he listened to Lewis.

"The French and their Indian allies have been preparing. Dinwiddie's man, Major Washington, saw hundreds of canoes when he delivered the Crown's message. He also determined a strategic location for a fort." Lewis tied his mare to the hitching post. "A brave sort, him. Almost got himself killed crossing that terrain in the dead of winter."

"Who is he?" The name Washington was unfamiliar. Not a valley man.

"A connection of the Fairfaxes."

Probably rich, or would be, but he sounded interesting. "Will there be a more general muster soon?"

"The French are intransigent, and Dinwiddie has invested his own money in the Ohio lands. You tell me." Captain Lewis shrugged. "How fast can you reload a musket?"

"I trained with Mr. Preston last fall." Thanks to Mr. Russell, he had been able to do that much despite his youth.

"*Captain* Preston now." Lewis tapped his hat in salute before disappearing into the building.

The babble of children's voices drew James back to the present.

"Georgie, mind me." Izzy was bossy.

"Mind Ma, not you!"

Their mother's voice murmured a correction.

Mr. Craig's chin jerked up and he glanced in their direction, but his eyes seemed unfocused, his mind probably still on his text.

James tried to remember what word he was searching for. He scratched his head. Oh, yes. The Greek for baptize ...

"Having difficulties?"

"No, Mr. Craig ..."

"Distracted?" The minister's piercing blue gaze settled on him.

"Just thinking about Captain Lewis."

Craig leaned back in his chair. "The whole valley has gotten wind of the expedition. Ye wishing ye went?"

"I dinna ken." He was studying to be a minister, not a soldier. And yet ...

The minister rose from his seat, crossed to the door, and took down the rifle that rested beside it. He returned and handed the fine gleaming firearm to James.

James fingered the smooth maple of the stock. The butt end of the firearm was scored by a deep gash. The blow of a tomahawk? "Your long rifle." He ran his fingers over the mechanism, wondering what scenes this rifle had been privy to. Pinpricks went up his spine.

"My gift to you."

"What?"

"I recently acquired a Brown Bess."

A wonderful firearm, not quite as accurate as a long rifle, but with enough stopping power to take down a bear. Mr. Craig could still defend his family. "Still, this is ... generous."

"I ken ye're drilling with young Preston and the rest. Ye need a decent weapon."

"I'm too young for the militia."

"But not too young to defend your own." The minister pushed aside his sermon and pulled out Calvin's *Institutes*. "Time for theology."

It was a glorious July morning. Susanna lifted her face to the warm gentle breeze, rejoicing. They were leaving the valley today.

Da guided the mules past freshly harvested barley fields, and soon the familiar clickety-clack of the wagon wheels echoed beneath the Lewis Creek bridge as they neared Staunton. The courthouse appeared, flanked by Preston's ordinary and McClure's dry-goods shop.

Da pulled the wagon around to the back of McClure's shop. "Will ye ask what Mrs. McClure needs from Richmond?"

Susanna nodded, leaped down, and entered the building, making her way past barrels of foodstuffs and buckskins. Breathing deeply of the scent of tanned leather and tobacco, she sidled past boxes and shelves full of fishing tackle, traps, and trade shirts. Any luxuries would be on the cloth-covered counter. One month several bolts of Holland linen perched there; another time a painted fan; and once an outrageous plumed bonnet. What would it be today?

Ribbon. Several long lengths of satin ribbon lay on the counter, red, yellow, green, and purple. What a wonderful shade of purple.

The vivid colors brought back the memory of the cavern, discovered by Jamie Paxton the year before. They'd followed him to a hole in the ground near a chestnut tree. Da tied a rope to the tree and they'd gone down, even Susanna, the breeches under her skirt giving her confidence for the climb.

At the bottom, Susanna turned. The flickering light of a small fire illuminated great translucent pillars that seemed to hold up the roof of the cavern like a Greek temple. The very air smelled alien, the familiar fragrance of burning pine unable to penetrate the dank cold of the cave, shocking in contrast to the June heat above. She'd imagined dirt and bland rock. Nothing like this.

One of the pillars was a color she couldn't quite describe. It was white, but possessed a texture. Not the stark white of snow, but a full-bodied color, like milk straight from the cow. In the crevices it darkened to butter.

To her left a great projection fell from the roof, not meeting the floor. Here the white gave way to a soft rosy hue, with rusty tones in the fissures, and deeper streaks in the middle of the stone, if stone it was. It did resemble limestone, but like no limestone she'd ever seen.

"Miss Russell, may I help ye?" Mr. McClure asked, jerking her back to the moment.

"No, thank ye kindly." Susanna returned her gaze to the purple ribbon. She had no lavender garments anyway, only indigo blue, madder red, and walnut brown, the colors Aunt Agnes was capable of achieving in her steaming dye kettle. Susanna enjoyed helping her.

"Do you sell cochineal?" Susanna asked.

"Co—?" The man's wrinkles pressed upward in his forehead.

"A dye."

"Move over, ye lout." Maggie McClure displaced her husband. "Mr. Russell's ready to load the wagon." She smiled. "How may I help ye?"

"Mrs. May needs a better red dye. Cochineal is such a dye."

"Hmph. Very expensive. I dinna stock it. Agnes May has a fine hand with madder, does she need something stronger?"

"Mr. May's kilt has seen better days." They had the sheep for the wool, but not the dye.

Maggie pursed her lips. "Richmond has a few shops. Is your da going to Williamsburg? Of course they'd have anything there."

"Richmond, and then the Jeffersons' on the way back for a horse." How she wished she could see Williamsburg. Richmond was the next best thing.

"Does your ma have a list for Richmond?"

"Yes, cramp bark. She can't get it to grow here."

"Aye, such a useful herb." Maggie lowered her voice. Midwifery was not a subject suitable for men's ears. "I'm that glad for your ma. With my rheumatism I canna be riding all over the county anymore." The sturdy woman turned and studied the shelf behind her, laden with small containers—spices, tea, and herbal remedies. She turned round. "I need basil. Sometimes called basilicum powder."

Susanna nodded. Mother devoted a corner of her garden to the useful herb, but it died off every winter. "I'll tell Da." He'd have his own list from Mr. McClure as well. As soon as he'd loaded the man's whiskey and other goods bound for Richmond, they'd be off. Their own items for sale filled the other half of the wagon bed: Da's canes, toys, and cradles. A few buckskins and other pelts. Aunt Agnes's extra madder from her garden, Uncle Roy's leather goods, and her own ginseng, harvested from the slopes behind their home. "Anything else you need?"

"Salt. Salt is scarce. We've had no Indian salt since the trader came through last year. We depend on Richmond now."

Susanna nodded. That was no surprise.

An eerie wailing cut through the quiet of the town square, startling her. "What is that?"

Maggie McClure was already at the door, hands on hips. "Simon McKee, is what."

They both stepped outside. Two men were placing a third individual, howling and protesting, into the stocks.

Maggie harrumphed. "He's squealing like a stuck pig. Wonder what he did this time?"

Susanna had never seen Simon McKee close up, only his family. Mary McKee was thin and pinched, and the children barefoot. Several times a year Mother made some kind of excuse to visit, always hiding stockings or even moccasins below the bread in her basket. Susanna had accompanied her once, but Mother had cautioned her that it was "indiscreet" for the husband to know about the visit. He was a drunkard and had been fined twice by the constables. And he didn't want charity.

Several folks came out of the ordinary to watch the spectacle. "What's he done?" someone shouted.

"Thievery," one of the men said.

That wasn't good. He could lose an ear.

Da and Mr. McClure joined them. "Stay here, Susanna," her father said softly. He crossed to the courthouse and engaged the constables in a discussion.

By the time he returned, McKee had quieted.

"What's happening?" Susanna asked.

"I asked if he'd been caught in the act, if his accuser was here. They said no, so nothing can be done until the sheriff gets here, which is any time." He paused. "Even the constables canna take the law into their own hands. There must be evidence. A hearing, at least. Colonel Patton will decide the matter."

Dust flew up at the end of the road. Two men on horses approached. Susanna recognized the lead horse, a mare with a huge blaze on her face, named Whiskey for the golden chestnut color of her coat. She was Russell bred and now belonged to Colonel Patton, sheriff of Augusta County, militia officer, and surveyor.

As the men drew closer, the other man came into view. Patton's nephew, William Preston, on a bay colt.

Watching them approach, Susanna thought about their own horses. Da had assured her that Ian MacLeod had a good hand with animals and not to worry. "Dinna fash," he'd said, "even Cricket likes him." The new indenture, almost at the end of his contract, seemed to like it on Russell's Ridge.

"Ho, what's the trouble?" Patton dismounted and approached the stocks with easy grace despite his age, betrayed only by his neatly trimmed silver beard. His nephew had much lighter coloring, but his confident, easy stride marked him as a relation. The constables joined them in conversation.

"Well, now," her father said, "the sheriff will take care of matters. I'll fetch the wagon."

Da guided the mules around the log building, but she was distracted by another horse and rider trotting down the road, the animal's forequarters darkened with sweat. Susanna didn't recognize the horse but thought the rider looked like one of John Lewis's sons. As it drew closer, the animal's lathered flanks alarmed her.

"Captain Lewis!" one of the bystanders said. "What news?"

"WAKE UP, LAD."

Branches lashed at him, beating him. Wake up? Had he fallen asleep in the saddle?

James opened his eyes to darkness. No, he wasn't mounted, riding along barely discernible deer paths, up and down, the jolting constant, twigs thrashing him. They'd camped for the night. He'd been dreaming.

His body felt nailed to the ground, and subtle aches suffused his limbs. If only he could sleep longer. But no, Mr. Craig had said they needed an early start.

Why, he couldn't remember. He pushed his body to a sitting position. "G'morning, Mr. Craig." Was it morning? He peered through the foliage to the east. Just over the darker black of the Blue Ridge the morning star—Venus—shone brightly. Sunrise would soon follow.

The fire had died and they didn't bother with breakfast. Mrs. Moore had wrapped up journeycake for them before they'd left the Moores' place yesterday. James nibbled on the last crusty piece as they rode over Buffalo Gap toward Staunton. Mr. Craig hoped to be there by midmorning to sell the beaver pelts they'd been given by the Foyles.

Gray tinged the far skyline. The aching stiffness began to leave his muscles now that they were moving. The trail opened up and they rode side-by-side.

"Mrs. Craig asked for linen diaper at McClure's. Have ye any idea what else she'd like?" the minister asked.

Mr. Craig adored his wife, but sometimes he was simply too distracted to notice her needs.

"Flour," he said. "Flour and honey, if there's any. Or some other sweetening, like maple syrup."

The man's face looked startled in the early light. "Good thinking, lad."

They rode silently for a time, the bright morning sun now over the top of the Ridge. James pondered the trip. Almost a week in the saddle to visit two families. Both had babies whom Mr. Craig had baptized. He'd spoken from the Scriptures each time.

Mary Foyles's face came to his mind. Her husband had appeared indifferent to Mr. Craig's sermon, but she had soaked in every word. The oldest child had listened, too.

The difficulties of the trip faded when he thought of that woman's face. Still, why did they live so far away? And they weren't the only ones. According to Mr. Craig, the Greenbriar River was dotted with homesteads. But land west of the Shenandoah Valley was disputed territory. Claimed by Virginia, the French, and the Shawnee. And without Mr. Craig they'd never hear the Word.

Something else niggled at him. Baptizing the babies. Mr. Craig had sprinkled them, but John Calvin said immersion was the proper mode.

James had another question. Why did they baptize babies at all? He knew what John Calvin said, he knew what Mr. Craig said about Old Testament circumcision, but there was no straightforward description of the custom in the New Testament.

He that believeth and is baptized shall be saved …

The Gospel of Mark was as familiar as the back of his hand. And much of the rest of the New Testament too. Why was it all other doctrines seemed easy to defend from Scripture, but when it came to the baptism of babies, he felt muddled?

Surely it would clear up in time.

"Almost there, lad. Almost there."

James needed a bath. Maybe he'd go down to the creek behind the Craigs' home. After stopping at McClure's it was just a few miles to the Craigs' property. Already he could see the courthouse, a dark gray smudge in the distance.

"What's the stramash?" Mr. Craig asked.

He looked again. A dozen people, give or take, were in the street near the courthouse. The minister kneed his horse to a trot, and James followed his lead, though the mule snuffed in protest.

They finished the last mile in time to view a grimy Andrew Lewis in the center of a knot of people, including Colonel Patton, William Preston, John Russell, and his daughter Susanna. James and the minister reined in and dismounted.

"The Half-King of the Mingo Indians smashed the skull of the French leader with his tomahawk," Lewis was saying. The tale was long, sordid, and confused. Apparently the French had gotten to the prized river fork first, and Major Washington had retreated to another location, where he'd erected a palisade named "Fort Necessity."

"It rained. And rained. Then the French Indians attacked, and we held them off with cannon. By the time the French regulars attacked, the Virginians from Winchester were soused with drink, ye see—"

"No!"

"Cowards!"

Lewis's brown hair was dark with sweat. "Without them we didn't have enough men, so Washington ordered us to retreat behind the palisade. We were coons up a tree. We surrendered with decent terms, thanks to the Major, but then, on the way back, the savages fell on us and stole our provisions!"

Howls of outrage filled the street.

"The men of Augusta County would never turn tail or slouch in their duty!" boomed Colonel Patton.

A cheer went up at this.

James ran his hand over the stock of his rifle and surveyed the crowd. Susanna stood next to the Russells' wagon.

Her dark eyes were on him. And she looked worried.

Suddenly the excitement filling him was replaced by a lead weight in his stomach.

The war had begun. And he wasn't sure of his part in it.

5

I cannot live without books.

—Thomas Jefferson (1743-1826)

Books covered the wall. Shakespeare, Newton, and Defoe stood side-by-side with authors Susanna did not recognize, on all sorts of subjects. Five volumes comprising *The History of England* nestled close to books on law and agriculture. She cautiously brushed the leather spine of Trent's *Astronomy* with a finger, then retreated, fearful of damaging anything. She'd been to Shadwell plantation a number of times but had never ventured into this room crammed with maps, books, and instruments.

She turned and saw a man.

No, only a painting on the opposite wall. Hazel eyes stared straight at her. The artist had rendered Peter Jefferson seated in a chair, graceful fingers posed above the armrest, face slightly angled, as if Jefferson had more important things to think about and could only offer her a brief glance.

Susanna frowned. The real Peter Jefferson had freckles and a warm, sunny smile. The man in the painting looked like a stranger, dressed in Williamsburg finery. But the clothing drew her. How did the painter get the satin so shiny and *real?* How had he executed the fine details of the lace? And the simple folds of the coat looked like they would pop out of the canvas.

Depth. Da purchased sketch paper for her every year in Richmond, and she tried to show depth in her drawings, but this magic astonished her.

"Like it?"

"Tom! I mean, Thomas—?" He was as tall as she was. No, taller, with huge hands and bony wrists projecting from too-short linen sleeves. He was no longer her old playmate.

"Only my mother calls me that. Call me Tom, same as always." He flashed a smile, his hair as red and wild as ever. But his voice had changed. No longer reedy, it rumbled with maturity. "Come. My father is taking the stallion out of the barn."

Susanna followed him outside. She'd spent a week with her aunt and uncle at their home near Richmond while Da had journeyed on to Williamsburg. He'd gotten a good price for her ginseng but hadn't said much about his other errands, only that he'd met Major—now Colonel—Washington and thought him a fine young man. Now he hoped to purchase a stud from the Jeffersons.

They watched from the paddock fence as Mr. Jefferson led out the horse her father hoped to buy. The stallion's reddish coat gleamed as it lifted its head to sniff and snort. Her father approached the animal slowly, holding out a fist for it to smell.

"See its knees?" Tom asked.

The knees were large and knobby, but the animal moved well. "A problem?"

"Some gentlemen prefer prettier horses. But the true difficulty is the creature's temperament."

The horse's nostrils flared, and its ears danced. Da had a way with horses, but it could take a while. "What have you been experimenting on?"

"'Tisn't an experiment, precisely."

He led her to the edge of a tobacco field, broad leaves green under the sun. The top of a post was studded with metallic objects.

He lifted one and showed her. "A rain gauge to measure precipitation. Every farmer must study the weather. I keep precise records." His gaze scanned the heavens. "What I truly desire is a barometer."

"Baro—?"

"Sometimes called a weather glass, it measures the pressure the air exerts. Expensive, though." He replaced the rain gauge. "These past few years I've been preparing for college. Latin, mathematics, history, French. Not much time for my collections. Only the weather."

He didn't sound as if he hated the thought of college. "I've never heard French." Da said Indians sometimes knew a few words of it. Grandda didn't teach it—only basic Latin.

He lifted her hand and bowed over it. *"Je suis enchanté de faire votre connaissance."*

Her cheeks warmed. "What did you just say?"

"Literal translation? Or the general meaning?"

"You sound like my father."

He smiled. "If a soldier engages in reconnaissance, what is he doing? *Connaissance* is a French word for knowledge—but a deeper knowledge than *savoir*, a more general word."

"Now you sound like my grandfather."

After several minutes she was able to say the phrase herself. With a curtsey.

"What an innate ability," he said, his long arms flapping with enthusiasm. "You have an exquisite accent."

"Thank you," she said, embarrassed. "I'm only imitating you."

"Come to the house, I have no more need of my French primer. My new tutor has me slated for Montesquieu." His lanky legs set a rapid pace.

She struggled to keep up. "But Tom, how will I learn pronunciation?"

He whirled and frowned. "Have you a tutor?"

Her shoulders sagged. She already had more learning than any other lass her age in the valley. "No."

"I see. My cousins in Williamsburg all have tutors. And my mother's sister Anne."

"What do they study?" Surely not what the young men were taught.

"I believe most do learn French, as well as dancing and music."

"Might they study art? Painting?" *If only ...*

Tom grinned. "Painting? Whyever not? If a woman may play the harpsichord, then the arts would be appropriate. Or should be." His expression shifted. "I shall speak to Mother. My aunt Anne is lonesome now she's the only unmarried sister left in Uncle Thomas's house. If a year in Williamsburg would please you, she might like the company."

Susanna's lips parted. Was she dreaming?

"If Mother approves, you will hear from Father."

They fetched the book and looked at Tom's collections, but Susanna barely paid attention. If all went well, and Da approved, she'd get to see Williamsburg.

She frowned. If Da approved. Her father didn't like Williamsburg, and she wasn't sure why.

"WHAT ELSE IS longleaf pine good for?" James asked. He wasn't truly interested in wood. What he really wanted to hear about was John Russell's trip to Williamsburg.

Mr. Russell slid a thumb up and down the worn leather of the reins. "The heartwood is good for furniture, but it doesna take a finish well, not like oak or walnut. But for building it is the best pine there is, sturdy and tough. Won't rot."

The load behind them in the wagon bed was destined to become siding for Mr. Craig's cabin. The day was still mild, the morning sun not yet over the Blue Ridge, but the work ahead of them promised to be sweaty in the August heat.

A thin stream of gray smoke purled from the Craigs' cabin just ahead. "Which side of the cabin?" James asked.

"I am thinking the north, to seal the cabin against the wind. But I'll ask his wishes."

James always needed extra stockings in the winter while studying at Mr. Craig's table. The cabin was not as well built as the Russells' house or even their original cabin, now inhabited by Susanna's grandfather. James had worked to patch the chinking more than once.

"Ho, the house!" Mr. Russell's smooth voice could carry when he meant it to.

Izzy and Georgie tumbled out of the cabin, followed by their father. "Welcome."

They discussed the particulars, and soon the long pine boards were aligned correctly. Mr. Russell handed James a hammer. "We'll start at the bottom, and overlap the planks as we go up. Ye'll see."

The boards weren't thick, but even so, it was backbreaking work. By midmorning sweat began to trickle into his eyes, but they were only half done.

"Lad, let's have some switchel." Mr. Russell fetched a jug from the wagon.

James set down his hammer gratefully and sat beside the older man, opening and closing his fists to ease his fingers. "Thank ye." He swallowed the sweet-sour beverage from the gourd jug, wondering if he'd ache on the morrow. Probably.

"What did Colonel Washington say?" He wished he could've met the man.

"A general named Braddock will be coming, as well as troops." Mr. Russell tipped back the jug and swallowed. "It's no' just a matter for the Virginia militia any more."

"Will militiamen be fighting as well?" Somehow the image of red-coated British regulars fighting in the backwoods struck him as incongruous.

"Possibly." The man faced him. "I told Colonel Washington I was willing if he needed me."

James didn't know what to say. He'd like to volunteer, but there were so many obstacles. His age, for one.

A brown blur caught his eye. A bird, circling. "Is that an eagle? Or a hawk?"

Mr. Russell's dark head jerked up. "I dinna think an eagle. Red-tailed hawks I do see now and again. If the sun catches it just right, ye'll see the red."

The distant bird looped closer. James took another swallow of switchel. A second bird sailed over their heads. "Another!"

The second bird's tail shone red in the sunlight. A *scree* pierced the air as the bird approached the first one. The two birds circled, closer and closer.

"The red-tail defends its territory," Mr. Russell said.

The second bird suddenly closed the distance. A screech sliced through the air. The first bird swooped down and away. Something fell, perhaps a feather.

Another movement caught his attention. A man on a horse, trotting from the direction of the forks. Mr. Russell called to the minister, alerting him to a visitor.

James made out the face under the hat. Captain Buchanan.

"Ho!" Buchanan drew rein and dismounted, a rivulet of sweat running down his face. "Word from down valley." He took a breath. "Bad news."

They'd already had bad news in the surrender of Fort Necessity. Mr. Craig emerged from the cabin and joined them.

Mr. Russell handed Buchanan the rest of the switchel. "What word?"

The man upended the gourd and swallowed. "The Foyles. They've been killed by Injuns."

James's mouth went dry. The Foyles. He'd been there only last month. Their faces were bright in his memory. "The whole family?"

"Aye. Well, not sure about the children. Sometimes they'll take a child captive."

He wanted to vomit.

6

John and James McColoch Was taken Captive by the indins from Canagogige July the 26th 1756... Weep ye not for the dead neither bemoan him but weep sore for him that goeth away for he shall return no more...

—James McCullough, *Journal*, 1756

Red Hawk halted. Father's dun pony had stumbled coming downhill, and he knelt to examine her feet. No, the animal seemed sound; she was just tired from traipsing over the hills, sides laden with cargo. Tired and thirsty, just as he was. He led her down the last few feet to a familiar creek, a final landmark before home.

The summer heat reminded him of that day last year when he'd observed the white men. Were they still marking out territory with their chains? The silver-bearded one rode an especially beautiful horse, strong and well muscled. Undoubtedly younger than this creature.

He untied his leggings, kicked off his moccasins, and splashed water on his hot face. Grandmother would be pleased with his find. She'd taught him which clays were good for pigment, which ones for pottery. White was the finest clay for creating pots. He'd seen her work moist clay between her hands, lengthen it into a long rope, and coil it. Few women desired large pots as they coveted the white man's iron kettles, but Grandmother's smaller containers were highly regarded.

Red Hawk rolled his leggings and packed them into one of the bags on the pony. He slipped his feet back into his moccasins. After spending three days in the hills, he looked forward to a cooling, cleansing swim in the river. Laughing Wolf must have returned by now. Red Hawk had declined the young man's invitation to hunt, wanting time to search for clay and stone. Plus, he didn't fully trust him. There was something about Laughing Wolf that didn't seem right. Even his name caused him to wonder. The wolf was made by He-Who-Creates-By-Thinking, but the animal could also be a bad omen.

It all depended. If you shot at a wolf and missed, your bow or musket was cursed for six moons. Laughing Wolf's father, Elk Tooth, must have seen a wolf during that critical period after the birth of his son. The wolf was his totem animal, ordained by the spirits.

"Red Hawk!" Buffalo Robe was the first to greet him. "Good hunting?"

"Yes, a deer." He'd skinned it, wrapped most of the carcass inside, including the head of the doe. Dark Water would want the brains for tanning.

"Want to go fishing later?" Buffalo Robe's dark skin glistened, a bead of sweat visible at his hairline. Such strange curly hair. His mother, She-Who-Sings, was Lenape, but no one knew anything about the father. Grayfeather had given the woman refuge years ago, and no questions were asked. Buffalo Robe was Shawnee now.

Red Hawk envisioned wading into the river behind their fishing weir. A perfect choice for a warm day. A swim, and fish to bring home. "Sure."

Grandmother was sitting in her usual spot in front of her wigwam, the thick buffalo skin door covering folded up above her head. She had something in her lap, probably sewing quills or shells into a garment. She looked up and smiled, her old face crinkling like an overripe pawpaw.

"I've brought you something." He deposited the carcass near the fire pit. Then he removed the other bags and parcels from the pony, which lifted its head as if to say thanks. One of the bags he placed before his grandmother.

She loosed the tie and touched the clay inside with a knobby fore-finger, then picked up a chunk and kneaded it with both hands. "White." She smiled again. "You know the path to this place?"

Of course he wouldn't forget. "It's near a good place for stone," he hedged. He didn't want to gush with pleasure like a child.

Her eyes shone like the coal she used to fire her pots. "You found stone?"

"Darker than usual. I'll ask Father about it." Hopefully, it was good chert. Whatever they didn't use could be sold to a trader. If he didn't ruin it all. Father knapped arrowheads twice as fast as he did and rarely spoiled a single one.

The pony stood naked now, with one hind leg cocked, her back dark with sweat. He needed to take her to the river to let her drink and wipe her down.

"Go." Grandmother's eyes twinkled.

Red Hawk was halfway to the river when he heard a commotion behind him. He turned. A horse and rider were trotting into the village. The rider looked like Laughing Wolf, though the horse was unfamiliar. The animal looked terrible—nostrils flared, coat lathered. It must have been ridden far and fast.

Yes, it was Laughing Wolf. A buzz filled the village. Women stood before their homes, shading their eyes to see. A few of the children approached the new horse, bubbling their welcome. Father emerged from Grayfeather's wigwam—so that's where he'd been.

Red Hawk strode to his father's side. And that's when he saw them.

Two scalps dangled from Laughing Wolf's belt. One was brown. Long golden hair cascaded from the second.

His stomach twisted.

~

THEY DIDN'T GO FISHING AFTER ALL.

Red Hawk kicked off his moccasins, parted the cane, and stepped into the water. Familiar silt and pebbles massaged his feet, but he found no joy in the beauty of the river. Father had gone with the other elders into Grayfeather's lodge. The scalps were on everyone's mind.

He scooped up a handful of sand and scrubbed himself. It occurred to him that the sweat lodge might be his next bath. The way men prepared for war. But surely not. There had been no provocation. Laughing Wolf had been the aggressor.

He dunked his head and finger-combed his dark hair. Ice stabbed his innards. Would the Long Knives seek them out?

He stood and let the water drip off his skin. Last year, after the men with chains had come, the chiefs had agreed on peace. The other divisions of the Shawnee were content to align with the British. Becoming mercenaries for either side was distasteful, according to Grayfeather. Their own grievances—intrusions by the white men—were not worthy of the warpath.

Most felt that way, but not all. Elk Tooth and his son, Laughing Wolf, were some notable exceptions.

Afternoon shadows were slanting over the village when he returned. The women ducked in and out of their dwellings, preparing food. A few of the younger men lounged about, talking. It could be any other day, but an invisible tension vibrated through the air as everyone waited for the result of the meeting.

Dark Water had stretched the deer hide on a rack. Now she sliced the meat into strips, preparing to smoke it over the fire. Red Hawk crossed to the woodpile, looking for something to do, to keep from thinking. His aunt was particular about wood for smoking, and occasionally asked him to chop a branch from this or that tree. He grabbed a couple of likely looking pieces and tossed them in.

"Here." Dark Water held up the deer's head. "Split this open."

Grandmother disappeared inside, and the aroma of her stew wafted out. His mouth watered as he dealt with the problem of the deer's skull, difficult to penetrate. He wasn't interested in stopping to eat, but his body betrayed him, hunger pangs assailing him. What would the elders be saying? Elk Tooth would want to turn this into an excuse for raiding. How, he couldn't fathom.

As Red Hawk handed the cracked skull back to his aunt, motion caught his eye. The men were emerging from Grayfeather's wigwam. Red Hawk breathed a prayer to He-Who-Creates-By-Thinking. He didn't think his own totem animal was strong enough to do much about this. On the other hand, he wasn't sure if the Creator heard him.

Father's steps were slow and sure as he approached. He jerked his chin in command and ducked into their wigwam. Red Hawk followed, and Dark Water served them portions of thick stew.

When their bowls were finally empty, his father spoke. "Grayfeather will join the Ohio chiefs traveling to Penn's village."

Red Hawk nodded. At the Bread Dance, he'd heard rumors. The Catawba had formed a new treaty with the whites, a surprising development. But at the time, he'd been more interested in the archery contests and footraces. "Is the chief of the Virginia Long Knives in Penn's village?" He had only a vague notion of the political boundaries of the whites.

His father tapped the ashes out of his pipe. "No. But the consensus is we should do as the Six Nations and deal as a unified people with all of the whites. Penn's Forest comprises white men living to the north of Virginia, near the Six Nations. It is said the white men of Penn's village are more equitable than the Virginia Long Knives. And they have influence with the rest of the whites."

Red Hawk didn't see how this was related to the scalps but waited for his father to continue.

"Even the Catawba have publicly aligned themselves with the British. Right now, the British see the French as their enemy, not the Shawnee."

He wasn't sure about that. As long as he could remember, there had been a cold hostility between white men and Shawnee. It had just never broken out into war.

Father wiped the bowl of his pipe and set it down. "If we present ourselves as peaceful, the actions of a few may not bring wrath upon us."

Laughing Wolf.

"Stealing a horse is one thing. Killing and scalping is quite another."

"Grayfeather is wise."

"It wasn't his idea. But now we are joining the embassy."

We?

"I will accompany him, with She-Who-Sings as interpreter. North to Sawkunk, then east, almost to the ocean."

Red Hawk frowned. "That's a long journey."

"We leave the day after tomorrow."

7

What made the times distressing and unhappy to all the frontier was the French and Indian war, which lay heavy on us…

—Rev. John Craig, *Autobiography*

November 1754

Susanna tried again. She treadled the spinning wheel more quickly this time—too quickly. The wool thread flew out of her hand and wrapped around the bobbin.

"Oo, now, come tae." Agnes retrieved the end of the yarn.

For some reason, Auntie Agnes's mock scoldings didn't irritate her. Mother wasn't loud or harsh, but her instruction just hadn't worked, and Susanna didn't know why.

She frowned at the carded fleece in her hand. Normally, she loved this time of year: gathering chestnuts and walnuts, hunting for ginseng whenever she could. Even plucking goose feathers wasn't that bad, since one day they'd have enough for another mattress. She already had a down pillow of her own, which made her feel like a princess.

But this autumn was different. Tension tightened the shoulders of the men when they went out to hunt, and Mother was unusually quiet. Susanna had even overheard Agnes muttering to her husband he was too old for the militia.

Susanna glared at the spinning wheel. No one told her anything.

"Lass, it's almost time for supper," Agnes said. "Will ye mix up the hoecakes for me?"

"Thank you." Susanna stood and stretched the ache from her shoulders, grateful the lesson was over. She reached for her favorite bowl, a large stoneware dish, and brushed her fingers over the glazed green and brown surface. Beautiful. How were such colors achieved?

"Only two eggs this morning," Agnes lamented. "Gabby is going into the pot soon." The woman stirred the brose in the kettle as she continued to ramble on about the vagaries of chickens, a soothing sound.

Susanna ladled a generous amount of warm milk into the bowl. They'd have extra folks at the table tonight. Stirring in the molasses, she thought of Kitty Kerr.

Kitty was only a year older and could spin both wool and flax with ease and skill. She even helped her folks on the loom. Now *that* would be more interesting than spinning. What would happen if indigo flax on the warp were mixed with red wool on the weft? No, that would look strange. Green and blue might work.

Sam Robinson had been hanging around the Kerrs' place, ostensibly to give them a hand with fencing, but everyone knew better. Kitty would be married within a year.

Marriage. Well, Susanna had no interest in that. Not for a long while, at least. And whom would she marry? Sam Robinson was pleasant enough and a hard worker, but he barely knew how to read, much less write a coherent sentence. Many valley lads were like him, their families too poor to allow their sons time away from the fields for study.

She added the meal, and scooped out a cup of flour from the bottom of the barrel. Poverty was nothing to be ashamed of, Da had said more than once. But she'd want to marry someone she could *talk* to ... talk about books, ideas, maybe even painting. Jamie Paxton was educated. But all he'd want to talk about would be the Bible or theology. Not like Tom Jefferson, whose mind wandered in every direction with glowing enthusiasm.

She poured the batter into the greased skillet, wondering when everyone would be back. Da and Uncle Roy had gone to Staunton. Perhaps there would be mail. Might there be a letter from the Jeffersons? Tom had promised to ask his mother, but so far there'd been no answer.

The door creaked. Mother entered, cap askew, and wiped her feet on the mat. The basket over her arm bulged with roots from the garden.

"G'een to ye, Mrs. Abigail." Agnes had been instructed to address Mother as "Abigail" instead of Mrs. Russell, but it hadn't quite worked. The Mays' indenture was long since fulfilled, and Arch served for wages now, but in reality they were like family.

"The garden is turned over." Mother dumped carrots, turnips, and what looked like chicory roots into a bucket. "I had help." She tugged off her ancient gardening gloves.

A blast of cool air from the open doorway accompanied Jonathan, face smudged, followed by Ian MacLeod. When George Morgan had signed over the balance of MacLeod's indenture to her father, Susanna had wondered. The young man seemed so distant. But now he seemed attached to the Mays, living with them in a new addition to their cabin.

"Looks like someone needs a wash." Agnes handed Jonathan a water bucket. "Fill this up while ye're at it, will ye?"

He disappeared out the door. Ian picked up another bucket and followed.

A clatter announced the arrival of the wagon. By the time the corn cakes were done, the whole population of the little rise where they lived was crowded around the walnut table, including Thomas Kerr, the weaver. Mother poured ale and cider, while Susanna scrounged for more cups. Uncle Roy and Aunt Lizzie had brought their children, who joined her younger brothers.

Susanna turned, arms laden.

Jamie Paxton, stray bits of flaxen hair framing his face, sat at her father's side. She hadn't noticed him enter.

The men's faces were clouded and their voices low. Something had happened, perhaps bad news in the mail. But her father led the family in prayer same as always, and they ate every last drop of Agnes's stew.

"Gae on, the lot of ye." Agnes rounded up the children and led them to the parlor, Hannah bringing up the rear, dragging a threadbare blanket. Jonathan remained in one corner alongside Ritchie, Uncle Roy's eldest.

Arch May leaned back in his chair. "So, what news from the governor?"

Da pulled out a newspaper from his satchel and unfolded it. "An act, for raising levies and recruits to serve in the present expedition against the French on the Ohio."

Recruits. Susanna's pulse quickened. Did that mean soldiers? Militiamen? But many men in the valley belonged to the local militia already.

Every man sat at the table still as death as her father read the notice. Most could read, but they'd want Da's commentary as well, which was sure to follow.

" ... sheriffs, under-sheriffs, and constables ..." Sheriffs were to enforce the act. Did that mean Colonel Patton? But the language was confusing. What exactly would he be doing?

" ... maimed or wounded ... upon their return, be supported at public expense."

Her father finished.

"Patton would choose?" Questions filled the room. "Who would serve then?"

Da lifted his hand for patience. "This doesna apply to our own defense here, only the Virginia militia, which will assist the regular army. And the governor has made many exceptions. No landowner must serve, which applies to most here."

Ian MacLeod scowled. "I willna serve with a redcoat."

Susanna blinked. Ian had always been quiet, though upon reflection, it was more of a wary carefulness. No wonder, given his background. He was lucky to be alive.

Arch May snorted. "And ye willna, lad, if I mun hie ye away to live with the Injuns." He lowered his voice. "But dinna let folks hear such talk. Ye may not be in Scotland, but King George reigns here too, and a valley man was fined just for blessing the Bonnie Prince."

"Dinna fash," Da said. "Colonel Patton is no fool. He willna kidnap respectable, hard-working members of the kirk. Or those under my protection. I suspect if I simply say Ian is my groom and I canna get by without him, he will find someone else. Remember, Patton is elected to the positions he holds. He will tread carefully."

And Ian did help her father with the horses. But who would be selected?

"Who, then? Wastrels and drunkards?" Uncle Roy asked.

Her father shrugged. "I dinna ken."

But she saw in his face that he suspected.

"What will ye do?" Jamie asked quietly. Everyone knew Da had met Colonel Washington.

"In Williamsburg I promised Washington my help if he requires it. I will write him."

Jamie's face was full of unspoken questions. Surely Jamie would not join the Virginia militia. He couldn't—he was too young. But she suspected he might find a way.

She stood and began clearing away bowls. She had to find something to do.

SUSANNA OPENED HER EYES. Gray light revealed the comforting line of dried herbs along the rafters. She stretched her limbs, still tired after last night. The men had talked for hours.

Giggles penetrated the wall. Nathan, by the sound of it. Her memory returned. Da had offered Jamie a place to sleep. Right next door, in her brothers' room, only a few feet away.

She sat up abruptly. It was cold in the little room underneath the rafters, and she longed to return to the warmth of the bearskin, but she forced her feet to the floor. If Jamie was here, she couldn't go downstairs with her hair mussed.

It was the Sabbath, another reason for Da's invitation. They would all go to the meetinghouse, and Jamie could return with Mr. Craig. But why had he come in the first place? It almost certainly had something to do with the militia.

Susanna fastened her stays, drew on her best petticoat over her shift and fastened the tapes. She added her woolen bodice and overskirt in quick succession, anxious to get warm and start on her hair.

She turned and peered in the mirror. Not an actual mirror, as Mother had, but a small shiny piece of tin, good enough for most purposes. Wisps of dark hair stuck out on either side of her head, come loose from her heavy braid. She unfastened her hair and brushed it out.

More giggles from the other room. A low rumbling voice. Jamie.

Susanna hurried. The wall wasn't a real wall, but thick canvas nailed over a pine framework stretched from floor to rafters, sufficient for privacy but certainly not soundproof.

She pinned her coiled braid and slipped it into a snood. She smoothed her walnut-brown overskirt and decided she looked well enough. She snorted. Why would she care what Jamie thought?

But he wasn't the same Jamie Paxton she used to know. Not the skinny child who ran about with the other lads at wedding frolics, accepted by the other children but never exactly popular. He was always a little too serious, a little too bookish. He was still quiet, but now he was tall, almost as tall as Da. And his face …

She opened the door, launched herself into the narrow hall, and collided with a solid warm object.

Susanna gasped. Jamie Paxton. He overbalanced on the edge of the steps, and they both stumbled. They ended up together on the tiny landing, limbs tangled.

Susanna's cheeks heated as she scrambled to her feet. *Oh no.* In her haste she misjudged the location of the next step. Strong arms halted her slide.

Warmth flooded her face. Stiffening, she disengaged his helping hands as quickly as she could while making it down the remaining stairs. She'd get a lecture for sure.

Mother stared as they entered the kitchen. How much had she seen?

Susanna reached for her hair. The ribbon was only slightly disturbed, the netting of her snood intact.

"Ma'am." Jamie was all politeness.

"I slipped on the steps." She couldn't see Da, and good thing too.

Mother's expression was strange, as if she'd just seen something unexpected. "Porridge and hoecakes are almost done, but I need more water."

Jamie took the bucket and Susanna the kettle. They made their way outside and walked briskly to the spring.

Susanna was still embarrassed. "Sorry about that. I wasn't looking."

"Och, no need. I have sisters."

Is that how he felt towards her? Like a sister? Something deflated inside. "Will you be joining the militia?"

"Too young. I'm only eighteen."

She heard the disappointment in his voice.

At the spring they filled their containers. Jamie touched the side of the little springhouse. "Beautiful work."

Da was known for both masonry and carpentry. "It's small, but it's all we need for our milk and butter." Susanna was proud of the wooden doors and raccoon-proof latch. Her father had created a base with gently mortared natural stone that blended into the hillside like it had sprung into being naturally.

They returned to the house, walking more slowly. Brown leaves blew around their feet.

"You're studying to be a minister." Susanna disliked the thought of him being part of the militia, now or ever. But she wasn't sure why.

"Aye, but it is the duty of every man to see his own safe."

They came around the bend in the path. Da stood in the open doorway, his blue gaze on them.

Susanna studied his face. Did this count as being alone with a lad? But her father didn't seem troubled, only bemused.

JAMES STRETCHED his limbs and tilted his face toward the sun. The coming winter was rumored to be bad, and indeed the ridges to the west glistened, clothed with early snow. Folks milled about the Tinkling Springs meetinghouse yard. He didn't know everyone here, as his own family worshipped at the stone kirk.

Children danced about, happy to be free from the restraints of listening to the lengthy morning sermon. It'd been a good one, surveying the offices of Christ: prophet, priest, and king. All formally divided into subheads, with multiple Scripture references.

Susanna Russell approached, and he straightened, still vaguely embarrassed about the collision on the stairs. She looked distracted. Was she still troubled?

"Miss Russell?" He swallowed.

She turned and saw him, the strange look fading away. "Oh, hello, Jamie. I mean, Mr. Paxton."

"Hope I didn't discommode you terribly—"

"Och, dinna fash, as my father would say." She spoke more like her mother, or perhaps a blend of the two. "Would you join us for dinner?"

He smiled. The Russells generally served good food, especially on the Sabbath. "Thank ye kindly."

They strolled in the direction of the Russells' wagon.

"What did ye think of the sermon?" he asked.

"Prophet, priest, and king? I am still thinking on the subheads. Da will ask, he always does. Tonight, or tomorrow evening."

James suspected few lasses were instructed quite as well as Susanna. "Is it terribly tedious to remember them all?"

She chuckled. "Why, how can I admit such a thing to you, the minister's lad?"

The minister's lad. His nickname. He was grateful she even spoke to him. Most lasses didn't. They *did* have eyes for William Preston. "I'll tell ye a secret. Sometimes Mr. Craig tears his hair out composing the thing."

They arrived at the wagon where Agnes May bustled about.

"Here, lad." Mrs. May piled fried pork, buttered bread, and a small Scottish meat pie on his plate. "Blackberry jam?" She didn't wait for an answer, but slathered it on his bread.

She served her husband and Ian MacLeod next, the former wearing a faded red plaid kilt.

"Is Mr. MacLeod a Highlander like the Mays?" The question sounded foolish to his ears, but he sought to make conversation as they found a place to sit on the low stone wall bordering the cemetery.

"Yes. His father was killed at the battle of Culloden. Then they arrested Ian and he was transported."

That explained a lot, but the Scottish uprising was almost ten years ago now. "Did he fight for the Bonnie Prince?" He felt her nearness acutely, and was glad for such a topic of conversation.

Susanna swallowed a bite of bread. "No, just being in the vicinity was good enough for the Redcoats. He was only fifteen."

"Sounds cruel." James took a final bite of the meat pie. Delicious. "I wonder what he thinks of Mr. Craig's preaching." Most Highlanders were Catholic.

"Want an apple?"

"Thank ye." Apples were far and few between. Must be from the Mays' orchard.

By the time they'd finished, folks were wandering back into the meetinghouse. As James followed Mr. Russell into the shade of the eaves, a rumble of voices floated around them. Not ordinary conversation. Sharper somehow.

"Did ye ken the McCulloughs were leaving? Selling their place?"

"And the Smiths, I heard."

"Naw, that's just a rumor."

The men left off their discussion as they entered the building behind the Russells.

James slid onto the front bench near the Craigs' children. To his right, William Preston took a seat next to his mother. Colonel Patton sat on the end. The murmur of voices settled as everyone took their seats behind them.

Despite John Russell's strong baritone coming from the second row, the singing was sluggish, everyone full from the meal. If Tinkling Springs was anything like the stone kirk, some would fall asleep during the afternoon sermon.

Mr. Craig crossed to the humble minister's desk and opened his Bible. He didn't look up as he arranged his notes. If anything, he seemed to be stalling for time, which was unlike him.

He eyed the congregation, his gaze landing most often on the prominent men of the area. Then he started to speak. Several moments passed before James fully comprehended the minister's words.

"Ye have heard of war and rumors of war ... some would flee. The richer sort have more ability than the poor to do so."

The Foyles were not the richer sort. Even if they had wanted to, it would have been difficult to leave their homestead. Now they were dead.

"It is a want of faith and an evidence of cowardice to turn tail and run when rumors start." Mr. Craig's eyes fastened upon each man in turn. "There are men of ability among ye. Determine to erect forts or fortified houses, such as would withstand small arms."

The cavern would do for the families near the Russells, just as the stone kirk would suffice for his own. But more places of refuge were needed, especially in outlying areas.

"Turn to the book of Joshua." Everyone was fully awake now.

James fumbled with his Bible, but all he could see in his mind's eye was Mr. Craig's scarred rifle.

8

Put them in mind of the freeness and eternity of God's electing love, and be instant with them to lay hold of the perfect righteousness of Jesus Christ by faith.

—George Whitefield, *Letter*

December 1754

"I've a letter," Mr. Craig said.

The Craigs' cabin was freezing, worse than usual, and James wriggled his toes inside his boots. He tried not to be obvious as he slid his hands into the opposite sleeves of his shirt to warm his fingers.

"It's from the Reverend Samuel Davies." The minister eyed him and threw a chunk of pine on the fire. "He's the first Presbyterian minister to receive a license to preach in the Tidewater."

James straightened. He'd heard of this man.

Mr. Craig sat and began to read in the uncertain light of the candle on the table. The first part was ordinary, consisting of greetings and general news. Then the topic changed. "'My own training consisted of schooling under the Reverend Samuel Blair. My family had no money and no means to send me to a proper seminary. However, the Synod did not see that as an obstacle as you know.'"

James's lips parted. *No money, no means* ... Well, that certainly described him.

Mr. Craig paused his reading. "Reverend Davies is a New Side man. Not my first choice."

Mr. Craig labeled New Side Presbyterians, who supported the outdoor preaching of George Whitefield, as "enthusiasts." Not a compliment.

"But, from all accounts, he is solid. No one finds fault with him. He is a great advocate of literacy for the purpose of reading the Scriptures. Even the African slaves."

"And he received a license to preach in the *Tidewater?*" James doubted slave-owning planters would care for such opinions.

Mr. Craig chuckled. "Aye, well, I dinna ken whether he'd explained all that ahead of time."

James approached the fire and stretched out his hands to warm them, the bright, resinous smell of burning pine in his nose. Mr. Craig was about to draw his threads of logic together.

"Anyway, the man's name has been bandied about for a place at Princeton. Not that he'd accept. He cares for two assemblies."

So in Mr. Craig's view, the man's credentials were impeccable, despite the lack of seminary. *So?*

"Would ye consider studying under such a man?"

Tears started in James's eyes. He swallowed. "Me?"

"Let me finish the letter. 'I am pleased to offer my services as tutor to the young man in question. He would supply half a day's labor on my property and otherwise as required.'"

"I dinna ken what to say." James collapsed into his chair. It was a generous offer.

Mr. Craig's eyebrows shot up in merriment, but his eyes were suspiciously shiny. "First ye need to learn to speak. 'I know not what to say.'"

The tightness of his chest bubbled over into laughter. "I *daresay* you are correct."

Their chuckles died away and the crackling of the fire filled the silence. The minister turned the letter over in his hands, as if he didn't know what it was.

"I'll miss ye, lad."

WHITE PUFFS MARKED the mule's breath in the frigid air as James rode along the South River. He'd study Hebrew under Reverend Davies, certainly. Expository preaching? Mr. Craig had taught him basic Greek, basic hermeneutics, and church history, but James suspected he'd be examined in all those points and more. Theology, especially. His schooling seemed to stretch out indefinitely before him like the blinding blanket of December snow. He longed to preach.

James squinted against the brightness. The Blue Ridge reigned silently on his left, a green, blue, and woodsy brown slope frosted with pristine white. It was ten miles to the Russells' homestead, and for the entire distance he'd wrestled with the offer.

The crumbling limestone wall appeared ahead, yellow and gray against the brilliance of the snow. The landmark.

"Haw, Libby," he murmured, but without a saddle the mule knew what he wanted with the barest nudge. They turned toward the Ridge.

He longed to preach. But how could he shirk his duty to defend his own and run off to the safety of the Tidewater?

Lord, direct me.

SUSANNA LUGGED Hannah to her chest. "You can sit with me." Without supervision, the toddler would have pie and currant cake all over her face, hands, and clothing.

The dinner dishes soaked as they all sat for coffee, sweets, and gifts. Auntie Agnes circled the table, pulling out items from a canvas bag. Christmas was her domain, and each man received a scarf.

What puzzled her was Jamie's presence. Surely no student of Mr. Craig would countenance anything to do with the Romish Christ Mass. Come to think of it, her father was normally strict about such things. But then, there was no popery here, only a roast goose and gifts.

"How did ye manage that?" Arch May held up a length of red plaid above the table.

"My secret." His wife bubbled her pleasure. "Well, I canna keep it now. Mr. Russell fashioned me a table loom."

Her true secret was the cochineal, Susanna knew. She looked more closely at the scarves. They were woven, not knitted. "What else can you make?"

"I dinna ken, maybe sew several together for a shawl or blanket."

Even Jamie received a pair of wrist mittens. She studied him surreptitiously as he tried them on. None of the lasses she knew ever mentioned his name, but then, his family worshiped at the stone kirk ten miles away. Maybe one of the lasses there had set her cap for him.

"Here, lass." Agnes dropped a small bundle next to Susanna's cup of chicory.

Bound up with a sheer fabric, the herbs inside released the sweet scent of lavender. "Thank you, Auntie. Where did you get the lavender?"

Mother answered. "From McClure's. A nice smell for your linens. Keeps away pests as well as pennyroyal."

Several embroidered pillowcases nestled inside a new cedar chest at the foot of Susanna's bed. Her cheeks heated. "Thank you both." She didn't want to even *think* about her next project, a shift of fine linen, not with Jamie Paxton looking at her. She occupied herself with feeding Hannah the last bits of the squash pie Aunt Lizzie had made.

"I've news, Mr. Russell." Jamie's voice.

She listened as they discussed his opportunity to study under a minister near Richmond.

"When will ye leave?" her father asked.

"Summer, most likely. First I need to speak to my folks, then write back."

Susanna wiped Hannah's face with a rag and let her down. Jamie leaving? But she hoped to go to Williamsburg herself. She had no reason to feel unsettled.

"I've news, too." Her father stood and reached for a shelf near the door. "Some letters."

The room quieted.

"Colonel Washington wrote."

"What's he say, Son?" Grandda asked. Concern flashed across his features.

Da cleared his throat. "He's resigned his commission with the militia."

A murmur arose.

"Why?" Uncle Roy asked.

"Washington says when General Braddock arrives, he will have need of aides who know the country. Washington intends to take such a position and will need at least one assistant." Da paused and looked around. "He's offering me that position."

"I see," Grandda said.

Mother appeared composed. She already knew.

Jonathan circled the table to his father. "Ye're going off to *war*?"

Da's arm circled her brother's waist. "Looks like it." His gaze met each man's around the table. "I canna ask ye to care for my family while I'm gone. Not with things as they are now. My sister lives near Richmond. I'll write her."

But the land and the horses—they couldn't all just leave. And her father, off to war? Ice stiffened her insides. But no. He'd be with Washington, and Washington was only an aide. Da wouldn't be fighting. No, surely not.

"I'd be honored to help with your horses," Ian MacLeod said.

Da's brows lifted. "Thank ye kindly."

"Ritchie and I can see to those sheep of yours." Roy frowned, clearly sorting out tasks in his mind.

A line appeared between Mother's brows. "Mrs. McKee will have a hard time of it without her husband."

Rumor had it Simon McKee had enlisted with the Virginia militia.

"Seems to me she does anyhow," Mr. May said.

Da's lips pursed. "My suggestion is to invite her and the children here. That way, birds won't build a nest in the chimneys."

"And they have a dog," Mother said. "Yes, I would feel better about leaving if someone were here. She could help herself to the garden ..." Her throat worked.

"Tell her it's a position. Housekeeper or something. So it's not charity."

"I'll have more students," Grandda said. Perhaps he was trying to console himself—and Mother. "But ye said letters. Plural."

"Och, aye, I did." Da opened a second missive. "From the Jeffersons."

Susanna's heart leapt. She was almost afraid to hope.

"Susanna has been invited by Anne Randolph, Mrs. Jefferson's sister, to spend a year in Williamsburg, for instruction. 'Typical subjects, taught by tutors in chaperoned settings, as befits ladies.'"

A grin spread across Grandda's face. He was on her side.

Da studied her face. "Ye concocted this with the young Jefferson, I kent that all along. 'Typical subjects'? Just what were ye hoping for, lass?"

Susanna studied the wood grain of the table. "French?" She braved his face. "And mayhap painting?"

Her father's expression closed and his shoulders sagged. "Where will ye attend services?"

She didn't know. Well, that was the death knell.

"I'll tell ye where ye'll attend. The Church of England. Half Papist it is."

Poor Ian. He never spoke of it, but he was undoubtedly Papist, and he was listening to this.

"Isn't Mr. Whitefield Church of England?" Mother asked.

Her question seemed to surprise everyone, including her father. Susanna had heard good things about the preacher. Da had used his sermons for family worship, and she could still remember the main points of "The Lord Our Righteousness." If Mr. Whitefield belonged to the Church of England, then surely it couldn't be all bad.

Da's face gentled. "Why, ye're right at that." Inexplicably, his eyes filled with wetness when his gaze returned to Susanna. "Ye may go, lass." He set the letter on the table and stared at it. "Ye may go."

IT WAS late in the season for deer. James adjusted Mr. Craig's rifle against his shoulder and headed up the slope. He'd left the mule, Libby, loosely hobbled down below and given her a feedbag as partial compensation for hauling him to Buffalo Gap and waiting for him in a snowy glen.

He wasn't sure why he was here. The bucks would be tired and lean, and he hated to shoot a doe swollen with young. Maybe he'd chance upon a yearling.

Mr. Craig had studied him silently when he'd offered to hunt. "Dinna forget what I told ye about breathing. On a long shot it'll make all the difference."

But he wouldn't shoot at a deer over fifty yards away. No, Mr. Craig wasn't referring to hunting. John Russell was waiting for the muster. When that would be no one knew, but it would be soon. As soon as the worst of the cold loosed its grip on the hills, most probably. James ached to go with him.

A flicker of motion caught his eye. A cardinal alighted on a thin branch. In the still forest, where evergreens mingled with sleeping brown oaks and poplars against a white background, the cherry-red bird brought a startling contrast to the scene.

The color of blood. The color of life. The color of death.

James stared and his shoulders sagged. He crossed to a rocky outcrop and sat, resting the rifle across his lap.

Oh Lord, please direct my paths.

He'd rarely doubted his call to the ministry. He'd always been more bookish than his brothers, and when at fourteen he'd gained a full assurance of faith, the gospel became such an integral part of him it almost seemed strange anyone would *not* want to preach the Word.

What could be more important? And yet, Mr. Craig had once warned him, that if he could do anything else, he should do it. The office of minister was a serious thing, with special qualifications and great burdens of soul.

Special qualifications … *the husband of one wife …*

He would need a wife who could help him carry those burdens. He cringed a little thinking of Susanna, with her warm brown eyes and spry manner. She was intelligent and sensible. Well taught in the Scriptures.

Would she ever look his way? Yes, they were friends, but he couldn't imagine anyone looking at him the way the Smiths' daughter made eyes at William Preston.

And now lessons in Williamsburg? He was of two minds about it. It was safer, physically, than the valley, and yet …

James fingered one of the wrist mittens, knitted of soft, undyed Russell wool. Why was he even thinking of her? He was in no position to court a young woman until he could support a wife.

He ran his fingers down the long barrel of the rifle. Perhaps he could accompany Mr. Russell as *his* assistant. Lead a pack mule, carry water, run errands. Surely armies needed folks like that. A foray against the French, and things would be peaceful again. Maybe it would settle his mind about the ministry. Give him perspective.

Whatsoever thy hand findeth to do, do it with thy might.

Yes, perhaps that was the answer. He'd lay it as a fleece before the Lord. If his folks approved, if Mr. Russell approved …

A gentle peace fell upon the woods around him.

9

Our mother-country is at a great distance, and before we can receive help from thence, our country may be overrun, and fall a helpless prey to our enemies.

—Rev. Samuel Davies, *In Time of War,* July 20, 1755

April 1755

Rain sluiced over the carriage window. Susanna pressed her nose to it, attempting to see the landscape. The trees were smaller here, and farther apart, and even the ground had changed color. Lumps resolving into cabins appeared.

Surely this wasn't Williamsburg. These homes were mere hovels. The rain slackened and she tried to focus through the drizzle. A sagging chicken coop, a droopy mule, a small garden patch.

"Almost there. These are the outskirts of town," her uncle said.

A dog yipped, and a carriage clattered past them going the opposite way. Surely only parts of Williamsburg looked like this. Maybe the rain made everything so forlorn.

The carriage turned slightly.

"Duke of Gloucester Street." Her uncle peered out. "The main road. To your left is the college."

Several buildings were just visible behind a screen of trees. The College of William and Mary. Where Tom meant to study.

"The Governor's Palace is up that way."

Stately two-story whitewashed homes now lined the road.

"You can't see it, but at the end of this street is the new Capitol, where the burgesses meet."

The carriage made several turns before they pulled up in front of a large two-story home. Four large glass windows graced the front, with dormers above. Da would love the dormers, as well as the fine brick foundation, probably enclosing a cellar. Fine brick steps led to an imposing door. Now *this* was Williamsburg.

Uncle James knocked, and a dusky face appeared under a mobcap. "Please do come in, Missus be right by."

The servant led them to a parlor lit with a crackling blaze in the fireplace.

Susanna stepped closer to the fire, warming herself. Green walls contrasted pleasantly with the fireplace's white trim. She yearned to touch the heavy fabric of the curtains. They must have cost a fortune. And the chairs looked too beautiful to sit in. The servant lit a candelabra, though it was still daytime. Costly beeswax candles, she was certain.

"Welcome, welcome," a hearty male voice said. A dark-haired masculine version of Tom's mother stood in the doorway, fully dressed in waistcoat, stock, and coat. After exchanging introductions with her uncle, Mr. Randolph bent over her hand. "We have been expecting you."

"Miss Russell?" A young woman swept into the room. "Forgive my tardiness. Please, do have a seat. I've asked Cook to send tea."

Anne Randolph's manner was charming and commanding at the

same time. Her splendid gown, a buttery yellow with white trim, complemented her pale peach complexion and hazel eyes.

"Thank you, Miss Randolph." Susanna eased herself into a chair. Da would have loved the craftsmanship, the exquisitely turned legs and carved back. She smoothed her simple brown skirts, heavy from the damp.

"Thank you," Uncle James said. "Then I'll be off to the Raleigh, to hear the gossip." He seemed uninhibited by the finery.

"The war, you mean," said Mr. Randolph. "In any case, you can gossip with me. Please abide here, you are more than welcome. We have plenty of room."

"Thank you kindly. What can you tell me of this man Braddock?"

The men began to discuss the war.

"Please call me Anne," his sister said to Susanna, sitting next to her. "None of this 'Miss Randolph' nonsense." The servant brought a tea tray, and Anne began to pour.

Susanna smiled. Despite the strangeness, she felt welcome. "Susanna to you, of course." She absorbed the pattern of the speech—the clipped consonants, the flat, formal intonation. Here was an opportunity to use her gift of mimicry. Once she'd spoken the Mays' Highland speech to Ritchie, complete with their Gaelic idioms, and received a scolding for her efforts.

"Ye may think nothing of it, lass," Da had said. "But others may think ye mock them."

And he was right. Ritchie had roared with laughter, thinking it a grand joke. But now it seemed a useful skill. She didn't want to sound like a backcountry farmer's daughter.

Which she was.

THE MIRROR above the dressing table drew her. Susanna marveled at the size, bigger than Aunt Sarah's pier mirror, and much bigger than Mother's. She extended her hand to touch the glittering frame and hesitated. Was it gold? Early morning sun caught the top, where a glittering lion raised a paw in regal splendor.

In the mirror a serious girl peered back at her, a tiny furrow between her brows. Tousled dark hair framed the pale oval of her face—winter pale, unlike her summer's glow. Dark eyes. A strong jaw culminating in a cleft chin—her father's chin. Anne Randolph had a soft, feminine face.

Susanna fingered her bodice's trim. Her summer Sabbath gown was the only other garment she owned that wouldn't look like servant's clothing here in Williamsburg.

A tiny scratch on the door presaged the entry of the maid, Callie. "Brought your water." She filled the jug on the dressing table. "Anything else you be needing? The master breaks his fast at nine."

"No, thank you."

Callie nodded and left.

Susanna tugged the bed linens and rug-like blanket into place and returned to splash water on her face. What would she do for clothes? Mother had instructed her to buy fabric for her next sewing projects for her trousseau. Might she sew a gown instead?

A tap echoed in the room. "May I come in?" The round glowing face of Anne Randolph appeared in the partially open doorway.

"Of course."

"What an interesting gown. The green trim complements your coloring. Honestly, I was not convinced you would be awake. Not after traveling." Anne wore some kind of dressing gown belted at the waist, and her hair hung in a long braid down her back.

"I wake early as a rule."

"A farmer's daughter." Anne's smile was infectious. "Your father is a gentleman farmer, I hear. He would be if he spends much time with my Uncle Peter."

Susanna wasn't sure what "gentleman farmer" meant. Perhaps a man with slaves, like Peter Jefferson. "We raise crops, breed horses and sheep, but presently, my uncle is minding the livestock." Her mind slid to her father. Where was he exactly?

"Are you worried?"

"Yes. Yes and no." How to explain? "Washington is an aide to General Braddock, and my father will be with him. I know not what an aide might do, but surely he's not marching with the infantry."

"He might be copying dispatches. He might sprain his hand." Anne tossed her head. "And from the little I hear, we outnumber the French by massive numbers."

Susanna smiled. It was good to be here.

Anne sat on the bed and curled her feet underneath her. "Tell me about your gown. I have not seen such a style before." She seemed to admire Susanna's patchwork garment.

Susanna relaxed and joined her new friend on the comfortable featherbed. She'd tell all. "It's not a style," she said softly, as if communicating a secret. "'Tis a rescue mission. My mother made this when I was twelve. She made it large, thinking it would fit for several years at least."

"Well, look at you now. I believe you are taller than Jane." Anne's pleasant face dimpled.

Susanna's heart warmed. "Mother took it apart and added trimming."

"An accomplished seamstress."

"Thank you." Susanna hesitated. "I may need more clothing." She left the bed and opened her small trunk. "I've simple skirts and bodices, things I would wear in the valley, and naught but the two gowns. Might I shop for fabric?"

Anne crouched and examined her clothing. "Let's hang these. I do love the red color of this skirt."

Soon Susanna's clothing was properly hung in the wardrobe, next to several gowns. Anne drew one out, a gorgeous blue muslin.

"This was my sister Dorothea's. As I mentioned, this is her room. But after two children, well, she informed me to make use of her old gowns. I haven't bothered, as it would take some work to make them fit me. She's as tall as Jane." Anne squinted at Susanna. "We could let out the hem, or add trimming. The color would flatter you. Stand straight and let me see."

Susanna obeyed and Anne held up the garment against her shoulders. What a beautiful blue, dyed so evenly.

"I think we need some fabric for trimming. I'll ask my brother about loaning us the carriage for the day. We'll see Williamsburg and get the necessities taken care of before any dreary lessons."

"Thank you, 'twould be wonderful."

"HAVE YOU BEEN PROMISED?" Anne asked.

Susanna tore her gaze away from the Capitol building receding behind them as the carriage made its way toward the market district. "Promised?"

"Back home? Or somewhere else?" Anne looked proper in her gown and gloves, but her eyes twinkled.

"N-no."

Anne's eyebrows rose. "There *is* someone, isn't there? You have a tendre."

Jamie's face flashed into her mind's eye. His thoughtful gray-blue gaze, the look on his face the last time she'd seen him, the day he'd come to the house asking to come with her father as a servant of sorts.

And her father's quiet face as he considered the request.

"No, no. I'm much too young to think of marriage." She *liked* Jamie, but couldn't imagine life as a minister's wife. She knew how Isabella Craig lived. Oh, the Craigs had enough to eat, but it was a hard life, and surely a minister needed a woman who was especially devout.

"Not too young to *think* of it. Some families negotiate marriage from the cradle. Thankfully my brother is open to my suggestions." Anne smirked. "Nothing's been decided yet." She pointed to the window. "Over here is the church."

The meetinghouse startled her. A steeple rose high above the street, and even the main building boasted a high roof. "'Tis ... large."

"We have an organ, installed just last month."

Susanna searched her mind for what that might possibly be.

Her face must have given her away. "A pipe organ is like a pianoforte only …" Anne fluttered her hands. "With pipes. Very beautiful. The largest in all the colonies."

"I look forward to the service." It seemed the polite thing to say, even if the Church of England was "half-Papist," as Da had said.

Soon they were at their destination, the millinery. The coachman, a lean but decently clad white servant, assisted Anne down from the carriage and turned to Susanna. She clutched at her skirts to raise them above the filth, the edge of the road still muddy from yesterday's rain.

The smell of the street assailed her, manure overlaid by something more putrid. The jingle of a harness from her right signaled the approach of a shining carriage, drawn by six beautiful bay horses. The vehicle turned on the next street, and several ragged children ran after it.

"The governor's coach," Anne said.

What a study in contrasts Williamsburg was. Susanna turned and followed Anne into the shop.

Bolts of linen, wool, and cotton covered several tables. Lace, ribbon, fans, and ornaments festooned a long counter. Cloaks, sashes, shoes, and hats lined the far wall. She stood still for a moment, drinking in the sight.

A table nearby boasted several types of fine linen. Susanna identified one bolt as Holland, another as something similar, perhaps suitable for the handkerchiefs she meant to sew.

Another table overflowed with color. "Anne, do look." Prints of every color and style swam before her gaze: gaudy red birds, sedate blue flowers, green stripes.

Anne joined her. "Printed muslin. Costs as much as silk." She indicated another table piled with several bolts of dyed cloth. "These are not so dear. This pale blue would contrast nicely with the gown. What do you think?"

"And a yard of the printed for a kerchief?" The blue flowered cloth was a shilling more per yard than the ordinary blue, but Susanna had enough and to spare, thanks to her ginseng money.

"That *is* pretty."

Anne purchased some lace, Susanna paid for her items, and they left the shop.

"Is that a print shop next door?"

"Why yes," Anne said. "They also sell a large assortment of books from London. Have anything in mind?"

They entered the shop. "Not especially, though my father asked me to look for sermons."

A multitude of newspapers, pamphlets, and books fought for space in the narrow shop. Beyond a half door a workshop of sorts. The printing press.

A stack of the *Virginia Gazette* lay to her right. Broadsheets were tacked to the wall behind. Farther down the counter, pamphlets of various sorts perched in jumbled piles.

"May I help you?" A gray-haired man squinted at her behind spectacles.

"Have you any sermons by Mr. Whitefield?"

"Whitefield?" The man examined her more closely. "The fellow from England who preaches in the fields?"

Susanna couldn't recall much of what Da had said about the man. "My father enjoys his sermons."

"Franklin." A sudden thought seemed to wash over the printer's face. "Mr. Franklin prints them. I must have a few here somewhere." He tore through the stacks of pamphlets. A few slid to the floor and Susanna bent to retrieve them.

"Ah, I knew it." He grasped a thin pamphlet. "Here you are."

Christ the Only Rest for the Weary and Heavy-Laden. "Thank you, thank you very much." Da would be pleased.

She turned to find Anne browsing the shelves on the other side of the room.

"Might your father enjoy this as well?" Anne asked. "I have heard of it but never read it myself."

The Pilgrim's Progress. "Yes, we have read it." Susanna recalled long winter evenings reading a strange tale. "Father loved it, but it was borrowed." The price was dear, but she had enough. "Thank you."

She scanned one of the shelves, full of theological works and collections of sermons. A thick pamphlet pressed between two large tomes seemed out of place. She tugged it off the shelf. *The Philadelphia Confession of Faith.*

Susanna frowned. This wasn't the Westminster. Or was it? She skimmed the pages, brightening at the familiar language. It must be the Westminster Confession, merely reprinted in Philadelphia. A gift for Jamie.

She brought the book and pamphlets to the counter and slid her coins across to the gray-haired man. The door opened and a whiff of manure from the street entered, along with two men.

"Miss Randolph." The older of the two nodded and bowed slightly, his hat tucked under his arm.

"Mr. Theus." Anne's curtsey was abbreviated. "I hope to see you at services again tomorrow."

The other man, a curl of dark hair loose against his forehead, gazed at Susanna. He seemed young, but older than Jamie, who still had a coltish look about him. She lowered her eyes, but not before catching interest in the man's gaze.

Anne's conversation with the older man was polite but brief. Susanna followed her as they left the shop and found the carriage.

"Who were they?" She settled her purchases on her lap.

"Mr. Jeremiah Theus is a painter from Charleston. He has a few commissions here in Williamsburg, and my brother decided to sit for a portrait. He will also do a miniature of me."

"You did not introduce me." A painter ... she could inquire about painting lessons.

"Well." Anne scrunched her nose. "As unmarried women we are limited in what is appropriate. If I had not been previously introduced, I would not have spoken at all, and neither would he." She slanted a glance at Susanna. "Is propriety so different in the valley?"

Susanna smiled. “No, just more plain-spoken. My father told me I should not be alone with a young man.”

Anne clapped a gloved hand over her mouth to stifle her giggles. “We shall be the best of friends.”

“Tell me about the painter’s companion.” That was what she really wanted to know.

~

THE DEEP THRUM STARTLED SUSANNA. Other sounds emerged, a fusion of harmonious metallic vibrations that finally settled into a melody. The pipe organ produced music, of a sort. Nothing like Rob Anderson’s fiddle. But, she supposed, only this kind of throbbing energy was suitable for such a church.

After the music mellowed and died, the service began. Sitting next to Anne in the Randolphs’ pew, Susanna studied the minister—rector was the term here. He was rotund, with round red cheeks and a bulbous nose, and wore what looked like a scarf draped over the front of his robes. He read from a book. Then, the strange preliminaries over, he began the sermon.

Reflexively, Susanna analyzed his logic. There were no subheads as such, only a general theme: the benevolence of God. He made a brief application, and she waited for the body of the sermon, for this was clearly an introduction.

It never came. The service concluded with a prayer. Suddenly everyone was standing and chattering.

“Is he finished?”

Anne frowned. “With what?”

“The sermon.”

Anne nodded, puzzled. “Benevolence is an appropriate topic as the parish is building a poorhouse.” She glanced about. “Perhaps my brother will introduce you to a few people.”

Mr. Randolph, cued by his sister, led them to a large group near the front. He exchanged pleasantries with several of the men.

"Relax," Anne murmured. "The Blands are cousins. Second cousins, actually."

Susanna's palms moistened beneath her fingerless gloves. By mimicking Anne's carriage and manner, she made it through several introductions. They all wore fine clothing; one of the young men sported lace on his cuffs.

Then it was over and she could breathe again.

"Mr. Theus is standing over there," Anne murmured. "Perhaps you'd care for an introduction?"

Susanna followed her gaze. Mr. Theus and the young man conversed with someone near the door. With a cue from his sister, Mr. Randolph approached them.

The young man looked her way. Assessing dark eyes. His posture straight, like a gentleman. But his coat wasn't as fine as the others', and he wore a simple stock instead of a lace-trimmed jabot.

Her pulse thudded, and her mind froze up.

"May I introduce Susanna Russell? A connection of the Jeffersons." Mr. Randolph made her sound important. She was no "connection," not in the usual sense.

Mr. Theus nodded over her hand. "Pleased to make your acquaintance."

She forced herself to respond and keep her attention on the painter while ignoring the young man.

Finally Anne's brother introduced him. "Miss Russell, Philippe Dupre."

He bent over her hand, curl falling over his forehead. "Enchanted."

"Je suis enchantée de faire votre connaissance."

It just came out of her mouth. The French phrase Tom had taught her. She hoped she'd said it right.

Philippe grinned. *"De même."*

Warmth stole up her cheeks.

SUSANNA FOLDED the note to her mother and tucked it into *Pilgrim's Progress,* wondering how long Da would be away from home. Would Mother be able to forward the letter and the book? And the pamphlet for Jamie?

She knelt at her bedside and prayed briefly, asking God for safety for her father. And Jamie. *Philippe.* His face intruded into her mind. What would Da think of him? A painter's apprentice? True, he was nearing the end of that relationship, desiring to obtain commissions on his own.

Maybe Philippe could teach her how to paint.

The wood pressed into her knees. She stood and rubbed them. The day had been strange. The simple service. The noon meal. Then … nothing. She'd chatted with Anne about their plans for the gown. Then tea—the rich, pleasantly astringent taste of Bohea was delightful. At home their tea was brewed at half the strength, when they had it.

Ham and cheese for supper, followed by light conversation, Mr. Randolph swirling Madeira in his glass. Anne poured Susanna a small amount of cordial, a fruity drink which stung like hard cider going down.

Now bedtime. It didn't seem like a Sabbath. Susanna found Mr. Whitefield's sermon and sat on the bed to read it, the well-trimmed beeswax candle spilling steady light on the page. Perhaps this would suffice for the missing sermon.

Two main points. Well, she supposed a man who preached in the fields would not want multiple heads and subheads. She lay back on the soft pillow. The first part was about Pharisees, a familiar topic. *Philippe.* Was he from Charleston as well? His name was exotic—was it French? Was *he* French? But no, his English was impeccable.

Her eyelids fluttered. Wondering when she would see him next, Susanna closed her eyes, her arm relaxing onto the covers.

The pamphlet slipped out of her grasp and slid under the bed.

10

Now they can go to balls and assemblies, play-houses and horse-racing; they have no thought of their sins; they know not what it is to weep for sin, or humble themselves under the mighty hand of God.

—George Whitefield, *Christ the Only Rest*

Slanting shadows fingered the grassy expanse before them. They'd been in the saddle since before sunrise, but James marveled that his backside wasn't sore. Well, his thighs would ache tomorrow, he knew that from experience. But the sorrel gelding under him ate up the ground in a smooth running walk, sparing him the bone-jarring trot Russell's mount broke into time and again. Behind them the mule shuffled gamely along, laden with foodstuffs, feed, and canvas for a tiny tent.

"Mr. Russell, is Red a pacer?" The man's face was backlit by the afternoon sun, low over the western ridges.

"Half. The stud was a hunter, gives him a bit more size, but the dam is a Narragansett. Moves well, doesn't he?"

"Ye gave me the best mount."

He chuckled. "Dinna let Cricket hear that. She's a fine mare, but her dam was a carriage horse. Of course, out here horses are asked to do a lot of things. Pull plows and the like. Cricket is an excellent brood mare, forbye."

They crossed a creek, and the trail ahead vanished into a wooded area.

Mr. Russell slowed the black mare to a walk and half-turned in the saddle. "We'll be camping for the night up ahead, near the river. There's a clearing."

James nodded. As they entered the shade of the trees, Russell straightened almost imperceptibly. James echoed the man's alertness by focusing on the animal beneath him. Red would scent any panther or bear before he would. Although four-legged creatures weren't the main fear here in the northern reaches of the valley. And not the French, with whom they were at war, for white men fought on battlefields, army against army. The chestnut's ears turned this way and that, lazily, the way his mule did when slogging home. There was nothing of interest here.

It was almost full dark by the time they'd found a place to camp, tended to the horses, and built a fire. Mr. Russell filled both a skillet and a kettle with water while James wrestled with the canvas.

"Dinna mind it, lad," Russell said. "Let's sleep on top of it, here near the fire. No rain tonight."

Indeed, it hadn't snowed much after Christmas, and the spring rain was thin this year, starting and stopping like the last dregs from a water cask. Bad for crops, but helpful for travel. "How far to Winchester?" Washington would meet up with Braddock and his men there.

"One verra long day." Mr. Russell stirred cornmeal into the pan. "From Winchester we'll be crossing the Potomac at Will's Creek. That's what I hear."

James pulled out a parcel wrapped in oilskin—the last of the food Mrs. Russell had packed for them. His mouth watered. Riding didn't seem like work, but he was famished. They shared a meal as the stars came out.

"Mr. Paxton, what did your parents say, exactly, when you asked their permission?"

He'd been a bit surprised at their approval. Maybe Russell was too. "My da simply said he could give me the mule, but not his musket." He fingered the scarred rifle that Mr. Craig had given him. "My ma … she said I could go. And she said her door was open to brave men, but forever shut to cowards."

"Och, sounds like she's a right courageous woman herself."

"Her family escaped Scotland when Claverhouse harried the land."

"Hmph."

Looking up at the stars and hearing the fire snap, it was easy to talk to this man. "She's a Wilson, kin to the Margaret Wilson who was staked in Solway Firth to drown."

Russell was silent for many long seconds before he spoke. "My sins and faults of youth, do Thou my Lord forget; after Thy mercy think on me, and for Thy goodness great."

It sounded like the psalter.

"Some of that lass's last words. D'ye ken the history?"

"The Killing Time, aye. Mr. Craig spent a week on it. Part of church history."

James remembered the lessons vividly. The minister had shut his volume of *Foxe's Book of Martyrs* and said, "What happened next isna contained in any book." Eyes welling, Mr. Craig took a deep breath. The valley was populated by the sons and grandsons of men and women who had been persecuted under the reign of Charles II, and the tales were close to their hearts. "Ever hear the song, 'Loudon Hill'?"

"Clavers coming to kill the Covenanters."

Mr. Craig cleared his throat. "Aye."

The king had tried to rule their worship. Some had died for their faith. Others had escaped to Ulster or the colonies.

And now Highlanders had joined the emigration, some against their will.

"What does Mr. MacLeod think of the preaching?"

Russell added several trimmed branches to the fire and poked at it until he was satisfied. "Arch May's taken him under his wing, aye?" He settled back on the canvas. "My father purchased the Mays' indentures, years ago, before I married Susanna's mother. We wondered then what you wonder now. Highland Scots and Lowland Scots have never been precisely friendly, and it's largely a matter of religion." He cleared his throat. "My father told us not to fret over things like the rosary."

James wondered what Mr. Craig would say to that.

"He spoke to the Mays about Christ, who He was and what He did for sinners. He spoke of grace. Free grace. The essence of false religion is laboring to please God, no matter what kirk ye attend."

James's heart leapt at the truth of the words.

"One day Arch May disappeared. Didna come back till late the next day. 'I see it now, I see it,' he said, tears running down his face and into his beard. 'I'm a great sinner, but the grace of Christ is greater.' He understood grace, and some of the Romish things began to fall away."

"All except Christmas?"

Russell chuckled. "All except Christmas."

"'Ho, every one that thirsteth, come ye to the waters, and he that hath no money; come ye, buy, and eat …'" Words, carried on the breeze, came from a man perched on a stump. James recognized the Book of Isaiah.

He squinted. The stranger was simply clothed, like a farmer. "Who is that?"

They drew near and Russell dismounted. "Let's have a listen."

Several folks clustered around the preacher. One older man, wearing a strange waistcoat, was probably German. The farms were close together here, and the road well traveled. Thick foliage nearby marked a stream.

James didn't mind the halt. The horses needed the water. After seeing to the animals, they sat down within earshot.

Russell pulled out dried meat from his saddlebag and handed James half. "He's a Baptist."

"How can ye tell?" The sermon was ordinary, if rather simple.

"Can ye imagine Mr. Craig preaching in a field or by a roadside?"

James swallowed a well-chewed bite. "Well, no. Not unless the meetinghouse burned down."

A rumble of hooves signaled the approach of riders.

A line formed between Russell's brows. "Look yonder. McKee and some other militiamen pressed into service." He didn't take his eyes off the man. "Be canny, now. Back home he's a nuisance. Here he's dangerous."

So far they were unnoticed, partially hidden by the foliage, but that wouldn't last long. The men would want to water their mounts.

The preacher kept speaking. "For whosoever shall keep the whole law, and yet offend in one point, he is guilty of all." A bead of sweat rolled down his face, despite the gentle spring air.

Some of the newcomers dismounted. McKee remained on his ill-favored bay, eyes fixed on the minister. A scowl twisted his face as the preacher spoke of sin and the need to repent. McKee spoke to the others and they began to jeer. Those on foot picked up stones.

Russell straightened and found his rifle. James did the same. McKee still hadn't noticed them. "Lad, follow my lead. Stay close. Bullies tend to frighten easily but ye canna always tell for sure."

Russell stepped out into the sunshine, equidistant from the preacher and the ruffians. "Welcome, McKee, ye're almost to Winchester."

The hubbub quieted. Even the minister stopped preaching.

McKee's expression slackened, then firmed. "Well, if it isna the meddler of Augusta County, John Russell." His gaze shifted to James and he cursed in merriment. "And the minister's lad, with a gun." He turned to his comrades. "A proper entertainment, I tell ye!"

McKee faced Russell again. "Did ye leave your bonny wife home with her witch's brews?" A few men chuckled. "Or ..." His next suggestion was lewd.

Russell's jaw muscle rippled. He made a show of fondling his rifle and priming the pan. "The water upstream will be better for your health." His voice was surprisingly calm.

Aghast, James primed his own weapon. Surely it wouldn't come to a fight. He darted a glance to his right. The peaceful members of the crowd had closed ranks in front of the preacher.

A man next to McKee shouted, "His preaching is illegal. And we're the militia."

McKee smiled. "That's right, Russell."

The muzzle of Russell's rifle dipped. "What do ye propose?" He advanced several steps, shoulders relaxed.

James's pulse throbbed in his ears. Surely he wasn't going to relinquish the preacher to a mob.

A man uncoiled a horsewhip. "Forty lashes?"

"Sixty!"

Dust rose from the horses' hooves as the ruffians argued, their mounts agitated.

"Who's your captain?" Russell scratched his head, seemingly unperturbed.

The voices faltered. "He sent us on ahead," someone said.

"Aye, well, we'll need a magistrate in any case," Russell said, as if disappointed. He turned to address the farmers. "Who's your sheriff?"

The man in the strange waistcoat lifted a hand, and Russell spoke to him for several minutes before turning back to the militiamen.

"The sheriff is in Winchester and willna be back today." Russell indicated the gray-headed man in the waistcoat. "This man's a constable. He'll take the lawbreaker into custody."

Murmurs of discontent rose from the group.

McKee spat into the dust. "We'll see you again soon."

The mob departed, trailing complaints.

James joined Russell and the others. The preacher was unharmed, though one of the onlookers pressed a handkerchief against a gash on his forehead.

"Aaron Walker." The preacher held out his hand to Russell and James in turn. "Thank you. 'Tis an honor to be beaten in the service of my King, but my flesh cares not for the experience." He pulled out a cloth to wipe his sweaty face. "Either way, those men—some may not survive. I read about Fort Necessity. They needed to hear the truth."

"Aye, I ken that. Ye're in good hands with the constable."

The constable spoke to Russell in a mix of German and broken English. James caught several words, enough to realize they were invited for the midday meal.

"We'd be pleased, Herr Henkel. I canna forget your wife's good cheese."

Ah, friends, then. And probably Dunkers—German Baptists.

Russell addressed the preacher. "Which way are ye headed? I assume your detention will be verra temporary. A fellow Baptist will find reason to commute your sentence to time served at the dinner table."

"Philadelphia. I'm to meet with several ministers there. There is a small group of Baptist churches in the area. They've formed an association, and published a statement of faith. Something the brethren farther south could find of use as they establish churches."

"I wish ye well." Russell's smile slackened. "I take it Philadelphia's unlicensed ministers are no' beaten nor jailed?"

"But Mr. Russell," James said. "Pennsylvania doesna license anyone."

There was steel in Mr. Russell's blue gaze. "Precisely."

James thrust a small piece of honey locust wood into the sputtering fire. A fresh billow of smoke wafted up to the red wool coat perched above it, propped on a number of carefully planted sticks. Hopefully any lice in Private MacKenzie's coat would be discouraged. But the bitter tang of the wood smoke did little to hide the stench of two thousand unwashed men camped in a palisade for weeks on end.

MacKenzie's chin nodded on his chest. The thin soldier had drawn fourth watch last night. James was certain Lil' Mac, as he was sometimes called—the other names were unspeakable—drew duty more often than he should. His regiment had fought against the Scots in the recent uprising, and the older soldiers hated Highlanders like MacKenzie. The lad was one of several who sometimes hung around their fire, preferring his and Russell's company to the drinking and card playing rampant among the members of the Forty-fourth Infantry.

James set the kettle over the glowing coals. Russell insisted they not drink the water from Will's Creek. Some were already sick. Their ale and cider were gone, so they drank sassafras tea and sometimes splurged on the coffee in the mule's packs.

At present Russell was in the main cabin with the general and his aides-de-camp. Hastily constructed like the rest of Fort Cumberland, daylight shone through the chinking. Colonel Halkett emerged from the structure. The gold braid of the man's uniform gleamed in the sun; his white stock was bright and clean above his polished gorget. Some sort of English lord, James had heard. The man commanded the Forty-fourth Infantry and James did not envy him the task. Halkett lifted a handkerchief to his nose, perhaps to ward off the stench, then walked off.

Mac stirred, and James added dried leaves to the kettle. Russell was hoping to get leave to forage again as they couldn't live on the salt beef and stale biscuit that made up the "king's provision." General Braddock was furious no one came to the fort to sell fresh produce, not realizing there were few farms out here, and what few there were grew mainly Indian corn and tobacco.

Another man emerged from the ramshackle cabin: Colonel Washington, elegant in poise but not clad in red coat, having no commission. Apparently Braddock considered a voluntary position a reward in itself.

Meeting Washington in Winchester had been a shock. Why, the man was no older than William Preston, and fresh-faced and handsome, apart from a few pox scars. James could tell just by the way he'd dismounted that he was a good horseman.

"I am that pleased to meet ye again," Russell had said.

"Though the circumstances leave much to be desired," Washington affirmed. For such a young man, he possessed grace and presence.

"Aye, I'll give ye that." Russell turned to James. "My assistant, James Paxton."

Washington's blue eyes twinkled despite his erect posture and proper persona. "Mr. Paxton." He nodded slightly.

James tried to bow properly. "Your fame has preceded you."

"Good or ill, I wonder? I have yet to win a battle."

James swallowed, mortified.

"I have no illusions about myself, nor the task before us, which will be difficult considering the terrain." He turned to Russell. "I can use as many true-hearted Virginians as I can find. Men like yourself." His eyes slid to the horses. "What a beautiful sorrel."

James tugged at Red's reins and brought him closer to the man.

Washington quirked an eyebrow. "Narragansett?"

Russell recounted the animal's bloodlines. "Good size and wonderful gait."

Washington stroked the horse's neck and turned to Russell. "Tomorrow we leave for Will's Creek, where the militia has built a fort. Some of the troops have already departed." He motioned toward a carriage. "The general will take the coach, and we'll accompany him, along with the cavalry."

James studied the carriage. Could it manage the journey? Many roads could barely accommodate wagons. Washington wore an impassive expression, concealing his thoughts. Russell had said the man had done a lot of surveying in the backcountry and knew the land, despite his Tidewater manners. Would Braddock listen to Washington's advice?

Washington nodded and departed for his quarters, the tail of his fine blue coat swinging.

"Rattlesnake colonel!" someone jeered.

James turned. A knot of infantrymen lounged on the street, eyeing Washington. Clearly they despised colonial militiamen.

The memory brought a foreboding to his heart. There was little chance a grand English general would listen to a mere "rattlesnake" colonel.

They'd arrived at Fort Cumberland after several days on the trail. General Braddock's carriage had somehow survived the trip, though there was no question of it going farther. There was no road to Fort Duquesne, only a footpath. Men with axes were sent ahead to create a passage wide enough for wagons.

But Braddock's army possessed no horses and wagons to carry needed foodstuffs and other supplies for the march. James didn't know where they would come from. Even if they had wagons, how would they get through the terrain? They sat waiting, day after day, week after week, for wagons that might or might not be helpful.

The kettle whistled, and James poured tea into a cup. "Hey, Mac, have some."

The scrawny soldier clutched the cup. "Thank ye kindly."

Motion caught James's eye. A filthy man dressed in buckskin entered the palisade, and Washington and Sir Halkett spoke to him. Probably a scout or messenger bearing bad news, like more French reinforcements at Fort Duquesne.

After several minutes, Russell headed for the fire. "Some good news for a change. Mr. Franklin has arranged for wagons, and they should be here within the week."

Benjamin Franklin the printer? James had heard his name more than once. He must be an influential man.

"Sorry, lads. I canna get away. But ye may go foraging, Mr. Paxton, and I asked Colonel Washington for a certain regular to assist." Russell's gaze slid to MacKenzie.

Mac's face brightened.

"He asked your commander. I've a pass for ye."

"Thank ye kindly." MacKenzie stood and threw on his coat, still warm from the fumigation.

They went to the gate where Mac showed the pass to an indifferent sentry.

Once outside the twelve-foot walls, Mac cleared his throat. "Ye ken anything about the Indians? Where did they all go?"

Braddock's Indian scouts, once a large group camping outside the fort, had thinned dramatically. Only one Indian hut remained in a dusty area once filled with the structures. Several half-naked men squatted around a single campfire.

"General Braddock decided the Indian women couldna stay. So they left, as well as most of the men."

"Canna be good."

They reached the tree line.

"Hmph. Ye're catching on," James took a deep lungful of clean air. "We're about to be ambushed by Indians and we could use some scouts, not to mention warriors, on our side. Braddock treats the friendly Indians like dirt and expects them to help him. It willna happen."

The trees grew tall and close together, the sweet spring air cooler underneath the canopy. Green shoots poked through last year's soggy leaf litter.

"Ever had to forage for greens before?" James asked.

"Aye, in Scotland."

"After the Rising?" James guessed. The Highland Scots had been slaughtered at the Battle of Culloden. Afterward, men had been harassed whether they'd been part of the rebellion or not. Crofts were burnt. Whole families had starved.

"My father fought at Prestonpans. D'ye ken we captured Sir Halkett? Didna harm him, released him on parole."

MacKenzie seemed to want to talk, but the memories were obviously hard. Ian MacLeod's father had fought too, and the young man often wore a guarded expression. Like a dog who'd been kicked too many times.

A clearing spread out before them, dotted with red. "Strawberries!" James would never take berries for granted again. Not after weeks of salty rations. "Come, eat up. They dinna keep, so just eat them."

They settled on the grass.

"What happened to your da?" James asked, after they'd eaten several mouthfuls.

Mac gazed into the distance. "He died at Culloden. My family, well ... it's a long story. No one had enough to eat. After my ma died, my sister and I signed an indenture. *This* was a mistake." He indicated the red coat. "I couldna imagine another year of working the tobacco, and when the Army offered to buy indentures, it seemed like a good trade." He popped more strawberries in his mouth. "But they dinna shoot at ye on a plantation."

They stood and headed back into the trees. "Pokeweed." James pointed. They stuffed leaves into their bags.

"See that creek?" MacKenzie asked. "There may be fiddleheads."

They walked down the slope and followed the bank, searching.

"My sister lives in North Carolina." MacKenzie turned, greens in his hand. "Her name is Janet."

Janet MacKenzie, presumably. Why was he telling him this?

"Will ye post a letter for me? After?" His Adam's apple bobbed. "I dinna think I'm coming back."

He didn't sound fearful, only sad. What should he say? MacKenzie was probably a Papist, he might want a priest, but no, he needed Christ.

James's pulse thudded in his ears. What would he say to a man who might be dead in a matter of days? He remembered Russell's words to him about Arch May.

"Mac, what think ye of Christ?"

11

To be SOLD… A Plantation in Augusta County, on Shenandee River, containing 450 Acres more or less, 100 of which are extraordinary rich low Grounds; as also, Ten choice working Slaves, with Hogs, Horses, and Cattle…

—*The Virginia Gazette*, September 5, 1755

The morning sun glinted off the silver chocolate pot and bathed the discarded newspaper in a patch of yellow light. Susanna wondered if there was any news of the general. Was her father safe?

"Here." Anne nudged the butter crock to Susanna's side of the gleaming walnut table. "Eat up." Her lips twitched with merriment. "My brother has secured a French tutor, and he's coming today."

"Truly?"

"Of course. Now eat your bread, 'Tis not that stale."

Susanna sipped her chocolate and buttered her bread, then reached for the *Gazette*. The tutor was good news. But she had to see if anything was written about Braddock. Or Washington.

Constantinople ... *Corsicans* ... Who cared about those places?

Susanna flipped the page, careful to keep her elbows off the table. The book of manners hadn't said anything about newspapers, but if Mr. Randolph read the *Gazette* at the breakfast table, it couldn't be a serious breach of etiquette. At least not for men.

There, on the top left, something about Braddock. One hundred Indians and a mention of wampum. Two weeks ago, General Braddock had talked to some friendly Indians. But no real news. The next line down proclaimed the results of a cockfight. A *cockfight*, of all things.

"Susanna?" Anne wore a strange expression. "Bad news?"

Susanna sighed. "I should not complain. No news of a battle is good news."

"The tutor is coming at ten. He's a student at the College."

The rest of the newspaper consisted of legal notices and classifieds. Susanna's eyes lingered over the notice of the sale of land on the Shenandoah River. She closed the paper.

"What say you we practice our posture with the rings?" Anne said.

Susanna tried to keep her face pleasant.

"Just for a few minutes, while we wait for Mr. Martin."

"Very well."

They crossed the hall to the parlor. Anne handed her one of the wooden rings and placed the other on her head, and Susanna followed suit. Anne proceeded to sit gracefully in one of the chairs, keeping her head and chin level. Her ring didn't budge.

Susanna had barely mastered the art of keeping the thing on her head, and now she had to perform acrobatics with it? Stiffly, she minced her way to a chair, backed against it, and lowered herself.

She slipped off the edge of the chair and fell to the floor, her legs splayed unladylike across the wood planking. The ring spilled off her head and rolled to the open door, where Callie now stood.

"Missus," the maid said nervously, "Mr. Martin be here."

A man stood behind the maid, clutching a hat.

Susanna scrambled to her feet, her face hot. Anne's expression was perfectly composed, except for a twinkle in her eye.

The young man looked flustered, big blue eyes darting nervously in a pale face. "Good day." He bowed.

"Welcome." Anne took charge, and soon they were arranged about the dining table.

"I've brought a book," Mr. Martin stammered. He looked young, no older than Jamie. The thin seams of his wool coat betrayed its age.

Susanna straightened in her seat, ignoring the ache in her tailbone. "I've a primer I've studied. Conjugations, mostly."

"The regular verbs? Irregular?"

"The three regular forms and a few of the most common irregulars. *Je suis, tu es, il est*—"

"*Très bien!*" Mr. Martin smiled, revealing crooked teeth. He pronounced the phrase strangely, but he knew more than she. Didn't he? "We shall continue with irregulars and introduce vocabulary."

After forty minutes she was tired. "*Répétéz, s'il vous plait,*" over and over. And she fought each time to remember the way Tom spoke. The way Philippe Dupre had slipped her a phrase.

"What does '*de même*' mean?"

Mr. Martin's eyes stayed on the text. "*Comment traduisez-vous 'de même' en anglais?*"

She repeated the sentence, fighting against his clunky pronunciation.

"Literally 'of the same.'"

"As we would say, 'Likewise'?"

"*Exactement*." He looked up. "By the way, your pronunciation is passable."

Passable?

She needed a *good* tutor. This young man barely knew more than she.

Anne interrupted. "Mr. Martin, would you care for tea or cider?"

He brightened. "Yes, thank you. Tea, if you would."

Anne slanted a wry glance at Susanna and left.

"Mr. Martin, may I ask you a question?"

The puppy-dog look on his pinched face melted away her frustration. "Of course."

"My father is with Colonel Washington, but the *Gazette* has no news. You must hear things."

Anne returned bearing a tray of scones and a crock of jam. Callie followed with tea.

Mr. Martin's eyebrows lifted at the sight of the food. "Yes, well, I did hear one item." He added a dollop of jam to a scone. "But you mustn't be concerned. There are always difficulties in executing military maneuvers. We know this from history."

"You've read Plutarch." Grandda had read excerpts to them.

The tutor choked on his scone but recovered. "And *Caesar's Commentaries*." He eyed her. "Wagons. There was a problem with wagons. Braddock requested them from the governor, who couldn't find any."

Wagons clogged the streets of Williamsburg. She raised a brow.

"Planters won't allow a driver outside of their own county, much less the Commonwealth."

Susanna saw the problem instantly. Slaves couldn't be trusted to return. And wagons wouldn't drive themselves. She nodded.

Mr. Martin sipped his tea. "Excellent tea, Miss Randolph, I do thank you." He slid his glance to Susanna. "Pennsylvania is supplying the wagons. Not a true problem, just a delay."

"But how would they get wagons into the mountains?"

"Mountains?" the tutor asked, perplexed.

Something was wrong.

"WATCH OUT." Anne extended an arm and pressed Susanna back, away from the edge of the street.

"Yee haw!" Hoofbeats thudded to their left. Two horses came into view; riders perched over their withers, galloping toward the Capitol.

Anne clucked her disapproval. "There is a perfectly good racetrack outside of town."

The young men were probably drunk, or nearly so. The horses' hooves stirred up the dust of the dry street as they thundered past. Susanna dared a glance at her hem. The newly altered blue gown remained pristine.

Mr. Randolph frowned at the racers but followed their course with his gaze. He offered his arms. "Shall we?"

Susanna's innards tightened as they entered the building. Hadn't Mr. Whitefield's sermon condemned the theater? And horse racing? But this was Shakespeare, wasn't it? And Da had given her *Julius Caesar* to read.

They'd discussed it. "What d'ye think of Brutus?" he'd asked.

"He seemed noble. Wanting the best for Rome."

"Had he the right to kill Caesar?"

Grandda leaped into the conversation. "Was Caesar even a lawful ruler?"

Then Da and Grandda had wrestled over that question, agreeing that crossing the Rubicon was a fatal mistake. Susanna had lost the thread of the logic at that point, not remembering what the Rubicon was. Some river. But how could a river be important?

Anne tugged at her elbow. "Mr. Bolling has come with his wife. He is a descendant of the Indian princess Pocahontas."

Pocahontas? That was more interesting than the endless web of cousins and second cousins that knit Williamsburg's prominent families together. "What is the name of the play?"

"*Twelfth Night*." Anne greeted a young woman, then fixed her gaze over Susanna's shoulder. "Mr. Theus and young Mr. Dupre are in attendance."

It was time for the play to begin, but the perfumed crowd seemed more interested in socializing. Anne nudged Susanna, turning her. She found herself face-to-face with Philippe Dupre.

He kissed her hand. "*Bien soir*."

Susanne swallowed. "*De même*."

"I believe Mr. Randolph has scheduled a sitting next week." His dark eyes mesmerized her.

"I look forward to it."

"Until then." He dipped his head.

Then he and Mr. Theus were gone, swallowed up in the crowd.

"Mr. Dupre is rather forward, don't you think?" Anne said. She hooked her arm in Susanna's and led her to her seat. "But he is good-looking."

Susanna's pulse quickened. "I do think he'd make a better French tutor than the one we have now."

"The one we have now is cheap. But I agree, Mr. Martin's pronunciation is execrable. I will approach my brother. I know how to throw hints."

"Thank you, Anne." A wave of giddiness washed over her. She struggled to act with decorum. Not like a silly schoolgirl.

Dinna be alone with a lad.

Her father's words. Well, she wouldn't be alone, would she?

The curtains opened and the prick of conscience vanished.

RED HAWK FINGERED his chin and found another stubby hair. He plucked it out and moved to the next. He wished he had Straight Arrow's skin—the man had no facial hair whatsoever.

The afternoon sun warmed his aching thighs and shoulders as he relaxed in front of the wigwam. He'd finished clearing Dark Water's field yesterday. His aunt was now planting the corn.

The move had been rough. Before Grayfeather's departure the elders had decided to move the village all the way to the Kanawha River. A few of the women wept; the plum trees and strawberry patches had just begun to bear well, and now they had to start all over again. It was a three-day journey southwest. Grandmother and a few others lagged behind, but Red Hawk didn't mind spending the journey in Straight Arrow's company, whose grandmother was also feeble.

At least the weather had been favorable. Snows had been light all winter, and hunting was good. When the land awakened from its frosty sleep, scouts were sent ahead to stake out the village, unhindered by the remnants of slushy snow. An elder accompanied them, needing to locate the most propitious site and plant the western post.

Grandmother had explained the process. "The ancient ones brought this knowledge," she said. "The evening star must be honored, and the whole village aligned to the four directions."

Red Hawk plucked out another hair. The sun was descending over the elders' new lodge, which held the place of honor near the western pole. The doorway faced east, just as it was supposed to. Everything was in harmony.

Dark Water came into view, carrying water and her digging tools. "Lazy good-for-nothing," she said, concealing her gratitude, even though it was expected warriors would help in the fields when new land was planted. Girdling trees was not a task for women.

Red Hawk rolled his shoulders. "I could use some of Grandmother's salve."

They went inside and sat around the hearth. After they'd eaten, the old woman reached into a bundle and pulled out a small covered pot.

"Here." Grandmother motioned him closer. She anointed his shoulders and massaged in the salve, her fingers surprisingly strong.

It felt good. Something came to mind then, something he'd been turning over in his mind all day. "Grandmother, when did the Creator make the Shawnee people?"

"He-Who-Creates-By-Thinking made the Lenape first, after the Great Flood." Her hands dug into his upper arm.

The Lenape were related to the Shawnee. "The grandfathers."

"Yes." She kneaded the other arm. "What are you really asking?"

"When did the Creator make white men?"

She let go of his arms. "I do not know."

But Grandmother knew everything. She'd taught him the old stories and the ancient truths: the four directions, the twelve witnesses. "The Creator brought everything into being."

"Well, the Uchee say the first man was created just after the earth was formed. They also say that death came about because of disobedience."

That made sense. "The Muskogee and Uchee speak different languages, they are different from us in that. Are white men simply another group?"

"Some say they are a result of mischief on the part of Cloud Boy."

"But surely only the Creator can make a man."

Grandmother sighed. "I think you ought to go on a quest. Your spirit is unsettled."

RED HAWK LEFT two days later just before dawn. He'd spent the previous day chopping firewood from the branches of the oaks he'd girdled. Now there was a stack next to Grandmother's wigwam, curing for next winter. Couldn't have too much wood.

The early morning mist cloaked the world and dampened every sound. Red Hawk wore his buckskin poncho against the chill but carried little: a gourd for water, his personal medicine pouch, and some cedar chips. A bag for herbs was slung across his back. Grandmother was too old to forage and Dark Water didn't always have the time. He might come across some on his way home.

He stepped through the foliage, listening. Wolves, attracted by scraps, had been common around the old village. Once a tiny girl had gone missing and her mother had wailed for days. Red Hawk hadn't heard or seen any trace of the animals around the new site, but it was only a matter of time. Their noses and ears would draw them.

Wolves. A powerful spirit animal, yet not always good. Had it been like this from the beginning? Grandmother said the Uchee believed death came from disobedience. Whose disobedience?

Surely the Creator was good. How had all the evil happened?

Pausing now and again to listen, he climbed. The village was well west of the steepest mountains, but the land undulated with ridges and hills, the little valleys between them full of bright green foliage and secret springs. Red Hawk emerged from the mist and gained the summit of a knoll, speckled with rocky outcroppings and flanked by pine.

He sat, pulled out the cedar, and arranged the fragments on a flat rock. The Creator saw the Shawnee from the sky, was pleased by good deeds, and could be approached in several ways, not all of which were open to Red Hawk. But he knew of one way. Cedar was a special wood. The smoke of burning cedar would ascend and perhaps the Creator would take notice.

Perhaps.

Red Hawk used flint and steel to start the fire, finding irony in using the white man's iron to perform such a sacred task. But the Uchee trader had explained that iron was smelted just as copper was. They both came from Mother Earth.

A tiny gray curl of smoke rose above the chips.

A hawk screeched somewhere nearby. Red Hawk started at the sound, normally a good sign, but a shadow descended over his heart.

Was his father still well? They'd been away so long.

He took out his medicine pouch and pulled out a smooth dark glittering stone, a treasure from the mountains and emblem of Mother Earth. Next, a feather. A hawk feather, tinged red. Emblem of his spirit guide.

Did the Creator take notice of him? If not, perhaps his spirit guide would.

He stayed on the knoll until the cedar turned to ash and the day warmed. His spirit seemed as empty as his stomach when he rose. Branches lashed his face as he descended into the next valley, but he welcomed the sting. He stumbled upon a tiny deer track and followed it downhill into a small clearing.

There, in the middle of the grass, lay a hawk. Its head was angled in an unnatural way, and the breeze ruffled its feathers.

It was dead.

12

These savages may indeed be a formidable enemy to your raw American militia, but upon the king's regular and disciplined troops, sir, it is impossible that they should make an impression.

—General Edward Braddock to Benjamin Franklin

The Monongahela River, July 1755

The setting sun glared behind the western ridge like a baleful orange eye. James slipped the headstall over Red's ears and eased the bit out of the gelding's mouth. "Glad to make camp, aren't ye, fella?" he crooned.

Nearby Russell struck flint and steel to start a fire, a seemingly incongruous goal in the heat, but they needed to cook and heat water for tea. Some of the soldiers behind them didn't bother, merely drinking their fill at a nearby stream and collapsing under the trees to rest. Each day's march covered little ground, but the days were long, hot, and draining, especially for a foot soldier wearing a wool coat and carrying supplies.

But despite the fatigue of the march, the mood was different tonight. They couldn't be more than ten miles from Fort Duquesne, and the French wouldn't wait for them to arrive and set up cannon. The infantrymen preparing for sentry duty looked grim.

James pulled the strap of his satchel over his head. The bag contained his Bible, the books Susanna had sent, and more bandages than they could possibly use. Mrs. Russell had insisted on herbs as well; her husband carried those, and James hoped the man knew all their uses. Was yarrow for fever or bleeding? James couldn't remember.

He traced the hard lines of the books through the canvas with his fingers. Russell was well pleased with Bunyan's allegory, and they'd started reading it together after the package had arrived at Fort Cumberland. But on the march everyone's mood had darkened, and Russell preferred to conduct a simple worship service each evening, either reading a passage of Scripture or reciting some of it from memory.

The other book, the *Philadelphia Confession*, nagged at his mind. Why had Susanna sent it?

James joined Russell at the fire just as the sun disappeared, leaving salmon streaks across the western sky. Clinks, thuds, and grunts sounded before and behind as the soldiers settled in for the night.

"Why do you think Susanna sent the confession?" he asked, finally.

Russell handed him a hard biscuit. "I dinna think she meant to instruct ye in theology. She probably didna even understand it was a Baptist confession."

A bubble rose from James's innards. He wanted to giggle from tension. Discussing the vagaries of a lass's mind in the face of battle provoked a desperate amusement. "I suppose ye're right."

"She must have thought it a suitable gift for a minister's lad."

"Hmph." He dipped the biscuit in his cup to soften it. If he survived this—if he survived his training for the ministry, for that matter—he'd want to court Susanna. But would she be married to another by then? "Mr. Russell, I would ask your leave that I might write and thank her."

The light had faded to pewter gray, but James could still distinguish Russell's features. The man's gaze was fixed on him.

"I'll relay the message."

James's shoulders slumped. He refilled his tin cup, needing something to do.

"I understand."

"No, ye dinna understand," Russell said. "It's nae lack in ye, lad. Ye're like a son to me as it is. It's Susanna."

"I ken she's in Williamsburg—"

"But ye dinna ken why." Russell packed away the food.

"To study French." What else was it? Painting?

"I dinna think she understands herself why she went. Not precisely. But she's running. Away from the valley ... Away from God."

A ball of dread landed in James's stomach. Suddenly he wanted to grieve. Over Braddock's stupidity, dragging them over ridges and splashing through streams, day after day. And over Susanna. He hadn't realized how he'd kept her in his heart until now, like a secret kept even from himself.

"I'm sorry," Russell said, his voice thick. "Now then, it's full dark. It may be MacKenzie will join us again."

The thought of the thin soldier distracted him. The man absorbed the Scripture like a babe, not understanding much, but returning again and again. "What passage tonight?"

"Mac may have more questions. If no', we'll go to Romans chapter five."

The snap of a twig presaged Mac's arrival. He wore his red coat open, unbuttoned; even when properly attired the man seemed swallowed up in his clothing.

"Good e'en," Mac said, and sat, folding up his body, knees near his chin.

James removed his loosely bound stock and splashed a little water from his gourd canteen down his back to ease the itch of drying sweat.

Strangely, Mac's countenance brightened more and more as they approached the French fort. The man seemed to live for the Scripture readings.

After Russell prayed, he began. "Therefore being justified by faith, we have peace with God through our Lord Jesus Christ ..." He quoted several more verses.

"What does 'justified' mean?" Mac asked.

The tension in James's gut eased, and something glorious took its place. Mac was coming to life.

THE NEXT MORNING James dressed carefully, checking and rechecking his powder horn and shot. Russell had scratched out a map in the dirt one afternoon, tracing the path of the Monongahela River and the Ohio. "Fort Duquesne is here." He'd pointed to the place where the smaller river joined the larger. "Water on two sides. But no' as secure as you'd think. Cannon will take it down easy. If we get that far." His lined face reflected his doubts.

Soon after breaking camp, the glint of water came into view. Braddock ordered the vanguard to cross the Monongahela. Axemen accompanied the first troops, in order to widen the path. Grenadiers and some militiamen, led by Colonel Halkett, pressed on next, along with several supply carts. Most of their supplies were far behind, with the other regiment. Only the Forty-fourth had come this far.

"Mr. Paxton," Russell said, holding Cricket's reins. The mare stood lazily, one hind leg cocked, accustomed to the stops and starts of the journey. "Look yonder. The colonel must be recovered."

James mounted Red and rechecked the mule's lead rein. "Aye, it's good to see Colonel Washington up and about." Like a number of others, the man had succumbed to the flux. Now he rode alongside General Braddock and the other aides, splendid in his blue coat, with no sign he'd been ill—except. Was that a pillow on his saddle?

Cricket snuffed once when Russell gained the saddle, her ears flicking this way and that. "Cricket can stand gunfire, at least my own. I'm no' sure of Red. Keep an eye on his ears. Remember, once things start, ye might not be able to see. Dinna shoot into the smoke, and if ye must, get behind a tree." He paused. "I'll try to assist Washington, cover for him."

Flying bullets weren't just dangerous for men. Horses, too. Worse, mounted men were clear targets. "Wouldn't fighting from behind cover be better in any case?"

James watched the grenadiers reach the riverbank, their strange pointed caps bobbing as they struggled to maintain formation on the trail. A fife and drum corps followed, striking up a merry tune. A group of mounted Virginia militiamen, clad in more sober colors, eased down the path after them. The sound of the fife echoed along the slopes, announcing their arrival to the French, who probably didn't need the information.

Russell's gaze was fixed on Braddock and his entourage immediately ahead. "Indians fight from cover, but the regulars are no' trained for it."

James didn't like the sound of that, but he was just a water-boy. Still, he checked his rifle and opened his powder horn. If Russell was covering for Washington, he'd cover for Russell.

"Dinna prime your pan just yet. The weather is dry, but still."

James nodded. The French might not show for hours, if at all.

RED NEVER BOLTED.

The first shots came from ahead where Colonel Halkett commanded the vanguard. James couldn't see much at first. Smoke floated over the troops ahead, and the *pop-pop-pop* of coordinated musket fire echoed in the hills ahead. The sound of Indian war whoops crawled up his spine.

The gelding's body tensed under him, echoing his own nervousness. "Easy, lad." Ahead, Cricket shifted her hindquarters and worried the bit, but Russell kept the reins taut, clucking to her. Smoke from a hill on the right seemed to indicate the location of the French, and yet, there was no way to be sure. The Indians might be flanking them on the other side for all he knew. Strung out this way, they were horribly exposed.

James glimpsed General Braddock, the gold and red of his coat further embellished by the eye-catching scarlet of a wide sash. The wigged man raised his arm but James couldn't hear what he said.

"Follow Washington," Russell said, his voice muffled under the sounds of shouting.

They advanced toward the melee, and James unstopped his powder horn. His hand twitched in nervousness, and black powder spilled on his leggings. He tried again, focusing on the priming pan, as Indian war whoops grew louder. Finally, his weapon was ready.

The clatter of musketry combined with the screeching and yodeling struck him like a physical force. Underneath him, Red quivered. Once, he laid his ears back but didn't lose his head. Ahead, Cricket broke into a trot obediently at Russell's command, but her tail was clamped tightly down, betraying her fear.

Russell took aim and fired at a target James couldn't see, the sound lost in a sudden crackle of musketry. Several Indians burst out of the woods, tomahawks raised.

He had no time to panic. James lifted his rifle and shot at a wild painted man.

He missed. The dark savage launched himself at Russell, who blocked the downward arc of a tomahawk with the stock of his rifle. James struggled to reload, anguished it took so long.

Pop!

A shot from behind him felled the Indian. James swiveled. It was MacKenzie.

A red-and-black face appeared, and a tomahawk curved toward the man.

"Watch out, Mac!"

But it was too late. The flashing blade came down on the Highlander's head. *Lord, no!*

Crack!

Russell had reloaded, and the man who killed Mac lay sprawled on the path. James stared at the bodies, entwined in death.

"Come, lad."

James's throat tightened. What about Mac's body? But his hands and legs obeyed Russell, urging his horse forward. He fixed his gaze on Russell, trying to anchor his mind against the nightmare enveloping them.

They caught up with Washington. A dead horse lay across the road, and the blue-coated colonel was leading a new mount to the general. Braddock was large, but he swung into the saddle with ease.

The smoke and hubbub increased. Sweating red-coated men filled the narrow road and the woods to either side. Some were hatless, some limping. Two soldiers helped a third to a cart. One crazed man, eyes wide with panic, ran past James.

"Halt! Close ranks!" Braddock's sword flashed in command. The general was flanked by Washington and another Virginian. His other aides had disappeared.

Beyond Braddock, a line of soldiers knelt and reloaded. The occasional pop of musket fire from the hill to the right increased to a steady rat-a-tat-tat.

"Fire!"

The British phalanx answered the hill. James checked his own weapon and scanned the trees for threats. Turning back, he saw a horse go down, slowly crumpling under its rider. Washington's mount.

"Lad—give Red to Washington."

James kneed the gelding and approached the colonel. Dismounting, he kept Red between himself and the French fire. "Sorry, lad," he murmured to the horse. It might be the sorrel's last day. "Sir, my gelding, sir."

Washington's blue gaze took in the horse. "Thank you. And thank Mr. Russell."

"Aye, sir."

Washington swung into the saddle, his blue coat marred with

several scorched bullet holes. Keeping his head down, James returned to Russell, now surrounded by Virginia militiamen.

"Let's get under cover," said one man, sweat streaking his grimy face.

"The injuns are shooting at us from behind the trees, and we need to do the same," another affirmed.

"Seems sensible," Russell said. "Can ye get Washington to approve it?"

"No time."

At this, several men melted into the woods. Others paused, waiting for Russell.

"Halt!" A red-coated lieutenant glared at the men. "Join the others. Anything else is desertion."

"I willna stand in an open place waiting to be shot, thank ye kindly," a man barked.

The fire intensified. The officer's head jerked, and cherry-red liquid fountained over his stock and saturated the yellow facing of his coat. His knees buckled.

Time seemed to slow.

Russell slid off Cricket. "Get down, lad!"

James's satchel thumped him in the back. A red sheet of blood covered the side of Russell's face, and James launched forward to grab the man and pull him to safety. Cricket shuddered, then sighed. She crumpled slowly to her knees, folding gently down, as if desiring a nap.

Something whistled by James's ear, and bark exploded from a nearby pine. Half crouching, he dragged Russell to the shelter of the trees. Was the man alive?

"Stay down, lad." Russell's voice was still strong.

An iron bar pressed James to the other man's chest. If Russell's arm was this strong, maybe he wasn't dying yet.

"Ye're hurt."

"Just a scratch."

They waited until the musket fire diminished. James braced himself on one arm and swung his satchel around with the other. He flipped it open by feel and grabbed a wad of bandages. They wriggled their way behind a tree, and James inspected the injury. Russell's scalp was creased above the ear.

"Here, lad." Russell unsheathed his knife, and when James handed him the bandages he cut off a length.

Then James saw the man's jacket. One side glistened with blood. "Your side," he croaked.

Russell knotted the head bandage and sighed. He pulled out a little flask. "Dump this on it first."

James crept to his side, his shin aching. He'd strained it somehow. With Russell's help he managed to expose the wound. Russell's side bled copiously, but the ball had probably glanced off a rib. Deer hit like this escaped.

"Argh." Russell winced as James sloshed whiskey over the area. Rinsed of blood, the injury looked minor. He packed it quickly with herbs the other man handed him. In a few moments, they'd tied off the second bandage.

A British officer sat slumped against a nearby tree. Was he also wounded? James had more bandages. He crawled toward the man, a metallic taste filling his mouth.

Flies buzzed around the officer's face. Blood splattered the gorgeous uniform as if mocking it. Recognition contracted James's heart. Colonel Sir Peter Halkett.

Oh no. They'd lost the commander of the Forty-fourth and the second-in-command of the entire expedition. Braddock's right-hand man.

Beyond the officer another body sprawled, limbs twisted. The dark-haired man wore the humble hunting garb of a militiaman. Surprise marked his sweat-stained face.

It was McKee.

James retched several times, his whole body aching.

"Ye canna help him now." Russell's voice, low and gentle. "We need to get to Washington."

James followed Russell, seeking cover behind the trees along the path as they approached the cloud of dust and smoke surrounding the general's entourage. But his leg wasn't working right. A white-hot pain lanced through his shin near his ankle and up toward his knee.

He grabbed a sapling for support and looked down. Blood covered his shoe. How had that happened?

Russell snaked his arm around him. "Come."

How could he fire his weapon like this? Had he loaded it? He stopped at the edge of the trees and brought his weapon to bear.

Pain stabbed him in the back. With shaking hands he opened his powder horn and sought to load his rifle. But his strength seemed to be leaking out.

"Lad." Russell's voice came from far away.

James looked up. The smoke had cleared, and Braddock was nowhere to be seen. Colonel Washington, mounted on the sorrel gelding, wore a brilliant red sash over his coat. He lifted his saber. "Retreat!" the man commanded. "Close ranks! Column of four!"

Coat dark with sweat, Red danced under his rider. But his ears were pricked forward. The animal was fine.

Good lad, ye're a good horse.

Then the reds and blues and greens swirled around him and sucked him down into blackness.

13

Our poor Virginians behaved like men and died like soldiers, for I believe that out of three companies that were there that day scarce 30 were left alive.

—George Washington to Gov. Dinwiddie, July 18, 1755

James was falling. He slammed into something hard and searing pain jolted him awake. The rattle of tongue and axle, clop-clop of hooves surrounded him. A wagon—he was in a moving wagon. A groan issued from a man next to him.

Above him stars circled. Or maybe they weren't circling. He blinked, trying to clear his vision, and slowly the dizziness subsided. The darkness was profound. He raised his left arm, strangely heavy, and touched the side of the wagon, the familiar texture of wood rough under his hand. His right hand felt instinctively for his rifle. No rifle, only fabric. Someone's coat.

He drifted off again. Tomahawks flashed, and flies landed on

Halkett's face. Where was Red? Where was Russell? He needed to cover Russell.

Someone sobbed near his feet. James blinked, trying to emerge from the fog. There was no moon, that's why it was so dark. A miasma of sulfuric gunpowder, metallic blood, and stale sweat filled his nose. Rustling, moans, and curses marked the presence of soldiers not far away. The army was on the march—at night? The trail was difficult even during the day.

Where was Russell? The last thing he remembered was McKee's dead face. James's stomach cramped just thinking of it. Losing Mac was one thing; he was convinced the man had peace with God. But McKee? It didn't bear thinking about.

And all the others ... no, he couldn't think about them either.

James sensed the presence of several men clinging to the end of the wagon as if for support or guidance. He didn't blame them. How anyone could find the way in this hellish darkness he could not fathom.

The sobbing intensified.

"Shut up," someone growled near the source of the cries. "You will bring the savages down upon us." A thin thread of panic suffused the voice.

The wagon halted. The harness jingled and an animal gave a familiar grunt. A mule was pulling the cart. James seized on the thought. Mules were canny, sure-footed creatures. A good thing.

Where was his own mule? Had she survived?

Muttering broke out into an argument somewhere.

"Come this way." Washington's voice rose above the rest.

His back screamed in pain as the wagon jolted into motion. A new smell choked him, the smell of the outhouse. James thrust down his nausea.

Eerie sounds swelled and ebbed away, the sounds of wounded soldiers. James heard one distinctive cry for water. Moans and grunts, and once, the scream of a horse. A pistol shot. An injured beast put out of its misery.

Help ... Lord.

James couldn't seem to pray. Panic and despair chased the army, and all he could do was strain for glimpses of the stars. But even they seemed cold and hard.

A strange sound floated over the groaning. A melody? A meeting-house tune.

"God is our refuge and our strength, in straits a present aid ..."

The familiar psalter tune diminished, then surged in strength.

"Though hills amidst the seas be cast ..."

It was Russell's voice. James mouthed the words, his lips stiff and cracked.

"God is in the midst of her ..." No one shushed the man.

James clung to the words, a slender thread of truth and sanity in the horror-filled night.

The sobbing ceased at his feet.

RUSSELL EMERGED out of the morning mist.

"Where are we?" James asked groggily. The horrible jolting retreat was taking forever. Someone had fashioned an oilcloth shade over them the first day, and he'd discovered that the man next to him was none other than General Braddock, his midsection wrapped in a blood-stained bandage. At least his mule, Libby, had survived. And Red still carried Washington. Were they out of danger? He doubted if Indians would follow them three days, but then, nothing about this situation made any sense.

"Here, lad." James drank greedily from Russell's canteen. "We're close to Fort Necessity. Your mule is grazing at a fearsome rate. See if ye can turn over," Russell said. "I need to look at your back."

The wagon was empty. Then James remembered. General Braddock had died the night before. The horrible rattle of his breathing had kept James awake half the night. He'd dozed, then discovered the other man quiet and strangely pallid at first light. The body had been removed, but a cold, heavy scent remained.

In the middle of the track several men thrust shovels into the dirt, digging a grave. Soldiers sat propped against trees, exhausted but still wary.

"I couldna dress it properly. I need to remove the ball."

That didn't sound good. But he was still alive, which was a miracle, Russell had said. A musket ball had gone through his satchel and lodged in his back. Slowed by *Pilgrim's Progress,* the piece of lead didn't penetrate far.

James managed to turn over, careful of his leg, which didn't hurt much if he didn't move it. His stubbled cheek resting on the rough wood, he tried to relax.

"It may sting, lad." They'd run out of whiskey but Russell must have procured something else.

James grunted as Russell lit his back on fire. He took a gasping breath.

"Rest easy. I'll be back."

James fished about in his mind for a verse of Scripture to think on. This was going to hurt.

Russell returned. "I cleaned my skinning knife. Here, bite on this."

James shoved the rag between his teeth. He loved the book of Isaiah. What was that verse? *Fear not: for I have redeemed thee, I have called thee by thy name; thou art mine.*

Fire stabbed his back.

When thou passest through the waters, I will be with thee; and through the rivers, they shall not overflow thee …

Incredibly, the pain intensified. Involuntarily, James groaned.

When thou walkest through the fire, thou shalt not be burned; neither shall the flame kindle upon thee.

"Hang on, lad. I see it."

James's vision darkened. The wood grain of the opposite side of the wagon seemed very important. Rough-hewn and graying with age.

Fear not: for I am with thee …

The words seem to glow on the wood's surface.

"Got it."

James latched on to the hopeful words. Then more fire smote him. He wanted to sob but forced himself to stay still. His teeth ground through the wad of cloth.

"Done. I need ye to lift yourself up a wee bit to bandage you."

As if watching from a distance, James saw his hands take the proper positions on the wood. Trembling, he raised himself. Russell's arms were strong and quick. Then James lay down, content to go without a shirt for the entire trip if need be.

"Poor lad," Russell murmured. "A bit of the satchel found its way in there, as well as the ball. It had festered a bit, so I had to wash it all out. Thank the Lord for Washington's wine."

"Thank you," James whispered, and meant it. Who knew what the regimental surgeon would have done. But Abigail Russell was a stickler for cleanliness, and her husband of all people would understand how to clean a wound.

A shadow crossed over the wagon, blocking his line of vision. Colonel Washington. His face was pale and there were shadows under his eyes. "Mr. Russell, how's the young man?"

"He'll do, Colonel. I dinna think he can sit a horse just yet."

Despite his wan appearance, the colonel maintained his poise. "After we reach Fort Cumberland, I intend to make for my home. Colonel Dunbar of the Forty-eighth will take over command."

Still lying on his belly, James couldn't see much, but he caught a glimpse of Braddock's red sash over the colonel's blue coat. Washington, the despised rattlesnake colonel, now commanded the army. The soldiers followed the sash and the stalwart personal force of the Virginian.

"We shall return to Augusta County." There was uncertainty in Russell's voice. Perhaps he wondered how they were going to get back on a single mule, especially if James was not able to ride yet.

"Sir, I am willing to escort Mr… "

"Mr. Paxton," Russell said.

"Forgive me. Mr. Paxton is welcome to accompany me to Mount Vernon. It is a salubrious place to recuperate."

James sought to bring his thoughts into order. "Thank ye kindly, sir, but the Reverend Davies is expecting me."

Russell harrumphed. "Not in your condition. In any case, a physician needs to see to your leg. I've bandaged it, and it's no' festered, but such an injury worries me."

James was too tired to argue, and he relaxed against the sour-smelling wagon bed. Words having to do with a funeral service floated in the air above him. The sun felt good on his tender back. He dozed.

The shadows were slanting over the campsite when he awoke to the jangle of harness and the rumble and clank of men getting ready for a march. The teamster was clucking to the mules.

A dark-headed man with a bandaged leg now sat in the wagon, an officer judging by his uniform. The wagon jolted into motion.

"Easy, there," muttered the teamster to the mules. The young driver, clad in a hunting shirt, spoke to James over his shoulder. "Gonna conceal Braddock's grave from the Injuns by running the wagons over it. I'll try not to jostle you more than I must."

The dark-headed officer cursed the savages.

Concealing the grave. What would Indians do to Braddock's corpse? James shuddered. In his mind's eye he saw the face of a savage, painted red and black, like a specter from the pit. They tortured captives and sometimes burned them alive. Were they even human?

THE MIDMORNING SUN was warm on Red Hawk's back. A good day to hunt. He glanced at Straight Arrow as they crossed the first ridge. "Does your wife burn your venison?" He wished his friend well but congratulating a friend on his marriage seemed womanly.

Straight Arrow's eyes danced. "You should marry." His chin jerked toward a faint track through the foliage. "I see how you look at a certain young woman."

Running Deer. Was it that obvious? "I don't know if she has eyes for me." There, he'd said it. She'd smiled at him once. But she was a pleasant young woman, patient and cheerful, and one smile meant little.

"Have your grandmother drop a word in her mother's ear."

Red Hawk mulled this over as they ceased their conversation, quieting their feet and bodies as well as their mouths. He drew two arrows from his quiver, slid them along his bowstring, and followed Straight Arrow down into a verdant glen untouched by the summer's wilting heat. Deer would love this place.

Finding the tiny creek in the heart of the lushness, they squatted behind an elderberry shrub and waited. Shafts of sunlight dappled the water with silvery dancing orbs. A bobwhite called, unconcerned. Red Hawk couldn't feel any breeze. Deer might not scent them.

His thighs were aching by the time a black nose appeared, followed by the great glossy eyes of a doe, glancing about, looking for danger. Beside him Straight Arrow drew his bow.

Red Hawk lifted a finger in warning.

Straight Arrow frowned but didn't take the shot.

The doe stepped to the stream and lowered her head, jerked it up, looked around again, then drank. Behind her a fawn emerged from the shady green womb of the forest.

And then another. Twin fawns. And they looked small, as if born late. Totally dependent on their mother.

Straight Arrow cut him a glance and lowered his weapon. They waited as the deer drank, stepped through the water, and left, her offspring trailing her.

"You are a prudent man, Red Hawk."

"It is only what my father taught me. What we all learn." Red Hawk knelt and drank. By preserving the mother, one of those fawns might feed them next year.

"Maybe." Straight Arrow dunked his head in the stream and tossed his hair back. "I saw an aspen grove on the way here."

"Yes, let's try for some grouse." Red Hawk slid into the stream and turned upon his back, relishing the cool respite from the fierce heat of blackberry moon. He closed his eyes.

"I think you would be a wise sachem one day."

Red Hawk sat up, dripping. "What?"

Straight Arrow finger-combed his hair and retied it. "Just what I said. You're related to Grayfeather, after all." He stood.

"My father is next in line."

"But who after him?"

Red Hawk followed his friend up the slope. They paused where the trees thinned.

Dark Water's son would by rights be the sachem after Red Pipe. But she had no son, only a daughter who had married a man in another village. "I-I don't think so, Straight Arrow."

His friend's dark eyes studied him. "Why not?"

Red Hawk shifted his stance. "I'm adopted." Everyone knew that.

"Pffft." Straight Arrow tossed his head. "What has that to do with it? It's not as though you are a recent captive. Do you even remember the gauntlet? You were a little boy. I recall that day, because I chased you through it with a stick."

Red Hawk smiled at the image. "I have only a vague memory. Rather like a nightmare, actually. But I do recall my father on the other end—Red Pipe, I mean."

"Yes, he was encouraging you to be brave and run fast. No one wanted you to be seriously hurt." His face stilled. "You are Shawnee now."

The gauntlet was a new birth, Grandmother said. It wasn't supposed to be pleasant, but it wasn't severe for children. Red Hawk couldn't remember much from before his capture and initiation, only a hazy memory of his mother singing to him near a crackling orange fire, like a half-forgotten dream.

He was Shawnee now. But what was he before? His mind shied away from that question, afraid he was Catawba or Cherokee. The enemy.

He turned. "Let's hunt."

They found the grove and flushed a dozen grouse from hiding. Straight Arrow's bow flashed twice in quick succession, bringing down two hens. Red Hawk was satisfied with the single male he'd killed; they were good birds for the pot. They found a place to clean the carcasses.

"Does your mother still do pottery?" Red Hawk asked.

"Hmm. Well, she would, but doesn't want to make another kiln. Says we'll just have to move again."

Red Hawk frowned at this. Women had their own type of wisdom, his father said. "I'm going to dig one for my grandmother. I'm sure she'd let your mother use it." He shook the blood from the gutted bird, and red drops littered the grass. His stomach clenched as he remembered the dead hawk. Was the omen a warning of something he could avoid? Or a curse he could never escape?

Headed for the village, they padded through stands of birch and poplar until the glossy green of maize leaves shone before them. Red Hawk stepped from the shade into the golden afternoon sunshine. Was this Running Deer's field? He thought so. Several times he'd tried not to be obvious as he watched her, bent over, weeding. Women were life-givers, suited for drawing life from the earth. She was beautiful.

He paused, drawing a forefinger over the broad curve of a waist-high leaf. He was lonely in a way Straight Arrow's company did not assuage. Perhaps—

A dog barked. A woman wailed.

Beside him Straight Arrow's body tensed. Red Hawk scanned the village, checking the far tree line, then the riverbank. Good, no canoes. He signaled his friend to stay behind him and crept to the river. They edged their way closer behind cattails and reeds, hoping to catch a glimpse of whatever was causing the disturbance without being seen.

His father—a worn shadow of his father, leading a pony. A woman—She-Who-Sings?—was upon it. He was speaking to those clustered around him, and when he paused, the women broke into weeping.

Red Hawk flung aside the reeds and sped toward his father. Where was Grayfeather?

He stepped around the women. Men had gathered, their faces stoic and hard. Before his father's feet knelt Dark Water, her body curled and shaking.

He met his father's gaze. "What happened?"

Anger flashed across his father's face. "The men of Penn's village killed all five of the Shawnee chiefs. They were hung in public to dishonor them."

Grayfeather dead? The village wavered before his eyes.

14

The shocking Scenes which presented themselves in this Nights March are not to be described—The dead—the dying—the groans—lamentation—and crys along the Road of the wounded for help ... were enough to pierce a heart of adamant.

George Washington, *Remarks*

Susanna examined her new green bodice in the gold-framed mirror. The sleeves had taken forever. Mother had taught her how to set a sleeve, but doing it on her own was a challenge. She stepped closer and peered at her left shoulder, but no ripple or pucker revealed the place where she'd had to pull out her stitches and try again. She couldn't afford material for a complete gown, but the new bodice went well with her walnut-brown skirt.

She tucked in her cream-colored kerchief. There. She'd fix her hair next.

Would Philippe attend the dance tonight? She hoped his attentions were more than politeness, but why would he be attracted to her? The reflection in the glass staring back at her was plain. Not to mention she was too tall.

A knock sounded on the door. "Come."

"You look well." Anne's cheeks glowed. Was that rouge or just the heat? She swept in, ringlets framing her face, a bag in her hands.

"What did you purchase today? You never told me."

Anne harrumphed. "You were so content in the bookstore, and then you kept your nose in your purchase—"

"Which I made for *your* household." Susanna lifted an eyebrow, enjoying the banter. "Your brother sick, with an empty simples cabinet, nothing but a few drops of laudanum and a bit of horehound."

"He recovered quickly." Anne sat on the bed.

"A good thing." Susanna grabbed the pamphlet-sized book from her nightstand and handed it to her friend.

"*Every Man His Own Physician,*" Anne read. She flipped through the pages. "'Dropsy.' 'Pleursy.' Very comprehensive."

"Mother's book is better. All about medicinal plants and how to prepare them. Things we can use, unlike bloodletting."

Anne tilted her head. "You said your mother was a healer? Or was it midwife?"

"Both, actually. So what have you in the bag?"

Anne produced a long metal object with handles, like a pair of scissors.

"What is that?"

"Have you never seen curling tongs before?"

So that was how women fashioned little ringlets. And gentlemen's wigs always looked tightly curled. "No, I have not. How are they used?"

"Hot coals in a tiny brazier. Nothing to it. Shall I prepare your hair for tonight?"

Reluctance fought with excitement in Susanna's belly. "Whyever not?" Her cheeks warmed with the thought of seeing Philippe.

Callie produced the coals, and soon Susanna was seated before the mirror, her hair brushed and ready.

"Tell me more about your family. Your brother Jonathan is next in age, correct? And Nate?" Anne asked, probably trying to distract her from the thought of hot iron near her tender skin.

"Nathan is six, almost seven. He has the sweetest color hair. Not a golden blond, like my stepmother's. It has a reddish tint, as if strawberries were crushed and mixed in butter."

Anne chuckled. "Wasted on a man." She wrapped a long piece of hair in the tongs and held it. "Your hair is a lovely color. Has your father dark hair?"

"Yes, but in the sun it looks rather red. My mother had dark hair."

Anne released the curl. "How did she die? Childbed?"

The room became still and heavy. The tiny eddies of breeze coming in through the window did little to assuage the July heat. "No, 'twas not that." She swallowed. "She was shot by an Indian."

Anne gasped.

"It was an accident."

Anne replaced the tongs in the brazier. "How can such a thing be an accident?"

"Da said it was all a misunderstanding, some Indians passing through were hungry. They killed some livestock and folks became angry. Next thing, the militia was called out and there was a skirmish. My mother was standing in the doorway of a neighbor's cabin." She recited the details of the event. She generally felt detached from it all, but not now. Studying her dark hair in the mirror brought it closer. "The battle came close to the cabin. A stray musket ball."

Anne toyed with Susanna's curls, her fingers gentle. "Do you remember her?"

"I cannot be sure. Maybe the idea of her." She did remember her father's uncontrollable sobs. According to Auntie Agnes, he'd grieved for a long time. "You would think I would resent the thought of a replacement. But I did not. My stepmother seemed like an angel from heaven."

"Even now?" Anne smiled.

Abigail Williams Russell would seem like a prudish backwater farmer's wife to the first families of Virginia. Susanna's conscience nudged her. Mother had more poise, knowledge, and simple gumption than any woman she'd met here. "She never raised her voice. But when I misbehaved, she'd show me the Scriptures. And then I'd have to scrub the kettle."

Anne hooted. "We should invite your family here."

"She would not care for dancing or the theater. But I believe she would enjoy your company." Susanna flashed her a grin. Then she sobered. What would Mother think of Philippe?

"We shall make plans. My own mother will be here when the weather cools." Anne reached for her bag. "*La pièce de résistance.* Ribbon." She withdrew a length of green satin and fixed it about Susanna's neck. "It brings the color up to your face."

It did. "You should learn painting alongside me."

"So Mr. Dupre has promised? Already you are making great strides in French. I can barely follow the conversation."

"After a trip to Charleston. They will leave soon and return in October or November. *What* are you doing?"

Anne had removed Susanna's kerchief. She tugged her own out from her bodice and handed it to Susanna. "Try this."

Anne's kerchief was an expensive bleached muslin, a brilliant white, whereas her own was a soft ecru linen.

"The colors, the contrast," Anne pointed out, when the kerchief was securely tucked.

It was true. The white and green flattered her—and the feminine curls softened the effect. "You should paint. You have a keen eye."

"A woman's eye. See, the softer cream works well against my skin." Anne tucked Susanna's kerchief under the edge of her own bodice.

Susanna fingered the ribbon, middle green like a fresh basil leaf. It coordinated with the deeper green of the bodice. "I cannot recompense you for this." She'd spent her last shilling on the booklet.

"Nonsense. You hear the drought everyone's talking about? Well, some plantations have suffered failures, but not ours. We will have a decent harvest. But tobacco prices are three times higher. Can you imagine? Three times! I saw a brocade at the millinery that would flatter you so perfectly—and my brother will have no reason to turn down a request for new gowns."

Fabric was expensive. But maybe she could accede to Anne's suggestion after all.

"Susanna, consider. You do need something suitable for the governor's gala. 'Tis not for months yet. We have plenty of time to prepare. We are bosom friends, are we not? Sisters in heart."

"Of course. Lead the way, sister."

SUSANNA'S STOMACH growled under her stays as the carriage pulled away from the house. The Raleigh must have food—it was a tavern, after all. She hoped they served something substantial. Beside her, Anne chattered on about who might be attending. On the opposite seat, Mr. Randolph, his fine jabot edged with lace, stared out the window, ignoring his sister.

Susanna's borrowed fan was inadequate in the enclosed space. But in a few short minutes the driver halted in front of a large building, at least at big as the Randolphs' home. Mr. Randolph led the way out of the carriage, assisting first Anne, then Susanna.

Her shoes crunched on a shell walkway before the large covered porch that fronted the tavern. Swirling gusts of salt air from the east puffed against her heated cheeks, washing away the street's stench of manure and emptied chamber pots. She'd bathed this morning, but in the July heat, ordinary morning ablutions with pitcher and basin were inadequate. For an instant she longed for the sheltered pool near their house in the valley, a place where the stream bent its course and the water stilled and deepened. Her only consolation was the herbal sachet Anne had given her, now lodged in her stays.

Several men conversed on the broad pine porch fronting the

Raleigh. Susanna followed Anne inside, where the smells grew thick: savory cooking competed with the acrid undertow of sweat. Tall glass windows illuminated a number of tables; around one several men sat, pewter tankards before them.

"'Tis unusual to have such an event in July." Anne tucked her arm in Susanna's as they followed her brother into another room. "Everyone stays on the plantations during the summer."

The tension on the frontier was felt even here, and the burgesses had been in session. "Because of the French?"

"No, not just the conflict with the French. Strangely enough, the rise in tobacco prices has thrown the burgesses into turmoil. I cannot grasp what the to-do is about." Anne waved her fan before her face. "Neither do I care to."

They stepped into a long, broad room, painted in a subtle green and dominated by a painted fireplace at one end. Golden light filtered in from tall windows and spread across the pine floors. A servant lit a candle in a wall sconce then turned his attention to an overhead brass chandelier.

Along one wall several women stood near a punch table, conversing. A finely dressed man leaned over another table nearby, filling a small plate with food.

Anne tilted her fan toward the supper table. "There's cousin Peyton. I do hope the men can avoid politics for the evening."

Peyton Randolph was a prominent member of the House of Burgesses and also somewhat corpulent. More men joined him at the supper table.

"Mr. Scott, the cabinetmaker on Gloucester." Anne seemed pleased to see a man in a bottle-green coat. He looked as old as Anne's brother, but then, her brother was a still a bachelor, so perhaps Mr. Scott was as well. Maybe Anne had her eye on this man.

"We should visit his shop sometime," Susanna said.

Anne grinned. "Why that's right. Cabinetmaking is in your family. We have an excuse."

From behind Susanna a fiddle sang out a note. Another instrument chimed in, tuning with the first. She turned to see and found instead a tall dark figure staring down at her.

Philippe Dupre.

She nodded a brief curtsey, blinking. She'd been hoping to see him, but now her stays were too tight.

"Miss Russell." He bowed over her hand. "Might I offer you some punch?"

Anne raised her brow and swept her fan over her smile, giving tacit permission.

"I-I thank you," Susanna said.

Philippe took her elbow. "The gentlemen's punch is to the left. I believe there is a fruit punch for the ladies." A servant girl handed him a cup, and he handed it to Susanna. "Tell me how it tastes."

She sipped it. Sourness tickled her tongue, followed by a fruity sweetness. Then a hint of hard cider stung her throat. "Wonderfully refreshing."

Philippe sipped at his own drink. "Would I need to ask your uncle's permission to paint your miniature?"

Susanna choked on her punch. Permission? Oh, not *that* kind of permission. "I-I—"

"At the same time we can begin the first lessons in painting. I believe there is time before I leave for Charleston."

How wonderful. "I would be honored." She set down her cup. He wanted to paint her. Surely this meant—

"Might I have this dance?" Philippe's gloved hand reached for hers, and Susanna felt absurdly glad that her nails, visible while wearing fingerless gloves, were finally now buffed and perfect.

The violin settled into a tune. A flute's warble joined in. Several couples lined up in formation. This was not a reel. No, it was the minuet.

Susanna swallowed with trepidation but allowed Philippe to lead her into a group. The minuet was precise, the gestures elegant, totally different from the dancing in the valley. The dancing master had gone over the steps again and again, and she and Anne had practiced them. But she'd never tried the dance in public.

Well, some of her mistakes would be cloaked by her skirts, wouldn't they?

The dance began, and she watched the others for clues. Across from her, the portly Peyton Randolph managed quite well, his green waistcoat bobbing. Next to him his wife sailed through the motions, graceful and precise. At least this dance was not physically demanding, unlike the reel, which would not be popular in this heat.

The next part of the minuet began. Susanna found herself circling Philippe, their gazes locked. Was this why Mother didn't like dancing? This part seemed so … close. They were in public, the movements so formal, and yet—

The door to the room burst open and several men strode in.

"News!" one of the men said, his voice loud enough to carry over the music. He was still wearing spurs on his boots.

The music ceased with a final plaintive note, and the dancers halted. Murmurs rose. Susanna's heart quickened. Was it about the war?

"News from the frontier." The dusty man in a threadbare coat waited until the excited voices ebbed. "General Braddock is dead."

Susanna felt arms around her. Philippe. Philippe was guiding her to a chair. Questions flew through the room.

"What about Fort Duquesne?"

"Colonel Washington? How did he fare?"

The messenger held up his hand. "Here is what I know. The army met the French about ten miles from the fort. The Indians fell upon our men in a dastardly fashion and the army was forced to retreat. Braddock gave the command to Washington, who guided the men out safely."

Susanna found herself on a chair, voices buzzing throughout the room. Her vision seemed hazy. Was her father safe?

And what about Jamie?

15

When General Braddock was defeated and killed, our country was laid open to the enemy, our people were in dreadful confusion and discouraged to the highest degree.

—Rev. John Craig, *Autobiography*

Mount Vernon, July 1755

The flashing blade of the tomahawk descended toward James's neck. Laughing eyes in a paint-blackened face loomed over him as he sought to twist away.

He couldn't move!

The savage turned and chopped at James's leg instead. He could feel every blow.

Throb, throb, throb.

James flung out his arms and gasped. He opened his eyes to the yellow fabric of a bed's canopy. His fingers curled over twisted, damp sheets.

It was a dream.

Throb, throb, throb.

The throbbing ache in his leg was real. What had the physician said? Everything seemed hazy—the trip here, the first day.

Where was Colonel Washington? James couldn't remember seeing him since their arrival. The man had managed to secure a carriage in Frederick after the hellish trek by wagon to get there. Then he'd curled up on one bench and given James the other.

Russell. He'd been injured. Was he home yet?

Wait. How long had it been since the battle? How long had he been here?

His gaze shifted to the fabric billowing about the partially opened tall glass window to his left. It was a luxurious room. The mattress under him was huge and incredibly soft. To his right, a single ladder-back chair sat next to a table dominated by a pitcher and basin. Other items circled the basin: jars, a tiny brown bottle, scissors, and linen.

He frowned at the chair. A woman sometimes sat in that chair. His memories were cloudy but there was a woman in the haze: tall, commanding, with cool, sure hands.

And a man. A physician wearing a dark coat. And spectacles. He remembered spectacles. And pain.

Throb, throb, throb.

Yes, the physician had treated his leg. And they'd given him laudanum. The medicine didn't really take the pain away, it just made him not care as much. And then, of course, he'd slept. He'd slept and dreamt awful, red-and-black painted dreams.

"Good morning." A woman appeared, the tall woman whose hands he knew. Her dress was ordinary, much like Abigail Russell's.

James attempted to sit up but failed. "Good morning, ma'am." At that moment, he felt an acute need for the chamber pot. *Oh no.*

"No need for proprieties, Mr. Paxton." She studied him a moment, the way a general scanned the terrain. "Would you care for tea?"

"Thank ye kindly, ma'am." His mouth was parched. "How long have I been here?"

"You arrived with the colonel three days ago, then we sent for the physician. He dug a ball out of your leg the next day. He also took three ounces of blood because of fever."

"I dreamt two men were holding me down ..."

"The colonel and Caesar." Her gaze slid to the table. "The colonel gave you brandy and we followed that with laudanum."

Brandy. He had a vague memory of choking down something strong. Like cider on fire. "And the colonel? How does he fare?"

For the first time he discerned a smile. "He is much improved. He went for a ride on a sorrel gelding earlier this morning, which he tells me you gave to him in the heat of battle."

Tears sprang to his eyes. "Red. He made it back."

"Methinks you love horses as much as my son does."

Of course. "Mrs.... Washington? Please forgive my manners." They must have been introduced, but he had no memory of it.

"No need. Anything you require?"

The chamber pot. "Well ..."

"I'll send Caesar to assist with the necessities."

His shoulders slumped in relief. "Thank ye ma'am. And might I trouble you for a bit of paper? I need to write my mother—"

"Certainly. I'll bring you a writing desk." She seemed pleased with his request.

James tried to keep the valley out of his speech. "Thank you very much."

She departed, patterned brown skirts swishing. Mrs. Washington reminded him of his own mother, a kind woman but one not to be trifled with.

But what would he say to his mother? And by extension, the rest of the household? His father could barely read and write, and so the business of correspondence belonged to her, as well as religious instruction. Da wasn't fussy over family worship. Chapters of Scripture were read in tandem, each family member taking a few verses, when it was accomplished at all. His father presided over mealtime prayers, but his mother made sure they all knew the catechism.

Da might be the head, but Ma was the bedrock of the family. Da might be disappointed James had missed the one Indian he'd fired at, but his mother would ask deeper questions.

He hadn't panicked, hadn't run away. But he'd *felt* like a coward.

~

THREE DAYS LATER, James hobbled his way toward the back door with the aid of a cane. Once in the doorway, he took a deep breath. The scene was beautiful.

The ground sloped away before him, disappearing into lush vegetation. Past the line of foliage beckoned a river, placid and glittering in the morning sunlight. A gentle breeze touched his cheeks.

The head of the cane digging into his palm, he sidled toward a bench near the doorway and sat. His leg still throbbed, but the ferocity of the pain was gone.

James opened the book he'd tucked under his arm. The Baptist confession. He needed to make use of his time; the physician had made it clear yesterday he'd be going nowhere soon. And he might not be a Baptist, but it was worthwhile to know what they believed, and why.

He opened to the first section. *The Holy Scriptures*. Why, this was familiar. Just like the Westminster, with scripture proofs after each statement. After several minutes of perusing the contents, he flipped to the section on baptism and scanned the page.

Clearly he had study ahead of him. If only he could talk to one of these men, one of the elders of these Baptist churches that had published the book.

Might he be converted to their way of thinking? He was halfway there already. And if he were, what would Mr. Craig say?

Motion caught his eye. Colonel Washington was riding Red across the slope in front of him. Gladness flooded James's heart. He made a sudden move to rise, but a sharp jab of pain forced him to grab his cane. *Easy does it*.

The colonel turned, approached the house, and dismounted. "Mr. Paxton, good morning."

Red nickered, his ears pricked forward.

"Good morning, sir." James studied the horse. "Hey, Red, there's my lad." He stood, keeping his weight on his good leg. "Such a canty, braw lad." He stroked the horse's nose and peered at the animal's ribcage. Underweight, but not terribly so.

"He served bravely," Washington said, a smile playing about his lips. "He gets oats with cracked corn in the morning and a bran mash at night. And plenty of good grass. He'll recover in no time." He ran his hand over the animal's ribs.

"Thank you." James eased himself down again. "And I thank ye for your hospitality. Mount Vernon is a pleasant place."

The colonel looked tired. No, not tired. He looked like he'd aged ten years in the past month. A muscle twitched in his cheek as he sat on the bench next to James. "Salutary for both body and soul."

"I've had nightmares," James blurted.

Washington took a deep breath and kept his gaze fixed on the river. "We lived a nightmare."

That horrible first night… "How many men did we lose?"

"Most of the militiamen did not make it back."

James swallowed. His own inner wrestling seemed trivial. "The infantrymen?"

"I am not privy to those numbers. But casualties were high. You were there."

Mac's face filled his mind. "Braddock—"

"General Braddock possessed admirable qualities." Strain filled the man's voice.

James nodded. The man had made foolish decisions, but they would not speak evil of the dead.

"Your letters are on their way." Washington stood and reclaimed the reins. "I've had my own correspondence to attend to, as you might imagine." His gaze fixed on James. "Are you acquainted with Colonel Patton of Augusta County?"

"Oh, aye—I mean, yes, sir, I am. His nephew William Preston is a friend. We studied mathematics and history together."

Washington was a surveyor too, wasn't he? Even the color of the colonel's hair was similar, though not quite as golden a blond as William's. "Preston? Yes, I know of him. Virginia is vulnerable in the valley, especially down south, where Patton's new land grant is located. I've written the colonel about erecting fortifications for the inhabitants."

James nodded. If the Shawnee went on the warpath, there was no other way. Russell's home had been built with them in mind, as well as the stone meetinghouse and other structures. "Your ideas will be welcome, I am sure. Every family needs a hiding place." He thought of the cavern.

"Even so." Washington paused. "You are training for the ministry, I am told."

"Yes, I hope to resume my studies soon." James frowned at the book in his hand. "I have a question ye might think strange."

Washington nodded for him to continue.

"I would like to correspond with one of the members of this association." James handed him the confession.

"A Baptist association." Eyebrows lifting, Washington opened the thin volume. "'Printed by B. Franklin.' Mr. Franklin would know. I will send word." He handed the book back. "You are not Presbyterian?"

"I am, but I have questions." James shrugged.

"I only have one question. Are you a praying man?"

"A poor one, but yes."

"Please pray. We will need the wisdom and the intervention of divine Providence to make any headway against our foes."

"I will."

As Washington rode away, James consoled himself. He might be weak and confused, but God was neither.

RED HAWK PLUNGED into the river and swam several strokes, then kicked to the surface. He opened his mouth and sucked in a mouthful of water, swished it around, and spat. He'd cleansed his mouth several times after drinking the vile purging brew they'd all swallowed yesterday. The men had been sweating and purging to focus their minds and purify themselves before the Creator, a necessity before going on the warpath.

A cloud of gloom lay over the village. Wails had given way to sobs and then to a simmering wrath. Grandmother, normally such a bulwark of strength, sat faded and silent before the hearth. All the men sharpened their tomahawks. But not all were going on this raid; six of them would join the party from the Ohio, who'd camped at the edge of the village this afternoon.

Red Hawk swam closer to the bank and stood, water dripping down his neck and back. White men were deceitful and cruel, worse than a warped bow. He wiped the water out of his eyes. At least he could think more clearly after the rituals. He ran his hands through his hair, squeezing out the excess water and pulling it back. He retied it. In the morning he'd oil and plait it properly.

He pushed through the reeds, stomach grumbling. Well, he hadn't eaten since the horrible news had come three days ago, but now it was time to strengthen his body. And perhaps knap a few more arrowheads.

The decision had been quick in coming. The elders met, then the women's council. The details decided.

Red Hawk entered the village and proceeded to their wigwam.

Father was fletching arrows. "I am leading the raid."

"Not Elk Tooth?"

"I am now sachem. Elk Tooth makes battle decisions and the young men will follow him in the raid. But I must also prove myself."

"Prove yourself? You are the best man I know."

His father had rubbed an old scar on his upper arm. "I am respected but untested as a leader."

Red Hawk filled a bowl from the cooking pot and sat, but for long minutes he simply stared at the food. This raid wasn't only a raid, and it wasn't just a test of leadership. There was something else his father hadn't said, but which they both knew.

Their retribution was just, but Red Hawk could see beyond the haze of his rage. Retribution would beget retribution.

16

Above all creatures in the world, the Indian was dreaded the most...

—*The History of Jonathan Alder*

It was very early. The waning gibbous moon shed stark white light on the village as the men gathered quietly. Horses shifted and grunted while the men tied packs on them. Once again Red Hawk opened the flap and felt the contents of the bag packed on his father's pony. Extra dried meat ... pots of pigment. Everything was ready.

Except he had no token for protection. His hawk feather was still in his pouch, but what did that signify? The panther and the owl, the Shawnee totem animals, should have some influence. And his father would not go if he had not a good expectation of success.

He looked up at the stars, silent and hard. Spirits resided there. And the Creator, of course, far away and distant. He could only hope He-

Who-Creates-By-Thinking saw the justice of their actions. It wasn't just Grayfeather's death they were avenging. He'd turned it all over in his mind again and again. The white men were intruders, slowly stealing the land, year by year. Even the horrific Beaver Wars, resulting in the Shawnee being forced south by the Six Nations, were ultimately the white man's fault.

Silver Beard. The image of the man rose before his mind's eye. Red Hawk's blood warmed to the thought of killing the man who was staking claim to land not his own.

He followed the others, traveling single file along the river. The terrain was easy here, and they'd covered a good distance by the time the sun spilled orange over the mountains ahead. The second and third day would be more difficult; Red Hawk had never been to the Great Valley, but he'd hunted in the river valley just west of it, and the ridge-top trails were narrow in places.

No one spoke much, although Laughing Wolf boasted and joked with the Ohio men now and again. His sly chuckles filtered back from the dark bobbing heads in front. They watered the horses frequently, but never stopped to eat, occasionally pulling mouthfuls from their pouches as they walked.

When the sun touched the western hills his father conferred with the Ohio band's leader, and they chose a spot to camp for the night.

Red Hawk unpacked the pony, led it to water, and hobbled it. He joined his father at the edge of the clearing. On the other side, a winking light marked someone's cook fire.

He stretched his sore muscles and sat. His father handed him a small branch laden with blackberries he'd saved from the trail.

"Thank you." Red Hawk opened the food pack and handed his father a piece of Dark Water's pemmican. He drank deeply from his gourd before taking a bite of the rich traveling food. "How big is the white man's village?"

"It's not a true village." His father drank from his gourd. "Maybe twenty families have settled in the area to the east—you remember the chain men?"

He nodded. Hair-Like-The-Sun and Silver Beard.

"We sent scouts and spied on them from time to time. Other men have come with their families. But their houses are not close to each other."

"That's foolish."

"Makes it easier for us to slip in, slip out."

"Father ... what exactly do we mean to do?" The mention of families troubled him. For days he'd run his thumb along the shaft of his tomahawk, imagining the throw, the blood of a man's neck. But women and children?

"This is your first raid. Your test as well as mine. The scalp of your enemy is a good proof of your manhood. Captives are an honorable spoil of war, but remember, grown men will always try to escape." His father glanced at the fire across the clearing. "The Ohio men brought plenty of horses. They may mean to bring back as much spoil as they can. Food, weapons, children."

Children. Red Hawk stared at the last blackberry in his hand. "Silver Beard seemed to be the leader."

"Silver Beard?"

"When I saw those men, two were in charge, an older and a younger. Both tall and strong, the older exceptionally so, with dark hair and a silver beard." And a handsome horse.

"Father and son?"

"Perhaps."

"I will speak to the Ohio man. If we locate this Silver Beard and kill him first, it may disorganize their defense."

Red Hawk popped the last blackberry into his mouth and lay back. Silver Beard, horses, children ... "Father?"

"I am here, Son."

The stars above him were bright against the moonless backdrop of the night sky. "Who am I? I mean, which people did you capture me from?"

His father was silent for many heartbeats. "Do you know the scar on my upper arm?"

There was a round, puckered mark on his father's arm he never boasted about. Usually men told the stories of their scars. Even if they were from accidents they could serve for a good laugh. But Father had never explained. "Yes, I know it."

"I have never told you the story. It is all of a piece—the story of your capture and the story of the scar."

And his father had been silent about both.

"When I was young, I fell in with several fellows from a village up north near Sawkunk. They wanted to go hunting. The first two days we caught very little, and we began to get hungry. We stopped at a white man's cabin. He was frightened but gave us food, hoping to get rid of us. One of my friends asked for firewater. The white man was reluctant but finally gave us a jug.

"It was nasty tasting, and I swallowed but a mouthful. My companions imbibed freely as we continued our journey. Then we spotted a man and his wife and young son. Hiding ourselves, we argued about what to do. I wanted to stay hidden as the man was well armed with a rifle, and besides, what quarrel did we have with them? The others lusted after the fine horse the woman and child rode, not to mention the firearm.

"Their drunkenness drowned good sense. One of my companions attacked the man while the other grabbed the horse's bridle. I am not sure how it happened, but the next thing I knew the woman was on the ground, dead. The child I picked up, partly to keep it safe from my companion, who stood over the body of the woman, and partly because I knew the boy's father would not endanger his son by shooting at me. For he'd shot my other companion, and was now reloading. I fled and heard a shot. I never saw the other man again."

"That child is me? Is that when you were shot?"

Father sighed. "I wish that were the end of the story. You see, the man was enraged at the loss of his wife. He followed me, perhaps thinking I had killed his woman. And I had captured his son. He was an excellent tracker."

Red Hawk's chest seized up. He possessed only a wispy faded

memory of branches lashing at him. Of sobbing uncontrollably. It seemed like a dream. "Did he find you?"

"Yes. I think he hid and watched the village for at least a few hours, because he knew exactly where I lived. He struck just after dark and killed—" A choking sound came from his father's dark shape.

"Moonglow."

"He took my wife for his."

Red Hawk blinked away tears. He knew bits and pieces. He knew she'd been killed. He swallowed. "The scar?"

"I did not wait to grieve. The trail would grow cold. I followed him. But it took many months to catch up to him. I came across him in the Great Valley and he shot me. But later I surprised him and killed him."

"Why did you never tell the story?"

"Several reasons. For one, it was a tragedy caused by firewater. And there was something else. I couldn't bring home the man's scalp."

His father had warned him about firewater more than once. "Because he was a worthy opponent?"

"Not entirely. You see, I surprised him at the very spot where a wise woman doctored my wound." He rubbed his arm. "When I was shot, a woman discovered me, weak from the injury. She may have saved my life."

"A wise woman?"

"Yes, a white woman with great knowledge of herbs. And much courage. It was a special sign that I found him at her cabin. I would have offended the spirits if I took more than my blood debt."

"A *white* woman cared for you?"

"Yes." His father then proceeded to describe the exact location of the woman's house. "Do not harm them, lest evil befall you."

"Yes, Father."

Red Hawk stared at the stars. No wonder his father had been slow to tell the story. A numbing grief, a charmed location—and no scalp to bring home.

He took a long breath. His mother, crumpled on the ground, killed for no reason. Though he could not remember her, he grieved. And he determined not to do the same. He would not raise his hand against the helpless.

But his father hadn't answered his question. Well, maybe he had. He'd told the story of a worthy man, a good tracker, who'd died under some sort of spiritual protection. Whether he was Catawba or not made no difference.

His eyes closed. Maybe one day he'd journey to that special place, the house by the spring.

Just to see.

RED HAWK DUCKED HIS HEAD. "Father, a rider."

The band had split into several groups to scout the area. His father squatted next to him behind a screen of myrtle and honeysuckle vine. They watched silently.

The rider crossed a small grassy patch on the ridge opposite. The rising sun caught the man's figure from behind.

"Hair-Like-The-Sun," breathed Red Hawk. There was no mistaking the form, the golden hair.

His father said nothing until the rider disappeared behind the trees. "Silver Beard will not have his son by his side to help him."

"He might have others." The white paint on his forehead itched.

"We shall see."

They remained in hiding until the others returned.

"We found the place," Straight Arrow said, his eyes ringed with yellow and green. "It's foolish how far apart their homes are."

"We found the horse you described," Laughing Wolf squatted next to them. "Another man left the house. This Silver Beard is trapped in his cave." He gave a sly chortle.

Elk Tooth returned with several others. "Most of the men of the settlement have departed their homes for the fields."

Captives and spoil for the taking. But Red Hawk hungered to fight a man. "Father, I wish to accompany you to Silver Beard's home."

Laughing Wolf glared at him as he cradled his musket. "I claim that right."

Elk Tooth cleared his throat. "Four or five need to go."

Father spoke. "I will lead my son and Laughing Wolf. Straight Arrow may come. Anyone else?"

One of the Ohio men joined them and they followed Laughing Wolf to a clearing. A large house sat alone, smoke curling from a stone chimney. A chestnut horse with a large blaze was tied nearby, saddled and bridled, just as Red Hawk had seen it two years before. The animal lifted its head, ears pointing toward their hiding place.

Some horses were sensitive to strangers; this one might squeal an alarm. "Father, if I go to the right and approach the horse, the rest can circle around the other way."

Father nodded.

Red Hawk circled and took several steps toward the horse, which lifted its head and flared its nostrils. He paused to let the animal settle. He'd managed to deflect its attention.

The others burst from cover, and rushed the house. Red Hawk sped to attack from the other side. He fitted an arrow to his bow. The horse squealed.

A giant of a man emerged and stood in the doorway, glittering sword slashing.

Silver Beard. A dark blue coat didn't seem to impede the movements of his massive shoulders as the man wielded an impossibly long weapon.

Red Hawk found a position behind and to the right of Laughing Wolf, who raised and aimed his musket. Red Hawk's gut tensed waiting for the discharge.

Nothing happened. Laughing Wolf cursed and fumbled with the firearm.

Light glinted off the silver sword as it swept another deadly arc. The Ohio man grunted and slumped to the ground. Another man—Red Hawk couldn't see who—faltered but jumped back.

There was no way to get close to a man with that kind of weapon, not with a tomahawk. The sword swept left and right, then left again.

He aimed and let loose. His arrow hit Silver Beard's arm, but the man plucked it out. The man's clothing was thick.

Red Hawk blinked away salt from his eye and drew back the next arrow with every ounce of strength. The man was a bear. Red Hawk's bowstring twanged and the arrow lodged in Silver Beard's breast. Better. But how many would it take?

Another arrow left his bow. Why were Straight Arrow and his father still so close? Laughing Wolf leveled his musket, the side of his face dark with black paint.

Fire, you fool!

The *pop* from the musket sounded insignificant amidst the war cries of the men. Light gray smoke obscured the scene for a moment. Red Hawk glanced over his shoulder and checked the tree line. He imagined Hair-Like-The-Sun galloping in with a similar sword … but no. The tree line was clear.

He looked back, where the last wisps of smoke were dissipating. Silver Beard was down. Laughing Wolf was drawing out a scalping knife. Straight Arrow—where was Father?

He dashed to the house. "Father?"

Father was on the ground, bloody and motionless.

In a daze, Red Hawk followed Straight Arrow through a stand of poplar, the reins of Silver Beard's mare in his grasp. But when the trees thinned, the animal jerked and dug in her heels. Was she smelling blood? Red Hawk had failed to retrieve his father's body, the nervous mare refusing to stand still for a blood-scented burden. In the end, Straight Arrow had jerked him away, unwillingly, from the scene.

Before them stood a log cabin, its door hanging open on its hinges. Straight Arrow bounded out of cover and checked the area, peering inside the house. Pewter plates and small items of clothing littered the ground in front; apparently the Ohio men had been here before them. Cooking smells mingled with the copper of blood.

Straight Arrow gave a motion of his hand. *No danger.*

Red Hawk tugged at the horse's reins, forcing himself to hurry. The mare snorted, and he finally saw the reason. An infant lay to one side of the log structure, bloodied and dead. Stomach clenching, he turned his gaze away and stroked the horse's head. The raid was a succession of horrors but somehow his heart felt numb.

Straight Arrow disappeared inside the cabin and emerged again moments later with colorful fabric in his hand. A blanket. "Nothing here, they cleaned it out."

White feathers fluttered in the dirt nearby. Red Hawk stepped closer. No, not feathers. They were leaves, the strange leaves bound together, like Hair-Like-The-Sun's. He snatched it up. Did it belong to that man or someone else? He shoved it in his pouch. "Let's go." The white men were sure to return from the fields any moment.

Once past the smell of blood, the mare became tractable, and they made good time to the rendezvous point where they'd left the pony.

"Straight Arrow, will you take Father's pony?"

Straight Arrow took the rope and drew his brows together. "My grief goes with you."

Red Hawk looked away. *If only.* If only he'd stayed with the others, shot his arrows from a closer position, perhaps Father would be alive …

Laughing Wolf shoved a bag in their faces. "Nice horse. I've got a better prize." The canvas bag bulged with something round and heavy. He chuckled and opened the blood-rimmed sack.

A man's head lay inside, severed at the neck, gray wisps of hair speckled with blood. An old man. Not exactly a prize of honor.

"I had to test this long knife on a Long Knife." Laughing Wolf grinned at his macabre joke. Spotted with dried blood, Silver Beard's sword danced against Laughing Wolf's leg. He turned and rejoined his friends among the Ohio men.

Red Hawk and Straight Arrow followed the others down the narrow track. Ahead, noises filtered back: the low murmur of quick discussion, the snort of a horse, a child's whimper, a woman's soft reply.

It wasn't until they'd camped for the night that Red Hawk shook off the haze and began to think. With Father dead, the village had no sachem. He knew himself to be too young for such a role, even if he had the necessary spiritual strength and the wisdom.

No, such a position was unthinkable, the more so after he'd seen the omen of the dead hawk. And now the Creator had deserted him too.

17

> The sight of so many perishing souls affects me much, & makes me long to go, if possible from pole to pole, to proclaim redeeming love.
>
> —George Whitefield (1714-1770)

Susanna squinted at the words on the page. The early evening sunlight was all but gone, and shadows filled the parlor.

Grenier.

She flipped open the French dictionary in her lap and scanned a page.

Callie entered the room, lit the candles, and slipped out.

Attic. Now the sentence made perfect sense. The girl slept in an attic. When Philippe had lent her Charles Perrault's tales several days ago, she'd been dubious, but he was right. Reading stories, no matter how silly, was much more diverting than studying a text.

"How is the book?" Anne adjusted the fabric in her lap, already recognizable as an infant's gown.

"I have never read anything like it." In the valley, the whole family had enjoyed *Robinson Crusoe*. This was different. "I think they are children's tales. *Cendrillon* is about a mistreated girl."

Anne frowned. "A story for children?"

"A fairy godmother shows up." Susanna scanned the page.

"A fairy? Sounds very French." Anne stabbed the muslin with her needle.

"She ends up going to the prince's ball after all. There is some kind of special shoe involved. The prince sees her—"

"Of course, and he falls in love. I could tell a tale of a beautiful woman who falls in love with a cabinetmaker—"

"Anne!" Of course it would be a cabinetmaker. Mr. Scott had made an excuse to visit just yesterday, full of talk about the newest fashion in chairs, ostensibly for Mr. Randolph's benefit.

Anne smiled. Although, perhaps she was merely trying to cheer her. Braddock's defeat had cast a dingy, gray film over the world.

Father ... was he even alive?

Susanna ran a finger down the novel's fine-textured paper page. The story had distracted her for a time. Everyone was so kind. But no one could help, except maybe God, and He seemed far away. Unreal.

Sighing, she gathered the books and stood. "I think I shall turn in early."

A line formed between Anne's brows, and she jerked her chin toward the candelabra. "Take a candle."

Once upstairs, Susanna secured the candle, put the books away, and knelt by the bed. The old familiar pressure of wood against her knees brought back a corresponding ache to her heart.

Williamsburg was wonderful. There was so much to see here, and the governor's gala was approaching. But when she'd left the valley, she'd left something else too. Or had she left it even before that?

The dancing candlelight formed patterns on the bed covers. She used to pray every morning and evening—short prayers, usually, but real. Now she never did.

Lord, help …

Her heart felt like stone. Why would God hear her? She'd ignored Him for what seemed like years. When she was eleven she'd made a profession of faith. The Scriptures had become alive, and Mr. Craig's preaching was no longer dull. Well, sometimes overly long, but always meaningful.

She'd lost that fresh excitement. And since coming here she hadn't opened her New Testament more than once or twice.

Susanna bent her head and tried in vain to pray. She knew what she'd find if she opened the Bible. Condemnation.

Their heart was exalted; therefore have they forgotten me. That was in the Old Testament somewhere.

Forgotten. She'd forgotten God.

She lowered her hands to the floor and paper brushed against her fingertips; something was under the bed. She pulled out a dusty pamphlet.

Christ the Only Rest for the Weary and Heavy-Laden. George Whitefield's sermon. How had it gotten there?

Susanna rose and sat on the bed. She opened the booklet and angled the pages toward the light. "Now they can go to balls and assemblies, play-houses and horse-racing; they have no thought of their sins …"

Yes. She understood. The first time she'd read this, Whitefield had seemed needlessly particular about such things. But now she saw his point. "The talk of sin and judgment is irksome to them, because it damps their mirth."

Such people were idolaters, worshiping pleasures and using such activities to shut out the voice of conscience.

Was she an idolater?

And where was the remedy? Her heart was already sore with guilt.

She turned the page.

ANNE GLIDED into the dining room the next morning even livelier than usual. "Susanna, a letter."

Tied with string, it was thicker than a letter, the direction written in Mother's fine hand. Susanna pushed her pewter plate to one side, grabbed a knife from the table, and sawed through the twine holding it together.

Several linen packets fell to the tabletop. *Seeds.* Then several letters. Planting instructions as well as notes on how to prepare and use the herbs. "Here, Anne, the medicinal herbs I suggested for your garden." Susanna thrust the packets and sheet of instructions toward her.

She focused on the two remaining sheets. Her father's beautiful scrawl spilled over the first. He was alive.

She blinked back tears. *Thank you, Lord.*

The second was in Mother's hand. Susanna took in a deep breath and swallowed.

Dearest Susanna, Enclos'd you will find Seeds and Instructions. Your Father wrote twice, once from the Fort and again from the Valley but they Both arriv'd about the same Time. I am including the Second Letter. He is Safe ...

What about Jamie?

She scanned the rest of the letter, but found nothing about him. Perhaps in her father's—

"Good news?" Anne's voice was unnaturally tight.

Susanna nodded, unsure of her own voice. Another breath. "Mother says he's safe and included his letter."

Anne poured some chocolate and sat.

Susanna picked up her father's letter, creased and spotted. There was a circular spot on one edge. A tear?

Dearest, I am happy to Report that no Indians have attacked our Settlement. The main Danger is North where the French provoke them to War. I hope for Peace in our Valley despite a few Incidents in the Mountains. Sadly, though, there is no Treaty with the Wild Animals. A Panther killed Samson while I was away. The valiant Beast defended his Ewes and the Noise woke Mr. MacLeod, but he was too late to save the Ram's life.

Susanna blinked. The ram stank but had done his duty. And they had a good crop of lambs every year.

I purchased two Piglets from Mr. Stuart. Once half-grown They can forage for Themselves. I have preferred Sheep to Swine but the Exigencies of Farming press me in that Direction. Perhaps we will obtain another Ram next Year, but for now we have Sufficient for Wool.

Mrs. McKee wept when I told her of her Husband's Death.

What? Simon McKee dead? He must have been killed in battle. His face sprang into her mind. And the image of his sickly-looking children. She struggled with the notion of his wife grieving over his death.

"Susanna?" Anne held a piece of toast halfway to her mouth.

"A neighbor was killed in that battle. Braddock's defeat."

"I am sorry to hear it."

Susanna wasn't sure she was sorry. Her first reaction was *good riddance*. But she could almost hear her father saying that only good could defeat evil. That we should love our enemies.

She tucked that thought away and returned to the letter.

You will be happy to learn that her Children are Fatter. They hide behind her Skirts when They see Me but I have seen them Smile. Their Dog is still Suspicious but looks better Fed. Please Tell Susanna the Horses here are well, but her beloved Cricket gave her Life most Bravely. She will understand what I mean. Horses can Panic, but ours acquitted themselves well.

Cricket. *No* ... She swallowed, her throat tight.

My Trivial Wounds have healed Nicely, thanks to Mr. Paxton, who dressed them so ably. I have receiv'd a Letter from him. He is recuperating at Colonel Washington's home on the Potomac River. He says it will take several Weeks due to the Nature of the Injury: a Ball Broke his Leg, and it was by the Grace of God the wound did not Fester. Please tell Susanna that her Gift of The Pilgrim's Progress in all Likelihood saved his Life ...

Susanna's heart contracted with the description of Jamie's other injury. There was now a sooty hole all the way through the stout volume. But he was safe.

Thank you, Lord.

She closed her eyes and a tear leaked out.

"Susanna?"

"Everyone is safe. Our mare Cricket was killed, but my father and Jamie are safe."

"Jamie?"

"James Paxton—"

"Yes, you mentioned him." Anne's gaze sharpened with interest.

The good news was a gift. An undeserved gift. She smoothed the letters before her, images filling her mind. Cricket, Jamie ... was he in pain?

Could she pray for him? God seemed distant still.

But when she climbed the stairs to her room, words from Whitefield's sermon returned to her. *Let me beseech you to come unto Christ, and he will give you rest ...*

She didn't have that rest yet, but she had hope.

18

> You may be said, my brethren, to be weary and heavy laden, when your sins are grievous unto you, and it is with grief and trouble that you commit them.
>
> —George Whitefield, *Christ the Only Rest*

Sitting at the walnut dining table, Susanna watched Philippe as he bent over the tiny portrait across from her. He'd explained the process of painting miniatures, but she couldn't understand how he could get so much detail into a three-inch-high ivory oval.

He glanced up, and a wisp of a smile stirred his mouth. Then he exchanged his tool for an exquisitely fine paintbrush and swirled the tiny tip between his lips. A dark lock swung over his forehead as he focused on his craft.

She'd seen another of his miniatures, and compared to his mentor's portraits, they were true works of art, always revealing an aspect of the personality in addition to hair color and face shape.

Abruptly, he sat up.

"May I see?"

"'Tis not dry, but yes."

She crossed the room to his side of the table, where the smells of linseed oil and turpentine overwhelmed the bergamot of Philippe's cologne. Before him lay the tiny portrait of a beautiful girl dressed in a deep rose bodice. This was her? Dark hair, dark eyes, and yes, the cleft chin. Beautiful yet determined. Is this how Philippe saw her?

"*C'est magnifique.* So detailed. But ..."

Philippe smiled. "But what?"

"She's so pretty."

"And you are not?"

Heat flamed her cheeks. Where was Anne? Shouldn't she be here embroidering? "You are better than your master."

"Indeed?"

"I have seen two of his portraits. He creates realistic fabric, but the faces are lifeless."

His eyebrow lifted. "And yet you accuse *me* of not being realistic?"

Her shoulders slumped. She didn't want to talk about how beautiful the girl in the picture was. "You capture more than line and color. The essence of personality lights up her features." *Her features, not mine.*

"And yet you do not accept this is you?"

Susanna looked down. Philippe's gaze was intense. She wanted to learn to paint, and yet his presence always brought something *more.* That something drew her, and yet ...

Philippe's gaze shifted. "What is this?"

She'd left some of her sketches on the table. "This one I made while waiting for you. Just a line drawing."

He turned it using a clean fingertip and drew in his lower lip.

"'Tis nothing."

"Who is this?"

"My father and a friend." She'd depicted her father riding Cricket with Jamie following on Red on their way to join Braddock.

Philippe turned and studied her. "I have a piece of canvas."

In moments, her sketch was pinned to the artist's fabric.

"Now trace the lines. We'll make a copy we can paint."

After a quarter hour, Susanna finished. "Now what?"

"Watch." Philippe took his palette and added a dollop of brown to white, then swirled his brush in linseed oil and mixed that in. "A background wash. I've thinned the paint out a little."

Much of the background took on that pale hue, and then he dipped the brush in sienna. "Let's darken the edges."

"Because the eye must go to the center?"

"Bravo, *mon élève*. I mean, my student." He mixed a subtle brownish-green with swipes of the brush.

"Why aren't you speaking French?" She did need the practice, but they'd been speaking English since he'd arrived.

He sighed, his eyes still focused on the canvas. "The tensions with France. Everything French is suspect, even people with French names who have been born here, like me. I have begun introducing myself as Phillip Dupray."

She frowned. The Anglicized pronunciation grated on her ears.

"Smile. The conflict cannot last long. Why, I will be back well before the governor's gala and surely by then we can all speak French without looking over our shoulders."

She peered at the canvas where the background colors forced her attention to the sketch of the riders. "Beautiful, 'twill be beautiful."

"Your lines created the focus. Without focus, there is no art. And character. Do you see your father's face?"

She nodded. She'd drawn him erect, facing forward.

"He is a stalwart man, bent on his duty. The horse is similar, although her ear ..." He pointed.

"Yes, she's obedient but can be nervous. She does well with my father. He isn't afraid, so she takes courage from him." Or she did. Poor Cricket. She hesitated to mention the loss of the horse. Despite the ordinary weave of his frock coat, Philippe seemed too refined to understand.

"The younger man, he has a different attitude."

Susanna hadn't thought about what Jamie might have been thinking but had sketched from instinct.

"He's glancing about. Not timid, exactly—"

"Jamie is a thinker. He is studying for the ministry."

Philippe's gaze slid to hers. She'd used Jamie's first name, a mistake in polite society. Would he remark on it?

"You are a natural." He took a deep breath. "I wish I had more time to spend. We must pack to leave tomorrow."

"Thank you, Philippe. Mr. Dupre." She bit her lip. "Mr. Dupray."

He chuckled. "Until then."

IN THE EARLY MORNING COOLNESS, Susanna stepped close to the stable's open door. A warm, woodsy smell enveloped her, competing with the familiar scent of manure and horse. Anne had planned their day, but Susanna had escaped to the peace of the garden and stable while she could.

She stepped inside. The carriage horses already knew her, as well as the two kept for riding: Mr. Randolph's sleek gelding, and Anne's mare, Socks, a chestnut only about fourteen hands high.

The gelding snorted. Susanna approached the little mare instead. "Here, girl, I have a treat for you." She extended her palm, fingers flat. Velvet lips swept across her hand, and the sugar was gone.

Poor Cricket. She would miss that faithful mare. And her foals … Whiskey was her favorite, her broad blaze and golden coat a match for her solid conformation. No wonder the sheriff had purchased her. Did Patton treat her well?

The gelding whuffed.

"I'm coming, be patient."

"Be careful of his teeth." A male voice behind her—the groom's.

She turned. "I will. He's got a mind of his own, doesn't he?" She gave the remaining chunk of sugar to the horse, which bobbed his head as if in thanks.

"Not a bad 'un, just a wee bit strong-willed." The groom's familiar Scots accent smote her heart. "I came for the carriage horses." He remained stiffly at the door until she exited.

"I should go inside." She needed to pin up her hair properly and get her gloves. Anne had promised a trip to the Capitol.

By the time her ribbon-trimmed bergère hat was secured on her head, the carriage was waiting out front.

Mr. Randolph, a newspaper tucked under his arm, handed her up into the carriage. Anne followed her.

"You said this was an important session?" Anne asked her brother.

He harrumphed. "We may receive information on the state of the troops, exact numbers and so on." His brows drew together.

"General Braddock's?" Anne asked.

"Yes, the regulars. We know the state of our own militia," he intoned darkly.

Few of them had returned uninjured, Susanna knew.

Mr. Randolph lapsed back into silence. He was normally reticent, but now he seemed downright serious, despite the good health of the family's finances. Not all Virginia planters had weathered the drought as well as he. But the war lingered like a dark cloud on the horizon.

The carriage halted, and they stepped into the breezy August morning, a bank of thick clouds covering the southwest sky.

Susanna studied the redbrick building before her. She'd seen the Capitol in the distance several times, a solid edifice with two round wings. Up close, it was imposing.

"Finished two years ago," Anne said, following her gaze. "The last one burned down."

The windows were gorgeous. Most were tall with arched tops; some were octagonal. They stepped into the dim interior. Spicy and fruity perfumes competed with the now-familiar odor of greasy wig pomade.

Voices sounded from the large room to the left. Anne's brother signaled them to enter. Gentlemen stood about conversing, most in colorful clothing with lacy cuffs, a few in humbler browns and grays. A railing, open in the middle, separated the foyer from a double row of pew-like seating that circled the room.

Mr. Randolph guided them to a bench on one side of the doorway. On the other side of the entryway a familiar man with spectacles sat on a rickety chair with a writing desk on his lap. The printer, probably taking notes for the *Gazette*.

The atmosphere was decidedly masculine. "Anne, I suspect ladies do not attend often."

"Hmph. If they did, there would be comfortable seating. And lemonade." Anne smirked as she took out her fan.

A rotund man sat in a strange chair with a tall back, sunlight winking through the octagonal windows on either side of him.

"Mr. Scott made Speaker Robinson's chair," Anne whispered.

Susanna nodded. There was no doubt Anne had a special affection for the unprepossessing cabinetmaker. But then, such a solid, staid personality would serve as a perfect foil for Anne's volubility.

Who would serve as her own match? Philippe?

She shook her head to clear it.

The speaker recognized a man on the floor, who stood, the silver buttons of his waistcoat glittering in the light.

"Generals ..." One dead general, none wounded, none safe. Braddock?

Apparently, the burgess was reading a list of casualties. "Colonels and lieutenant colonels. One killed, two wounded, none safe."

Her lips parted as the enormity of what he read sank in. No officer above the rank of captain had survived the battle unharmed. She focused on the numbers as she would points in one of Mr. Craig's sermons. Da would want to know.

"Surgeons and mates. One killed, five wounded, none safe."

Privates had done better, but more than half were dead or wounded. Susanna took a deep breath. How had her father and Jamie survived?

A murmur swelled in the room, the sound magnified by the echoing walls.

"The army is destroyed!"

Several cursed General Braddock.

The speaker pounded something. "The House will come to order."

The muttering slowly died down. The speaker slid from his seat and spoke quickly to a man nearby. The room darkened, and outside the octagonal windows the sky was gray.

A solemn quiet reigned when Speaker Robinson retook his chair. "We have further news of the war." He recognized another man, who shrugged off his coat when he stood.

The burgess read from a letter. "The western colonies are in great consternation and tumult on the death of General Braddock...."

Discussion ebbed and flowed. All the colonies, it seemed, had something to say about Braddock's defeat—and how their own militia would have done better.

Then someone made a motion regarding the Virginia militia.

"Questions?" Speaker Robinson said.

"Will Colonel Washington resume his duties?"

"Yes. But he needs more men."

A lengthy discussion ensued while the light dimmed even further. Thunder rumbled.

Anne fanned more briskly and shifted on her perch. The room was warm despite the clouds, and the musk of sweat clashed with perfume. Bright waistcoats emerged as men removed their coats.

A wigless gentleman sitting next to Anne's brother spoke. "What news of the other generals?"

Other generals? This was the first hopeful piece of information Susanna had heard. At least they were not all dead. Rain pummeled the roof as more discussion ensued.

"The street will be muddy," Anne murmured, clearly ready to leave.

The heavy door to the chamber opened with a sharp report like a gunshot, and a man strode into the foyer. He halted, dripping, between the two railings, almost close enough to touch. Spurs hung from filthy boots. He removed a shapeless hat, revealing golden-blond hair darkened along the hairline by sweat.

Recognition rolled over Susanna. William Preston? What was he doing here? The sober lines of the young man's face poured ice into her belly. Did he have news from the valley?

Murmurs rose, most disapproving.

"Mr. Speaker, I bring a report from the New River area."

The New River ... Susanna exhaled in relief. The New River was far to the south of her home.

The murmurs subsided.

"You may speak."

"Colonel James Patton, member of this body, has been killed ..."

What?

Preston stood tall and straight but his jaw muscle rippled. A collective sigh spread over the room.

"Killed by Shawnee Indians in a most perfidious massacre."

Sheriff Patton dead? The Shawnee at war?

The Shawnee were just a few days' journey over the mountains to the west. The entire valley was open to their depredations if they so chose.

The room wavered before her eyes.

19

The Holy Scripture is the only sufficient, certain, and infallible rule of all saving knowledge, faith, and obedience...

—*The Philadelphia Confession of Faith,* 1742

James made his way to the stable, the firm pressure of the cane's head under his hand. The pain in his leg had lessened, but he wondered if he'd always need the length of stout hickory.

Did it matter? He was sure of one thing. He had no calling to be a soldier.

Colonel Washington met him at the outbuildings, but his eyes were on the house, lit up in the golden morning light. "I shall add a full story. And extend each wing." His gaze shifted to James. "And build a proper staircase with a walnut banister."

The man was a visionary. How he was going to accomplish all that while directing the defense of the Commonwealth was more than James could imagine. "Are the burgesses agreeable to your requests?"

Washington's brows twitched. "Yes, they will give me more militiamen."

Hopefully enough to construct the line of forts the colonel had planned for the valley. "You wanted to see me?"

"Mr. Russell agreed to a proposition I made him regarding his gelding. A mare of your choice for the sorrel. I need a faithful saddle horse, and I lost two of my best. He has agreed most generously."

John Russell bred horses. If the mare were young and sound, it would be more than equitable. "Of my choosing?"

"I have two you might find interesting."

James followed Washington to the paddock behind the stable. Two animals nibbled the grass. At their approach, a blue roan raised her head high. Her lines were clean and her eyes intelligent, but she reminded him of an Arabian he'd seen once. Temperamental.

A moment later a chestnut turned her head, observing them without interrupting her grazing.

James hobbled closer to get a better look.

"You like the chestnut?"

"Is she sensible?"

"Yes. Not as flashy or as fast as the other. Only six years old."

After taking her through her paces, James made his decision. John Russell would want a sure-footed, good-tempered addition to his stable.

He looked forward to the journey to Hanover County to begin his studies with Reverend Davies. Riding made him feel whole again, and he looked forward to the company. The last letter he'd received from Philadelphia contained welcome news. A Baptist minister was traveling south.

South to Hanover County. James's brow furrowed. Hanover County and Reverend Davies.

~

MORNING MIST ROSE off the Potomac in the half-light of predawn. James slipped on the bridle over the chestnut mare's head and turned to address Aaron Walker. "When Mr. Jones sent word you were the one traveling south, I was surprised."

The Baptist minister smiled. "There are no coincidences."

They mounted and directed their horses down the lane to the main road.

"You said you'd studied over the confession?" Walker asked. They hadn't spoken much since the man's arrival last evening.

James was glad for the minister's company. When he and John Russell met him on the way to Winchester, Walker was traveling to Philadelphia. Now, it appeared, he rode south in order to encourage and instruct Baptists in both Virginia and North Carolina. "I know little of Baptists so I was glad to see a friendly face. And yes, I've given the sections on baptism extra consideration."

"Much of the rest is similar to the Westminster."

James nodded. The trees thinned as they approached another plantation on their right. Birds chittered. "Aye. Otherwise I might have been more cautious."

"Thinking us to be heretics?" Walker chuckled. "Of course that begs the question. Is the Westminster our authority? Or the Philadelphia?"

"Neither, of course. The Scriptures are the only infallible rule."

"On that we are agreed."

A gentle breeze brushed against his neck. It was cool and damp, golden light skimming the treetops, but later it would turn sweltering, even now in early September. James worked hard in Mr. Craig's fields in the summer, but it was hotter here, the air heavier.

He glanced at Walker's face, weather-beaten above a loosely knotted kerchief. "How did you end up a Baptist?"

"It's not complicated. I was studying to become a Presbyterian minister much as yourself, but I could find no warrant for infant baptism in Scripture."

No warrant ... "You mean no positive commandment to do so?"

"Yes. You would think something we put importance on should have at least one clear example."

James frowned. "But several times we are told someone 'and his household' were baptized in the book of Acts."

"I do understand the position of my Presbyterian friends. In fact, if this were the only consideration I might have simply acknowledged the difficulty of the matter and dropped my objections."

"What convinced you?"

Walker cut him a glance. "There are positive commandments regarding baptism. 'He that believeth—'"

"'—and is baptized shall be saved.'"

Walker cleared his throat. "So, what are the implications of that verse?"

The man sounded like Mr. Craig. "Well, the passages on baptism all presuppose believing." Which had nagged at him for a long time.

"So why baptize infants?"

"To bring them into the protection of the covenant relationship." This was tricky. Church members were brought in through baptism even though some turned out to be rogues later. But the visible church was composed of both true and false believers, wasn't it?

For an hour they tossed verses back and forth as James wrestled through the knots of his doubts. To the left of the road trees grew sparse and grasses rose yellow to the horses' knees.

"Remember," Walker said. "I may make it sound straightforward, but in actuality my convictions were built over many months."

That was comforting to know. They traveled in silence until the next landmark, a broad river, where they led their horses onto a ferry.

Sunlight danced on the ripples produced by the ferry's passage across the Occoquan River. James's leg ached as he stood at the gunwale, one hand on the rail, the other rubbing the mare's leather reins between his fingers. Salty, dank air brushed against him from the east. They weren't far from the sea.

The chestnut mare nosed his back. Nutmeg, her name was, although in James's opinion, her color was closer to cinnamon.

The water claimed his attention. *Water* ... Water baptism was a picture of the death, burial, and resurrection of the Lord Jesus Christ. And yet, it was more than a symbol. It didn't save a person, that was true. According to the Westminster, it was a sign and seal of the covenant of grace, and not absolutely necessary for salvation. But it was so close to the heart of the gospel ... He just had to get it right.

Walker joined him at the rail, his gaze focused on the southern shore.

"What is the meaning of baptism?" James asked rhetorically. He was approaching a point of no return and had to make doubly sure his convictions were well grounded in Scripture.

"Like the Lord's Supper, it is a sign of His work of redemption. Unlike the Lord's Supper, which is a remembrance and meant to be repeated, the ordinance of baptism is a one-time act of obedience and identification with Christ."

Obedience. Yes, that was the crux of the matter. But there was something else niggling at him, something he hesitated to bring up. "Tell me, Mr. Walker, how do you define courage?"

The other man did not respond immediately. "What was the battle like?" he said finally. "I've only heard rumors."

"Like a nightmare, only worse, because it was real." More he could not say. It was as if the words were frozen in his throat.

"I suspect every soldier feels fear. Before a battle, if not during."

James mulled this over as they led their horses off the ferry and remounted. "None would admit such a thing."

"Perhaps not. But all are flesh and blood. When a man follows the path of duty despite fear, that I call courage."

Now that he thought about it, the fear he'd experienced during battle did not compare to the apprehensions assailing his mind during the ghoulish retreat and horrible nightmares. "You mentioned obedience earlier. But if I canna recall my own baptism, how can I obey the command to believe and be baptized?"

Walker sighed. "I daresay you know the answer to that."

But what would happen if he dared request baptism? Mr. Craig's face sprang to mind. All the babes the man had sprinkled, traveling for days in some cases.

It wasn't just the man's approbation he cared about. The vision of his heart was to preach the gospel. What if his new stance on baptism shut down that opportunity?

They rode without speaking for a time, and James lifted up his heart in silent prayer. Tall grasses and cattails cloaking pools and ponds swept toward the sea on his left. A few brave trees, maple and oak, lined the western side of the road. The distinctive cry of a bittern floated through the air.

James broke the silence. "If I were baptized, would Reverend Davies reject me as a student?"

"Hmm. Perhaps not. Remember, Presbyterians are also considered dissenters in the Commonwealth of Virginia. In fact, the notable Baptist John Bunyan never found the issue a matter for division."

"Bunyan? Ye know him?"

Walker's eyes twinkled. "He's been with the Lord many a year. Have you heard of him?"

James recounted how *The Pilgrim's Progress* might have saved his life.

A smile crept across Walker's face. "Praise the Lord. He wrote that story while imprisoned for preaching without a license." The smile vanished. "Here in Virginia the same thing can happen."

James recalled the day when John Russell had delivered Walker to the constable, who'd proceeded to feed the man. Not all constables and sheriffs would be so forgiving. But James had no intention of preaching publicly. "How did your Presbyterian friends react to your new convictions?"

"I discussed these issues with several ministers. In the end, they were amiable about it. I think they understood my desire to serve Christ fully, according to my best understanding of the Scriptures."

"According to your conscience."

"Just so."

They urged their horses to a brisker walk in the morning sunshine. James mulled over the question, but his heart burned with conviction. Even if Mr. Craig cast him out, he had to obey God rather than man.

Finally he came to a decision. At the first sizable river or stream, he'd ask to be baptized.

Peace flowed over him.

20

Surely I can fill sheets of paper with the sufferings of the Baptists...

—Jonathan Sprague, 1721

Williamsburg, October 1755

"Can you tighten your stays?" The milliner's assistant asked softly, though there were no other customers in the shop. And they were in a back room, besides.

Susanna debated. She hated boned stays to begin with; their only sensible use seemed to be on the Sabbath, when they'd poke or pinch her when she slumped. Usually she wore the comfortable quilted variety. "Perhaps a little."

Muttering, the seamstress ran the tape one more time around Susanna's waist. Behind the woman's back Anne made a face and rolled her eyes. Susanna pressed her lips together to keep from smiling.

"You'll be beautiful, no doubt," Anne's mother said. "These ladies are renowned for their skill and eye for fashion. I overheard Mrs. Bolling say the gowns sewn here are the equal of any from London." Mrs. Randolph was a soft, older copy of her daughter, with laugh lines framing her eyes.

The assistant's taut face relaxed. It was the perfect thing to say.

The chosen bolt of silk damask lay on a table nearby. Red flowers over a subtle golden-green background. Red and green did not mesh well, in her opinion, but here they did. When Philippe returned she'd ask why a bold crimson served as the perfect counterpoint for such a gentle tint.

Finally the seamstress was satisfied, and Susanna followed Anne and her mother out of the shop. A chilled breeze ruffled their curls as well as the ragged clothing of a man, thin as a fence rail, walking on the other side of the road. But the others seemed not to notice.

Once in the carriage, Mrs. Randolph addressed Susanna. "Is your family's plantation in the Northern Neck or near Shadwell?"

"Not far from Shadwell," Susanna said. "We typically stop there when visiting relations near Richmond." True enough.

"Dear Peter." Anne's mother looked pensive. "When he desired to court my eldest daughter, I opposed the match."

"There were stories about Uncle Peter, you see," Anne said.

"Legends, you mean," said her mother. "Lifting hogsheads and the like. Just like a country backwoodsman." Her tone was derisive.

Susanna cringed inside. How could such a pleasant woman say such things? Yes, there were some in the valley who were uncouth. Drunkards, even. But most of the Ulster Scots were strong, steady people who valued education even if they didn't have it themselves. At least Anne was sympathetic, and neglected to clarify Susanna's background.

"Despite his father's property, he owned only one decent coat. I think I was the only one who noticed his limited wardrobe. But he was charming to all and sundry, and your papa liked him. Jane was besotted."

"He had a good name, and he wasn't penniless," Anne said.

"Even now he invites savages to his table. Imagine!" Mrs. Randolph said.

Susanna cringed, thinking of the Indians around the Russell table.

"But it did prove to be a good match after all," Anne's mother conceded. "Peter Jefferson may be eccentric, but there are worse things."

The carriage halted, and the groom assisted them down. Once in the house Callie took their wraps. The warm aroma of hickory, ham, and cloves greeted them.

Callie returned. "Ma'am, there be a letter for Miss Susanna on the hall table."

Susanna spotted the worn packet lying on the gleaming mahogany surface. She stepped forward and picked it up. "From Mother."

She ran her finger under the seal and unfolded the paper. This time, no letter from her father was enclosed.

"I need to supervise supper preparations." Mrs. Randolph glided out of the hall and Anne followed.

Glad for the privacy, Susanna crossed to the parlor and sat. In a previous letter Mother had acknowledged the news of the death of Colonel Patton in the massacre down south. What it all meant for them was uncertain.

She untied the packet and unfolded the paper.

Dearest Susanna, your Father spent several Days here while delivering Goods and fine Woods to your Uncle. Apparently some of our Relations believe a War will increase Need for Wood of various Kinds, including Masts for Ships.

Her stepmother continued with news from the valley. Aunt Lizzie's new baby, and Kitty Kerr's first, a boy.

A long labor, but a well-formed Child, with the Robinson Nose. Mrs. May is raising Pullets, and Mr. MacLeod has a natural Way with the Animals, according to your Father.

As the names emerged from the letter, Susanna's throat tightened. She missed everyone.

Your Father has discussed the Matter of the Indians with John Lewis and his Son. The Danger seems to be well to the North and West of Staunton. Our Home is even farther East and unlikely to see Harm.

Silas Sloan had been killed in front of the cabin by a Shawnee Indian, but hadn't he been singled out for retribution? Surely Da was right.

He has decided that since he will be to Home and well able to Protect us, we might return. He will come to Richmond in the Spring for that Purpose.

She swallowed. What about her painting lessons? And what about Philippe? The governor's gala would be this winter. The painter had said he would be back by then. Perhaps then she'd know if he merely possessed a *tendresse* for her or if there was true intention on his part.

She continued reading.

Auntie Agnes sent more Yarn, Red and Blue. She is proud of the Red. Have you used the Loom yet?

She'd already fashioned several scarves, her donation to the Bruton Parish's poorhouse committee. Hopefully some of the ragged children she'd seen upon her arrival wouldn't be as cold this winter. It was hard to understand how a place as prosperous as Williamsburg would need a poorhouse in the first place. At home they took care of their neighbors. She smoothed the letter under her hands.

We attended Meeting in a new place, Hanover County, on account of a ~~Presyb~~ good Minister there.

Susanna smiled. "Presbyterian" was a challenge for any writer.

He proved excellent, though the drive was over two Hours. You may be glad to hear James Paxton is his Student. He still walks with a Limp but seems well. He informed us he is studying Hebrew.

Jamie. Jamie standing in the doorway of the house in the valley. Jamie colliding with her and falling halfway down the stairs, their limbs tangled. Jamie discussing a sermon with her at Tinkling Springs.

Was he in pain? Did he use a cane?

Your Father thanks you for the Sermon you sent. He reminds you to read your Testament. He prays for you Daily, as do I.

The letter concluded simply.

Susanna folded the paper slowly. Her father prayed for her. For once, she was heartily glad for it.

Anne stood in the doorway, an uncertain expression on her face.

"'Tis good news, Anne. Father judges the valley safe enough for us to return in the spring."

"But I shall miss you!" Anne's mouth puckered. "Do write, I pray thee!"

"I have not left yet. Not till the snow melts, I imagine."

"Hmm. Mother asks if you wish mulled cider in place of ale."

"A warm drink sounds wonderful."

Anne half-turned to leave. "You've time to freshen up before supper is laid."

Susanna nodded her thanks and stepped to the stairs. Anne could sense when she needed time alone.

Once in her room, she ignored the mirror and crossed to the bedside table where her New Testament lay. Last night she'd found hope in the Gospel of John.

But guilt still plagued her.

She remembered a verse about forgiveness, somewhere in one of John's epistles. She flipped open the volume and carefully made her way to the short letters.

There it was. *If we confess our sins, he is faithful and just to forgive us our sins, and to cleanse us from all unrighteousness.*

She read it over and over.

Lord, forgive me for forgetting You.

RED HAWK STRUCK the flint firmly. Too firmly. The antler billet slipped, and the stone fractured the wrong way, spoiling the tip. He threw the tool down in disgust.

A shadow fell across the litter of ruined arrowheads in front of him.

Gusts of autumn breeze stirred Buffalo Robe's buckskin poncho. "Your face looks like a storm cloud."

Red Hawk stood and wiped bits of stone off his leggings. He gestured to the mess without speaking.

"You excel at everything else. Look. I'll trade you some of mine if your grandmother will give us some herbs for my mother."

She-Who-Sings wasn't that old. "Rheumatism?"

"When the weather changes, like today."

Red Hawk scanned the sky. It would rain soon, which could be good for hunting the next day. Soft ground made it easy to track deer. He bent and picked up the single good arrowhead he'd made and rubbed it between his fingers. "I have enough arrows. Thank you anyway. I'll remind my grandmother about your mother." Grandmother seemed like a shell of her former self, but she still dried herbs and combined remedies for people. "I'm going hunting tomorrow if the weather clears by morning. Want to come?"

His friend cocked his head, and Red Hawk followed his gaze. Laughing Wolf was leading his horse through the village. He stopped at the wigwam of Running Deer's family.

Red Hawk's throat constricted. Twice in one moon the man had brought Running Deer gifts of meat and furs. He couldn't imagine how any woman would welcome Laughing Wolf's advances, but clearly the man could provide, and with no proper sachem, Elk Tooth, Laughing Wolf's father, was the village leader.

He recalled Big Turtle's words at the Bread Dance, where all the villages of their band assembled together.

"I've spoken to the elders, Red Hawk. A sachem will emerge in time, as grass in the spring. In the meantime, the band's medicine bundle is here and all may come to inquire."

Big Turtle's village was two days' away. Not very far. But the words seemed hollow now. Elk Tooth's words swayed the elders, and Laughing Wolf curried favor in every way he knew.

Buffalo Robe cleared his throat. "Laughing Wolf wanted to sing a spell over my mother to banish her aches, but she chased him away."

Good for her. But it was an alarming development. "Will he now style himself as a medicine man?"

"He's gone into the forest for meditation and visions." His dark friend shrugged. "Do you think he wants to be sachem?"

"He is by no means old enough."

Running Deer emerged from her wigwam and smiled at Laughing Wolf.

Red Hawk tasted bile.

IN THE SHADOWS of the hearth's orange glow, Red Hawk rummaged underneath an old deerskin and laid his hands on the special bundle. Wrapped in a piece of woven cloth, he'd kept the object safe.

He opened the cloth and studied the rectangular object nestled within. It was not much larger than his hand. The cover, leather of some kind, was scuffed and bruised—possibly in the raid. But most of the inside was intact.

Gently, he opened the cover and turned the thin white leaves. Black marks, marching in even rows, covered each surface. Red Hawk scooted closer to the fire. Each mark was a unique shape—but no, here were two alike.

The thought flashed through his mind like fire. It was a code of some sort. Hair-Like-The-Sun had been recording what he'd seen in something like this. Recording so he would not forget.

He nearly dropped the object. This was as potent as any medicine bundle. Perhaps this would explain his dream.

Grandmother slipped inside, and behind her Dark Water. He needed to know what Grandmother would say.

Dark Water spoke first. "What is that?"

"I think it's like a medicine bundle. Something powerful."

The women sat before the hearth, their expressions cautious.

"Where did you get it?" Grandmother said.

"On the raid to the Great Valley." The terrible raid, the raid in which his father had been killed.

"White men's medicine?" Dark Water's face was hard.

"I had a dream the other night, a very strange and vivid dream."

Grandmother's shoulders relaxed. "Tell me."

"I saw a beaver. A white beaver."

Dark Water's face showed reluctant interest.

"He stood upright like a man and wore a purple wampum belt. He wanted to show me something, so I approached."

Grandmother nodded for him to continue.

"He showed me something in his hand." Red Hawk swallowed and lifted the bundle. "It was this." He unwrapped the object and opened it so the white leaves showed. "In the dream, the leaves glowed with a beautiful light. Then I awoke."

Fear and respect mingled in Dark Water's expression, but Grandmother's face gave nothing away.

Red Hawk closed the object so the tougher leather protected the leaves. "Grandmother?"

"You wish me to give an interpretation. Very well." She chuckled. "Realize, though, what I tell you is common knowledge. This vision is meant for you in particular. When it is fulfilled, you will know."

She coughed noisily. "First, the beaver is white. A symbol of wisdom and spiritual knowledge. The white color marks the dream as significant."

Red Hawk nodded. He understood that much.

"He walks upright. He symbolizes a man. An important man, perhaps even a chief."

"Because of the purple."

"Yes, purple is a sacred color of power and mystery."

He held up the bundle. "What about this?"

Grandmother's eyes twinkled in the light of the hearth. "One thing I can tell you. That is not medicine the way we think. It is called a *book.*"

Red Hawk tried to say the word. "B-book?"

"We have no word for it in our tongue. The book is their language painted on an object. The way I decorate pots or put patterns into beads."

He couldn't help grinning like a boy. "It makes better sense now. But this is medicine, in its own way. Don't you see? Grandmother, your herbs for remedies, I could paint them in a ..."

"Book."

"B-book. Then no one would forget."

Dark Water frowned.

"And all the Shawnee stories." He wanted to preserve all the wisdom of his people. If only he had the power of the code.

"Trapped in some piece of skin?" His aunt could be contrary sometimes.

"Daughter, let him find his own path." Grandmother fixed her eyes on him. "It is a good dream. Be patient and wait to see how it unfolds."

Wait. He would try. One thing was certain. The dream was the only ray of hope he'd had in a long time.

21

That I from thee no more may part,
No more thy goodness grieve,
The filial awe, the fleshly heart,
The tender conscience give.

—Charles Wesley (1707-1788)

Hanover County, November 1755

Gasping, James blinked at the oak beams above him. The gray of early morning slowly brought him back to the real world, where damp, twisted sheets entangled him and the sound of a small boy's nasal breathing filled the small space of the loft.

He'd had another dream. He could still see the red paint and smell the greasy stench of the Indian. And Mackenzie's face loomed in his mind like a specter.

James unwound the sheets and sat up. Little Willie slept on, his thumb in his mouth, something his devoted mother tried to keep him from doing. He was six years old, and not a babe, she maintained. When he slept he was impervious to noise—a good thing, James decided.

He slipped on his clothes, slid down the ladder, and carefully opened the back door. The kitchen hearth was stoked; Mrs. Davies had probably already started breakfast or perhaps the midday meal, but he didn't see her.

He found himself at the side of the cantankerous cow, whose grunts indicated he was late for milking. She could be contrary, but he generally succeeded in filling a tin pail morning and evening. Only once had Bluebell kicked him.

He sat on the low stool and soothed her udder with salve, but she tried to shift away from his cold fingers. "Whoa, lassie." It was pleasantly warm in the little barn, and his fingers would be soon.

Samuel Davies had regarded his arrival as providential. His indentured servant's contract was completed, and he needed help. When the minister learned James had helped Mr. Craig with labor in the fields and around the property, he rejoiced. "I'd feared a student would be next to useless. I should have known, seeing as you're a lad from the valley."

His hands were warm now, and the milk flowed easily. The comforting smell of the beast and the rhythmic swoosh and patter of the milk as it hit the pail helped to counteract the aftereffects of the dream.

James stripped the teats one last time and brought the milk in to strain and settle. The house was nicer than Mr. Craig's, but not huge. The single large kitchen fireplace managed to warm the four rooms downstairs plus the loft he shared with the couple's only child.

He ducked outside again into the chill pearly-hued dawn with the water bucket, his stomach rumbling. He hoped there was buttermilk for breakfast. Day-old cornbread crumbled in milk equaled anything served at Mount Vernon.

Once his chores were completed, James washed and entered the kitchen, where Willie sat at the pine table, owlish eyes blinking up at him. His mop of fine brown curls haloed his head like a fairy wig.

His mother brought a stoneware pitcher to the table. "Mr. Paxton, will you ask the blessing for us? Mr. Davies is at prayer."

James sat and ignored his stomach while praying for the food, also asking God's blessing of the preaching of the Word as the minister was always in the habit of doing. Everything Samuel Davies said or did was somehow flavored with a love for the Scriptures and the souls of men.

"Thank you." Jane Davies passed him the buttermilk. "Mr. Davies says to meet him in the study after breakfast."

Not unusual. Sometimes Reverend Davies needed a full day to study and pray over a text, and those days there were no lessons, but most days James brought his books to the small room made smaller by a large desk and several bookcases.

"Mr. Paxton," Willie said around a mouthful of cornbread, "why is your hair white?"

Mrs. Davies raised her brows at her son.

"'Tis naught but a family trait, you see." He shrugged at Mrs. Davies to show her he didn't mind the question. "My brothers and sisters all have light-colored hair, and mine is the lightest."

Willie's single dimple made its appearance. Normally he was not allowed to speak at the table.

James stood and thanked Mrs. Davies for breakfast, deciding to escape before he got in trouble too. "I'd best be getting my books now."

Once inside the study, Mr. Davies waved him to sit. His brown hair was casually tied back, the gentle curve of his dark brows giving him an appearance of continual surprise. "Hebrew first."

James opened the text, battered and creased, an ancient relic used by several generations of students. "*Bara* compared with *asah*. Two verbs with the meaning of to make or create." He studied the inkwell on the desk, stained with layers of drips. "There doesn't seem to be much difference."

Mr. Davies stared into space. "Perhaps they seem interchangeable in Genesis the first chapter. But tell me, is *bara* ever used to describe the work of a man?"

The Hebrew lesson ground on. James compared learning the subject to plowing a field. Sweaty and painful, but once in a while a sweet morsel emerged from the text, a shade of meaning indiscernible in the English translation.

Next they tackled hermeneutics. "Back to Augustine. What did he mean by the literal meaning of a text?"

James pulled out the previous day's lesson from the fuzzy recesses of his mind and responded to the question.

Mr. Davies picked up a quill and twirled it between his fingers. "Mr. Paxton, you did not tell me you've been re-baptized."

He tensed. The time had never seemed right, and even now he didn't know how to explain. "The subject was on my mind a long time."

"Does Mr. Craig know about this?"

"Not the baptism, no. But we did discuss the topic. Calvin had no problem with immersion. Mr. Craig seemed to think the mode indifferent."

"That is not the issue." Mr. Davies tapped the quill on the open book before him. "The very nature of the church is related to the doctrine of baptism."

James quailed under the questioning but forced himself to respond. "I agree with the Westminster on the doctrine of the church." He stared at the book. "I knew I would need to discuss baptism with you eventually."

"Eventually." The minister sighed.

Guilt swamped him. He'd known there would be practical issues but hadn't realized there were theological ones as well. "I apologize, Mr. Davies. I knew I had to obey the Scriptures for myself, and thought I'd deal with the rest later."

The minister turned the quill around and examined the tip. "Some things you could not have known, perhaps. Baptists have a slightly different view of the church. The ones theologically inclined, anyway." Lines creased his forehead. "Some Baptists have no training whatsoever. They preach in every imaginable venue, licensed or not, and drift into error."

James clasped his hands in his lap, rubbing his cold fingers. Reverend Davies was a supporter of George Whitefield, who'd been known to preach in open fields. But James wasn't George Whitefield.

Mr. Davies fixed a thoughtful gaze on him. "Enough hermeneutics. I have two assignments for you. First, write an essay on the history of English Baptists, including those here in the colonies. Second, read this book."

The man turned to the bookshelf on his right and pulled out a thin volume. "Ever hear of Jonathan Edwards?"

"Yes, I've read his *Religious Affections*."

"Then you know how solid he is. He also wrote this." The minister pushed the book across the desk.

James picked it up. *The Life and Diary of David Brainerd*. The cover was scuffed and some of the inside pages dog-eared.

"In the meantime, you are welcome to stay and complete your studies."

Thank you, Lord!

"On one condition." A line appeared between the man's brows. "I must never hear of you preaching in the open air or doing anything to otherwise bring attention to yourself."

"I certainly have no intentions of such, sir." James knew Mr. Davies had to be careful, or he'd jeopardize his preaching license.

"Good. I truly do appreciate your labors on behalf of my family."

"Thank ye kindly." Chopping wood was no sacrifice, just ordinary service. He stood and examined the volume in his hands. "Who is David Brainerd?"

"He preached to the Indians."

He almost dropped the book.

~

James opened his eyes, the last words of the minister's closing prayer still sounding in his ears. The congregation was dismissed, and a low swell of chatter began to fill the meetinghouse.

A familiar sound of relaxed breathing caused him to glance at Willie, seated next to him on the hard pew. The child was sleeping in the most unlikely position, fully upright with a slight sideways slouch. The child's neck was kinked at an angle that made James wince.

He suppressed a grin as he rose from his seat. Mrs. Davies was speaking to another woman, oblivious of her child's condition.

He scanned the room. Had Mrs. Russell come again? Last time he hadn't inquired about Susanna's welfare, thinking it too forward of him.

No, only the regulars in view—except for one stranger, a redheaded youth whose hair resisted the discipline of the queue. Wisps framed the young man's face as he spoke to Patrick Henry. His light coloring contrasted with Henry's dark hair and fading summer tan.

James approached them. The Henrys were enthusiastic supporters of Mr. Davies's preaching and most of the family was converted. The elder Mr. Henry rarely attended, but his son was close to his own age and an agreeable companion.

"Impressive oratory," the stranger was saying.

"Mother made me recite his sermons after meeting for years," Patrick said. "You won't find a better logician."

They caught sight of James at the same time.

James inclined his head to the stranger. "Welcome. James Paxton, at your service."

Patrick laid a hand on James's shoulder and gestured with the other. "Mr. Thomas Jefferson. On his way to the College of William and Mary." He waggled his eyebrows. "To study law."

Ah, that explained the obvious camaraderie. Young Henry desired to study for the bar himself. But who knew when he could find the time, after the responsibilities of a wife, young babe, and the farm. "Mr. Jefferson. I hope you found the sermon profitable." The name sounded familiar.

The lively hazel eyes shuttered. "I always appreciate a well-constructed line of reasoning."

Now he remembered. "Are you acquainted with a Mr. John Russell?"

"The Russells are friends of the family. Their daughter is studying in Williamsburg with my mother's sister."

"A valley connection?" Patrick asked James.

"Aye. I accompanied Mr. Russell up north last year. We assisted Colonel Washington."

Both faces lit with interest.

"I knew you'd been injured in that battle, but not the circumstances," Patrick said.

James shrugged. "I survived." He'd always found himself reluctant to speak of it.

Jefferson's gaze was keen for one so young. "Many have good things to say about Colonel Washington, despite the defeat."

Thank you for changing the subject. "Indeed. He was stalwart despite … everything." Mackenzie's face flashed before his mind's eye, as it usually did when thinking of the battle. "Speaking of the Russells, I do not see Mrs. Russell today."

"Her relations, the Bashams, do not attend on a regular basis." A faint crease formed between the young Henry's brows. "I heard talk at the tavern of a Baptist minister in the area. His name is Woods, and his circuit brings him nearby every couple of weeks. I heard the name Basham—I believe he preaches near their farm. Perhaps they worshiped closer to home this morning."

James blinked rapidly. How he'd love to speak to the man. "Thank you." He decided to leave the young men to their discussions of law and philosophy. Then he caught Mr. Jefferson's thoughtful gaze upon him. "Might I ask a favor of you when you go to Williamsburg?"

"'Twould be my pleasure."

"Might you look in on Susanna? See how she fares."

Jefferson inclined his head, hazel eyes lively. "I was planning on it."

"Thank you." Suddenly his clothes felt too warm. Surely Thomas Jefferson was too young to be pursuing any young woman.

22

Thy word is to my feet a lamp,
and to my path a light.

—*The Scottish Psalter,* 119:105, 1650

Williamsburg, January 1756

The red satin shoes were beautiful, like a dream. Susanna slipped them on, thinking of the cinder girl in *Cendrillon*.

"Jane's," Anne said. "Do they fit?"

Of all the finery encasing her body, the shoes were the only comfortable part. Her stays were too tight, the large bumroll tied about her middle felt cumbersome, the red ribbon about her neck made its presence known every time she swallowed, and the brocade of her gown was stiff and heavy.

"Yes. If anything, they're a tad loose." They reminded her of her moccasins back home. "Thank you."

"Tom just arrived."

Thomas Jefferson was escorting her to the governor's gala. Philippe would be there, a guest of the Carters, and the thought made her sweat beneath the fabric.

Anne swept through the bedroom door and glided down the steps. Susanna followed, testing out the shoes. Yes, they would stay on.

She gripped the banister tightly as she began to descend. The curls Anne had insisted on bounced against her cheeks. She flushed thinking of the rouge. Apparently powder and a small amount of color was appropriate for a formal dance, but Susanna still felt like a strumpet. She was glad her father couldn't see her now.

Now they can go to balls and assemblies … Whitefield's words returned to her, smiting her heart.

Something wasn't right. Philippe's image came to her mind, along with a niggling finger of guilt.

Lord, help me. Lord, forgive me.

A TALL STRANGER wearing a crushed green velvet coat stood in the foyer. His gaze found her face when Susanna approached.

"Tom?" Lace sprouted from his sleeves and bubbled from his jabot, and his waistcoat boasted gold stripes. Most shockingly, his red hair was gone, submerged in a layer of pomade and white powder. "Is that really you?"

"I might ask the same, my lady Susanna." He bowed, his arm gesturing theatrically.

She rolled her eyes. "Your aunt dressed me."

His expression sobered. "Most beautifully."

"Now where have you been, and where did that coat come from?"

Tom raised his hands in defense. "You well know my studies consume me."

Not that he minded, she was sure. He'd been in Williamsburg over a month but had come by the house only once.

"As for the coat …"

"Horse racing?" The track was a popular draw for the students of the College.

"In the snow? No, cards." He shrugged. "I was lucky."

A feminine voice resonated in the hall. "I see our company is complete." Anne's mother sailed into the foyer, a thick shawl over her arm. "Susanna, you will travel with Mr. Jefferson."

Tom crooked his arm in invitation, and she accompanied him outside where two vehicles waited, one looming large in the moonlight, the Randolphs' coach; the other only a riding chair pulled by a single horse.

"I apologize. I have no grand carriage. Only my friend's riding chair —rather chilly in winter, but I have a lap blanket."

She gathered her skirts and stepped up inside. "The moonlight is grand, Mr. Jefferson. See how the snow and ice twinkles?" They sat close together in the tiny open carriage, but she didn't mind. The remnants of the snowstorm were ugly in daytime, mixed with the soot of many fires and the mud and manure of the road, but the filth was cloaked by the evening darkness, giving rise to a fairy-like landscape. Above them, stars were scattered like silver dust across the darkened canvas of the sky.

Tom urged the horse to a brisk walk. "I should have known a valley lass would not consider creature comforts."

She settled back. Tom was easy to be around. "How are your studies faring?"

"My mathematics professor is a gem."

"Mathematics? You jest."

Tom waxed eloquent about the subject until they reached Palace Street. He reined the horse right. "I have heard this professor is in accord with Montesquieu with regard to religion."

"*Explique-moi.*"

He replied in French. "Montesquieu says all forms of religion should be equally tolerated under the law."

Interesting thought. "My father pays tithe to the Church of England though he worships elsewhere." Everyone in Virginia did. It was the law.

"I have heard of Baptists beaten for their faith." He shifted to English. "Susanna, your French is better than mine. Who is your tutor? You sound like a Frenchwoman."

They were approaching the Governor's Palace, illuminated windows looming high above street level. "A painter's apprentice, actually. His *maman* was born in France."

Tom glanced at her but made no reply.

Susanna's heart quickened as she studied the grand building. Was Philippe already here?

EVERYTHING SPARKLED. Even the walnut banister gleamed. And the chandeliers—Susanna hesitated in the ballroom's doorway, staring.

A soft glow from a multitude of candles illumined the largest room she'd ever seen, half-full of glittering people and the warm buzz of conversation. Feminine titters flowed over the undercurrent of men's voices. The walls were teal with white trim, and the tall windows reflected the gleam of the interior.

Tom's faint pressure on her arm woke her to the presence of two individuals ahead. She stepped forward. An older man in a huge powdered wig stood next to a younger woman perhaps Mother's age.

Tom bowed low before the man and introduced Susanna to Governor Dinwiddie and his wife.

Susanna curtseyed as deeply as she could. When she rose, she noticed the woman was smiling.

"Miss Russell? You make me feel like a queen with that curtsey." Garnets swung from the woman's ears, and her overskirts fell over a wide structure that caused her gown to extend sideways. "Call me Rebecca."

"Je suis enchantée de faire votre connaissance." Susanna blurted out the greeting without thinking.

"Mr. Jefferson, have you brought a Frenchwoman into our midst?" The governor's voice possessed an echo of Scotland, despite his precise King's English.

Susanna's cheeks warmed. "I am no spy, sir."

"Indeed." The governor's tone was cheerful underneath the bluster.

"My father fought with Colonel Washington."

His wife raised a brow. "Was he injured?"

"He has recovered."

The governor smiled. "Well met, daughter of Virginia. Enjoy yourselves."

As if signaled by the governor's words, the strains of several violins pierced the hubbub of conversation.

"May I have this dance?" Tom asked.

She grinned at him as they stepped into the throng. "Part of me feels like I'm playacting, that it can't be real."

They joined the swinging figures of a reel. By the time they were done, Susanna wasn't winded at all. Williamsburg reels were tame.

Tom glanced over her shoulder.

She turned. "Philippe! Or should I say, Mr. Dupre." She scrambled to find her manners and made introductions. "Mr. Thomas Jefferson, of Shadwell."

"Phillip Dupray, if you prefer." The painter's dark gaze swept over Tom.

She caught a hint of his favorite cologne, and her heart thudded in her chest. But she truly did not know how to feel anymore.

"After this unpleasantness with France is over, none of us francophiles will need to watch our tongues." Tom dipped his head and departed.

"May I have the pleasure?" Philippe led her to a group for the minuet. When the steps of the dance brought them close he said, "You look beautiful tonight."

"I am glad to see you." It was warm in the room.

They retreated to the line. As the minuet continued, Susanna couldn't help but admire Philippe's broad shoulders under his fine coat. When the violins ceased, his gaze met hers.

"Have you seen the gardens?" he asked.

"No, I have not had the pleasure." Susanna wondered if it might be too dark to appreciate them but allowed herself to be led outside.

Philippe's arm supported her firmly as they descended the steps into the rear gardens. Lanterns set along the crushed shell walkways illumined the paths between large designs created by evergreen hedges. In the shadows other couples strolled. The cool air soothed her heated cheeks.

"Through that gate is a maze," he said, indicating the direction with a jerk of his chin. "Back the other way are the orchards."

"Perhaps we could sit." A painted wrought-iron bench looked tempting. If she was careful, she shouldn't soil anything. Everything along the walkways was clear of snow and mud.

"Indeed." Philippe sat at an angle, facing her, and clasped her gloved hands in his. "I was hoping for a bit of privacy."

Oh. Susanna compressed her lips together nervously, fighting for composure.

Philippe fumbled inside his coat and brought out an object. "Your miniature."

Which he'd painted "for the practice," he'd said. She wasn't totally fooled by that; the Carters had engaged him for a full-size portrait. He was gifted.

"I made a copy."

"Thank you." Her image looked back at her. "I will treasure it."

A line appeared between Philippe's brows. "I told my mother about you."

Susanna closed her fingers around the tiny painting. She'd *wanted* him to express truly serious sentiments, but now …

"She asked if I had spoken with your father."

Restlessness seized her. "Might we stroll toward the orchard?"

His dark eyes gazed at her tenderly. "Of course."

She placed the miniature deep in her pocket as they stood, and tucked her other arm through his elbow. "My father is returning this spring to Richmond."

"Business related to the war?"

"Not precisely. He has been seeing to the needs of the property and the tenants." Not to mention Rockfish Gap was sometimes impassable during the winter. But Philippe had no notion where they lived.

"'Twill be a relief once this 'unpleasantness,' as your young friend labeled it, is over. Such a disaster the militia broke and allowed such a setback last summer. Had we taken the French fort, Braddock could have advanced to Canada and brought the conflict to an end."

The militia's fault? Most were frontiersmen like her father. Granted, some were ruffians like McKee, but all could handle weapons. And few were cowards. No, the mountains weeded out cowards. "Most give Colonel Washington credit for leading the army out."

"Yes. But George Washington is not a common Irishman."

Her right hand curled into a fist at the sneer in his words. Philippe didn't even realize that almost every immigrant from Ireland was, in fact, a Scot.

The trees of the orchard glowed before them in the light of the palace windows. The walkway curved toward the front of the building. Several couples blocked the path ahead. They paused.

Philippe patted her arm. "Irishmen have been flooding the ports for decades, and recently Jacobite Scotsmen—traitors to the Crown—have joined their ranks." He sighed. "I'm glad many of them settle west of the Blue Ridge. At least in the mountains they can do little harm to us here."

What? She drew her arm away. "The Irish immigrants are actually Scotsmen."

He scanned the path. "There are more gardens ahead, though no flowers at this time of year." His gaze found hers. "Scotsmen, did you say?"

She nodded. *And you're looking at a Scotswoman,* she wanted to say. Every muscle in her body grew rigid.

"That explains the debacle. Scotsmen are uncivilized rabble."

"Rabble? How dare you!" She stepped back and launched the entire weight of her body against him in a single, mighty shove.

Philippe tried to stay balanced but tripped over a root. He fell onto his backside in the mud under a tree, his mouth agape.

Susanna stumbled but caught herself, one foot landing in the cold mud. "How dare you insult my father!"

Philippe frowned in puzzlement and sought to stand. Someone hooked an arm under his elbow and helped him up.

Susanna blinked back sudden tears. A small crowd had gathered. She lifted her skirts and wound her way through them, not knowing where she was going.

She wanted to be anywhere but here.

"SUSANNA!" A familiar voice.

Frigid air bit through the fabric of her gown as Susanna slowed her steps. Behind her the sucking squish of a horse's hooves in mud signaled the presence of a carriage. She stopped and turned. The lights of the palace were still visible in the distance. What was she thinking? She couldn't walk all the way to the Randolphs'.

"There you are." Tom jumped from the small open vehicle and shrugged off his coat. "You must be cold." He wrapped the warm velvet around her and gently guided her to the cart.

Susanna took little heed of her hem as she clambered aboard. Both her shoulders and her mind began to thaw. "T-thank you. You saw me?"

"I gave you ten minutes outside with that gentleman, then followed." He slapped the reins on the sluggish pony's rump. "I did not hear much. But I saw the finale."

"I just want to go home." She didn't care if her father scolded her. She wanted to see the valley again. It seemed so distant in the bitter darkness.

"I sent a servant to inform the Randolphs we were departing early and I'd see you safe home."

"Hmm."

"I have your shoe. You left it behind in the mud."

Jane's shoe. Her bare foot pulsed with pain, a welcome distraction from the ache in her heart.

23

Oh, if ever I get to heaven, it will be because God will, and nothing else; for I never did any thing of myself, but get away from God!

—David Brainerd, *The Life and Diary of David Brainerd*

Kanawha River

Cold air puffed against Red Hawk's face as Dark Water entered the wigwam and closed the buffalo skin door. Frowning, she knelt next to Grandmother.

"Any news?" Red Hawk asked his aunt.

"Laughing Wolf is awake. Not only that, he's asking for a meeting."

The man had been brought into the village slung over his horse the day before. His companions said he was on the verge of death from the amount of firewater he'd drunk on their raid.

Grandmother's eyes flickered in the light of the hearth. "A meeting with the elders?"

"No, with everyone. In front of the elders' lodge. Something about a vision," Dark Water said.

Red Hawk's gut tightened. Not everyone liked Laughing Wolf, but visions and dreams were not to be discounted. Although in his opinion, anything from the lips of Laughing Wolf came straight from the evil one. If the man had died it would have solved a lot of problems. Especially his own.

Despite the chill, almost the entire village turned out for the meeting several hours later. Mothers sat in the back with infants; warriors stood about, faces impassive; older men took the places of honor in the front.

"A miracle ..."

"A sign."

Murmured comments met Red Hawk's ears as he drew near. He found a place next to Straight Arrow and shot the man a wary glance.

"Apparently his recovery was unexpected," Straight Arrow said softly.

Red Hawk grunted and crossed his arms over his chest.

Elk Tooth led his son to the middle of the circle where a fire had been built. "Laughing Wolf has a message for us. An important message."

Laughing Wolf's hair gleamed in the winter sunlight. Stray patches of red and black on his face and neck spoke of his recent raid. "All hail, people."

Red Hawk wanted to roll his eyes but he dared not betray the faintest emotion. He scanned the crowd. Running Deer knelt next to her mother, her gaze fixed on his nemesis.

"I had a vision. A terrible vision." Laughing Wolf struck his chest with his forearm. "The words burn in my heart and I cannot keep them back."

The rustles of the crowd ceased. Running Deer leaned forward.

"We stand guilty before the spirits. That guilt must be expunged."

Red Hawk stiffened. This wasn't what he expected.

"White men are a curse upon our land."

Now he had everyone's attention. Several men nodded.

"We will destroy them." Laughing Wolf gestured for emphasis. "But first, we must purify ourselves. Purify ourselves from the white man's stench." His gaze went from man to man. "We must put aside the poison of their firewater. We must put aside the poison of their ideas and traditions. We must put aside the cloth the traders bring and create our own clothing as our ancestors did."

A low murmur of approval rose from his companions.

"Red Shirt, hand me your garment."

The man in question disrobed and handed Laughing Wolf his signature red trading shirt.

"We will give Red Shirt a new name today, the name of a true warrior of the People." Laughing Wolf cast the shirt into the fire in front of him. "I name you Piercing Lance."

A cheer arose from the young men. Someone dumped the contents of a jug into the fire and a blue flame engulfed the fabric.

Red Hawk shivered, and not just from the cold. Something was terribly wrong, but he didn't know what.

As the fire gained intensity, strange shadows flitted across Laughing Wolf's face. "We will purge these mountains with blood … and with fire!"

ANNE STOOD in the bedroom doorway with packages in her arms. Her eyes were shiny.

"Come in, Anne." Susanna closed the lid of the chest and rose to her feet. Had she forgotten anything?

Anne placed the bundles on the bed and turned to her. "I shall miss you. Will you write?"

"*Bien sûr,*" she blurted, without thinking. Even the French language had soured on her tongue. "My direction is simple. Everyone in or near Staunton knows my father."

"I stopped by the apothecary yesterday for the herbs you recommended. I bought you a few things too."

Susanna slid a finger under the paper and looked at the packets inside. Jesuit bark, wormwood, and a large bulbous root … Ginger? "Mother will love these. Thank you."

"And this is for you." Anne pushed a small package toward her hand.

"Logwood. I have not heard of this."

"The man said 'twas a dye. A purple dye. I recalled you said your aunt dyes her wool and linen and—" Anne gestured to the table loom next to the chest. "I thought you would enjoy another color."

Susanna laid the package down and wrapped her arms around her friend. "Thank you, Anne. For everything."

Anne drew back and wiped an eye. "Have you finished packing?"

"Yes." The simples and logwood went into her satchel. Sliding her left hand into her pocket, Susanna felt the outlines of the miniature. She wasn't sure what to do with it. Giving it back meant communicating with Philippe. She took a deep breath and her gaze fell upon the New Testament on the bedside table. "Just one more thing." She lifted the small book and slid it into her other pocket. Now she was ready.

Noise sounded from downstairs. "Someone's here," Anne said. "Your uncle?"

Scooting out the door, Susanna lifted her walnut brown skirt and descended the steps. But the man in the foyer wasn't her uncle. "Tom!"

He wore student's attire, an ordinary frock coat and a plain linen stock casually tied at the neck. A book nestled under one arm. "Good morning, Miss Russell."

"'Tis good to see you, Mr. Jefferson. My uncle is coming at any time."

"Have you space for one more item in your baggage?" He held up the book.

"Thank you." She drew nearer and he placed the volume in her hands. "*Traite des Maladies des femmes grosses.* A book on midwifery, written by a man? I have never heard of such a thing."

"In France trained male midwives are called to assist ladies of importance."

Susanna snorted. "A woman would let a man near her at such a time?" But the gift was wonderful. The first time she'd come along to a birth she'd been terrified. "I do appreciate this, Tom. You are a true friend." Tears threatened. She'd miss him too.

A strange expression skittered across Tom's face. "Speaking of friends, I met one of yours in Hanover County."

"Oh?"

"Mr. James Paxton, the young man studying under the Reverend Samuel Davies."

"Jamie? Yes, I know him. How is he?"

"Quite well. I suspect he would not mind seeing a familiar face."

Her cheeks warmed. "Well, of course I shall. Mother has mentioned attending Reverend Davies' meetinghouse."

Tom's stance became formal as he sketched a brief bow. "Enjoy the book with my compliments." He turned as though to leave.

"Tom, I hope you get your ... baro ..."

"Barometer?" His lips traced a faint smile. "Yes, perhaps one day."

And then he was gone.

"THANK YOU FOR MEETING WITH ME," James said.

"I'm blessed to meet with a lad such as yourself, studying for the ministry. This place have decent ale?" Jeremiah Woods peered at the sign over the Hanover Tavern. The lower part of his weathered face was suntanned, and a neatly trimmed beard testified of the difficulty of a daily shave as he journeyed from place to place. A broad-brimmed wool hat nestled under his arm.

"Their small beer is excellent." James refused to drink anything stronger. Several times he'd accompanied Patrick Henry here, and his friend always refilled their tankards at his own expense. Two tall tankards of regular ale made him sleepy.

They walked in and sat at an empty table scored by scratches and knife gouges. An apron-clad lad plunked down their pewter tankards, foam sloshing and dripping down the sides.

"Where do you hail from, Mr. Woods?" James asked.

"The Blue Ridge. The family owns a large place on the east side."

Woods was a familiar name. "My family lives near the Triple Forks of the Shenandoah."

A broad grin lit the man's face. "Neighbors, then. Right across the Ridge." He took a long pull of his drink. "Your note said you were in a difficult place."

James recounted the struggle to understand baptism and his eventual decision to be immersed himself. "As Mr. Davies said, I didn't realize the implications. I can't be ordained a Presbyterian minister."

Woods lifted his brows, and deep furrows appeared in his forehead. It was hard to tell how old he was. "Why are you studying for the ministry in the first place, Mr. Paxton?"

James swallowed. "Well ... at first partly because I loved the Scriptures and wanted to know more. And I didn't seem suited to farming like my brothers."

The man's gaze seemed to bore into him.

"But when I saw faces lighten at the sound of the gospel, my heart warmed." *Warmed* was inadequate. The feeling was inexpressible.

Woods said nothing, so James continued. "I went with another man to help Colonel Washington last summer. There was a soldier." He paused, stomach tight. He couldn't think of MacKenzie's face without emotion. "He was a Catholic from Scotland."

"You preached to a Papist?" Woods lifted a brow.

"I didn't know what to say. He thought he would die. So I spoke to him of Christ. And my friend read the Scriptures every evening when we camped. MacKenzie came to our fire and soaked up the gospel like a sponge."

"Was he killed?"

"Yes." His gut contracted, thinking of that day. "Sometimes when I study Hebrew, I feel like Samson grinding grain for the Philistines. So I think of MacKenzie to keep me going. There are more who need Christ."

Woods drained his tankard and gazed out the grime-laced window. It was a full minute before he replied. "You still lack one thing. A specific direction. A calling. Seek God for a calling—where and to whom you should preach." He sighed. "I can't give that to you. No man can. They can train you and ordain you, but they can't give you that." He leaned forward. "That knowledge of God's call will keep you through endless days of hardship and darkness. For the man of God is called, like his Master, to suffer for His Name's sake."

James fingered his half-full tankard. He couldn't deny the truth of the man's words. But what form would that suffering take?

24

Awake to righteousness now, at the gentle call of the gospel,
before the last trumpet gives you an alarm of another kind.

—Samuel Davies (1723-1761)

Richmond, February 1756

Afternoon sun glinted off the second-story windows of the Bashams' house. The sight cheered Susanna despite her fatigue from the two-day journey from Williamsburg, and she jumped from the carriage eagerly. Waving her on to the house, her uncle joined the coachman in leading the horses to the stables. She stepped up the walk, eager to see everyone, even Hannah.

The savory smell of baking bridies welcomed her as she crossed the threshold. Her aunt and uncle's house wasn't home, but it was halfway there, and soon they'd all be going back to the valley.

"Susanna!" Mother sprang from a chair, yarn and knitting needles flying, and embraced her.

"Zanna?" echoed Hannah from the floor.

Susanna held out her arms to her little sister, a peculiar tightness in her throat. She picked up the three-year-old, kissed her, and put her down again. The child was heavier than she remembered.

She studied her stepmother's form. "Mother?" There was something different about her. Had she gained weight? Or …

"You look well." Mother gave a small smile. "And yes, we shall have an addition to the family this summer. I am glad to have you back."

To assist her? But what about Mrs. McClure?

"Dear Maggie will come, but she will need help." She'd read the question on her face.

Aunt Sarah appeared, towel in her hands and flour on her face. "I kent it was you. Welcome, and I'll get ye some ale."

Cold air and a clatter announced Uncle James's entrance, laden with her things. "I will take these to your mother's room."

The Bashams' house was larger than their own in the valley, with several glass windows downstairs and smaller ones upstairs in the bedrooms. By Randolph standards it was quaint, but to Susanna, it was comfortable, with several examples of Basham woodworking adorning the parlor. "Thank you, Uncle."

Mother retrieved her knitting, and Susanna hesitated before an unfamiliar ladder-back chair. It was a strange design, with narrow boards under the legs. "What is this, Mother? I fear to sit in it." She set Hannah down, wondering where her brothers were.

Her aunt stepped in with the ale. "A nurse chair. They're all the rage now. The rockers on the bottom are like a cradle. It's safe. Now sit and try it out." She turned to Mother and held out a tankard. "Here, Abigail, put down your knitting for once."

Susanna gingerly tested the chair and finding it stable, reached for her drink. "Thank you Auntie." She sipped while testing the chair, pushing gently with her feet.

Mother smiled over the rim of her tankard. "I am not used to it myself, but Sarah threatens to send it home with us."

"I could see how this would be a boon to mothers," she said, thinking of babies. "Mother, I have a book you might be interested in." She reached for her satchel and pulled out Tom's gift. "Thomas Jefferson gave it to me." She tilted the cover her stepmother's way.

"'Tis French, is it not?"

"'Tis a book on midwifery." She handed it to her stepmother.

"I have always wanted something like this." Mother flipped through the pages. "I cannot read French."

"But I can."

"This well?"

Susanna nodded. "I learned quickly. Even Tom was impressed. We can go through it together." It would be like a school in midwifery, translating and then hearing her stepmother's comments. But she suspected not everything a man in Paris might recommend would be approved by Mother or Maggie McClure.

Was this her true calling? She hadn't had a specific plan in going to Williamsburg; she'd merely wanted to escape the restrictions—or what she thought were restrictions—of the valley. Painting was a pleasant diversion, but she'd never imagined making it something more. Only men painted portraits.

She'd never imagined herself as a wife and mother either, assisting a yeoman farmer in his labors like so many did in the valley. But Mother was that and more.

"Susanna, if the study of midwifery pleases you, you could be a great help to me. Maggie is infirm, and a new family lives just beyond the Stuarts' now. They moved south to escape the raids up north."

"I would be willing to try." She slid her gaze to Hannah, playing now with several wooden toys on the floor. If families were moving south to escape Indian raids, perhaps Augusta County was safe after all.

THE SUN WAS low behind the bare tree limbs when Susanna left the house, basket over her arm. Aunt Sarah's bridies were as good as

Agnes's and the kitchen still overflowed with the leftovers. Sally, the Negro housemaid, had packed a basket of the small meat pastries intending to take it to the stables, but Susanna had intercepted her, desiring fresh air after the long carriage ride.

The Basham stables were a favorite retreat, as well as the large pasture, where witch grass grew past the knees of the Connemara brood mares. She hesitated at the entrance, breathing in the warm, deep scent of horseflesh. She glanced about, looking for the groom who also served as coachman. "Joe?"

"Ma'am?" The voice came from a dark corner where the Negro servant stood with a harness in his hands.

"Hello. Your wife sent these from the kitchen."

"Wife?" He stepped into the golden light coming through the doorway. His eyes were large in a face of indeterminate age; his frame looked shrunken somehow, as if left too long in the sun. "I have no wife here."

But Sally the Negro housemaid was clearly solicitous of the man's well being. "Oh, I'm sorry. Sally packed these bridies for you." As she handed the basket over, she considered the man's cryptic statement. "Your wife is elsewhere?" she asked, surprised at her boldness. The knowledge that slaves were bought and sold troubled her vaguely, but she'd never truly questioned it. Now, looking at this flesh-and-blood man, it irked her that a man could be separated from his wife.

He cut her a wary glance. "Thank you, I's partial to these little meat pies." He turned and hung up the harness, then settled onto a stool.

Susanna studied the ears of the nearest carriage horse and held out her fist to sniff.

"Dolly there be right gentle," Joe said. "Phantom be fussy now and again."

"Hmm. I wonder if carrots might help."

"Sally thinks food might help, but I's done told her I's married."

Susanna remained silent, her attention on the horse. She stroked its nose. Would he tell her more?

"A plantation in the Northern Neck be doing poorly. The owner going sell most of his people. One of them have an Indian woman to wife, and they have a son."

Was the Indian a slave too? That seemed unusual, but she knew little of slaves. She dared a glance at the corner where Joe sat with his basket on his lap, the food untouched.

"The man done tell his wife to run away before she could be sold."

Susanna reached up and scratched the mare around the ears, waiting for him to continue.

"He knew she could go over the mountains, live with the Indians there. Be free and happy." He paused for a long moment. "And she done take her son, little Joshua."

Susanna's eyes filled with tears. She dared not speak.

"The boy have an Indian name too. It mean Buffalo Robe."

"JONAH." Samuel Davies twirled his pen and laid it down. "Any difficulties in the translation?"

What a question. James ran his mind over the past month's exhausting translation of the tiny book, laboring over verbs and sentence structure. "The fish."

"A very general word. You wonder what kind?"

"A whale?"

Mr. Davies leaned back and laced his fingers over his stomach. The Henrys had donated a ham in addition to their usual offering last Sabbath, and breakfast had been hearty. "Perhaps. Does it matter?" Mr. Davies leaned forward. "What is the message of Jonah? The main theme?"

James's stomach tightened around its unaccustomed load of ham. "Jonah ran away after being given a command to preach to Nineveh. He was thrown off a boat and swallowed by a fish or whale. A very large creature. He prayed—"

"That is not the theme. That is a summary."

James trapped his hands under his thighs and tried to focus. "Certainly we see the sovereignty of God in directing the steps of His servants, even against their will." Jonah's rebellion was almost comical.

Mr. Davies picked up his quill pen and quirked an eyebrow. Not impressed.

"Jonah was to preach judgment to Nineveh which resulted in mercy, revealing God's nature. It is a pattern for preachers today."

The quill spun lazily in the minister's hand. Getting closer, perhaps.

"Jonah is referenced by Christ as a type, a picture of Himself. Just as Jonah was three days—"

"Good. But there is more."

James reviewed the text yet again in his mind. Jonah was told to preach to Gentiles, something he didn't want to do as a Jew. They were his enemies. What did other texts say about heathen nations? Isaiah contained a number of references, and the Psalms—

Declare his glory among the heathen, his wonders among all people.

Why, of course. "It was also a picture of the gospel going forth to all nations. We are Gentiles who have reaped this blessing."

"Even so." Mr. Davies laid the pen down. "Have you finished the book about Brainerd?"

"Yes." It had taken a long time. There were so many other things to do.

"This time, I just need a quick summary."

"After being expelled from Yale for a minor infraction, David Brainerd continued his studies independently while at the same time preaching in various locations. Sometimes to the Indians, sometimes to the Irish, and by that he must mean Scots from Ulster."

"Was he eventually ordained?" Mr. Davies always knew the answer to his own questions.

"Yes. Afterward he met with more success in his preaching. He had a number of hindrances, though. His health, for one, and he also seemed to have a melancholy nature. He mourned over his own sins often."

The twin arches of Mr. Davies' brows lifted. "Why did he preach to the Indians?"

"I do not know, but he must have felt a call. He lamented over their heathenish practices, but in one place wrote of them as 'my' Indians." The choice of words had struck him at the time. "And a few times ..."

Mr. Davies waited for him to continue.

James finally found the right words. "There were instances of Indians being powerfully struck with the sight of their sin before a just and holy God, and then seeing the sufficiency of Christ to cleanse that sin away. Very dramatic conversions."

"But not many?"

"A small group grew, and eventually they numbered seventy." For some reason his mind conjured MacKenzie's face, eager to hear the Scripture at their campfire a lifetime ago. "But I suppose the numbers did not matter to him."

"No, he possessed a great heart for souls." Mr. Davies breathed a deep sigh. "Your assignment is to write a sermon appropriate for a heathen Indian."

What? For months James had run through various texts in his mind, toying with outlines and applications, eager to try his hand. He always imagined preaching before men like Patrick Henry or women like ... like Susanna Russell.

But this would have to be a different kind of message. Why Mr. Davies thought this necessary he didn't know. Granted, some were called to this sort of thing. Brainerd had been. Surely not him.

He opened his mouth to protest, to ask why, but found himself saying, "Yes, Mr. Davies. I shall have it finished next week."

25

So I saw in my dream, that just as Christian came up with the cross, his burden loosed from off his shoulders, and fell from off his back, and began to tumble... and I saw it no more.

—John Bunyan, *The Pilgrim's Progress,* 1678

Hanover County, March 1756

"Let us view the returning sinner under his first spiritual concern."

Susanna forgot the minister's formal appearance, his powdered wig and clerical robes. The sermon drew her in, reminding her of Sabbath mornings in the valley meetinghouse.

Mr. Davies continued. "We shall not find him as usual, in a thoughtless hurry about earthly things ..."

Whitefield's sermon also came to mind. Oh, this was so much better than the homilies at Bruton Parish. She scanned the front row again, but didn't see Jamie. He must be here somewhere.

"'After I strayed, I repented; after I came to understand, I struck my thigh in grief!'"

Yes, so true! She'd wandered from the Lord, not realizing how it cost her. And now, returning, she felt regret. The minister continued to expound on the text, for how long Susanna was insensible. Time ceased to be important.

Mr. Davies turned the corner in his message. "Return you perishing prodigals! Return! Though you have sinned against heaven, and before your Father, and are not worthy to be called his son ..."

These words were sweet as he began to speak of God's love to His people.

"You will not stay angry forever but delight to show mercy. You will again have compassion on us; you will tread our sins underfoot and hurl all our sins into the depths of the sea!"

Susanna slipped her hand into her pocket for a handkerchief. She almost never wept, but her nose was needy of attention. Her stomach grumbled, and she realized the message had been long, at least two hours by her estimation.

"Susanna?"

She jerked to her feet. "Jamie?"

He stood before her, hat tucked under his elbow. His familiar gray-blue eyes startled her with the intensity of their gaze. The face above a crooked stock seemed to have grown more angles. His hair ... Something was strange about his hair.

"H-how was Williamsburg?" he asked.

"Jamie Paxton, what happened to your hair? Have you powdered it?"

"My ..." He ran a hand over his hair, tied back in a simple tail.

She kept her voice low as the members of the congregation milled about them. "Your hair is white."

A line formed between his brows. "But it's always been—"

"I know what color it is. Or was. It's not just blond anymore. You look like you're eighty years old!"

~

HIS HAIR? What could be wrong with his hair? Eighty years old? James fingered his locks again, more tentatively this time. "What?"

Susanna tilted her head and inspected him. "Your hair has gone completely white. When did this happen?"

James thought quickly. He'd had no access to a good mirror for a long time. Mount Vernon must have had a mirror, but he hadn't shaved himself while there. Later he'd acquired a scrap of polished brass, which gave everything a yellow cast. No one had said anything, except for wee Willie.

He turned and glanced at the child, standing at his mother's side and rubbing a sleepy eye. Yes, Willie hadn't been too polite to make mention of a person's strange hair color.

He turned back to Susanna, standing before him in a well-cut blue gown. She seemed different. "I haven't looked in a mirror in ages." *The battle*. It must be. The horror of the long night retreating and the sobs and cries of the men. The screams of horses. Yes, that must be it. "I dinna ken when, but I ken why."

Her gaze was upon him, large brown eyes searching and sympathetic. "How is your leg? I heard you were injured."

He swallowed, feeling awkward, but glad beyond words to see Susanna. "I still use a cane, but it doesn't trouble me much." Even the nightmares were less frequent. "Going back to the valley soon?"

"I suspect Da will come after barley planting."

James had just plowed Mr. Davies' barley field, leaning on the plow handles like crutches. "I dinna suppose it will be long then."

"Jamie, eat with us. We brought enough for a wedding ceilidh."

"I'll ask."

He slipped away to speak to Mrs. Davies, who shooed him off with her blessing. Susanna led him to a wagon outside, where questions were quickly flung at him from left and right.

"How many Indians did you kill?" This from the lad with reddish-blond hair wisped about his head, his innocent question slicing his innards. But he was so glad to see the Russells he thrust the pain aside.

"Your da killed at least one that I saw. He's a brave man." James sought to remember the lad's name. Was it Nate? Nathan?

"Are ye recovered from your injuries?" The older brother had grown since he'd been to the Russells' home. Jonathan was his name.

James flourished his cane and grinned at the boys. "I can plow well enough, but for a Sunday stroll, a gentleman requires a fashionable walking stick." His leg did ache upon exertion, but no one needed to know that.

Mr. Basham found him once plates were filled, and they discussed the conflict with the French.

"What will happen once war is declared?" James asked after swallowing the last bite of his pork. A formal declaration was only a matter of time. As far as all Virginians were concerned, they'd been at war with France since the Battle of Fort Necessity, which seemed like eons ago.

Susanna's uncle set his empty plate down upon the canvas they'd spread out to sit on. "The current machinations in Europe will define the scope of the conflict. Ironically, tensions in places like Austria and Germany will force King George to move decisively against France, and that can only help us." He turned to James, his hazel gaze intent. "But the Indians have no interest in the dealings across the ocean, so they are less predictable. For instance, why would the Shawnee attack the Drapers' settlement?"

James set down his plate. "I dinna ken." Colonel Patton was killed well south of Staunton. The French never went that far. "But then, Indians have no king. D'ye think a single chief simply took it into his mind to attack?"

"Hmm. No, the raids are too numerous and widespread. I wonder if they have reasons of their own."

Susanna knelt and scooped up their plates. "Uncle, you have stolen my guest for too long."

James used his cane to help him rise, hoping no one noticed his lingering infirmity.

Susanna returned but waited until her uncle had departed to speak. "Jamie, I want to know everything."

He fought against a smile. "Thank you for the books. One of them saved my life, and the other upended it."

"What?" Susanna's eyes widened. "I knew about *The Pilgrim's Progress.*"

"The other book, the confession."

"Was something wrong with it?"

"The Philadelphia is a Baptist confession."

"Oh." She didn't seem troubled by that.

"Susanna, after studying it, and much prayer, I decided to be baptized." He held his breath.

Her eyebrows lifted slightly. "So you're a Baptist now."

"Yes."

There was silence for a long moment as she stared at the meetinghouse. She adjusted her shawl higher, and her gaze fastened on his face. "You will not be able to preach in either meetinghouse."

She meant the valley meetinghouses. Her thoughts had bounded ahead faster than he'd expected. "True, I willna be able to assist Mr. Craig." The minister bore the weight of preaching to two congregations. James had assumed that he'd be able to help the man in his labors, or perhaps be called to a similar position elsewhere. But that door was closed to him now.

"Where will you preach?"

It seemed easy to unburden his heart to Susanna. "I dinna ken. I need to pray. The Lord has led me this far."

"How can you tell, Jamie?" Her mouth worked. "How do you know if something is God's will, or just your own idea?"

A few yards away a servant harnessed horses to the Bashams' carriage. She would be leaving soon. "God only gives us light for the next step, I think. It keeps us humble."

Her expression was thoughtful.

"Susanna, will you attend service here again before you leave for the valley?"

"I doubt it. Next Sabbath, Mr. Woods preaches in the back pasture."

"Mr. Jeremiah Woods? The Baptist minister?"

"He's a Baptist? Mother only said his preaching was sound."

He smiled. Somehow he'd find a way to visit.

IN THE END, it hadn't been hard to take a trip to Richmond. After trying to think of an excuse that didn't include some element of deception, James had simply told Mr. Davies the truth. He'd wanted to hear Mr. Woods preach.

"A wonderful idea," the minister had said, surprising him. "And the family, are they kin?"

"Almost." He'd explained who John Russell was.

"His daughter seemed very attentive to the sermon."

Mr. Davies noticed things like that. But James made no reply, not knowing her spiritual state, and unable to explain the special camaraderie he felt when speaking with her.

"Ask Mrs. Davies what she needs from the shops there." With that the minister had dismissed him with a wave of his quill.

Upon his arrival, Mr. Basham directed him to the stables. "I hope you do not mind a pallet in the parlor. I would give you a proper bed, but my house is full of Russells, as you can well imagine."

"No need. Thank ye kindly for your hospitality."

James watered the mare and found a curry brush in the stables. The animal lifted her head and pricked her ears at a sound. He turned.

Face flushed, Susanna hesitated at the entrance. "What a sweet chestnut."

"She is. Nutmeg is her name. Brought me here from Colonel Washington's home on the Potomac. The colonel gave your father this mare in return for the pacer." He checked the animal's feet.

"Da will love her."

"She'll make a fine brood mare, I'm sure. I'll bring her when I come home this summer." He backed her into a vacant stall.

Susanna darted off and returned with a bucket half full of cracked corn. "What will Mr. Craig say?"

"About my baptism?"

"Yes."

"I dinna ken, but he willna be pleased. Mr. Davies upbraided me some, but he's been very kind."

"You are following your conscience, Jamie. Surely he will see that even if he rails on you."

He was startled by sudden wetness in his eyes. How was it that she understood so well—and took his side? "Will ye pray for me?"

She removed her hand from the mare and faced him. "Yes, I will." Her gaze dropped. "But I have a confession to make."

He swallowed, not knowing what to say.

"I came to Williamsburg thinking I wanted certain things, not realizing the true motives of my heart. I was not trying to do evil, but you know how Mr. Craig always preaches that the heart is deceitful?" She looked up, her eyes glistening.

He nodded.

"I filled my mind and my heart with all manner of things. Forgetting God. Ignoring Him. I suppose I knew what I was doing but deceived myself into thinking it inconsequential. I had not committed any grave sin or rejected the truth of the Scriptures. Who was to judge me if I was less devout or strict?"

She went on, describing a sermon by George Whitefield. And seeking the Lord every evening. Finally finding forgiveness and peace in her soul.

"Mr. Davies' sermon was wonderful." She wiped an eye. "'Twas an exposition of my own life. And to hear the love of God for sinners. I do not think I will ever tire of it."

"That's a happy confession." He felt a smile spreading on his face.

She looked away. "They'll be wondering where you are." She started for the doorway, brown skirts swaying. "Come for supper, Mr. Paxton."

His heart felt light. "At your service, Miss Russell."

JAMES BREATHED deep of the biting March air, exhaling white puffs in the morning chill. The sun cast long shadows over the fields, but the sky was clear, and the afternoon promised to be pleasant, but for now, winter's remnants still kept them in warm wool and thick shawls as the family made their way to the back pasture, accompanied by Mr. Woods.

A huge walnut stood at one end of a clearing, a natural meeting-place, cheered by the song of an early wood thrush. James helped unload stools for the women from the Bashams' wagon. Neighbors set up chairs or spread out blankets. Some leaned against trees; many of these were dark-skinned.

Hatless, Mr. Woods stepped onto a low crude table under the finger-like bare canopy of the walnut. Conversation already muted by the moist morning air died out completely.

"Let us pray."

The minister's voice sounded weak and hoarse. Would his preaching be heard clearly?

Mr. Woods opened his Bible. "My text is—" He coughed. "Paul's second letter to the Corinthians, chapter three." He removed a handkerchief and coughed into it.

James cringed inwardly, hoping his new friend could manage. On his arrival the night before, Mr. Woods had pleaded fatigue but hadn't appeared ill. James pondered the text. The old covenant versus the new. It wasn't exegetically difficult, merely a matter of having the strength and presence of mind to preach.

Mr. Woods read the passage, stumbling. A few among those seated or standing cut glances this way and that.

The minister looked up and fixed his gaze on James. "Mr. Paxton, would you kindly lend your services?"

James went numb as the minister's request sank in. Mr. Woods was not going to be able to deliver his sermon. His feet obeyed, and he walked to the pine platform.

What was he doing? He was not a licensed minister. He would be breaking the law. Heart thudding, he received the Bible from Mr. Woods and found the passage.

He opened his mouth and began to speak.

26

Whenever I find myself in the cellar of affliction, I always look around for the wine.

—Samuel Rutherford (1600-1661)

Leaning against the wagon, Susanna watched Jamie ascend the crude platform. A lump rose in her throat. *O Lord, help him.*

At first, his voice quavered. But after several introductory remarks, he seemed to warm to his subject, and his words reached the trees.

"Why is the Law of Moses then called a ministry of condemnation? Is there something wrong with the Law? Elsewhere, Paul writes that the Law is holy, just, and good."

Somehow he managed to keep to a logical structure of thought despite no preparation. Even better, the words he used were clear and simple, suited for landowner and slave alike. Her heart swelled with pride and amazement.

Mr. Woods stood near the tree, arms crossed, nodding occasionally.

Everyone in the clearing was attentive, despite the cool morning and wriggling babes in arms.

"If the Law that condemns us was glorious, how much more the gospel of Christ—"

"Halt!"

Susanna turned to see whose voice dared interrupt. Behind her, two men strode up to the gathering; one was well dressed in coat and stock, the other looked like a tenant farmer with a battered broad-brimmed hat of uncertain color.

"Halt! I must see your license," the better-dressed man said to Jamie. "I am the Sheriff of Hanover County."

Jamie stepped down and stood silent. One hand twitched at his side.

"I have a license," Mr. Woods said. "Mr. Paxton is a student." He fumbled in his coat and withdrew a piece of paper.

The sheriff snatched it and scanned the document while his assistant stood by scowling. "This is a license to preach in Goochland County. You're in Hanover." He thrust it back. "In any case, you were not preaching, he was." He pointed to Jamie, whose face was pale. "You are both coming with me."

Murmurs rose as the assistant marched up to Jamie and grabbed his arm. "Come easy-like, and maybe I won't tie your hands."

Jamie stumbled. Shocked, Susanna covered her mouth. He recovered, but there was a hitch in his stride as he was dragged along. *His leg* —were they going to march him across the county on foot?

The horsewhip coiled on the man's belt froze Susanna's innards. She tugged at her uncle's sleeve. "What can we do?"

Her uncle frowned, his jaw working. "I will speak to the sheriff." He approached the two men and their charges.

A child wailed somewhere. Uncle James spoke to the sheriff in low tones. Around the perimeter of the clearing, men and women stood, eyes on the spectacle. But most of the slaves had slipped away.

Her uncle returned and they all gathered around. "I pleaded with him that this is private property. How a man's own private worship could be against the law, I know not." He shook his head. "There is a gaol of sorts near the county courthouse. They will be held there until a hearing."

~

THE ROAD to the gaol was torture. James walked behind the constable's horse, his hands tied and knotted to a length of rope in the man's hands. He focused on keeping slack in the rope; any sudden changes in the horse's movement could jerk him off his feet.

Early on, he heard Mr. Woods attempt a song behind him, but the minister's voice was hoarse. The sheriff hollered at him to shut up.

The morning sun rose above the height of the longleaf pines on either side of the road. Despite the bracing air, sweat trickled down his back. His mind became hazy, and his thoughts congealed into a single idea. One foot in front of the other. One foot in front of the other. *The rope. The rope. Don't let the rope grow taut.*

Pain stabbed his leg, and fear clamped him like a vise. Above the haze he fought for a resting place for his soul.

The prophet Jonah came to mind. *When my soul fainted within me I remembered the Lord …*

More verses came to him, one after another. They didn't take away the pain, but they took away the encroaching panic.

If only he were fit. Back in the valley a ten-mile walk was nothing. Pain shot up his leg with each step. *In everything give thanks …*

There must be something to give thanks for. He focused on the tiny swirls of dust the horse's hooves stirred up. The snow had melted, a good thing.

Rejoice, and be exceeding glad: for great is your reward in heaven: for so persecuted they the prophets which were before you.

Rejoice, rejoice. He didn't feel like rejoicing. *Help, Lord.* Watch the rope. Watch the rope.

The horse shied and lunged forward a few steps. The rope jerked his hands forward and his shoulders ached with the sudden jolt. His feet slipped, and his body flew forward and hit the ground. The impact forced a grunt from his lips while dirt flew into his face.

"Hullo, Sheriff! Catch some bandits?" A new voice.

The rope slackened, and James rested his cheek on the cold dust of the road.

Thank you, Lord, for the rest.

LYING BACK on the straw bedding, James realized the gaol was a smokehouse. Instead of a hole directly above him, several large openings had been cut at the top of the walls. Large enough for smoke, but not quite big enough for a man to squeeze through. This place would be miserable in a thunderstorm. Pain lanced through his lower leg with each heartbeat.

"I prayed for you," Mr. Woods said. "And the Lord answered. Just as you fell the feller comes up and wants to know who we were. Bless my soul if he wasn't the judge's nephew."

James hadn't heard much of the conversation. He'd only rejoiced in the result—him on the horse, and the constable leading. But now other thoughts intruded. Mr. Davies. What had his mentor commanded? Not to draw attention?

The minister coughed. "I don't mind a walk on a fine spring morning, but …"

"Here, Mr. Woods, if we scoop up the straw some, it will be warmer." James levered himself to a sitting position and helped the older man get comfortable. The shed's dirt floor was cold. In his opinion, the minister was in worse shape than he. A simple case of catarrh could become pneumonia.

"Your message was fine. I think you have a gift."

James searched the man's face for signs of fever, but Mr. Woods lay peacefully on the straw, gazing at the roof. "The text is uncomplicated."

"Maybe. I wondered if you would refuse. Not everyone can preach without notes or preparation." Mr. Woods slid a glance toward him. "And I doubt you've much practice."

"It was my first sermon."

The minister smiled with his whole face. "I'll take a nap now."

"No, Susanna, there is naught we can do until tomorrow." Uncle James removed his woolen cap and scarf. "I went to the tavern and inquired. Even if I called on the judge, he would not rule on the case until it comes to court."

Susanna wondered how warm Jamie's clothes were. He hadn't worn a cap or scarf to preach, and it got cold at night. "Did you see the gaol?"

"'Tis a shed, about the size of my smokehouse."

"They will freeze in there!" Aunt Sarah joined them at the doorway. "And Mr. Woods was already coughing."

Her uncle crossed to the parlor and collapsed in a chair. "You ladies prepare food, drink, and whatever else they might need. We'll load the wagon, and I'll leave at dawn."

Susanna clenched her jaw but helped Mother and Aunt Sarah gather foodstuffs.

"They need tea." Her stepmother selected several items from the simples cabinet. "Horehound, mullein, and coneflower." A line appeared between her brows. "I hope he's not feverish, but I'll add willow bark just in case."

Susanna stuck out her tongue at the mention of horehound. "Can you sweeten it?"

After an hour the wagon was ready, with food baskets, gourds of medicinal tea, and blankets in the bed. Susanna lingered outside, watching the sun slip below the horizon, crowned by swatches of orange and scarlet. In the northern sky salmon-pink clouds lifted their heads, deceptively cheerful. Sudden puffs of chilled air brushed her cheeks. In the distance, tree limbs swayed. A storm was approaching.

"Joe?" She stepped into the stables where the slave lived in a tiny section of the loft.

"Miss Susanna?"

"We also need oilcloth. Is there an extra lantern?" She'd look for a tinderbox, trivet, and kettle in the house.

Joe departed to find the items. Susanna frowned. Jamie and Mr. Woods needed these things tonight.

Would Joe help her?

"I'SE GOING BE in trouble for sure," Joe muttered.

The jolts of the wagon, the creak of the harness, and the clop-clop of the horses' hooves sounded unnaturally loud in the darkness. A full moon overhead illuminated the road enough to drive safely, but a line of clouds edged close to the bright disc, threatening to obscure it. A gust of wind tugged at Susanna's cloak and she pulled it closer. "Never mind, I'll take the blame."

"Hmm."

At least they had the road to themselves, and Joe was not alone, which certainly would have raised questions. At this rate, they'd be at the courthouse in a little over an hour. But how would they get the supplies to the men inside? Surely the gaol was locked.

She worried her lip. *Help, Lord.*

What would her father do?

"Why should the children of a King …" She sang, her voice sounding thready to her ears. "Go mourning all their days …"

One of the horses swiveled an ear. Joe said nothing at first, but after the first stanza of Watts' hymn he began to hum along.

Peace settled upon her like a cloak.

"JAMIE!"

Poised to race, Susanna stood in the grass behind the Andersons' barn, her linsey skirts swirling about her bare ankles. He tried to join her, but he couldn't move.

"Jamie!"

He jolted awake. His movement dislodged his coat, which he'd shared with Mr. Woods as a covering. The minister murmured in his sleep, and James adjusted the garment over him. Could that be Susanna's voice? Or was it part of the dream?

"Jamie? Are you in there?" Yes, it was Susanna's voice, not much louder than a whisper.

He stood. "Yes, I'm here." Confused, his brows contracted. Why had she come? Was her uncle here?

"H-how are you?"

"Mr. Woods is ill."

"Jamie, I'm going to pass some things to you through this gap in the wall. Can you reach it?"

"Yes." Just barely. Susanna was tall, but not that tall. The creak of a wagon axle on the other side of the wall told him the story. She must be standing on a wagon bed. "I can't see, the moonlight's gone." Gusts of wind whipped through the cracks in the shed.

"I've a lantern." In moments a glow illuminated the gaps between the logs and threw shadows through the hole on top.

"Dinna give yourself away." Sudden fear gripped him. Clearly she was alone, and he didn't trust the men who had locked them up.

"'Tis a dark lantern. Here, Jamie, this is a blanket."

A dark lump penetrated the space above. He reached for it and welcomed the musty smell of wool. One by one she passed him oilcloth, a kettle, trivet, and several packages of food.

"Mr. Paxton?" Mr. Woods was sitting up, looking puzzled. "I heard a woman's voice."

"Mr. Woods, my mother sent you tea," Susanna said.

Several gourds came within reach. "Thank you, Susanna. Thank your mother for me," James said.

"A tinderbox. And a couple of candles."

His throat tightened. Even a tiny fire would make a huge difference. "Thank you, Susanna. Now get on back before someone notices."

"I'm praying for you."

The jingle of harness and creaks of the wagon signaled her departure. He listened for several minutes, making sure no one had noticed or had given pursuit.

Rain pattered against the roof, eased off, then returned with greater force. James felt through the pile of blankets and soon they were bundled snugly with the oilcloth on top.

"She's a rare woman," Mr. Woods said as they sat side-by-side. He coughed.

"Here, drink this." James opened a gourd. He rummaged through the food basket and his fingertips encountered a bumpy surface. *Bread.* Good wheat bread. His stomach cramped with forgotten hunger. He tore off a large chunk, divided it, and passed one piece to the minister.

"Thank you."

James murmured his reply. A rare woman? Susanna had always been different, special, but now she possessed something else. Hardiness. Courage.

Total darkness settled upon them as the wind increased, groaning and whistling, sending sharp fingers through the gaps in the logs. Stinging ice-cold raindrops pummeled James's face with every sudden gust. It would have been miserable indeed if Susanna hadn't come.

In the morning he'd chip off bits of bark from the log walls with his pocketknife. *Thank you, Lord, they didn't take my knife.* He'd created a fire with less likely fuel.

When would Mr. Davies find out? The meetinghouse and parsonage were close by. And if folks in the nearby tavern knew, everyone knew. James had no reason to think the minister would overlook this. The man had to abide by the terms of his own preaching license.

And what about Mr. Craig? James would be *persona non grata* in the valley after this.

Out of the depths have I cried unto Thee O Lord …

The darkness pressed upon him. He'd followed his conscience, thought he was following the Word of God, and now he was alone.

The advice he'd given Susanna on the will of God seemed so trite now. *One step at a time.* He thought he'd been obedient to the Lord's will, but what if he'd been mistaken all along?

27

May it please the court, what did I hear read? Did I hear it distinctly, or was it a mistake of my own? Did I hear expression as if a crime, that these men are charged with? What! 'For preaching the gospel of the Son of God.'

—Patrick Henry (1736-1799)

The Shenandoah Valley, April 1756

The Craigs' cabin was chilly as usual, the scant early morning fire having sputtered to embers by the time James arrived. Mr. Craig welcomed him, his lined face betraying little. The children crowded around.

"Jamie, Jamie!" Georgie jumped about his legs as James stood in the doorway. Jane, with her mother's dark curls, hesitated behind her brother.

"That's Mr. Paxton to the both of ye." Mr. Craig's admonition was mild. "Awa' with ye."

The children scampered into the kitchen.

"Come have a seat." The minister indicated the familiar table, adorned with a single candle.

It seemed like he'd never left. And yet everything appeared new and strange.

James lowered himself onto the cane chair. His leg throbbed as he slid his limbs under the table, reminding him of all the things that had happened since he'd been a student here. He ran clammy hands over his breeches.

Mr. Craig looked at him a long moment and cleared his throat. "I've a letter from Mr. Davies."

Samuel Davies had come the next day after their imprisonment with James's Bible and a package of cheese. But Davies had said little. When Mr. Woods and James were released a week later, Patrick Henry had a room ready for them at the tavern. James only returned to the Davies household for his things. The minister shook his hand gravely, wished him well, but gave him to understand that his tutelage was at an end.

He rubbed his fingers together. He had no idea what Mr. Davies had written.

Mr. Craig pulled out a folded piece of paper and opened it. "He sends his greetings. Then he says, 'Mr. James Paxton has excelled in Hebrew and in every other subject. It has been a great joy to instruct him, and my family has benefited from his physical labor. As to his conduct, he keeps a pure conscience as described in Paul's letters to Timothy. What pleases me best is his love to souls, which serves as the motive force for his efforts.'"

James's lips parted. This wasn't what he expected.

The minister continued reading. Mr. Davies spent several paragraphs supporting his claim that his student met the biblical requirements of a minister as set forth in the New Testament.

Mr. Craig cleared his throat. "'However, as a result of personal study, Mr. Paxton now holds to a Baptistic view of the Scriptures, at least with regard to the proper subjects of baptism. Therefore, I can no longer recommend him to a Presbyterian Synod for ordination. In every other matter of doctrine he is sound.'" Mr. Craig gestured with the letter. "He closes with well-wishes, but what good are those? What am I to do with ye?"

He'd dreaded this moment. "I spent a week in a cold shed with Mr. Woods asking that question."

"Ah, I heard of that." Mr. Craig's eyes narrowed. "Mr. Davies doesna mention it."

James described the chilly Sabbath morning and his subsequent arrest. "If Susanna hadn't brought us supplies that night, I think Mr. Woods would have died of pneumonia."

The minister's eyebrows lifted. "Susanna Russell?"

He described her boldness but glossed over the long days and even longer nights of his imprisonment. "The magistrate wanted a witness. He wouldn't fine us without one. The sheriff and constable had no clue what was actually spoken. Meanwhile, we stayed in the gaol." The hot bath Patrick Henry secured for him afterward was more than welcome.

"So what will ye do now?"

"I dinna ken." James studied the table with its familiar pattern of scratches. "I believe now more than ever that I am called to preach."

One verse from Isaiah had comforted him in the dark nights. *Who is among you that feareth the Lord, that obeyeth the voice of his servant, that walketh in darkness, and hath no light? Let him trust in the name of the Lord, and stay upon his God.*

"Hmph." Mr. Craig's blue gaze bore into him. "Other men must recognize that call." He flapped the letter against the table surface. "I ken that Mr. Davies thinks highly of ye, Baptist or no'. There is nae doubt ye must have more training. Ye havena preached. Tell me more about this Mr. Woods."

As James spoke, his spirit lifted. He couldn't imagine an itinerant ministry as his calling, but traveling with Mr. Woods would give him the opportunity to preach.

And he had to preach the gospel. It burned in his bones.

"Spend three months with this man and come back to see me."

Report to Mr. Craig? So he wasn't truly cast out after all. Gratefulness swelled in his chest. "Thank ye ... thank ye kindly." Careful of his game leg, he got to his feet.

"Hold on, lad." Mr. Craig turned to a shelf nailed to the log wall. "The letter came with a book. A gift I'm to give ye." He thrust a familiar scuffed volume to James's side of the table.

David Brainerd.

"What's wrong with ye? Ye look like ye've seen Bluidy Clavers."

James blinked. Yes, Brainerd had become his personal nemesis, and there was no way to explain. He picked up the book, slid it into his satchel, and said his farewells. But the volume seemed to burn against his side.

OAK, cottonwood, blossoming redbud, and dogwood trees spread their branches in welcome along the road. Stiff and sore from two days of riding, Susanna shifted in the saddle and inhaled deeply. The crisp air was full of delicate spring scents. The whole world seemed clean.

Her father drew rein, and she followed suit. The rest of the family, in the wagon, had fallen behind. Da's mare, Percy, stood patiently, chestnut coat gleaming copper in the morning sun, while her own mount, Rosemary, lengthened her neck to snatch at the blue-stem growing lush between the ruts of the narrow road, not much wider than a bridle path.

Da glanced back, his gaze fixed on her, his eyes the blue of the sky above the mountains, his tailed hair glinting copper.

"Tell me about the governor's dance." Beneath him, Percy stretched her neck and hunted for grass.

The first two days of the journey, Susanna had described Williamsburg and her experiences. Well, many of them. She looked back. The wagon, with Jonathan proudly driving the mules, was nearing.

"Young Mr. Jefferson escorted me."

Da's scarred eyebrow lifted. "Ye mean Tom?"

"He's at the College of William and Mary now."

Her father signaled his mare forward. Susanna gently tugged on Rosemary's reins to disengage her from the grass.

"Well, now. The lad is near your age, come to think of it." He slid her a glance. "Are his manners as fine as his French?"

She smiled. "Yes, Da. He regaled me with discussions of French philosophy. Tom is a good friend, but ..." How to explain? Tom was young, and besides, he seemed like a brother.

Da's gaze flickered to her, but he remained silent.

She told him about Philippe. About meeting him at the theater, the French lessons, and the painting. "And then he requested I sit for a miniature."

"And?" Her father's forearms knotted, and Percy snorted at the slight pressure on the reins.

"What I did not know was that he made two. He gave me one of them at the governor's gala."

"Where was Mr. Jefferson all this time?"

"He knew. At least, he ... he escorted me back to the Randolphs'. After I pushed Philippe in the mud."

"What?"

Susanna hesitated. Then she launched into an abbreviated version of Philippe's speech outside the governor's mansion. "Oh Da, I couldn't bear to hear him say those things."

"So ye treated him like ye treated Seth Robinson." Da chuckled, the faint white scar in his cheek appearing as he smiled. "Hmph. I was praying for ye, and your mother too."

She relaxed. She didn't know what she'd expected, but he hadn't lost his temper. "Thank you, I needed your prayers. And not just because of that."

His expression shifted to something she could not read.

She rubbed Rosemary's well-worn reins between her fingers, wondering how to continue. The realization of her bad spiritual state, finding herself in mire without knowing how she'd gotten there, and the slow journey out, clinging to God's promises. Where would she start?

"Da, my soul wasn't in a good place."

He said nothing.

"Mr. Whitefield's sermon helped, and then I started reading my New Testament." She cut a glance at him.

"I kent ye had wandered. I prayed for that too."

Her throat swelled.

"Pee-yew!" Nathan complained behind them. "Hannah's had an accident!"

Susanna smiled, relieved at the interruption. Da wheeled Percy, and she followed suit on her mare.

"Not to fret, we shall manage," Mother said.

"We'll stop here anyway. There's a stream right past that hill."

They had not yet reached the last push up to Rockfish Gap, but the ground had changed even in the course of the morning, knolls and gray-green rocky outcrops interrupting the steady course of trees to either side. Her father would keep them to a slow pace today, even if it meant arriving home after sunset. The mules were strong, but the east side of Rockfish Gap was difficult.

With Jonathan's assistance, her father led the animals to water, and Mother tended to Hannah in the back of the wagon. Susanna knelt to refill their canteens beside the stream, pushing her wool cloak off her shoulders. The sun shed welcome heat on her back. But the water was cold as ice, sending a shiver through her arm as she plunged the first container below the surface.

After their water supply was replenished, Susanna stood, clenching and unclenching her chilled fingers. To her left, a rocky knoll seemed climbable. Harness jangled behind her; the mules were being put back in their traces. She still had time. Gathering her skirts, she scrambled up the slope.

Earlier, she'd caught a glimpse of a cloudy horizon, the mist shrouding the Blue Ridge ahead. Rockfish Gap was often foggy, but the morning had warmed; there was a good chance she'd see it. At the top of the little rise, she peered west.

Yes! The clouds had dissipated, and the gentle cleft lay before them, the green shoulders of the mountains rising up on either side. Her heart lifted.

"See the gap?" Her father stood below with one foot propped on a gray ledge.

She nodded, and picked her way back down, her wool skirt dragging, but she cared little if she soiled it.

They recovered their horses and mounted.

"Susanna," Da said. "Shall I give leave for Mr. Paxton to write ye?"

Her thoughts tumbled past one another. "You spoke to him?"

"Aye, he brought me a mare just before I left the valley for Richmond. He explained he'd be joining Mr. Woods on his circuit, and would I consider giving permission to write."

Her uncle had explained the events of the past month to her father when he'd arrived. But now Jamie was joining Mr. Woods? "But isn't that illegal?"

"Hmph. A license restricts a minister to the county in which it was issued. But usually Baptist ministers suffer no harassment if they stay quiet, preaching to small groups or in private homes."

Still, she'd seen how dangerous it could be. That frightening night in Hanover County flashed before her eyes. For some reason, it did not dissuade her. "Yes, I'd like to write him. Thank you." Her heart warmed. Being given liberty to write was well-nigh to permission to court, and she wasn't sure what to think about that, but Jamie was a special friend.

Yes, she'd write. And pray.

"THE MEAT WILL TASTE LIKE FISH," Buffalo Robe whispered.

Red Hawk surveyed the area, plotting a strategy. The young bear in the clearing below, feeding on early strawberries, had undoubtedly subsisted on fish and small game all spring. And it was thin, besides—only a year old, he judged.

Buffalo Robe shifted his weight and indicated a direction, down and to the right.

Red Hawk nodded and pointed—he'd take the left side, along the slope. He took a deep breath, hoping he had the favor of the spirits. Fall and winter were better seasons for hunting large game, but he had his own purposes for desiring extra provisions, and Buffalo Robe had been eager to join in the special cleansing ritual necessary for a successful hunt. The bear was a good omen.

He slipped through the young yellow-green foliage, placing his feet where no stone would dislodge and betray him, gently pressing away the limbs and stems that plucked at him, easing them back into place as noiselessly as he could.

He hesitated. He was now close enough to hear the beast slurping as it devoured the berries. It was turned from him, turned from Buffalo Robe too. Both of them could take a rear-angled shot.

To Red Hawk's left rose a tall beech, limbs stately and strong. The lowest was easy to reach. *Good.* Should the bear attack, they'd need to scurry. Even such a youngster had formidable jaws. He selected an arrow and waited.

A muffled *thwop* was followed by a grunt from the animal. Red Hawk rose, drew the bow to its full reach, and aimed for the area just behind the ribcage. Causing the beast to suffer would anger the spirits. A strong shot to the vitals was essential.

The bear moaned and turned, spoiling the opportunity. Buffalo Robe's arrow might have merely irritated it. Red Hawk took several steps to regain the proper angle and released.

He ran forward, another arrow at the ready, but Buffalo Robe had released a second one. In moments the fletching of four arrows studded the animal's sides.

The bear faced him and growled, beady eyes fixed on him. A glistening drop of red oozed from the corner of its mouth. A lung shot, then. Red Hawk grabbed his tomahawk, ran forward, and plunged the sharp edge into the beast's neck.

The great vessels spurted blood, and the bear moaned once, eerily like a human. It sank to the ground, lay on its side, and stilled.

A faint breeze rustled the leaves of the beech.

Buffalo Robe advanced from the trees and knelt on the other side of the bear, now humbled in death.

Red Hawk knelt before the belly. Gratitude for the animal's sacrifice swelled up in him as he began the first words of the prayer.

"BUFFALO ROBE, do you remember the white man's tongue?" Red Hawk's skinning knife paused. "I have a book, and I want to learn the medicine of the marks."

A thin thread of gray smoke rose before the dark form of his friend, who was building the fire. Buffalo Robe threw in several twigs and sat back on his heels. "Book?"

Red Hawk pantomimed the opening of the leaves.

"Yes, yes, I remember now." His friend's gaze searched the forest as if needing an answer. "I can teach you some words, but that will not help with the book."

"Why?"

"I do not know the way of books. It was forbidden, you see. Only the white men were allowed their secrets, not us."

"That proves it. The medicine is so strong, white men keep it from those they wish to oppress."

The fire gained in strength and Buffalo Robe added several small branches. "The bear—do you want the teeth or the claws?"

Red Hawk considered. The spirits had given him a bear, a source of strength, wisdom, and courage. "I think we should eat the heart, and divide the liver for our families. The heart will give us courage."

"The claws?"

"This animal was young. He'll need his claws in the spirit realm." As a sign of respect, they'd be leaving the remains of the carcass on a simple platform in the trees. An intact head, with all four paws, was a good idea.

Buffalo Robe grunted his agreement and reached for the heart. "I will teach you the words I know. But you must never speak of it to Laughing Wolf."

Red Hawk slanted him a wry look. "On that we are agreed."

They propped the heart on sticks over the fire, and soon the aroma of roasting flesh filled the little clearing.

"Buffalo Robe, do you think the Creator hears us?"

His friend's eyebrows jerked up. "I do not know." He sliced into the heart to test for doneness. "Short Stick, in Big Turtle's village, mumbles thanks to the Creator. I suppose that is appropriate, but here is what I think." He settled back on his haunches. "The Creator sends rain on the earth. Yes, He provides for us. But He provides alike for all, even wicked whites east of the mountains. He is not a totem spirit. We can ask the totems of our tribe or clan to assist us." He snorted. "You know this."

"The Creator is the greatest spirit."

"But what good is it? If He is good to all, how do you gain power against your enemies?" Buffalo Robe sliced a chunk of steaming meat from the heart with a flick of his wrist. "I will tell you what I saw in Big Turtle's village when I was young, before I killed my first deer. Grayfeather had gone to consult the medicine bundle, and Big Turtle went into the sacred lodge. I was curious and crept closer. After a while I heard strange noises coming from inside. Light shone from the edge of the skin door, a strange light. When the shaman emerged and spoke, several strong warriors near the entrance fell to the ground. I was terrified." He gestured with his knife. "Now *that* is power."

Red Hawk grunted in response. True, the sacred bundle had power. But it didn't answer the emptiness of his heart.

28

From all that dwell below the skies,
Let the Creator's praise arise;
Let the Redeemer's name be sung
Through every land, by every tongue.

—Isaac Watts (1674-1748)

Sandy Creek, North Carolina, June 1756

James squinted at the page in the gray light of sunset. The Book of Revelation was difficult. No, not entirely. Some things were plain. The general gist was evident; Christ was revealed in this book through the lens of prophetic imagery.

The verse before him was plain. The apostle John saw the redeemed in heaven. "...every kindred, and tongue, and people, and nation ..."

Nation—the Greek word *ethnos*. Gentiles. Heathen. Pagans who spoke another language.

It was dark. He'd never noticed when night had fallen. James closed his Bible. He only read in firelight when he was desperate; the dancing shadows on the page gave him a headache. He had to snatch every moment he could for study and sermon preparation.

Jeremiah Woods tossed a trimmed branch on the fire and sat. "Glad for a night out of doors."

James inhaled the evening air and wrapped his arms around his knees. Even the poorest offered hospitality, but if the weather was good, a bed by the fire was preferable to the crowded, smelly cabins they'd slept in recently. He slapped his arm. Only the occasional mosquito marred the peaceful night.

"What did you think of Stearns?" Woods asked.

They'd spent the last night at the minister's house. Mr. Shubal Stearns pastored the largest Baptist congregation he'd seen yet. "He's different."

"His preaching style?"

"Yes, his voice ..." James didn't know how to explain it, and he didn't want to be overly critical.

"He's got a manner of speaking that would drive some of our proper Presbyterians up a tree."

"The content was biblical."

"You heard what he said, about the need for ministers."

James nodded. The crowd this past Lord's Day had amazed him, even though the church was only one year old. Some had traveled quite a distance. "I'll get the water."

He stood and grabbed the handle of the kettle while Mr. Woods rummaged in his saddlebag for their supper. James checked on his mule on the way to the stream. Was he meant to fill the need for ministers? According to Stearns, Mr. Whitefield's unconventional preaching had resulted in a number of new churches, Baptist as well as the so-called "Methodist" variety.

He breathed in the damp air above the stream as water gurgled into the copper kettle. If it were God's will, wouldn't he feel something? Preaching to these small groups—and once to the church at Sandy Creek—had been encouraging. The Lord was doing great things in the backcountry. The need for ministers was clearly great, but nowhere had he sensed even the smallest indication he should stay and pastor. The way ahead remained dark.

He trudged back to the campfire. No, only a leaden lump in his chest remained.

Susanna. He'd write her. Unburden his heart.

The thought cheered him.

STEAM ROSE from the wash kettle over the fire. Mrs. McKee advanced like a general, thrust her wash paddle down, leveraged the mass of sodden clothes up into the air, and pivoted to dump it into the rinse barrel.

Susanna glanced at Agnes, who slanted her a smile. "I canna say I want the job back, meself," the old woman murmured.

In the family's absence, tasks had been reassigned at Russell's Ridge. The young widow was good at washing clothes, and Agnes was getting too old for heavy labor. Laundry was also a way to make Mrs. McKee feel useful when it was quickly apparent that her housekeeping skills were poor. They'd arrived to a warm greeting, even from the McKees' thin dog, whose bones were beginning to subside beneath its coat. But the house had been mouse-infested.

"I would call this batch a success," Susanna said, staring at the oak bucket at their feet. Their first attempt to use the logwood dye had resulted in a color as black as the iron kettle they'd mixed it in. Agnes had scratched her head and suggested a different container. Now the surface of the liquid reflected a vivid purple; puzzling, but dyeing was tricky. Now, how deep of a color would the hemp fibers take up?

Agnes submerged the skeins of hemp and stirred with a wooden spoon. "I doubt if anything takes up dye as well as wool. But 'tis a bonny color."

Her father had traded for the retted hemp, and now an old cornfield had been dedicated to its production; already tight green rows of the plant shot skyward, narrow leaves circling a single stem. For those who resisted the siren song of tobacco farming, hemp was an alternative cash crop; the Bowyers sold theirs in Richmond to rope makers.

Spinning was still an unpleasant chore, but Susanna found it less onerous now she had weaving to look forward to. She returned to the house, thinking of her loom, stashed out of sight in her cramped bedroom. Campbell colors, green and blue, were stretched upon the frame; soon the shawl for Agnes would be finished, and then she could start on something out of hemp. A natural ecru would do well for youngsters' breeches or satchels. What she'd use the purple for she'd no idea. But everyone would have a gift come Christmas.

She crossed to the walnut table and studied the crock of leftover black logwood dye. Perhaps even these remnants could be useful. With a bit of gum Arabic or honey it might make suitable ink. She went to the parlor for the box of writing materials. Jamie had written a letter full of contradiction. Joy in the opportunity to preach, edged with melancholy regarding his calling. How she could encourage him she didn't know. She set the box on the table and took out an empty inkwell, the pewter cool beneath her fingers.

A creak and a rustle marked Mother's entrance, basket over her arm. "Mrs. Smoke is near her time."

She'd heard the new neighbor was with child. "Were you able to speak to her?" They were German, from the settlements up north.

Mother sighed. "Just enough to explain who I was." She set her empty basket on the end of the table and sat on her stool. "'Twill be difficult when her time comes."

Susanna carefully spooned dye into the inkwell. "*Kinder. Kinder* means 'child' in German."

Mother's blond eyebrows rose. "You learned German as well as French?"

"No. Remember the year I went with Da up to the German settlements?"

"Hmm. You want honey for that?"

Her stepmother began to rise but Susanna motioned her to stay seated. "I'll get it. Remember when your ankles swelled with Hannah?"

Mother chuckled. "Yes, madame physician. I shall rest a bit. Add a drop or two of whiskey. 'Twill preserve the ink."

Ink making was a common enough occurrence in the kitchen. Susanna retrieved the whiskey jug. "While Da traded his furniture I played with the other *kinder*—"

"And learned a few words that way. Well, I shall need your assistance. Doubly so." She slid her hand over the broad curve of her belly, then moved to the corner, put her feet up, and took up her mending.

Susanna finished the ink and pulled out a quill to cut. "Mother, how did you know you should marry Da?"

Her stepmother's blue eyes rounded, and her hands stilled for a moment. "Well, he did not mock my botany book."

Botany book. "The one of your own drawings?"

"Yes, 'twas not something a typical young woman would do."

Certainly in the valley that was true. Most women had no time for special pursuits. But Mother was a shopkeeper's daughter, born in Boston and raised in Philadelphia. "Da didn't mind?"

"Oh, no. In fact, he gave me the book on medicinals."

"The *Pharmacopeia*."

Mother's gaze sharpened. "But you knew some of that already."

She nodded.

"You are thinking about Mr. Paxton."

Was it so obvious? "I'm not thinking about marriage, exactly ..."

"You enjoy his company?"

Susanna smiled, relieved. Mother understood.

Mother's hands regained their motion. "I did not want to marry, either, when I met John. I was content to pursue my little studies in the free time I had when chores were done. Marriage seemed a sort of bondage."

Susanna finished the quill and laid it down.

"When your father courted me all that was pitched out the window.

I enjoyed his company, and he enjoyed mine. The Scripture describes the woman as a helpmeet—a suitable helper—for the man. Not a servant, but a companion."

"But the wife must obey her husband."

"Well, naturally. And the militia has only one colonel." Mother was unruffled by the objection. "But I daresay a husband and wife are meant to be friends in a sense that a colonel cannot be with his men."

"But I have seen—"

"You see sinful men and sinful women fighting God. Men will twist God-given authority and become oppressors at every level of society. Women also subvert their role, making their husbands' lives miserable or neglecting their children."

Susanna nodded silently. It shamed her suddenly, to have such hard thoughts of marriage when her father and stepmother lived out such a blessed union before her.

"I suspect marriage is a bit like the gospel. Unbelievers look at religion and think it bondage, whereas we who know the Lord enjoy liberty and love." Mother tucked an errant blond curl behind her ear. "Fret not. 'Twill be clear in time."

Not for the first time, James silently blessed Roy Russell for the new saddle, complete with special strap that kept it from shifting. Underneath him the mule plodded along, following Mr. Woods' horse through the thick forest along a nearly invisible track. But at least the unique gait of the animal did not necessitate periodic halts to re-saddle the creature. Who knew a simple strap would correct the problem?

James tugged at his kerchief and pulled it from his neck. It had rained during the night, and from the few glimpses he'd had of the sky, it was still overcast, but the air remained heavy and hot. He thrust a finger around the collar of his onasburg linen shirt, trying to get air below the fabric, but it made no difference to his sweating neck.

He raised his forearm to push back feathery cypress fronds threatening to pluck his straw hat from his head. As they traveled east the great trees were becoming more numerous, their strange buttressed trunks twice as wide as a man was tall, their tops disappearing in the canopy high above. The trapper's cabin they were headed to was located at the edge of the Great Dismal Swamp. Why anyone would want to live there he didn't know.

He shoved the linen kerchief into his saddlebag and pulled out Susanna's letter. Parts he had memorized.

Ian MacLeod came yesterday with a young Pig for the Widow McKee. She came to the Door, Laundry in her Arms. The wriggling Animal leaped at her, spoiling the Linens, and galloped about the House. Nathan thought it amusing, but Hannah cried. Mother took control and bid Everyone outside. She coaxed the young Pig with Milk and finally secur'd it. Up to this Point I knew nothing of this Courtship, for that it plainly is. MacLeod is happier now than last Year, if I am any Judge. He is also quite industrious, having staked out his Cabin on the few Acres Da gave him after his Indenture expir'd. He still works for us, and in exchange for his Labor Da says he is to receive the new Heifer. Mrs. May predicts there will be a Wedding by the end of the Year, and to see Mrs. Kee's Eyes when the young Man visits, I think she is right.

Mother needs my Help more than ever due to her Limitations. A new Neighbor will be in need of a Midwife soon, if I may speak so plainly. I am settled in my Mind that I am where God wants me to be, if only for now. I am reminded of Rockfish Gap. When we crossed this spring, it was clear on the Summit and one could see for Miles to the East and to the West. Da let us stop briefly to rest and eat a bit of Cheese. I drank in the beautiful sight as the Sun sank toward the Ridge in the West. I suppose there are Times when God's Will is as clear as the Gap was that day, but often it is not. Sometimes Travelers through the Gap are hindered by a dense Fog that settles on the Mountains. One can see only a few Steps ahead. Presently I see God's Will but only for the next few Steps.

James folded the letter and replaced it. *The next few steps.* He wished he knew more of God's will for his own life, but he was in a fog—or a swamp.

"Ho, James, boggy ground."

He scanned the ground as best he could over the shoulder of the mule. He couldn't see anything unusual, but a faint squish and pop of the animals' hooves revealed the moisture. To his left, a faint glimmer of water showed through the trees.

"Almost there, lad."

Mr. Woods was right. After a quarter hour, the ground solidified under the animals' hooves, and the gloom dispersed. The trees thinned, then stopped suddenly, and a small field planted Indian-style with corn and beans sat to their right. A dog barked. Ahead a weathered cabin was visible, and in the yard several buckskins were staked for tanning. The smell of hickory smoke cheered his heart. He was hungry.

A woman appeared from behind one of the skins, dressed in what looked like a pale leather gown that hung only to her knees and some kind of leggings below that. Her long braided hair was black.

She was an Indian.

29

The Lord carries on His work gloriously, in sundry places in this province, and in Virginia, and in South Carolina.

—Shubal Stearns (1706-1771)

The venison stew was surprisingly good, thick with beans and chunks of something James could not identify. His belly uncurled a bit, although the Indian woman's glare from across the narrow board table didn't help his digestion.

The trapper, Mr. King, pushed back his bowl. "What news?"

Mr. Woods leaned back in his chair and soon a discussion commenced on the war. Mr. King's sandy-blond eyebrows, thick like caterpillars, jerked when he found a comment interesting. The silver in his close-cropped beard betrayed his age. He must be fifty, at least, despite the young children playing in the corner.

His wife seemed younger, and quite handsome actually, with clear olive skin, full lips, and large dark eyes. A smaller lighter-skinned replica of herself stood behind her parents, ready to serve those at table.

James stifled a belch with his hand, and the woman's hard expression relaxed slightly, as if she approved—or was amused.

Mr. Woods opened his heavy Bible. They'd have "family worship" in which the preacher would give an "exhortation." The terms would see them clear of any magistrate's accusation, though James doubted they'd need to be careful in such a location.

But this evening, the exhortation was indeed short, a mere twenty-minute exposition. Then Mr. Woods turned to him. "Mr. Paxton, do you have a word for these good folks?"

James looked at the woman across from him, then at her husband. "How much English does she understand?" Despite her sharp gaze, it was hard to imagine her an enemy. Even if she was, what did the Scripture say about enemies?

"Enough," replied Mr. King. "But she says she worships He-Who-Never-Dies as the Catawba do. The white man's God is not her god."

The woman tilted her chin and looked at him slantwise, her expression hard.

James's thoughts tumbled. Then he remembered something.

SUSANNA UNLOADED the motherwort from her basket onto the cloth-covered table. "What are the uses?" The plant was a new addition to her stepmother's herb garden.

"'Twill strengthen a woman's pains," Mother replied.

"But why—"

A shadow at the open door announced Da's presence. He filled the doorway, large, sweaty, and smiling. "The hemp is twelve feet tall if it's an inch. Some say ye can see it grow, and I've half a mind to believe it. Mr. Bowyer will be over to dinner tomorrow—might ye scare up a bit more to feed him? He'll show me the way of harvesting the plant. Can ye imagine? Haying, then the barley next week, and hemp after that. Without Mr. MacLeod, I dinna ken what I'd do."

He wiped his feet on the mat and produced a few items. "Thomas Kerr went to town. I've the *Gazette* and a letter for you, Susanna."

Her father poured himself a tankard full of ale that disappeared down his throat in moments. Then he disappeared.

Susanna reached for the letter.

"I'll finish this," Mother said. "Go ahead."

Susanna crossed to the parlor and sat in the nurse chair. Drops of water stained one corner of the letter and smudges marked one side, as if the missive had traveled a hard road. She opened it. Jamie's writing quickened her heart. The familiar script was cramped and crooked in places, as if he'd written with very little light.

Dear Susanna, I thank you for your Letter of the 21st ult. It does cheer my Heart to hear of ordinary Activities, even Laundry and Dye. You have a great Facility with Prose, which I do not share, but I will recount a few Matters regarding this Journey, which I trust will come to an End in a Fortnight.

Since my last Letter one Event has stirred my Mind greatly. Mr. Woods and I rode to the Great Dismal Swamp, which I may tell you, is indeed dismal, even on the Fringes. We lodged one Night at a Trader's. His Wife is a Catawba Indian who seemed hostile to the Gospel. I was asked to speak, and at first I hesitated. You know how I have suffered at their Hands. Well, not this woman, certainly, and not even the Catawba. How strange and wicked is the human Heart, that I should resist doing Good to these poor Creatures!

But God was merciful to me even so. I remembered a Sermon I prepared while at Mr. Davies', based on Paul's speech to the Athenians. You recall he was among Men who had no Knowledge or Respect for the Hebrew Scriptures. He could not Reason with them on that Basis, but seeing an Altar "to the unknown God" in the midst of their Places of Worship, he preached about their unknown God.

In the same Way, I spoke about He-Who-Never-Dies, the Catawba Deity. Can you imagine? These ignorant Heathen already possess a Concept of their Creator which contains an Element of Truth, to wit, His Immutability. I cannot say whether my poor Exhortation was well received, but I believed the Woman listened.

I can tell you this. My own Heart was warmed. It was the greatest Encouragement I have received on this Journey as yet. 'Tis strange to me, I must say. What it means I do not know. Mr. Woods has said nothing.

Yr. Ob't Servant, James Paxton

Susanna blinked. What a heart-warming story. But what were the implications? Jamie preaching to Indians? Was that God's will for him?

She stood and paced the small room.

It was unthinkable.

THE BEARSKIN WAS READY. Red Hawk had pushed his aunt to the limits of her patience, asking her for an extra treatment of the hide with brains before he finished the process himself, rolling the skin with several large river stones to break it to unusual softness.

He ran his hands over it, thick black fur shading to a deep brown on the edges. He rolled it up easily, the heavy hide soft and supple in every direction. Time to present it to Running Deer.

The Green Corn Dance at Big Turtle's village had come and gone, and neither Running Deer nor Laughing Wolf stood for the marriage dance while there. Now Laughing Wolf was gone on a raid. Just as well.

Red Hawk stepped outside, the rolled hide tucked under his arm. Motion caught his eye from the east, something along the tree line.

It was Grandmother, hobbling back to the village with an herb bag slung under her arm—quite full by the looks of it. She took a few slow steps, and then stumbled.

"Grandmother!" Red Hawk ran to her side. Thankfully she hadn't fallen. But she could have fallen, alone, out in the woods, no one knowing where she was. "Where were you?"

He knew, of course. She'd been hunting for herbs and roots. He and Dark Water occasionally searched for them, but Grandmother had commanded him not to bring back any more ginseng. "You bring me young roots with no potency. Leave them to mature," she'd said. Harvesting herbs was a craft, he'd decided, best left to the women.

"You worry too much. And what else is an old woman like me to do?"

True. She had no babes to dandle at her knees, no young ones to teach the stories. She was too old to work in the fields, and even her production of pots and beaded moccasins had languished.

Red Hawk clenched his jaw. Marrying Running Deer would help. A young woman in the household could do the heavier work, fetch water, gather berries and nuts, assist in the fields—and maybe, just maybe—learn enough herb lore to be useful.

But it wouldn't solve all their problems, for he'd need to look out for Running Deer's family as well.

"Grandmother, I know what I will do. I will go on a raid."

She said nothing as they walked slowly to the wigwam.

"I will find a child." As he spoke, the idea took shape in Red Hawk's mind. "Not too young. A girl to help you. Train, even."

"Hmph."

But Grandmother didn't object. In any case, a young slave would be useful for common tasks. *Yes.* The more he thought about it, the more he wondered why he hadn't thought of it before. And a captive was just as good a coup as a scalp.

And maybe, just maybe, if the girl were old enough, she'd know the secrets of the code. Learning a few dozen English words from Buffalo Robe hadn't solved his problem. The book was still closed to him.

Once Grandmother was back inside her wigwam, he returned to his errand, the bearskin under his arm. The sun was past its zenith, and the air was hot and heavy. Running Deer would probably be back from the fields or the woods. Few worked long hours in the heat of blackberry moon.

At first, he saw no one at the entrance of the family wigwam. He called a greeting.

"Red Hawk." Running Deer's mother, Sun-on-the-Water, smiled at him. "Running Deer will return soon. She is gathering berries with her cousin."

Red Hawk felt awkward; his purpose was obvious. "I-I have a gift." A bearskin was more than an ordinary gift of meat. Receiving it was significant. He didn't mind too much that Running Deer was not here. Impressing her mother was critical.

"It's beautiful." Sun-on-the-Water's smile faded, replaced by a more serious expression. "Sit here, I will get you something to drink."

She returned quickly and poured a beverage into a cup.

He sipped it. Honey locust tea. His gift had been received, then. He savored the sweet fluid, glancing occasionally at the tree line beyond.

A shadow fell, followed by the scent of old sweat and something else. Laughing Wolf stood gazing down at him, glittering eyes revealing nothing. At his hip jostled two scalps, one half-blackened by fire, the source of the faint smell of blood and smoke.

"Was your captive very courageous?" Normally any drawn-out torture would be carried out in the village, for the others to see; Red Hawk had never witnessed it himself but had heard plenty of stories.

Laughing Wolf's lip curled. "He gave us plenty of sport. And the smoke appeased the gods. The Sun will look favorably upon us now."

Reportedly the man had made several pilgrimages to the Old Places to worship, to give homage to the Sun. Clearly he wanted to be shaman. Although in Red Hawk's opinion, Laughing Wolf cared nothing for the people. Only in gathering followers, which he had—two dozen young men accompanied him on raids.

He looked up. Running Deer approached with a basket held tightly in front of her. She greeted them both, her expression carefully neutral.

Red Hawk rose, nodded, and slipped away. He needed to plan his own raid. But he would invite only a few loyal friends who could be trusted to keep their purification secret. He could not trust Laughing Wolf on a raid. Arrows bore the signature of their owners, but musket balls did not.

And Laughing Wolf had a musket.

30

There are in life real evils enough, and it is folly to afflict ourselves with imaginary ones; it is time enough when the real ones arrive.

—Benjamin Franklin (1705-1790)

Lift, shuttle, beat, repeat. The rhythm of the small loom soothed Susanna. Here in the kitchen, air wafted in through the open door and eased the heat. She alternated the strands of purple hemp with narrow bands of white; not a fancy pattern, but it pleased her nonetheless.

A shadow darkened the doorway—her father. But it wasn't suppertime yet, and barley harvest had just begun.

"Need some switchel, Da?"

He shook his head. "I need your mother. And some ale for the gentleman."

Something was wrong. "Mother went to the springhouse for something."

He frowned and slipped out the door.

A stranger stood at the threshold, hat in hand, his chestnut hair darkened at the temples with sweat. He dipped his head in greeting. "Miss."

"Please come in and have some ale." Susanna moved her loom and found some tankards.

"Switchel, if ye have it."

His clothing was dusty from the road. "Is your horse in need of care?"

"Thank ye kindly, but a young man has seen to him. Please forgive me, name's Houston. Robert Houston, at your service."

Now she placed him. The Houston clan lived perhaps twenty miles away. The family had just completed a stone church on their property, useful for both worship and defense.

Da returned, his face tense, Mother behind him. "Roy's coming, and all the men. Mrs. McKee is keeping the children in the old cabin at the moment."

Soon Grandda and Arch May joined them, and Susanna fled to the parlor to fetch another chair.

"Your news, Mr. Houston?" Da asked. He probably already knew some of it and had guessed more.

The man took a deep breath, his face somber. "I dinna ken how much to relate with the lass in the room."

Da's gaze met her own. "She'll do. Susanna is a sensible sort."

"I was on my way to Fort Loudoun when a farmer apprised me of horrible news. I made a detour to collect information for the colonel." He took a long swallow of his switchel and set down the tankard carefully. "A large party of Shawnee attacked George Painter's home near Woodstock. Like yourself, he has a goodly house—he even has a stone cellar. All in the neighborhood took refuge there, but the Indians set the house on fire, and the folks came out to save their lives. The

Indians took the women, children, and at least one of the men captive, some say fifty total."

There was silence for a long moment.

"George Painter?" Uncle Roy asked.

"Dead. And the babes ..." Mr. Houston's eyes flickered to Mother's rounded form. "The babes didna survive either."

The babies didn't survive? Susanna didn't want to know what that meant exactly.

"Did any escape?" Arch May's throaty voice held an edge.

"A couple of lads. They couldna get anyone to follow the band, there were so many Indians."

A chill seeped through Susanna's belly. She focused on the tankards. Did anyone need more ale or switchel? But no one was drinking now.

"They gave a verra nasty report about what happened to one of the captives."

Da signaled Susanna with his gaze, jerking his chin slightly to indicate that she was to leave. She set down the pitcher of switchel, went outside as if to go to the old cabin, and then doubled back, creeping along the house. Leaning against the siding, she strained to hear what they were saying inside.

"They ordered little Jacob Fisher to gather dry wood. The poor lad sensed what was coming and cried out to his father, who couldna help him. They set the wood on fire and ... I would spare ye the details. His death was not quick, I am sorry to relate."

Sudden nausea engulfed her. Susanna leaned over and laid her hand over her mouth.

"Who else kens this?" Her father's voice.

"Everyone above the Triple Forks, to be sure. I've told Mr. Stuart, and next I mean to visit with John Lewis and his sons. The militia needs to know."

Susanna straightened and took a long breath to settle her stomach. Where did this happen?

As if reading her thoughts, Uncle Roy asked, "How far is Woodstock?"

"Sixty miles north, on the west side of the valley."

Northwest. Well, didn't Da say that's where the main danger was?

"Folks are panicking, some speaking of leaving," Houston said. "Colonel Patton killed at Draper's Meadow down south, now this. Truly, any place west of the Blue Ridge can be attacked at any moment." He sighed. "Savages dinna fight like we do. To kill wee bairns—" His voice broke. "Every man ought to be ready, and every family needs a fort or place of refuge."

"Tomorrow." Da's voice. "We'll send word to the Kerrs. We need to practice finding our way to the cavern quickly."

Susanna hoped Mother would be able to safely navigate the steep steps chopped into the sides of the entrance by her father's axe.

A hatless head, hair flying, popped into view from the path below. Kitty Robinson approached, legs churning.

"Susanna! Tell your ma, quick! Mrs. Smoke's pains have started."

SUSANNA RUBBED HER FACE, tired after the long night. The gray light of dawn illuminated the yard.

"Mr. Smoke, keep your wife quiet. The babe is well," Mother said. "He's small but not too small. Mrs. Smoke must not fret … for her milk's sake."

Normally a midwife gave these instructions to the mother, but this time language was a hindrance, not to mention the reason for the early birth.

John Smoke wrung the hat in his hands. "My Annalise is high-strung, and up near Winchester, well, we feared the Indians. So we moved here. Now it seems the danger is everywhere."

Hearing about the Indian attack had sent the poor woman into early labor.

"Has my husband told you about the cavern?"

"I've seen it—but there's no question of Annalise going anywhere for a few days."

Mother nodded. "Fret not yourself. Put your trust in God. We shall check on her daily for a few days, then when she is stronger, make the trek together."

A smile flitted across Mr. Smoke's face. "Thank you, ma'am. Here, take this." He thrust a wrapped object toward them.

"No, Mr. Smoke, I have no need of cheese, and your wife and babe do. However, I do have need of someone to help spin all our flax and hemp. When she is able, that would be most welcome."

Da emerged from the barn, rifle slung over his back. Hopefully he'd found a place to sleep for part of the night, at least. He harnessed the mules and drove them back to the house. He had insisted on accompanying them with the wagon, not allowing Mother to carry a single thing.

But Mother refused to go straight to bed when they arrived home. Everything needed to be cleaned and set to rights, and besides, she explained, she'd napped during a long spell when nothing much had happened.

"Now do you see the usefulness for motherwort?" Mother said.

The babe's position was what the French book called *postérieur,* and for hours there'd been no progress.

"Yes, Mother, although I wonder if kneeling or squatting would have turned it without using the herb at all."

They talked until the sun was well over the Ridge, Susanna filing away each nugget of wisdom. Studying her stepmother's rounded form, she decided to read over the French midwifery book one more time.

THE SINGLE, plaintive call of a wood thrush far upslope beckoned Susanna forward. The familiar dawn chorus was thinner now as songbirds hunkered down for late summer, just as people did. Da was already in the hemp field with Mr. Bowyer, using as many of the cooler hours as possible. All the men sat around the table after the midday meal resting and talking, sometimes dozing, waiting until the shadows began to lengthen before resuming their labors.

Mother had cautioned her to stay close, an easy commandment to obey after last week's mad dash to the cavern. It was only practice, but Mrs. McKee's little boy had gone missing, and precious minutes were wasted until they found him playing at the springhouse. Da's forehead had sprouted grim lines.

Basket over her arm, Susanna purposed to look for ginseng after claiming the plump blueberries in the clearing they always frequented this time of year. But in the back of her mind she tracked the distance to the cavern. Just in case.

She paced herself. The shoulder of the mountain didn't appear steep, but that was deceiving, and she was still regaining her strength after the months of relative inactivity in Williamsburg. If there was a bear, she didn't wish to give herself away by breathing hard.

She reached the birches her father tapped for beer and paused to enjoy the colors emerging from the gray-on-gray palette of dawn.

This is the day that the Lord hath made …

It was so peaceful. Hard to imagine danger here. She resumed her climb, slowing as she approached the clearing. From the shelter of a young cedar she scanned the area.

No bears.

It didn't take long to fill her basket, and she retraced her steps, meandering a little, focusing on the ground. Susanna doubted she'd find any ginseng so close to home; surely she'd already harvested anything in plain sight.

She circled a patch of rhododendron. *There.* The familiar pattern of leaves seemed to reach for her. The plant was large, at least five years old. Beyond it, a smaller specimen—too young. She knelt and thrust her spade into the damp loam.

Yes. The root revealed the proper number of scars. She shook off the soil and tucked the specimen in the basket.

Mother would fret if she tarried. Susanna circled back to the birch grove and began her descent.

A masculine shout echoed from below.

Heart thudding, she quickened her steps.

RED HAWK SIGNALED THE OTHERS, and they halted behind several pawpaw trees.

Face streaked with red, Straight Arrow emerged from the foliage. "There's a dwelling to the right."

"How many lodgings are here?" Cat's Eye asked. He was very young and a little too eager for his own good.

"We must use caution." Red Hawk peered through the branches. "We are near a place inhabited by a wise woman, and we must not incur her wrath." He'd decided not to tell them the whole story, only impress on them the potency of the woman's medicine.

Red Hawk's mare lifted her head, nostrils wide. Probably smelling other horses.

Time to finish instructing them—they were too tense to listen much anyway. "Do not harm any women or children. Take spoil for yourselves. Cat's Eye, look for a horse." The youth admired Red Hawk's chestnut, and if his attention was on animals, he might stay out of trouble.

Hopefully the men were out in the fields by now. Having seen Silver Beard's bravery, Red Hawk was loath to lead his friends to their death. But he couldn't say that; they'd think him a coward.

"Straight Arrow, take Cat's Eye to the right. The rest of us will go straight down. We'll rendezvous back here."

Straight Arrow nodded and they departed noiselessly.

Red Hawk led the others down the slope, looking for a stream, a spring near a gnarly walnut, and to the right, a cabin. The place where his father died.

Creator, please give me what I need.

The prayer sprang unbidden to his heart.

31

The jewel of faith is always put in the cabinet of a good conscience.

—Thomas Watson (1620-1686)

James woke to the gunmetal flash of a tomahawk against the gray half-light of dawn. But he wasn't frightened. He took several slow breaths, wondering about it.

He pushed away the bedclothes and sat up, careful to keep his head down. The loft was tiny. His oldest brother had taken over the bedroom they'd all shared, now that he was married, and all that was left for James on the family homestead was this little space.

His nightmares had become fewer over time, but always left him sweaty and trembling. He couldn't remember exactly what he'd dreamed about this time, but the sheets were dry.

A toasty aroma cheered him as he tucked his shirt into his breeches and slid down the ladder. Clanks and murmured conversation met his ears. Surely not everyone was still inside, not at this time of year.

His parents looked up at him as he entered the kitchen. His siblings must have already gone out for morning chores.

James grabbed a chair near the large stone hearth. "Good morning."

Real wheat biscuits were piled on the table.

"We've no jam, only the Andersons' honey." His mother pushed it toward him.

His father sipped his chicory. "Barley's in. Corn's still early. Might help in the kailyard. Your sisters are out there now."

James nodded while chewing a biscuit. He knew what season it was. His da was just welcoming him home.

"Thanks, Ma." He lifted the remaining biscuit.

She lifted her brows in response, then tugged a large bowl full of peas into her lap and began to shell them. "Jamie, where'll ye go next?"

His parents knew about his Baptist convictions, and he'd written his mother about his experiences while on the road with Mr. Woods.

He washed the rest of the biscuit down with chicory—heavily laced with real coffee—and considered how to answer. No one was going to understand this, not even his parents. "I was ordained by Mr. Woods and another minister. I was questioned by the other man on both doctrine and practice. Then he asked me what my calling was.

"'I'm not completely sure,' I said."

"'But you have some idea?'"

"I said yes, and he asked what it was." James poured another cup of the chicory. "I said my calling was similar to David Brainerd's."

A line formed between his mother's eyebrows. Had she heard the name?

"Who's David ...?" Da looked puzzled.

"A man who preached to the Indians."

His mother paled.

Da studied the inside of his cup. "Did these ministers seek to turn ye from this idea?"

"They told me to fast and pray, and if I was more certain at the end of that time, they would give their blessing on it." James couldn't look at his mother. "I did, and God gave me a peace about the matter."

"But Indians ..." His mother had regained her power of speech.

"Ma, I thought the same way. I still suffer from that injury."

"They're heathens. Savages!"

He looked at her. "Precisely. Would ye deny them the truth of God's Word and consign them to hell?"

Ma stood and peas flew everywhere. "Ye'll be killed, and for what!"

"Calm doon," Da said. "Let the lad speak."

"Ma is right. I could well be killed. I've thought about that. But my responsibility before God is to obey Him and my conscience."

His mother sat, her shoulders slumping.

"I studied the book of Jonah with Mr. Davies. The prophet ran away when God told him to preach to the enemies of Israel. I ran away for a long time, resisting what I knew in my heart to be His call."

There was silence for a long moment. Then his father spoke. "Ma, remember what ye said when Jamie left with Mr. Russell to fight the French?"

"Aye, I mind it."

"Ye said he'd best not darken this door if he turned tail and ran before his enemies. Seems to me this is a better war, a more worthy battle."

A single tear escaped his mother's eye and ran down her lined cheek. "Aye, that it is."

SUSANNA HESITATED BEHIND AN OAK TREE. To her left the twisted walnut tree was visible; straight ahead the browns and grays of the house; and to her right the cabin. Occasional shouts and strange screeches emanated from the direction of the Mays' home, and her gut chilled. Was anyone left in the house, or had they all fled to the cavern?

A tousled sandy head appeared. Ian MacLeod ran from the direction of the barn toward the house and—hopefully—the safety of the cavern beyond. Behind him danced the three-year-old colt, Charcoal, snorting with indecision. Several sheep bleated. Ian must have released the animals from the barn, saving them from a cruel death if the Indians should fire the structure.

Below, Mrs. McKee's little girl appeared in the doorway of the house, sobbing. How had she been left behind? Ian aimed for her, legs pummeling the ground in his haste.

Would any Indians see him? Susanna scanned the wooded slope behind her. She caught a glimpse of brown skin and leather.

No. The Indian was headed straight to the house. He'd probably see Ian, who scooped the child up against his shoulder and ran for the trees—and if he did, he'd follow Ian all the way to the cavern.

Later, Susanna could not remember making the choice. Her feet took her straight toward the spring. She paced herself, her basket bumping against her hip. Not too fast.

Please, Lord, let him follow me.

RED HAWK LED THE MEN, zigzagging toward an open space. He slowed, looking for movement. And a certain walnut tree.

A black horse circled, nostrils wide. He signaled Buffalo Robe, who darted left toward the animal.

Any men? He laid a hand on the handle of his tomahawk. His quiver was full, and his bow sat securely on his shoulder. From the sounds to his right, the others had engaged at least one of the white men. Blood pulsed through his body, and his senses sharpened.

A flash of red and a dark head moved beyond the foliage. Red Hawk darted closer. Man or woman? Tall enough for a man.

He was not fast, and Red Hawk closed the distance. Once in the open, he realized his mistake. The red flash was a skirt, not a shirt. Dark hair tumbled free. The woman was older than the girl he'd envisioned helping his grandmother, but his steps did not slacken.

In a few more strides he was upon her. His momentum knocked the woman down, and he placed his knee in her back. With his left hand, he grabbed her thick hair, luxuriant dark brown like a beaver's pelt.

The basket went flying, and out popped a plump ginseng root.

Beyond the ginseng the bulge of a large tree root led his gaze up the trunk.

He was beneath the canopy of the walnut described by his father, with its strange angled limb.

SUSANNA LAY FACE DOWN, a tremendous weight on her back, face buried in a scratchy clump of bee balm. Her head ached from the force of her hair being yanked back. She gulped air fruitlessly.

Was she going to die? Was this Indian going to scalp her?

Her mind calmed, strangely peaceful, while her heart raced and her body struggled to breathe.

The Indian released her head and spoke some garbled nonsense—his language, she supposed. Then a single sound: "Up."

It was perfectly recognizable English. She scrambled to her feet, keeping her gaze down, curious but terrified she'd anger him. In moments her hands were tied before her.

The brown-skinned man scooped up her ginseng root and placed it somewhere on his person.

Numbly, she wondered if he knew what it was.

A shot rang out.

THE SOUND of gunfire beyond the trees reminded Red Hawk of that day long ago when Laughing Wolf had taken so long to kill Silver Beard with a misfiring musket. That horrible day when he'd lost the only father he'd ever known.

And now he was standing near the spot where his true father had died. He'd died bravely, Red Pipe had said. Died in front of the wise woman's cabin.

He looked at his captive, seemingly still stunned. Was she the wise woman? No, that was long ago. Still, he would shed no blood in this place. He'd treat this one well, though she was beyond childhood and would attempt escape. He looped a rope around her midsection and knotted it, then tugged her along. Straight Arrow had a musket but knew not to use it unless necessary—the noisy report would bring the men in the fields. Had a white man fired on him? Either way, it was time to leave.

Red Hawk retraced his way, the woman stumbling behind him. Buffalo Robe was already behind the pawpaws, catching his breath. He'd not been able to catch the horse.

Red Hawk was tense, watching for the others. They needed to get away.

Straight Arrow burst through the foliage, blood running down his arm. He carried a sword and a dripping scalp. So it had come to that.

"Cat's Eye?"

"Dead, and I dared not drag his body here."

Red Hawk knelt, grabbed his captive's clothing, and used his knife to cut a long swatch of fabric. "We can't leave a blood trail. Once we're safe, I'll wrap this properly." He bandaged his friend's arm and boosted him onto his pony. "Let's go."

He tugged on his captive's lead but she was doubled over, vomiting.

WITH FLUID HASTE her captor jerked her to a sheltered spot high on the slope. Susanna gulped air, getting her breath after the climb. Another Indian was here, darker than the first, with curly hair like the Bashams' slave, Joe. The two men spoke in a strange language.

In the back of her mind, Susanna knew she needed to learn their tongue. For now, she let the cadences flow over her, her mind numb.

She needed to focus on their location and direction. Maybe find a way to escape. The sooner, the better.

Two horses stood tied to a tree, heads up and ears alert. The larger animal had a wide blaze splashed down its face.

Whiskey? She'd have to get a better look, but no, that blaze was characteristic. Colonel Patton's horse. Which meant this man—her captor—was Patton's killer. She shivered. The Indian hadn't harmed her yet, perhaps because she was female, but she determined to be very careful.

A third Indian burst through the trees with blood running down his arm. In one hand he carried a sword, and on his belt a scrap of hide dangled, oozing blood.

Susanna stared at that scrap of hide, fear niggling at her. It wasn't hide, it was a scalp. The only man with hair like that was Arch May.

She turned away and emptied her stomach onto the leaf litter.

OAK LEAVES, still moist with morning, struck Susanna's face. It was impossible to dodge all the low-hanging branches mounted on the tall mare. Her captor led the animal purposefully through the woods high on the slope of the mountain, as if following a trail. Perhaps he was. But the trees flanked them like drilling militiamen, and thickets of rhododendron and gooseberry nudged at the horse's legs, hiding any obvious track.

The others followed behind. Another man had joined the group at some point, laden with spoil. A rolled buffalo skin lay in front of her; she wasn't sure, but it might be her parents' bed rug.

Where were her parents? Where was Auntie Agnes? If Arch May was dead …

Abba, Father.

She couldn't think, couldn't really pray. She thrust her fingers through the soft fur in front of her, trying to move her hands without chafing her wrists against the rope. How she was going to attend to her bodily needs she had no clue.

Abba. She felt sure she'd done the right thing. Dodging in front of the house, luring the Indian toward the spring and away from the others. She couldn't bear to search the Indians' hips for more scalps.

But then, the raid had been short. At least, she thought so. Ten minutes? Fifteen? Time had seemed to lose all meaning. She was the only captive; that much was certain.

They were traveling south. Unless she was totally befuddled, they'd come to Rockfish Gap soon.

Would Da be able to follow her? He was a good tracker, and a better shot, but the thought chilled her. If he followed her, he'd be in danger.

32

I saw we was entirely at their mercy. They could kill us any moment they chose.

—*A History of Jonathan Alder*

Andrew Lewis galloped up to the kailyard fence, his face tight. "Injuns," he barked. "Up at Russell's Ridge."

James gripped his hoe. "How many?" Was it another Woodstock?

"I don't know. One dead, one captured. There's a gathering at the Russells' place. To track the savages."

"Who?"

"Arch May is dead, Russell's daughter captured."

James dropped the tool. "Susanna?"

Lewis nodded. "Get your things and let's be off."

He dashed for the cabin, gathered his satchel, powder horn, and rifle, and made for the barn. By the time he saddled Libby his father was there.

"We'll pray for ye."

Ma stood straight and quiet in the doorway of the cabin.

"Come home to your ma," Da said.

"Aye."

Lewis had gone on ahead, which was just as well; the mule was no match for the militiaman's hunter. James kicked her in the ribs, desperate for speed, but the best Libby could do was an enthused, jerky canter.

The miles crept by with agonizing slowness. It was ten miles to the Russells' homestead. Now nine.

Horrible images swept through his mind. Poor little Jacob Fisher. They'd burnt him to death. Other raids up north generally resulted in the death of any captive too troublesome to cart home.

Would Susanna be troublesome? She certainly had her own mind. She was a bonny lass—what did Indians do to women? He didn't want to know.

James kicked the mule again, urging her to speed. At least the beast wouldn't kill herself through exertion, as horses sometimes did.

He thought of Arch May then, leaving behind a widow, and his stomach soured. No doubt they'd be tracking the Indians soon. He hated the Shawnee in that moment. How dare they kill and steal? Cowards, too—sneaking in and refusing to fight like men.

Gusts of wind swirled about him, eddying up dust in the road. Grit flew into his face.

He grimaced. How could he even think to preach to these savages?

Libby switched her lead and stumbled. He grabbed at her mane and held on while she recovered her footing. In seconds the faithful animal was loping south again.

He was halfway there. James felt for his powder horn, snugged against his waist. Next to it was his satchel, worn along the edges, packed with shot. He thrust his hand inside, and his fingers met a hard edge.

That book. How could God expect him to preach after this?

~

JOHN RUSSELL'S face was pale but rigid as granite. "John Craig's with Mrs. May and my wife. I'll need a few men to stay back and guard the place."

James sat in a chair with his leg thrust forward, aching from the ride. He ran his fingers down the stock of the rifle across his lap, getting reacquainted with the cool hard maple. They'd be tracking the Indians; the only question was who would go, and where. Had they come from across the valley? Or up the slope?

A rustle at the door was followed by a woman, pushing John Russell aside. Agnes May stood before them, her eyes red-rimmed. "They came from the woods above our cornfield. The mountain." She pointed, then swallowed, elbows akimbo. "I was in the kailyard. Arch came bellowing from the cornfield. He ran toward the cabin, calling to me. Behind him two savages—one had a bow and arrow, and he aimed at me. But Daisy barked at him, came right up at him. Dog saved my life."

The McKees' dog, most likely.

"Arch grabbed his sword, and I ran for the cabin, thinking to use the musket."

She stopped and seemed to shrink into herself. "But it took forever to prime … there was powder everywhere." She sighed then, a great sigh of grief that reached into James's innards. "By the time I could fire, Arch was on the ground, the Injun over him. I'm afraid I didna aim so well."

The men around the kitchen were silent and grim. Even Susanna's grandfather had brought his musket. But some would have to remain.

Finally Ian MacLeod sighed. "Ye'll need someone to catch the sheep. I'll stay."

"I can get a few men from Staunton." Andrew Lewis's face was pinched.

"No, if they catch wind of our pursuit, they'll …" Russell broke off, and there was silence in the room for a few moments, as everyone considered the awful possibilities. "I just need one man."

There was no question of the eldest Russell going, but Roy Russell argued for a while before conceding.

John Russell looked at James. "Ye'll come with me, lad."

~

THE WIND SLAMMED against Susanna and rustled her torn skirt as her captor led Whiskey through the last screen of trees and into the gap. The weather was changing. Strands of loose hair flew in front of her face. She glanced about and saw no travelers; the Indians had scanned the area before edging down the slope, but still she hoped.

Over her right shoulder dark clouds loomed. A single fat raindrop splashed against her cheek, but the morning sun still shone warm on her face, illuminating the rocky outcrops only partially covered by grass and trees. Rockfish Gap was like a great saddle, a gentle dip in the Blue Ridge, but the gentleness was deceptive, for there were treacherous places, especially traveling the direction they were going. But the mare was sure-footed.

Behind her the injured Indian rode his pony, the only other man mounted. The others trailed behind.

With one more glance around her, Susanna surrendered to the shade of the oaks on the other side. How could she escape? There was a knife in her pocket—her eating knife, sheathed in leather. In the other pocket nestled the miniature. She'd put it in her pocket two days ago, thinking to give it to Jamie.

Maybe … If she could drop it somewhere, it would help to mark her trail.

But how to get her bound hands into her pockets she didn't know.

~

THE MANURE WAS STILL WARM. "Here—it's likely theirs." John Russell's gaze shifted to the undergrowth around them.

James looked about, as if Indians would spring out of the foliage at any moment. They were high on the shoulder of the Blue Ridge, and he was still getting his breath.

"Verra simple now. Be sharp, and cast about. We'll soon see which direction they took," Russell said. "With Indians on foot it's harder. Horses will create more of a trail to follow."

A twig hung strangely, snapped at eye level. "Here," James said.

Russell grunted his approval. They turned south.

Only one scalp. Only one scalp. Susanna tried to persuade herself Auntie Agnes and the others were alive. After all, the Indians hadn't even taken time to fire the homes. There had been no smoke—she would have noticed that, wouldn't she?

The scene replayed itself in her mind over and over as the Indians pushed along the invisible forest track. The male shout. Arch's bellow? She could imagine Arch May bellowing as he swung the heavy claymore. Clearly, he'd nicked one Indian. And warned the rest of them. Her heart squeezed. *Thank you, Arch May.*

Raindrops fell with an irregular tempo, and gusts of wind set branches waving over her head. Storm clouds darkened the sky as her captor led them down the slope. They would cross the valley here. Would her father be able to track them? Susanna took a deep breath, her legs stiff from hours of riding. A strand of hair got in her mouth.

She had an idea.

The Indians came to a fat stream crossing their path. The leader tugged at Whiskey's bridle and led the horse into the water, then turned downstream, but slowly, knowing perhaps, as Susanna did, that many of these streams were full of pebbles that could easily get lodged in a hoof or bruise the sole of the foot.

Her captor did not stop until they were at least a quarter mile downstream. Then he led them up the bank to a shady place thick with willows and beech trees. They camped, and the leader reached for her. Susanna was grateful to dismount. He led Whiskey to water, and she followed, her own lead wrapped around the man's forearm. The knot at her waist was firm; she'd never escape without a knife. Unless ... if her captor were careless when they slept, then perhaps ...

Rain pelted them despite the canopy of the tree limbs. She knelt at the edge of the stream and drank gratefully. Her captor needed a name. Bird Man, she decided, glancing at him surreptitiously, for the feathers in his hair. Dark Indian was easy to name; the injured one wore a necklace of sorts, so she called him Fancy Man; and the other had plucked out most of his hair, leaving only a patch at the crown, long and braided. Bald Man.

Bird Man prodded her from behind and turned her shoulders to face Fancy Man. Some of his gibberish followed, then the word, "Go." He slapped his thigh in seeming frustration and spoke to Dark Indian.

"Help." The curly-headed man seemed to be translating as he pointed to Fancy Man. "Help."

Susanna unwrapped the man's bandage. She had no medicine. What did they expect her to do? A curl of hatred rose in her throat. This man had killed Arch May. But she pushed the thought aside as she examined the wound. Without the pressure of the bandage, the edges of the cut gaped and oozed blood. It had to be painful.

Pain. There were willow trees all around them. She could at least do something for that.

RED HAWK FINGERED the bark of the cottonwood and tried to see beyond the thick screen of foliage to the grassy expanse beyond. Falling Leaf had scouted the area and said there was no one about; certainly the storm would hinder trackers, so Red Hawk didn't fear discovery. A bolt of lightning threw harsh illumination over the middle distance, and he could see that nothing stirred. They'd wait until the rain slackened to cross the Great Valley.

Rumbling thunder followed the flash, and a whinny met his ears. His mare was not high-strung but definitely out of sorts in the storm. The rope around his forearm tightened, and he pivoted to see the woman at the horse's head.

She was crooning to the animal, stroking its face and neck. The horse settled and thrust its nose into her chest. The woman was a good prize, Red Hawk decided. The bark Straight Arrow chewed on was familiar, but Red Hawk had forgotten that remedy for pain. Then she'd spotted a sassafras tree nearby, and packed the wound with the leaves before bandaging it. She kept her gaze averted, probably from fear, but she'd been firm and brusque in her motions when requesting help with the doctoring. He now carried extra sassafras leaves in his pouch at her insistence.

The mare lowered its head to snatch at a bit of grass, and Red Hawk made a decision. Straight Arrow would be walking soon; both his pony and the mare could carry spoil. Falling Leaf had been murmuring about raiding another place, and Red Hawk had no doubt the others felt the same. Still, it would have to be a lone cabin, perhaps after dawn, when the man of the house went to the fields for the day. Their numbers were too few for anything else.

The dim afternoon faded into night, and Red Hawk guided the woman away from the mud. He was exhausted, and the others must be tired too. They'd rest until the rain eased up, then cross the valley in the dark. Once the woman lay curled on the ground, he tied the other end of the rope around her middle to his own waist. In her place, he'd try to escape before they left the valley. He had no doubt she would try if she could.

He lay down. An hour later, a sudden tug and he knew she'd discovered the precaution. Then a gasping sob.

Yes, he'd been right.

~

"LOOK, LAD." John Russell stared, transfixed.

James kneed the mule closer. The morning mist had coalesced into glistening drops on a spider's web, strung between some branches. No, not a web—several strands of hair. "Susanna," he breathed.

"Aye." The man's voice cracked. "She's well."

"And thinking."

The storm had been both a blessing and a curse, the men agreed. It had hindered them, slowed them down, and obliterated the marks of the Indians' passage, but it had undoubtedly hindered the Indians too, and now, with the ground muddy, they'd have a better chance of tracking them.

Below them lay the valley. They continued downslope and came to a stream. Crossing it, they lost all sign of the horses.

Russell reined in Percy, and James drew alongside.

"They slipped us by going upstream or downstream, I canna tell which." A line formed between Russell's brows. "But I ken where they're headed, aye?" He pointed to the western ridge. A cleft dipped directly opposite them. "They need to cross the mountains and that's where they will go, most likely."

They urged the animals into a trot. James gripped the saddle with his thighs, protecting his weak leg. There was no way he could ride for long using stirrups. He wasn't certain why Susanna's father had chosen him to accompany him, except out of courtesy—he was nearly courting her, after all. No, there was no "nearly" about it. He *was* courting her, even if she didn't realize it yet.

They rode for an hour, sometimes separating to cast about for sign.

"Ho, Paxton!"

James reined his mule closer. Between two clumps of tall grass, an unshod hoof print, pressed deep in the drying mud. Horses had come this way.

They continued, stopping once to rest and let their animals drink.

Late in the afternoon, James spotted a thread of smoke. A cabin. Russell jerked his chin and they altered course.

A fine bay stood outside. Visitors, perhaps.

"That's Robert Houston's animal. He lives nearby." Russell knew horseflesh. "Ho, the house!" The strain in his voice revealed the man's worry.

James dreaded what they would find.

33

It is said that in some countries trees will grow, but will bear no fruit because there is no winter there.

—John Bunyan (1628-1688)

Susanna woke in the darkness to the soft snore of an Indian. The storm had ceased, but water continued to fall from the branches above, plump drops that pattered on the leaf litter below.

She'd left hair in several places, but doubted it would be found. The land was so vast, the valley so wide. The horses would leave a trail, though. Surely her father could find that.

Jamie. Would he come too?

If only she could get to her knife. Her pockets were tied underneath her skirt in such a way that the straps could be moved. Perhaps when she was relieving herself she could shift the pocket with the knife to the front and get a hand into it with her hand bound as it was.

Arch May was dead. Auntie Agnes had finally finished the new plaid, bright with cochineal red. Woven by Thomas Kerr on his ancient loom, the long yards of wool would never be worn as a kilt. Would it serve as his shroud?

Tears seeped behind her lids, but in her exhaustion she dozed. When she opened her eyes, she was unsure of how long she'd been sleeping. Voices murmured, and she listened. There was a strange lilt to some of the words. A tonal quality.

"Kweewa." She'd heard that word before. She decided to memorize the words and try to sort out their meanings.

The rope on her midsection tightened, and she scrambled to her feet.

It was still dark, but the clouds had dispersed, revealing winking stars above. The Indians loped west for the rest of the night, the landscape eerie under a silent moon; occasionally Whiskey shifted into a trot to keep pace with Bird Man. Susanna worried she'd catch a foot in a hole, but reminded herself that horses could see better in the dark than people. When daybreak threatened, they hid in a grove of cottonwoods near a stream. They had to be on the western edge of the valley by now.

A lone bird chirped as the men conferred quietly, and in moments they slipped away, leaving Susanna alone with Fancy Man. The rope was now wrapped around the injured man's forearm.

She studied him. Despite his injury, he was alert, and the gray light revealed a muscular torso. With her hands bound, there was no hope of getting away from him. Instead, she took several steps toward a thicket and tried to communicate her need to relieve herself.

He conceded and moved in that direction. She wouldn't have total privacy, but perhaps enough to move the pocket about. Maybe even grasp the knife.

After several minutes Fancy Man became impatient. Susanna rearranged her skirt. The pocket had slipped forward, and she'd adjusted the skirt as well, so the slit lay partway to the front. Maybe soon—

The others burst into the grove, and Bird Man grabbed her about the waist. She found herself on Whiskey, and several moments later, a screaming tangle of arms and legs was placed in front of her. Dark Indian stood on one side of the mare. He caught her gaze and placed a finger on his lips, telling her to quiet the child.

She wrapped her arms about the little warm body as Whiskey lurched forward. A boy, she realized, perhaps six or seven years old, with brown hair and wild blue eyes.

"Hush, now." She babbled nonsense to him as they moved off, Bird Man jogging at the horse's bridle, his dark braid dancing against the bronzed back. Ominously, a musket now lay cradled in his arms, apparently stolen from the boy's family. Were the owners now dead?

The child's screams turned to crying. She felt his ribcage expand and contract as he sobbed. He was thin.

An argument began behind her.

She realized suddenly the boy would become a liability if he gave away their position to trackers. He'd be killed. "My name is Susanna. What's yours?"

Slowly, the sobbing quieted as the child tired. He said his name was Sammy. She murmured to him about the horse, the horse's mother, and what horses ate, and while she rambled on, she glanced back several times. Fancy Man now led his pony instead of riding, the bearskin and several other items tied to the animal's back.

She looked for scalps but didn't see any. She thought back to the gray dawn. A very quick raid, only long enough for her to use the necessary.

She could at least hope no one had been killed.

JAMES DISMOUNTED but did not approach too closely, lest he confuse the sign. Russell studied the ground intently, his face pale and strained. Had the man been sleeping? He knew his own nights had been restless.

"Look, lad. See the hoof prints?"

James stepped nearer. Curved marks lay scattered over the streambank. One curve crossed over another. "Two horses?"

"I dinna think so. The overlapping prints are identical, both front feet." Russell squatted. "I canna find a single print, no' even a bent blade of grass, beyond this point. They've backtracked. Led the horse here, then walked him back, to trick us into thinking they'd left the streambed here."

James scanned their surroundings. They'd been traveling north along this narrow valley, having tracked the raiding Indians to this streambed.

North. Were these Indians from the Shawnee villages to the northwest? It seemed likely. His heart sank at the thought. The distance was great. And even if they could track them all that way, how would they get the captives back? The raiding band had taken another captive at the Wilkins' place; thankfully, the man of the house had taken his older sons to the fields, leaving only the youngest with his ma, who'd mercifully been spared.

"'Twas my brother come to visit. He took the musket and a keg of powder. He looked verra strange, he did. Why did he put feathers in his hair? And where is my Sammy? Have ye seen him?"

Houston's wife had been summoned to comfort Mrs. Wilkins, but she looked confounded by the strange delirium possessing the woman.

John Russell stood and James shook away his musings.

"I wonder if they've gone south," Russell said, gazing that direction.

"Aye, ye must be right."

They turned their animals and journeyed south, and in less than an hour spotted a familiar hoofprint. They continued, twice finding fresh manure. The second time Russell thrust a finger into the moist mass but found it cool.

The Shawnee lived west of these ridges. At some point they would turn west again, but where?

The sun sank below the western ridge, and Russell signaled a halt. They watered the animals and made camp below the stone of an outcrop.

"Mr. Russell, what happens if we find them?"

Russell leaned against the stone. "We both have Deckert rifles, aye? If we get close enough, we can kill two at once."

It seemed unlikely, and dangerous. Dangerous for the captives. "We're half a day behind them."

"Aye." The man's shoulders slumped and he looked old, his face drawn. "If we can establish the direction, there's hope that ..." He swallowed. "We can offer ransom."

"But how?"

"Maybe through George Morgan."

"I haven't seen the trader in a long time."

"Aye, I ken that."

After a few bites of journeycake, they bedded down.

Insects droned in the lonely darkness. James was still awake when the sounds died and a fat waning gibbous moon rose over the ridge, casting eerie shadows.

A strange noise startled him. He reached for his weapon, always near at hand.

A sob followed. Then an anguished, muffled groan.

John Russell was grieving for his daughter.

James wished he could pray for the man, and for Susanna. But right now his heart was hard as the stone behind them.

SUSANNA SAGGED against the stony outcrop at her back. The Indians had backtracked, finally heading south. The sun had disappeared, and they'd made a fireless camp in the dim light of dusk. The child sniffed at her side.

"Here now, Sammy." She attempted to wipe his snotty face with the lad's shirt. "Lie there and get some rest."

Bird Man had tied her lead to a tree. Once they slept she could cut it and be off. But what about the child? She could not leave him behind. Her heart sank.

The low murmur of the Indians' voices turned harsher. Bald Man prodded Fancy Man with a finger; she could not see Bird Man's face, but his stance was disapproving. Bald Man swung the jug he'd been carrying, his arms and legs pinwheeling.

Whiskey.

Bald Man moved toward her, swaying slightly. He lifted the jug to his lips, and it seemed to be empty, so he cast it aside. His gaze locked on her, and his eyes narrowed. Using her lead rope, he tugged her painfully to her feet.

Liquor fumes assaulted her. He grabbed her bound hands, and Susanna twisted to one side. If the man could push her hands over her head she'd be pinned, and she had no faith the others would care.

He pressed closer and her shoulder slammed against the rock. She cried out, a ragged sob of despair. She could only delay the inevitable.

Wandering hands explored her waist and hips. *Oh no.*

The Indian chortled and said something triumphant. He held up her knife and leaned close to her face.

A barking command sounded near her ear, and Bald Man's grip loosened. It was Bird Man, his gray silhouette tall and tense, beside her.

Holding up her knife, Bald Man replied, but from the sound of the conversation, Susanna knew he'd lost the argument. The drunken man left, snorting protests.

She sank down to the ground and folded her legs tightly in front of her. Bird Man seemed to study her a moment, then he prepared a sleeping place only an arm's reach away.

"Susanna?" The child's thin voice sounded troubled.

"Hush now. Hear the crickets?"

"We catch them for … for … fishing."

"Listen to the crickets."

Sammy quieted, and after a few minutes his breathing became regular. Susanna took a deep breath. The dark night seemed like an iron cage about her.

Lord? But the prayer died on her lips.

TWO DAYS LATER, Susanna opened her eyes to bright sunlight. She wondered at it. Previously the men had shaken her awake in the soft dark of predawn, eager to move. She sat up, her body aching from the hard ground, her mouth stale.

Below the broad rocky ledge where they'd camped wound a stream, edged with willow and cattail. They were deep in the mountains now. Probably past any hope of rescue.

Several of the Indians seemed to be missing. Yes, she couldn't see Dark Indian or Bald Man. She hoped they'd gone hunting. So far, they'd fed the captives sparingly, only handfuls of parched corn or some kind of jerky, and now Sammy whimpered from hunger.

"Chin up, young man." She'd give him her own breakfast, if it came. "Courage is the greatest of the manly virtues."

"Virtues?" He peeped weakly.

"Your ma tells you to be good, yes?"

His face brightened. "She whips me if I ain't."

"Well, God tells us not to murmur, not to complain. It takes manly courage to be patient when things are hard and your stomach is empty." She felt like a hypocrite instructing him when her own heart was dark and despondent. But maybe hearing truth out loud would help her, too.

Maybe. Susanna's wrists were red and chafed beneath the leather. They were many miles from the valley. Escape was unlikely now, and surely Bird Man knew that. Perhaps she could ask him to release her from the bonds.

She stood, wondering how to get his attention. Her lead rope was tied to a spindly shrub, and she could not move far. But over the past few days, she'd memorized the sound of their names.

"MASK-NIN-YE."

He whirled, the sound sending a thrill through his limbs. The captive was calling him.

"You know my name?" Red Hawk approached the woman, examining her closely. How could she know Shawnee? She was dirty, her beautiful hair mussed and tangled. She didn't respond, but only looked at him, her expression changing to one of astonishment.

SUSANNA BLINKED in the strong sunlight. Bird Man approached her, his chest broad and strong in the morning sun. Feathers fluttered from his hair. His eyes—no, it couldn't be.

His eyes were blue.

34

The Great Spirit made all things. He gave the white people a home beyond the great waters. He supplied these grounds with game, and gave them to his red children; and he gave them strength and courage to defend them.

—Tecumseh (1768-1813)

Red Hawk decided he'd frightened the woman somehow. "Red Hawk," he said gently, striking his chest with his fist. Then he pointed to her.

"Susanna." She said it slowly, which helped.

"Su-anna."

She seemed to collect herself then, and thrust out her hands. She made a request in her language. It was obvious what she wanted.

He warned her not to attempt to escape, hoping she understood his harsh tone. Of course she didn't understand Shawnee. "No go." It was all the white man's tongue he could summon.

She nodded and remained still while he sliced through the thongs with his knife.

Buffalo Robe hailed him from behind. “Two geese!”

Red Hawk turned, tension easing from him. They’d managed to get well away from the valley, and now they had food. “Excellent news.”

“Buffalo Robe.” Su-anna said, motioning frantically. What did it mean, that she knew their names? She was related somehow to the wise woman described by his father; did she have special medicine of her own?

His friend tossed down the birds and joined them, face inquisitive.

“Buffalo Robe, Red Hawk—” At this point she babbled on in her own tongue, and he could not follow.

“What’s she saying?”

“Something about your eyes.”

Su-anna pointed at the sky, then pointed at Red Hawk’s face.

“She says your eyes are like the sky. I think she means they are blue.”

Red Hawk frowned. “Blue eyes? That makes no sense.”

“This child has blue eyes. Just like you.”

What? How could he have blue eyes? He’d studied his reflection in a pool once, the ripples causing his black hair to dance. True, his eyes were not as dark as Buffalo Robe’s. “Laughing Wolf’s mother has light eyes.”

“Yes, they are light, but they are not blue.”

There were several captives in Big Turtle’s village with blue eyes, but they were white. He tried to remember everything Red Pipe had told him. Yes, he’d been captured, but he’d always assumed he was Indian. His hair was dark, his skin was not pale. “I am Shawnee.”

“Of course you are. So am I.” Buffalo Robe searched his face.

Red Hawk turned, curling his fingers into fists. His friend’s strange curly hair betrayed his mixed blood. Was it so important?

Was he a white man? He shuddered to think of it.

Worse, everyone who looked at him knew. They’d always known.

Susanna rubbed her wrists and watched the men. Bird Man was troubled. Didn't he know he had blue eyes?

Obviously not. The shock of her discovery, made after days of travel staring at his brown back and black braid, still coursed through her. He acted like an Indian. Was accepted as an Indian—he was their leader, in fact. Could he be as shocked as she?

"Siwinewi," Bird Man said. The word sounded like "Shawnee." He was affirming himself to be Shawnee. She mouthed the word, storing it away.

How had this state of affairs come to pass? She gazed at little Sammy, who stared in awe at the Indians. He'd lost much of his fear. Would they raise him to be an Indian? Would he forget his parents?

Maybe not, but what if he were younger? Five, perhaps?

She wondered how old Bird Man had been when taken. Four? Five? He'd even forgotten his language.

Would she and Sammy be assimilated in the same way? She had to think it through. If she cooperated, perhaps she'd find a way to escape when the time was right and they relaxed their guard.

She'd learn their language. But she would not become one of them.

The next morning Susanna begged a bath in the stream from Fancy Man, who was minding her while Bird Man hunted. Behind a light screen of willow branches she submerged herself, feeling cheered by the cool water. Wishing for soap, she dunked her head and kneaded through some of the tangles with her fingers. With her hands free she was able to access her pockets. She plucked out the miniature; this place was as good as any to leave it. She dropped it on the bank, fearing it would be swallowed up by the vast wilderness, a pointless token of her passage.

While clambering up the rocky slope behind the Indian, she heard an exclamation. She soon discovered Red Hawk had brought down a yearling buck; they'd have plenty of food.

They put her to work preparing the meat, and even Sammy helped by gathering wood. Soon a smoky fire was built. Venison wasn't Susanna's favorite under normal circumstances, but her mouth salivated as her stomach awakened to the thought of a decent meal.

At midday they settled near the fire to eat.

"Sammy, let's give thanks for the food."

They bowed their heads and Susanna led them in prayer. "Thank you Lord, for this provision. Please remember us as you remembered the Israelites in Egypt and delivered them from their oppressors."

"Amen," Sammy piped.

Susanna raised her head to see Red Hawk staring at her, his eyes a shockingly ordinary hue, the man himself a foreigner. What was he thinking?

His gaze shifted over her shoulder.

RED HAWK'S mind had struggled as he hunted, searching his fragmented memories for any clue to his early history. But a mother's murmurs and a flickering fire was all he could summon. He'd gone through the motions of tracking by rote, finding a soft print in the streambank and pursuing it, the faint breeze blowing away his scent.

He consigned the young buck's spirit to the skies, grateful for the kill. They'd make it the rest of the way and perhaps even have leftover for the family of Cat's Eye. He dreaded that conversation. But everyone took his own risks; they all knew that.

Back at camp the work went quickly. Even the young boy helped. Buffalo Robe's captive would be useful to his mother, She-Who-Sings.

Each man grabbed a chunk of the roasting meat when it suited him; Red Hawk sliced his own into several pieces and handed portions to the captives. He eyed Su-anna as she bent her head and spoke to the spirits.

What was her spirit? The gentle deer? The courageous bear?

But no, she was white, and would pray to the white man's god. His heart quickened. Did her god hear her?

Something moved in the middle distance. Brown skin flickered behind the foliage. Red Hawk stood and signaled the others. The village was less than two days' away—who was it?

Laughing Wolf. The man's broad cheekbones and narrow eyes irked him. An unpleasant face. An unpleasant man.

"I smelled the smoke of your fire." Laughing Wolf scanned the scene, his eyes lingering on the captives. Several companions came up beside him. They must have left their horses at the stream.

Red Hawk was carefully formal. "You are welcome to our fire."

"I thank you for your hospitality."

The men sat and availed themselves of the venison. Red Hawk hoped they didn't stay long. He wished to get started soon.

"A successful raid?"

Laughing Wolf's tone angered him. He was not a child to be trained in the manly arts. "Good enough, considering our small numbers."

Buffalo Robe's shoulders were tense. Straight Arrow's gaze flicked to Red Hawk's. His friends felt the same.

Laughing Wolf toyed with his knife as he studied the fire. "Make a sacrifice to the sun yet?"

SUSANNA SCOOTED against the rocky face of the cliff behind them, seeking to make herself invisible as the new Indians settled around the fire. Something was wrong, and more than ever she wished she understood their language. So far, she could only grasp a word here and there. Sammy was frightened, and she hummed to him. "Be still, now."

Throughout the long journey she'd studied her captors, seeking to understand them through body language even if she couldn't understand Shawnee. They were stoic, hard to read, but after a time she could see tension in their shoulders or mirth in a half-quirked eyebrow.

They were tense now, all of them. The leader of the new Indians spoke to Bird Man in a challenging way. And Bird Man didn't like it.

Scowling Man asked a question, a skinning knife in his hand. Then his gaze slid to her.

She trembled.

~

"I WOULD NOT TAKE it upon myself to offer to the sun." A shaman might do that, although Red Hawk had never heard of Grayfeather doing so. All gave homage to the sun and moon, but only the Muskogee were known to offer sacrifice. But then, Laughing Wolf's mother was Muskogee.

"The white men come from across the eastern waters," Laughing Wolf argued. "The land of the sun. Clearly the sun is angry and must be propitiated."

Surely the Creator was more deserving of sacrifice, but Red Hawk didn't feel confident to argue theology. He did know Shawnee customs. "Each man must walk his own path."

"Is the woman brave?" Laughing Wolf examined the blade of his knife.

Red Hawk stood. "She is my captive, and I will decide." This wasn't just about the captive. It would be expected for Laughing Wolf to succeed his father as war chief. He wanted the position of shaman too.

Laughing Wolf studied the woman. A sly smile touched his mouth. "Yes, I understand now. She will be a good bride for you."

Red Hawk's jaw clenched. Before he'd discovered his white blood, he wouldn't have understood the insinuation. He'd have taken it as mere rivalry for Running Deer's attentions.

Laughing Wolf rose fluidly to his feet and nodded to his men. Then they were gone.

~

Vitality drained from her while listening to the men's conversation. Susanna didn't need to understand Shawnee to gather the gist—Scowling Man's dark glances and sharp knife communicated his intentions more clearly than words.

And there was more. Scowling Man and Bird Man were enemies. Were they of different villages? Or was it the natural clash of leaders?

In the valley, James Patton's roguish ways had frequently run up against John Lewis's more sensible leadership. Her own father was influential around Russell's Ridge. The Stuarts, Robinsons, Kerrs, and now the Smokes all looked to him. Bird Man possessed the same quiet charisma, wrapped in savage clothing.

Bird Man's gaze followed the departing Scowling Man. He'd defended her, though for what purpose she was unclear. She was his captive.

But why did they take captives? Killing her would have been easier. The child they'd raise as an Indian hunter and warrior. But her?

A niggling suspicion grew. Did he want her as a bride? Or worse, as some sort of concubine?

Stomach tense, she turned this over in her mind as they packed the horses for departure.

As she mounted Whiskey, Jamie's face came to her mind, and she realized she loved him.

She had to get away. She would not marry a Shawnee.

The knotty wood of the pew pressed through James's breeches and into his flesh. This Sabbath was interminable.

He sat on the front row of the Tinkling Spring meetinghouse, near the very spot where Colonel Patton used to sit. On the other end of the bench sat Mrs. Preston, now bereft of both husband and brother. William was absent, probably off on some militia duty.

Behind him, in the second row, the Russell clan arranged themselves, shy now of two members. Sitting next to his swollen wife, John

Russell's eyes were clear but his face lined and lean. A vacant spot on the bench next to Russell shouted accusingly.

Mrs. Russell's situation had turned Russell from his purpose in the narrow mountain tracks. The man had proposed scouting ahead, with the purpose of sneaking into the Indians' camp as they slept.

"It's the only way," he said. "Slice open their throats."

James could see conscience warring with the love of his daughter in the man's blue eyes. Killing men as they slept was an act of villains or savages. Was it right to fight them by their own rules? But Abigail Russell's condition removed the temptation and they'd returned to the valley without Susanna.

"My fellow mortals! So I call ye, because mortality is the certain doom of us all." Mr. Craig's preaching was edged with taut emotion. "Now, I consider, it is more striking than usual, when calamity and death have made such inroads upon us."

France seemed ascendant in the ongoing war, and the minister alluded to this gloomy situation before focusing on the valley and their own torn hearts. "Our country has been ravaged, and bled in a thousand veins; our neighborhood has been turned into a graveyard, and some of us are the remains of families that have been thinned by death, and we are escaped, as brands plucked out of the burning."

Someone sobbed. Mrs. May?

Arch May, dead by the hand of a Shawnee. Susanna wasn't dead, was she? No, it couldn't be. But if she were alive, what then? Would some savage take her as his bride? He cringed. What a fate. He wanted to pray, but his heart was shriveled, like a cornfield after a drought.

His mind drifted as Mr. Craig launched his application. "Repent, reform, and turn to the Lord under these threatenings and chastisements… "

Remarkably, the minister finished in less than an hour. Then Mr. Craig turned his eyes on him.

"Mr. Paxton, will ye be so kind as to give us an exhortation?"

What? How could the minister be so hard as to ask that of him today?

In season, out of season … He couldn't pick and choose the times and places, could he? Then his gaze caught the empty spot in the Russells' pew. Anger coursed through him.

James stood, his worn Bible tucked in his hand. For a second he regarded the wooden minister's desk. Then he spun on his heel and walked out the door.

He just couldn't do it.

35

God indeed is remarkably frowning upon us every where; our enemies get above us very high, and we are brought down very low… What will become of us, God only knows.

—Jonathan Edwards, *Letter,* 1756

The village lay nestled in a lush bowl amid the rolling hills. They'd left the steeper ridges the day before, and the land beyond was gentle and well watered. To the left Susanna saw a river, and beyond lay fields thick with the deep green of ripe corn.

Grayish-brown shelters populated the area like mushrooms after a rain. As Susanna followed Bird Man into the outskirts, shouts of welcome met her ears. Naked brown children ran about.

Smells assailed her—smoke and cooking, a hint of manure, all overlaid with hints of human excrement. Strangely, much like Williamsburg.

Bird Man brought her to a rectangular hut almost as large as a cabin. Wisps of smoke curled from the top. Someone emerged, a woman with gray hair.

She was squat and wrinkled, like a plump currant. Keen black eyes glittered with intelligence. Susanna detected no welcome in her face, but something about her demanded respect either way.

"Good afternoon, ma'am." She curtseyed. "Susanna is my name," she added in Shawnee. At least, that's what she thought she said.

The woman's cheeks rounded in a smile.

Bird Man produced a knife, and in the space of a breath, she was free of the rope about her middle. He spoke to the old woman.

Anger rose in Susanna's heart. She was glad to be free of the rope, but she was still a captive in an alien place, amidst an alien people.

Help, Lord. She had to keep her head, use her sense. She needed Bird Man's favor, and she needed to know the language.

Bird Man handed the old woman the ginseng root Susanna had harvested, and something changed in the woman's expression. More discussion, but this time, the woman's eyes were on her.

Another woman approached, perhaps middle-aged, with a stony face. More conversation. Then the stony-faced woman selected several large gourds and thrust them into Susanna's arms. She pointed to a line of cattails at the edge of the river and spoke a command.

Were these for water? Was that her role, to fetch and carry? She turned to Bird Man for confirmation.

A blow from behind brought her to her knees.

RED HAWK WANTED to care for his animal, but first, the woman Susanna needed to be given to Grandmother. The elders would decide the rest. The day of the trial by gauntlet and adoption would be soon, probably tomorrow. There was no need to delay.

Grandmother's eyes lit up at the ginseng and his explanation.

"I believe the Creator led me to that place and gave me this woman," he said.

Dark Water joined them. She didn't seem pleased, but he wasn't sure why, as the captive would perform the heavier labor. She reached for the water jugs and thrust them into Su-anna's arms. Before he knew it, she was on her knees.

"What is this?" Heat suffused him. "What are you doing?"

"She needs to obey," Dark Water said.

"Did she understand your command?"

His aunt didn't back down. "It was plain enough."

"If she needs beating, I will do it." Had he crossed a line? Usually women were given full rein in their households. He wasn't sure about the treatment of slaves. "I may decide to take her as a secondary wife." Laughing Wolf's comment had given him an idea. If the woman needed protection, he could give it to her that way. But he never imagined she'd need protection from his aunt.

Dark Water's jaw worked and she stared at him for several long moments. "She is the enemy. She will knife you in your sleep."

"She faces the gauntlet soon. She will be adopted and then she will prove herself. And if I should take her, it is my business."

He looked at Grandmother. Her face was placid, her gaze lowered. But a tiny hint of a smile tugged at one corner of her mouth.

WOMEN AND CHILDREN armed with sticks defined a path that ended where Dark Indian squatted, face impassive. A woman stripped Sammy's clothes from him.

Don't cry, Susanna urged silently, sensing they'd want the child to be brave.

The boy's face screwed up, but no sound emerged.

Good.

Several young boys about Sammy's age appeared, clad in nothing but loincloths. Each carried a stick. At the other end, Dark Indian raised his brows to get the lad's attention. Then the howling started, and the boys chased Sammy through the gauntlet.

Susanna shrank into herself from her seat on the ground. A cry tore from the lad's throat. Then he was safe in Dark Indian's arms. A few chuckles floated in the air. She sought to see Sammy more clearly. Was he injured?

But no, he was actually smiling. A single welt lay across one arm.

It was her turn.

Stony Face jerked her to her feet and tugged at her bodice. Another woman joined her, and soon she was in her chemise. Susanna untied her pockets and dropped them.

The chemise joined her stays on the ground. Tears welled in her eyes. Was Bird Man watching this? She was humiliated. She'd told Sammy to chin up, to be brave. Well, then. She was John Russell's daughter, and she would not show fear. Or crumple from the shame. Smirking, Stony Face joined the other women in the line. Susanna knew her testing would be real, not the easy trial they'd given the child.

Help me, Lord.

Then she remembered the Lord's shame and suffering. All for her. Inexplicably, His gift of grace seemed more real than ever before. Peace settled on her.

She looked up once to focus on the other end.

Bird Man stood there.

RED HAWK AVERTED his eyes at the sight of Su-anna's nakedness. Then he stiffened, face forward. He would not—could not—show any sympathy for the captive.

Her hair straggled long over her shoulders, and her face shuddered once with shame. Then her expression stilled. Her gaze met his, and her eyes widened in embarrassment before tightening in pain.

She'd been struck from behind to drive her forward. He added his calls to the cacophony, willing her to speed. The faster she ran, the fewer blows would connect. Dark Water swung, and Su-anna lurched to the side. Soon her feet were under her again and she charged forward, shielding her head with her arms.

Just before she reached him, She-Who-Sings belted her in the ribs with a stout length of hickory, and the woman crumpled to her knees, groaning. She crawled, then regained her feet and managed to stumble past the last few women.

He covered her with an old Uchee robe of Grandmother's, then led her to Dark Water. The women would scrub her in the river to remove her white blood.

He hoped none of her bones were broken. Some of the women had taken a fierce joy in the assault. No wonder. They all hated the white invaders.

THE RIVER BATHED her with pain. Susanna was surrounded by women, how many she didn't know or care. They pushed at her, scrubbing her with river sand, stinging the uninjured places and tormenting her bruises. Fire shot down her left side, and her right arm she guarded, hoping against hope it wasn't broken.

A woman jerked her injured arm upward to scrub her side, and Susanna screamed. Hands shoved her down, down, until her head was underwater. She thrashed and pushed off with her feet, panicking.

She sucked in a lungful of air, and pain lanced her side. She looked toward the bank, needing to focus her mind on something. Beyond the reeds, two women stood, clutching something. Clothing, perhaps. The scene became surreal, a haze enveloping everything.

One woman on the bank was dark-headed, the other gray. Susanna felt herself observing the scene as if from a distance. Her body was pushed and prodded, then led through the reeds and out of the water. The two women reached for her, and she was clothed by the dark-haired one. It was Stony Face, she noted vaguely, who did not regard her injuries, but shoved her arms into a deerskin tunic.

A last whimper accompanied the pain, but the pain seemed far away.

Then it was gone.

~

SUSANNA OPENED her eyes to dimness and smoke and pain. She was lying in a wigwam; above her glowed the bright smoke hole. The fog in her mind slowly dissipated. How had she gotten here? The last thing she remembered was the river. She must have passed out.

She was lying on a fur pallet, covered by some sort of blanket. Flexing her limbs slightly, she tried to take account of her injuries. There was little she could do for broken ribs; they should knit on their own. A broken limb was another thing entirely—was her right arm broken, or merely bruised?

She used her left hand to probe for irregularities. Her right arm was horribly tender, but not obviously shattered. She flexed her right hand. So far, so good.

A voice startled her.

It was the old woman, sitting thoughtfully, her knees drawn up so that she blended gnome-like into her surroundings.

Susanna tried to rise, but pain coursed through her body, and she sagged back.

The woman babbled something and gestured, like an Indian version of Auntie Agnes caring for a sick member of the family.

Auntie Agnes. They'd killed her husband. And now, here she was, deep in Shawnee territory, out of the reach of rescue.

Despair fingered at her mind.

Out of the depths have I cried unto thee, O Lord.

Susanna focused on the light coming through the smoke hole. The darkness, the pain, were pulling at her.

God seemed far away. She shook herself mentally, remembering something Da had said about feelings. "Ye canna trust them. They come and go. But ye can hope in God, because Christ's work is finished, no matter the darkness of your heart."

But what about her sin? Yes, she was angry. She saw that now.

Did God love her even so?

Herein is love, not that we loved God, but that he loved us, and sent his Son as a propitiation for our sins.

That He loved us. The hard kernel of anger in her heart melted suddenly.

Thank you, Lord.

A soft rustle drew her attention. The old woman was preparing something. She brought Susanna a cup and thrust a bony arm under her head to help her drink. Bitterness assailed her mouth. Willow bark and something else she didn't recognize, mixed with honey or some other sweetener.

This woman was a healer. Susanna managed to finish the concoction and lay back and studied the roof above her. Dried herbs were tied to the poles bracing the structure. Some she knew, some she didn't.

She needed to communicate. "Susanna, I am called." With her good hand she pointed at the woman.

Smiling, the healer pointed at herself. *"Noke mis."*

For an hour Susanna asked questions, absorbing the vocabulary of the Shawnee.

It was something else to give thanks for. And something to do.

DARK WATER CROSSED her arms across her chest. "When will she be able to work?"

Red Hawk looked past her to the wigwam door, where Su-anna sat with Grandmother. "Tomorrow I'm to take her to gather herbs."

"I mean real work."

Many days had passed since the gauntlet, and still Grandmother protested that her charge was not strong.

Red Hawk lifted his eyebrows mockingly. "You nearly cripple her and wonder why she can't haul water. You can't have it both ways."

His aunt snorted. "She babies her."

"Su-anna is the daughter of a wise woman. Perfect to help Grandmother. We can't let the knowledge of the Shawnee die." Surely she knew the secret of the book. He wished he could communicate with her. How long would it take for her to learn his tongue?

"Why would a white woman help the Shawnee?"

Red Hawk took a deep breath. "You didn't hate me."

Dark Water's shoulders sagged. "That was different. You were so little." The brittleness left her tone.

"I didn't know I was white until very recently."

"Oh?" Her eyebrows shot up. "I don't remember speaking of it one way or the other."

"Red Pipe told me the story of my capture, but didn't mention that my parents were white. And I always thought mirrors were for women."

She chuckled.

"My heart is Shawnee. It may take many moons, but yes, this woman will become one of the people in truth."

He hoped so.

SUSANNA INHALED DEEPLY, steadily. It felt good to stretch her legs. She'd need to build up her strength to make it over the mountains. "Is there a stream nearby?"

Bird Man turned abruptly. "You speak Shawnee?"

"Grandmother taught me." After the first week she'd focused on verbs. The grammar was still a hopeless tangle, but she was making progress in making herself understood. Bird Man hadn't spoken to her in all this time; no wonder he was surprised. "I am still learning. I make many mistakes."

A wide grin made Bird Man look friendly. With his blue eyes, she almost thought him white. He *was* white. But he thought Shawnee.

Don't forget, he is your enemy. But what did the Scriptures say about that? To love your enemies? And yet, her father would have shot this man dead. It was confusing.

They'd climbed a knoll and now descended the other side. The foliage thickened as they approached the water. Susanna found several good specimens and placed them in her bag. Then she loosed her moccasins, left them on the streambank, and stepped into the water, enjoying the coolness and the roughness of the stones beneath her feet.

Bird Man joined her. "Do you know the secret of the book?"

Susanna turned. "Book?" Was he speaking English?

"Book." Red Hawk pantomimed turning pages. "There are marks on the leaves." The rest of his explanation was gibberish.

She frowned, trying to put the pieces together. "Words. In a book. Yes, there are words in books."

"Will you help me?"

Help him? Suddenly all the anger she'd tamped down for weeks loosed her tongue. "Why should I help you? You killed James Patton."

"Who?"

"The horse. You put me on a horse."

Bird Man's face shifted, comprehension dawning. "The horse was Silver Beard's."

Silver Beard. Of course the Indians wouldn't know the sheriff's name. But the man did have a hoary beard, much grayer than the hair on his head. "You killed Silver Beard."

"No. Laughing Wolf killed Silver Beard." Bird Man looked away. "Silver Beard killed my father."

What? Colonel Patton killed this man's father?

36

> Does he attempt to escape the savages, he knows in advance, that, if retaken, he will be roasted alive.
>
> —Marie LeRoy and Barbara Leininger, 1759

Susanna collapsed on the bank, stupefied. "Your father? Silver Beard killed your father?" Bird Man had been there. He must have been one of the raiders that day.

Bird Man sat on the stream's opposite bank. "Yes."

"But … but you are white."

"Red Pipe is the only father I remember. My true father."

Red Pipe. She understood that name. Bird Man's name started with the same sound. "What does your name mean?"

He took up a stick and brushed away the leaves from a patch of dirt on the bank. He traced a bird, some kind of raptor. An eagle? Red Eagle?

He tapped the tail. *"Mask-waa-wi."* Red. The color red.

A red-tailed hawk. She'd seen them in the valley.*"Mask-nin-ye.* I understand." She took a deep breath. She needed to know more of the language, and unlike French, there was no book to consult. "You don't remember your white parents at all?" At least, that's what she meant. She was surprised he didn't laugh at her terrible grammar.

His face stilled. "I believe I remember my capture. I was frightened. But most of the tale was told to me by Red Pipe. He said my white father died bravely."

That seemed to matter. She wondered who it was.

"He died in the very place I captured you."

She lurched to her feet. "What do you mean?" The only man who'd died on their property was Silas Sloan—could it be?

"I wanted to see the place."

"But you killed Arch May." The memory of his scalp tied to Fancy Man's loins inflamed her. "Why? Why couldn't you leave us alone?"

He blinked at her, his irritating blue gaze reminding her of Seth Robinson. "You are a woman and do not understand."

She clenched her fists and glanced at his feet. His stance on the slippery bank was vulnerable.

She drove her shoulder into his midsection. He slipped, and fell into the stream.

A moment later she was down and thrashing. She twisted and turned, but Red Hawk was everywhere, like a huge snake. A painful pressure immobilized her hands—he had both wrists in one large hand. She was pinned. On her back, she looked up at his face, fierce in the dappled shadows of the foliage. Steel flashed above her, his drawn knife a foot from her neck.

Fear flashed through her. He was not Seth Robinson.

Abruptly, he released her and sat back on his heels. "That was a foolish thing to do. Laughing Wolf would have enjoyed the opportunity to slit your throat."

~

His blood thrummed through his veins. The shame of his momentary vulnerability washed over Red Hawk. He took a deep breath. It was his fault—he'd lowered his guard. Instinctively he'd drawn his knife, but if she'd had a weapon he could be dead now.

Rivulets of water ran cold down his back. The strength of her grief and anger shocked him, though he wondered why he should be surprised. Who had Straight Arrow killed—a relative?

Red Hawk sighed. The woman had courage. She was going to try to run away, he was certain of it, and if she did, she would be killed. Slowly, over a fire. He replaced the knife. All he could do was keep an eye on her. She seemed to enjoy helping Grandmother. Perhaps by spring she'd become settled—but no, if she had a plan, she might wait until the first strawberries were ripe, when a traveler could live off the land, even if he had to eat sassafras and cattails.

Su-anna rose, one long muddy lock dangling over her shoulder. Her rage seemed to be gone, but he could not read her expression now.

He clenched his jaw. The silly wrestling match had seared something else into his mind. She wasn't just a white captive; she was a woman. If he didn't marry her, someone else would want to.

He turned away.

"What happened?" Grandmother asked.

Susanna quailed under the woman's keen gaze. "I ended up in the mud." It wasn't precisely the truth, but for some reason, she didn't want Red Hawk's behavior to be known. He hadn't hurt her, after all. And she had provoked him. They'd returned silently, with no more mention of his white father. Or the mysterious book.

"What did he do?"

Her lips parted. "I was angry."

"He said something to make you angry."

There was no escaping Grandmother. "Yes. And I pushed him into the stream."

The old woman's eyes crinkled, and her belly shook with restrained laughter. "I would like to have seen it. Red Hawk is a brave warrior. But he is young. Some men never do learn how to speak to a woman." She wiped her eyes. "Fetch some water for Dark Water. Then go to the river and wash."

"Yes, Grandmother." There were some things she liked about their ways, and bathing was one of them. In the valley most folks only bathed before the Sabbath. Once, she'd gone into McClure's and nearly gagged from the stench of the men inside.

Other things the Shawnee did perplexed her. The men lolled about, gossiping or smoking, while the women labored from dawn to dusk, working in the fields, tanning hides, and cooking. All the men did was hunt and fight, apparently.

Susanna took two trips to the river for water and returned for her bath. She found a place where willows and cattails screened her, then disrobed. Shawnee clothing was something else she liked; a tunic or short wrap skirt with leggings was much more practical than long skirts.

Slipping into the cool clean water, she sighed. She wished she had soap. Perhaps one day she'd persuade Grandmother to let her make some. Her arm, still mottled with the yellow splotches of fading bruises, ached afresh after her tussle with Red Hawk.

He could have hurt her, but he hadn't. In fact, he'd turned away. Was he angry? She didn't know how Shawnee men thought. She had taken a terrible chance, but she'd reacted out of grief. And anger.

She dried herself as best she could and dressed. It was one thing to push Philippe into the mud. She'd attacked a Shawnee warrior. Red Hawk was right. It was beyond foolish.

Something unexpected surfaced in her heart. It seemed strange to feel guilt over such a thing, but she was sorry.

Feeling like a mule, Susanna balanced the heavy basket of corn on her back, a strap across her forehead bearing much of the load. The cornstalks were dry and withered, their boastful green replaced with a dirty linen hue. Each time she entered the field, they rustled as she picked her way past the startling orange of swelling pumpkins between the stalks.

Apparently gathering and transporting the dried ears was not a favorite task, and now that she was deemed strong enough to labor, she labored like the other women did, from morning till night.

Grandmother encouraged her, saying that once the corn was in and they returned from the festival in Big Turtle's village, they'd make pottery.

Susanna unloaded the corn at the wigwam and returned to the field. She was supposed to help Running Deer next. She plopped down the huge basket next to the young woman. "Tell me what you want me to do."

Running Deer slanted a dark glance at her and merely jerked her chin at a pile of ears near her.

At least no one had laid a hand on Susanna since the day of the gauntlet. But the hostility of many of the women was difficult to bear. She filled the basket at a steady pace, fearing to wrench her back if she worked too hard.

A stabbing pain shot through her spine, and she stood upright and rubbed her lower back. In the middle distance several men shouted to one another in the river. They were fishing, with weirs or nets.

Her rubbing slowed. She'd rather be fishing.

"What are you looking at?" Running Deer threw an armful of corn at her feet.

Susanna looked more carefully at the men. Red Hawk was one of them. Was Running Deer jealous? "I have never fished in that manner."

"Red Hawk brings gifts to my wigwam."

That needed no interpretation.

"But my mother says he needs to bring a scalp if he is serious."

Susanna's stomach roiled in disgust. "Women are life-givers." That much she knew from Grandmother. "And you wish an emblem of death and hate?"

"You know nothing," Running Deer spat.

Running Deer would have preferred Susanna's scalp to her labor, that much was clear. She finished the work in silence and carried the load to the woman's wigwam. The sun was casting long shadows by the time she made her way back to the field. Maybe one or two more loads.

Hopefully she'd be exhausted tonight. If she were tired enough, sleep would claim her before she wept.

THE FIRE CAST strange shadows over Laughing Wolf's face as he danced with Running Deer. Red Hawk agonized at the sight, but he stayed put, sitting in the first row behind the dancers. The courtship dance did not always end in marriage; sometimes it served as a mere flirtation. It all depended on the words they exchanged, and he wouldn't hear them if he sat farther back.

The Bread Dance festival was almost normal. Plenty of food, footraces for the younger ones, archery contests. Bartering took place in odd corners. One of the elders of Big Turtle's village had surprised him with an offer for Su-anna. Ten beaver pelts. When Red Hawk declined, the man had smiled and winked.

Yes, almost normal. Only the occasional comments about Long Knives reminded him they were at war.

Red Hawk studied Running Deer's graceful form as she stepped and swayed. What did she see in Laughing Wolf? She spoke, praising his manly form, and Red Hawk cringed. This could go on for a while, the flirting. Then the man would speak of marriage, and the woman would agree—or politely shy off.

Some ornament was tied to her waist. She swirled slightly, and the light caught it A scalp.

Laughing Wolf had given her a scalp.

THE STRANGE PAGAN festival reminded Susanna of a valley wedding dance in some ways. There was a lot of food. And people. For once she was glad of her dark hair and eyes; after several months in the sun with no hat, she was almost as dark as a Shawnee. Even so, she kept close to Grandmother.

On the way home, the weather changed. Cold gusts of wind slipped under the deerskin shoulder cape Grandmother had made for her. Walking ahead, Red Hawk seemed impervious to the temperature; he wore no jacket. Behind her, Dark Water and Grandmother rode the mare, the younger woman chattering about people they knew.

Susanna had been surprised to see Running Deer dance with Laughing Wolf. Grandmother had explained the purpose of the dance. Judging by the reaction of the crowd, the dance ended favorably for Laughing Wolf. Were they married now? But what about Red Hawk?

Perhaps that explained his hard face and total silence as they walked home.

Home. She cast her gaze east, where the mountains edged the horizon. A hard-edged ache of homesickness washed over her. With or without Sammy, she'd leave in the spring.

37

The Indians are great believers in witches and witchcraft, in supernatural things, and in supernatural power.

—*A History of Jonathan Alder*

A wide basket on her hip, Susanna ducked under a bare dogwood branch as she followed Red Hawk through the trees. She fingered the fraying basket brim; perhaps Grandmother could teach her to make another, or to weave fabric like the beautiful but worn blanket in the wigwam. Baskets were plentiful enough in the village, but Susanna couldn't remember seeing another woven item like Grandmother's. Most Shawnee wore clothing made of leather.

Red Hawk carried an object wrapped in deerskin under his arm, but he hadn't said what it was, just that she would be collecting chestnuts.

He slowed and she drew abreast. She hadn't spoken to him since that day by the stream.

"Red Hawk, I'm sorry."

He faced her, a line between his brows.

"The stream." How to explain? She didn't understand her own feelings, but she wanted to do what was right, even if he was her enemy.

A corner of his mouth twitched. "I accept your apology."

"I know who your father is." She'd had a long time to think it through.

Red Hawk became very still. Then his chest rose, and he jerked his chin toward a fallen log. They sat beneath the shade of several chestnuts.

"His name was Silas Sloan."

"You knew him?"

"Not really. I was a child, and he died when I was perhaps four or five. But I know the story." She leaned over and tossed a few chestnuts in the basket. "I am not sure of some of the details, but he'd lost his wife to the Shawnee. He raided them in turn. But his grief and his rage embittered his mind. Because of his retaliation, a Shawnee came after him and killed him."

"He was a wicked man?"

He'd used a word the Shawnee applied to an unfaithful bow. "Yes. But before he died, he became good."

Red Hawk leaned forward. "How can this be?"

Susanna took a long slow breath. She knew enough Shawnee to speak of concrete things. Abstractions were more difficult. "Grandmother told me of He-Who-Creates-By-Thinking." She stood. "The Creator can make us good."

His gaze was riveted on her.

"I do not have the words." How to explain substitution? Or the incarnation ... or the Trinity? "The Creator's book speaks of it." Susanna hadn't read the Scriptures or heard preaching in months, and her heart contracted with the thought.

"Book?" Red Hawk stirred, clutching the bundle in his lap. He motioned her to sit. "I want to show you something. But you must not tell anyone."

She sat and watched as he unfolded the leather. Inside was a book. A Bible.

Her heart quickened. "May I?"

He passed her the Bible carefully, as if it might break. "I want to know the secret."

She opened to the Psalms and began to read. A tear trickled down her cheek. "Thank you, Lord," she said in English. She curled up over the battered volume and began to sob.

"What is it? Is something wrong?"

"No, I am so happy to see this book. It is the sacred book of the Creator."

Red Hawk's brow shot up. "But it is in the white man's language. It must speak of the white man's god."

She shook her head. "It was changed from another tongue." She wished Jamie could explain how the Scriptures had been translated.

He waved an impatient hand. "I want to know how to make a Shawnee book. I want to send words this way. And keep the stories of the Shawnee alive forever."

"Oh." She wiped her face. "Then I must learn your tongue." He was asking her to find a way to write down the Shawnee language, a huge undertaking.

"You speak Shawnee already."

"I need to learn more words."

Frowning, Red Hawk stood abruptly. "I will teach you—when I can. It is hunting season."

"I will ask Grandmother, too."

"Do not tell anyone of the book." He wrapped it carefully.

Susanna's innards contracted as she lost sight of it. "Why?"

"Laughing Wolf. He will say it is the white man's poison."

THE VALLEY behind him lay quiet under a mere dusting of frost, but here on Buffalo Gap, the snow lay thick. James directed the mule down the slope. There were deer in the valley, drawn by the fat fields of settlers, but for the wary bucks you had to cross the gap into the mountain hollows. Nowadays folks declined to take the risk, holing up in their cabins and refusing the bounty of the hills.

Ma declined to fuss at him. She worried, he knew, but she soon realized that her son's treks weren't just about stocking up for winter. He'd done that and more; the Craigs' larder was full too. James headed for a walnut grove he'd spotted on a previous trip. And he'd look for hickories as his mother was partial to hickory nuts. Hopefully, if the snow were thin or patchy lower down, he'd find some the squirrels had missed.

The lonely creak of the saddle sounded loud in the stillness of the woods. The story of Mary Ingles had circled the valley, how she'd escaped the Shawnee and survived a difficult journey home that would have daunted a healthy man. Made it back to her husband, who didn't recognize her, she was so thin and scarecrow-like.

James took a deep breath. Had Susanna tried to escape—and failed? What would the Indians do to someone who tried to escape?

He tried to pray.

Keep her, Lord. Protect her, Lord.

His heart quailed at the notion that she'd probably be married to one of the savages before long.

No, Lord. Not that.

He swallowed. His prayers seemed ineffectual, and no wonder. How could he expect an answer when he was only interested in his own desires, without regard for God's plan or purpose?

His prayers were totally selfish, springing from a hard, unthankful heart.

A tiny motion arrested his attention. He grabbed the cold barrel of the rifle slung over his back and slowly brought it forward.

A deer?

He dismounted carefully and felt for his powder horn. The barren oak branches before him couldn't conceal the motion of antlers, though they were strangely shaped. He ground-tied Libby and approached.

Where was his powder horn? Had he forgotten it?

He took several more steps forward, mesmerized by the huge rack before him. Brown fur—a huge eye—long antlers resolved into an animal much larger than any deer. Defenseless, he stayed close behind a tree and marveled at the creature. A bull elk, he was sure of it. He had never seen one before.

The great head rose slightly, and the ears searched for sound. With a slight roll of the eye the animal moved off, unhurried.

Still grasping the useless rifle, James slid to the ground against the oak. The forest was still again. And beautiful.

Break forth into joy, sing together, ye waste places of Jerusalem: for the Lord hath comforted his people, he hath redeemed Jerusalem.

The verse from Isaiah breathed a peace into him. A peace he did not deserve. No, he was a prodigal, spending his substance in a far country. Rebelling against the call of God.

But hadn't the father of that wayward son looked for him? Welcomed him? Why, he'd dressed him and feted him in such a way that his brother had become angry at the extravagance.

Lord, do You love me like that too?

Before the prayer took shape, it seemed he had the answer. A great joy welled up in him, a great thankfulness that washed away all his anger and rebellion.

The Lord hath made bare his holy arm in the eyes of all the nations; and all the ends of the earth shall see the salvation of our God.

He saw it now. For the first time, he understood that the call was not an onerous task, a crushing burden, laid on his shoulders. No, it was a sweet duty, a privilege, even. Truly, it was God's own work, his own mighty arm flung out to achieve a purpose.

If he went along, it was merely as a vessel, an observer, even. What was God's plan for the Shawnee people? For the first time, James wondered what the Lord would do.

~

MOTION from above caught Red Hawk's eye as they stopped at another chestnut grove. Ghost-like, fat white flakes swirled silently down through the branches. Su-anna crouched and tossed the brown globes into her basket rapidly.

The woman had wept over the book. She'd described it as sacred. The thought chilled him more than the snow. Of course, he'd said what any Shawnee would say—that the white man's god had no bearing on the Shawnee.

But doubts plagued him. If He-Who-Creates-By-Thinking created all men, then wouldn't it follow that such a book was a message for all people everywhere?

Su-anna finished and propped the basket on her hip, curling the fingers of her other hand into a fist again and again. She was cold. He jerked his chin in command, and they descended the gentle slope. Over the next knoll was the village.

A wolf howled nearby, and Su-anna hesitated. Barking yips echoed through the woods, swelling and ebbing. Then another howl, followed by sudden snarling. He pulled out two arrows from his quiver.

"Red Hawk, that is close to the village," she whispered urgently.

SUSANNA STAYED CLOSE to Red Hawk as they neared the village. The man's frame was tense, his steps carefully chosen.

A woman's scream pierced the air. Ragged wails followed, intermingled with the wolf chorus.

Her pulse thudded in her ears. Red Hawk broke into a lope, and she struggled to keep up. Someone was hurt.

Bursting through the last screen of trees, the village seemed like a disturbed ant mound, with people running everywhere. Women grabbed small children, and men clutched at their weapons.

Susanna made for Grandmother's wigwam. If anyone needed help, the old woman would probably be called upon. As she drew near, she spotted her. Grandmother was outside, shading her eyes, trying to see what the commotion was about.

"Grandmother, why are the men just standing there?" A number of Shawnee men faced the trees with weapons at the ready, but they seemed cautious. Her father would have gathered the others and sped through the trees without hesitation. Granted, a wolf pack was dangerous, but several men with guns could pick off a few at once and perhaps scatter the others. Half a dozen Shawnee could do as well or better.

"They do not want to curse their weapons during hunting season."

Another ragged scream—closer, this time. Susanna clenched her fists. She was ready to take up a branch and plunge into the forest herself. "Curse?"

"The wolf spirit is powerful and tricky. If you fire at one and miss, your weapon is cursed for six moons."

Several men disappeared into the trees. Susanna didn't see Red Hawk. Slowly Grandmother's words penetrated. "That's not true." Her father had killed many, especially in the early years, when settlers first came to the valley and wolves were plentiful. Several wolf pelts still lined the walls of the old cabin.

The old woman ignored her. "Here they come. It's Running Deer's cousin."

Red Hawk emerged from the trees carrying a woman. Even from a distance Susanna could see blood on her legs. As they approached, it became obvious the woman was with child. Another man trotted up, his arm bloodied.

Swiftly, Grandmother took charge. Susanna brought water; Dark Water tended the man—the woman's husband—outside, and Grandmother cleansed the woman's wounds before the hearth inside.

The woman moaned and wailed, but not from the pain. The wolves had taken her little girl. Horror filled Susanna's heart as she went for more water. Returning, she saw Running Deer at the door of the wigwam, weeping silently.

Running Deer took charge of the woman's husband. "It's not the place for a man." She led him away.

Susanna frowned and ducked inside. Grandmother had wrapped the injuries and now sat back on her heels. "Su-anna, do you know midwifery?"

It was a new word, but the components revealed the meaning. "Is her baby coming?"

A nod. "A little early, and the baby has not turned."

She noticed a wet stain on the woman's leggings—her waters had broken. "Where is the head?"

Grandmother extended a wiry hand and gently traced the middle of the woman's belly. "Up here."

The woman groaned and tried to sit up. Susanna placed several rolled skins behind her. "I don't suppose you have any firewater."

Grandmother smirked and pawed through her belongings. She withdrew a small gourd. "What would you use it for?"

"For cleansing. Do you think she would allow me to help?" Rapidly, Susanna's mind sped through the pages of the French midwifery book. There were several possible breech presentations, some worse than others.

Grandmother shrugged. "She might not notice anyway." She gave several instructions.

Susanna darted through the skin door and almost collided with Red Hawk. "Grandmother wants clean rushes from the river bank. And more water."

"She's not having the child in the birthing hut?"

"I guess not."

The minutes crept by with agonizing slowness as they made preparations. The laboring woman did not moan or scream with the contractions; her face merely tightened. Occasional sobs marked her grief. Why did the Shawnee allow wolves to get so close to the village? Their superstitions were destructive. They needed the truth.

Running Deer returned and sat by her cousin's side. She glanced at

Susanna but did not interfere. The dwelling was close with the smell of sweat, fear, and the faintly sour scent of broken membranes.

"I'm ready, Grandmother." She was as clean as she could get. *Oh, Mother, I wish you were here.*

The old woman nodded, and Susanna examined the woman. A tiny foot met her fingers.

She closed her eyes. *Oh Lord, help. Have mercy.*

A footling breech.

She took a deep breath and focused on a memory of her father, assisting Cricket. The mare's last labor had stalled, the foal inside her misaligned, with one foreleg curled back. Da had managed to reach it and pull it straight. Two tiny hooves had emerged, then a dark head, the body following wetly like a fish landing on a bank.

She felt for the baby's other foot between contractions. It seemed impossible. Her hand was too large—to do this with a mare was one thing. A person was much smaller. She prayed and hoped and tried again.

There it was. She used a fingertip to nudge it down without success. A contraction seized the woman and she bucked and writhed. Susanna took a deep breath and tried again. This time, the foot moved. Another long minute, and both feet emerged.

Thank you, Lord!

The midwifery book listed things that could go wrong and suggestions for each case. The chin could hang up on the pelvis—oh no, she didn't dare think of that.

The woman moved restlessly and pushed up with one arm. She wanted to push. Thinking of a diagram in the book, Susanna wrestled her to her hands and knees. Running Deer narrowed her eyes but did not protest.

Two tiny feet emerged. With the next contraction the legs followed, then the baby turned slightly. Susanna grasped the child as it emerged —only the head remained.

The woman grunted, and the baby dropped into Susanna's hands, wet and sticky and blue, with the cord around its neck. She removed the cord and cleared the child's mouth. Grandmother handed her something to wipe it down with.

Breathe, breathe.

"The babe is cursed," Running Deer said.

Susanna puffed into the baby's mouth. No response. She flipped the still form over and slapped its buttocks. An eternity seemed to pass.

Then, suddenly, the baby cried. The mewling sound was surprisingly strong. Its body pinked up, and its little fists began to move. "A girl," Susanna said. "You have a girl." She handed the child to Grandmother and attended to the afterbirth.

Running Deer helped to clean the mother. "I will take my cousin home."

"She should nurse first."

The new mother's face contracted into a scowl. "It is cursed."

Running Deer helped the woman to her feet. "She will not take the baby. Give it to the wolves."

They left.

Horrified, Susanna looked at Grandmother, who sat calmly, still holding the child. "What do I do?"

38

I very much desire to translate some parts of the Scriptures into their language… and teach them to read.

—John Eliot (1604-1690)

The Shenandoah Valley, April 1757

Mr. Craig ran his knobby fingers over the cover of the Bible. "Why, it's Eliot's translation into an Indian tongue. But dinna the Shawnee speak something different?"

"Massachusetts is similar to the Delaware language, which is similar to Shawnee," James said. The gift from Samuel Davies of John Eliot's Bible, arriving after the snows melted, served as yet one more encouragement in a string of many he'd received after that fateful day in the snowy woods.

Standing at the preaching desk in the dim meetinghouse, the minister flipped open the book. Everyone else had departed after the afternoon service; random eddies of conversation drifted in from outside.

"Why, here's the old Geneva translation on one side, the strange tongue on the other. What a piece of labor."

"Aye, it encourages me to see the work of another who's brought the gospel to the Indians."

Mr. Craig slapped the book closed and returned it. "Are ye prepared?"

The barley was planted. There were only a few decisions to make. "I've started packing."

"Leave your rifle home."

"What?"

"Take a rifle into Shawnee country and what do you think will happen?"

"But I'd need it—"

"Pack twice as much. Sell the rifle. Set yourself up as a trader. Get another mule or donkey."

James studied the question. Not only would the firearm make him appear hostile, a long rifle would be coveted. Few Indians had them.

"Preaching to the Shawnee is a dangerous proposition, ye ken?"

That went without saying. "Thank ye kindly, Mr. Craig." He turned to depart.

A shadow blocked the doorway. "How dare ye!"

It was William Preston, hatless and disordered. "Preach to the Shawnee?"

His broad fist came from nowhere, the blow blinding James, sudden lights and colors flashing; the shock coursed through his body. He lost his footing and found himself on his back over a bench.

"Taking sides with murderers!" Preston's harsh voice slammed into his heart.

James scrambled to his feet. Reflexively, he folded his hands into fists, but hesitated, only to run again into his friend's fist. Staggering back, he touched his face, and his hand came away tinged with red. His lip was split open, and the taste of copper filled his mouth. He could hardly blame Preston. His instinct to fight back was stymied by the truth of the man's words.

"Traitor! Turncoat!" Preston snarled. "After what they did to my uncle—"

"Aye, lad. We mind it." John Russell's voice broke in, low-toned, as if he spoke to a horse.

Backlit against the doorway, Russell grasped Preston's arm, and Mr. Craig took the other. Preston cursed as they wrestled him outside.

James turned away and found a seat. His face throbbed, and pain shot up his back where he'd fallen across the hard pew. If he was to be smitten and beaten, he'd rather it be by an enemy. Not by Preston.

At least the minister understood. Didn't like it too well, but he understood and supported him.

John Russell entered the building and came his way. "I dampened a kerchief in the spring."

Gratefully, James pressed it to his face. His eye was swelling up.

"Ye'll have a shiner for sure."

"William is my friend."

Russell sighed. "I ken that. And I sympathize with him."

"You, best of anyone." James half wondered why Russell hadn't joined in.

"I am not sure I understand why you should preach to the Shawnee, especially now, during wartime. But the Lord's ways are not our own. And ye must follow your conscience."

"There are moments when I lose my courage. Like now. I know what Preston has suffered. What you have suffered."

"My father once said that duty is the foundation of all good choices." He took a deep breath. "Your conscience, enlightened by the Word of God, reveals your duty, the path you are meant to take. And a clear conscience is the heart of godly courage."

The heart of courage. "Mr. Russell, will ye pray for me?"

"Aye, that I will do."

~

SUSANNA SMOOTHED the salve over her hands and rubbed it in. It wasn't exactly like Mother's lavender ointment, as she had no lavender, but marigold and bee balm and another unknown herb Grandmother had suggested mixed with goose grease soothed her chapped, roughened skin. It had been a long winter.

Various hues of green softened the hard fingers of the dark tree limbs that arched upward like a palisade around the village. She longed to escape, but though the weather would soon be warm enough, she had a new responsibility. A baby.

"Here, take this to She-Who-Sings," Grandmother said, handing her a bundle of herbs.

"Shall I give her some salve?"

Grandmother hummed an assent and handed her one of the small colored containers they'd crafted before the snows halted all such work. It was the green one. Her first try had cracked in the pit they used for a kiln. But soon she mastered the craft, making sure the clay was perfectly tempered with crushed shell, and coiling it carefully row upon row, blending and smoothing.

It was comforting work, not strenuous, like the stretching and scraping of the multiple hides Red Hawk had brought back from his hunting trips. The day he'd come into camp triumphantly dragging a buffalo carcass behind Whiskey she groaned out loud. Dark Water helped that time; it was a two-person task just to lift and tie the heavy hide. Until now she'd had no idea how hard Uncle Roy labored to tan and finish a single skin.

Susanna filled the container with the greasy concoction and reached for her thick otter skin leggings. She hesitated. It was breezy but not cold, and the extra warmth would not be needed. She'd been glad for them on bitter days when she'd needed to work for hours outside scraping hides.

Red Hawk had dropped the beautiful pelts in her lap one day after the first significant snowfall.

Alarmed, she'd glared at him, knowing that such gifts were typically part of courtship. "I cannot marry you."

His lips parted as he gazed at her, face expressionless. She felt Grandmother's presence at her side, heat from the open wigwam door warming her back.

His gaze slipped away. "I hunt for Grandmother, Dark Water, and for you."

She clutched at the thick brown skins and watched him walk away. He was strong and stoic, but sometimes he seemed lost.

In some ways she regretted her harsh words. Besides Grandmother, he was the closest thing to a friend she had here.

Jamie. Where was he right now? What was he doing? She prayed for him sporadically, but her spiritual life had dried up. It had been so long since she'd read the Scriptures or heard a sermon. The Scriptures ... perhaps there was a way to preserve those verses already hid in her heart.

She put the leggings aside. Living Water stirred in her cradleboard. Susanna decided to bring her along to She-Who-Sings's wigwam. It was almost time for her feeding.

She hoisted the cradleboard onto her back and went outside, steeling herself to face the woman. Few of the Shawnee were noticeably hostile now, but this woman was another story.

She-Who-Sings was sitting outside sewing. She looked up as Susanna approached, her dark eyes revealing nothing. Susanna was conscious of her ribs as she stood before the woman, remembering what she'd suffered at her hands.

"I've herbs from Grandmother."

"Sit."

"I've a salve too." She knelt. "I use it for my hands."

She-Who-Sings examined the contents of the little pot, dipped her finger in it, and smoothed it on one hand. She grunted.

Susanna loosed the baby from the board and began to feed her.

"How can you nurse this child?" She-Who-Sings stabbed the leather in her lap with an awl. Close up, the woman didn't seem as formidable as she had before. Her hair was threaded with gray. "You have none of your own."

The story of the wolf orphan, as she was initially known, had spread throughout the village overnight. "Grandmother gave me herbs." The first week had been horrible. The baby would have starved if a relative of Grandmother's hadn't snuck into their wigwam each evening and nursed the child. "The milk finally came in."

"You don't fear a curse?"

"No. My father killed many wolves."

"He is a good hunter, then." She-Who-Sings spoke Shawnee with an accent.

Susanna shifted the baby in her lap. "Yes, like men here, he hunted deer before the snow fell. Our ..." she fumbled, searching for a word to mean smokehouse. "Our house for the meat—"

"Smokehouse?" She-Who-Sings used the English word.

"Yes," Susanna replied. Her own language felt strange to her throat. She switched back to Shawnee. "Did you live east of the mountains once?" With a son like Buffalo Robe, it was almost certain.

She-Who-Sings remained silent for a long moment. "Does it matter?"

"I spoke to a man once. A black man who took care of horses. He told me a story about a woman and child. The child's name was Buffalo Robe."

She-Who-Sing's fingers stilled in her lap.

Susanna relayed the story. "The man's name is Joe."

"Is he well?" The woman asked, her voice cracking.

"Yes. He is owned by my father's sister. He insists he is still married."

A tear escaped the woman's eye and ran down her cheek. "The fool. He should marry."

Her throat tight with emotion, Susanna found herself unable to speak.

Buffalo Robe approached, accompanied by Sammy. The child bounded up to her.

"Look," he said in Shawnee. "Bow! Arrows!" He held up a small version of the Shawnee weapon.

Susanna's heart squeezed. "Very good." She'd noticed him moping at times during the winter, but he seemed alarmingly cheerful now.

She-Who-Sings shot her a warning look. "He is my son."

Susanna lowered her gaze. Were her thoughts so obvious?

Buffalo Robe's attention shifted. "Who is that?"

A tall man was leading two heavily laden mules to the edge of the village. A ground swell of conversation rose as the village awakened to his presence.

It was George Morgan, the trader. Susanna scrambled to her feet, balancing Living Water on her hip. The world swirled and tilted. She remembered that day by the river, her arms aching from wrestling that huge fish, the trader's gentle voice. Another time, another life.

The village solidified. She was here now—and so was he. Could he get a message back to her parents?

"The Uchee trader." She-Who-Sings rose. "It's been a long time."

Several women started toward the trader, but a man elbowed his way in front of them. Laughing Wolf.

The women shuffled back, uncertainty in their posture.

The sound of Laughing Wolf's voice filtered through to them, but not the words.

"What is he doing?" Buffalo Robe asked.

"Perhaps he's inviting the man to his lodge. To give the man hospitality." But She-Who-Sings' tone of voice was uncertain.

George Morgan nodded at something Laughing Wolf said. Then Laughing Wolf spun about and returned through the village. The trader began to move off.

A few murmurs rose.

"What just happened?" She-Who-Sings asked. "Why is the trader not staying?"

A muscle tightened in Buffalo Robe's jaw. "The man wears a shirt made by white men. Sells goods made by white men. I can guess."

She-Who-Sings spat into the dust. "Laughing Wolf takes too much upon himself."

"Hush, Mother."

Susanna stared at the trader, now leading the mules away. Even if George had looked straight at her, what would he have seen? A Shawnee woman, dark hair in plaits, with a babe on her hip. Not Susanna Russell.

She returned to the wigwam as quickly as possible, heart swollen with grief.

Why, Lord?

ONE MORE DECISION. James paused and looked north, his leg throbbing from the day's journey. North was the way he'd need to take if he wanted to travel to the Ohio, where most of the Shawnee lived.

But south was where Susanna's captors had taken her—at least, that's what Russell had concluded.

James decided to camp by the stream for the night. He hobbled the mules and pulled out his fishing tackle. If he could pull out a trout in the evenings, he could stretch his supplies; not that they were scanty, not by any means. He hadn't had the means to purchase much from McClure, only fishhooks, traps, and trinkets for trade. But his parents had given him a keg of salted pork, a bag of cornmeal, and beans; Mrs. Craig a cheese and some ham; and the Russells had outdone themselves.

"Here, lad." Scowling, Mrs. May had thrust a keg of cider into his arms. "Dinna get yourself killed."

Mrs. Russell held a package, her eyes glistening. "Susanna started making Christmas gifts before she was taken. This was for you."

It was a fine leather satchel with a strap made of purple canvas. *Purple?*

"She's right canny with dyes and weaving." Mrs. May said.

Unspoken was their desire that he'd find her and bring her back. But where did the Lord want him to go?

The wriggling char he pulled from the water was puny, but he hadn't much appetite anyway. After cleaning the fish and cooking his supper, he went down to the stream to scrub the skillet with sand. The simple task soothed his mind.

Lord, Your will be done. Show me what direction to take.

He slept uneasily, waking at intervals. The stars wheeled overhead, marking time during the long night.

A delicate birdcall roused him. He rubbed his eyes and sat up. Despite the mules' hobbles they'd wandered in search of grass, and he took them to the stream to drink. He splashed his face in the gray light, still weary. At least his leg was rested.

He began the process of loading the mules. "Well, Libby, shall I go south?" He had no clear direction, and Libby wasn't telling him. The other animal, slightly smaller with a dark coat and white belly, looked at him suspiciously when James strapped on the keg of salt pork.

"Here, Gunner." He handed the mule a wrinkled apple. "The laborer is worthy of his hire."

Libby crowded him. "Here, lass." Of course she'd want one too.

He grabbed a chunk of the cheese to gnaw on and led them south.

Lord, is this Your will? Or am I just following my own heart?

His leg began hurting at midday. He stopped and guided the mules down the slope to the stream. The rolling terrain was deceptive; he had to watch his footing. He refilled his gourd and studied the western ridge, so close he felt like he could touch it. There must be a gap at some point, the ones the Indians had used.

Libby scrambled willingly back up to the path while Gunner followed slowly, ears bobbing. It wasn't exactly a trail they followed, more like a collection of open places that paralleled the water below. Sometimes brush or tree limbs hindered him. But James could imagine Indians taking this path, even on horseback. Had Susanna come this way? And Arch May's killer?

Lord, have mercy on Susanna. And …

He frowned, conflicting emotions tangling in his heart. Agnes May's red-rimmed eyes …

It was one thing to pray for the Shawnee in general, to hope for their salvation as a group. But what about the man who had killed Arch May? Could he pray for this nameless man?

For the rest of the afternoon he wrestled, his aching leg pulsing in counterpoint to the turmoil in his heart.

Finally, he paused under the shade of a young oak, catkins dangling about his head. A renewed sense of his own sinfulness and need of Christ suffused him. He was not better than this man.

I am not worthy of the least of thy mercies… Lord, have mercy on Arch May's killer.

A great peace chased away the confused thoughts. He tugged at the mules' leads and resumed his trek.

Tired and aching, James was ready to stop once the sun descended below the ridge. Below, the stream slowed and widened into a pool behind a screen of willow branches.

It was perfect for a campsite. He led the animals down to the bank. Careful of his stiffening leg, he knelt and drank. Several feet away, something was half buried in the mud.

He reached for it. A three-inch miniature painting lay nestled in his palm. Susanna's face looked back at him.

She'd been here. A jagged sob tore from his throat.

39

Translation it is that openeth the window, to let in the light; that breaketh the shell, that we may eat the kernel...

—Miles Smith, *Preface to the King James Version,* 1611

Red Hawk hobbled the mare in the midst of a large patch of grass. She was winter-thin, her ribs showing through her coat, but the new growth would fatten her up quickly. "What do you think, Straight Arrow?"

Straight Arrow chewed on a long stem of grass. They'd exercised their horses and brought them to a clearing to graze. "Is the Uchee trader part white?"

"It never mattered before," Buffalo Robe said.

Straight Arrow removed the stem and gestured with it. "Well, other things matter now that didn't matter before."

"Perhaps it is time to consult Big Turtle," Red Hawk said. He wasn't worthy to be sachem himself. Nor did he have the kind of universal respect and support that such an office required. But a wise sachem would not have turned the trader away. Grandmother had been visibly angry. She'd needed more shells for her pottery.

"I think more people would follow you if ..." Buffalo Robe's voice trailed away.

"If I weren't white?"

Buffalo Robe sputtered. "No, it isn't that. If you had scalps on your belt, the young men would esteem you."

Straight Arrow plucked another piece of grass. "Especially now that there's war. Even Grayfeather took scalps in his youth. Maybe we could go on another raid." He looked hopeful.

"Hmm." Another raid was a good idea. Straight Arrow had brought home little from the first one. Why did his heart feel so sluggish? Sometimes the only thing that kept him going was the dream of the white beaver. And Su-anna. He needed to ask her to create the code in Shawnee. Surely she knew enough of the language by now.

Yes, that's what he'd do. As soon as the fields were planted, Dark Water would have no excuse to keep Su-anna working.

Straight Arrow tensed and shifted.

Red Hawk followed his friend's gaze to the foliage cloaking the stream below. Something was moving along the path next to the bank. An animal?

Conversation ceased as they watched the rustling branches. A man emerged.

A white-haired man. He didn't seem old, but his hair was snow white. A purple band crossed his front from shoulder to hip. Red Hawk blinked in confusion, thinking of his dream. The white beaver with a purple wampum belt. The man led two heavily laden mules along the path. He looked up, spotted them, and stopped.

Straight Arrow stood, tomahawk in hand.

THREE SHAWNEE MEN stood before him, naked above the waist. One grasped a tomahawk, his stance tense, but the one in front squinted at him in a curious manner. A lone feather was braided into his dark hair.

"Hello," James said. *Lord, my life is yours.* He placed a hand on his chest. "Paxton. I am Paxton." Would he live or die?

The Shawnee with the tomahawk took a half step forward, but the one in front stayed him with a hand motion and a comment.

"Paxton," he repeated. Shouldn't he be terrified? But these men seemed like men—not wraiths. Not the specters from his dreams.

The leader spoke, and James grappled with the sounds. As he attempted the name, the man smiled. It was then James noticed something strange. This Shawnee had blue eyes.

"Pak-ton," Blue Eyes said. "Book." He placed his hands together and pantomimed something. "Book."

Book? How did he know the word? But his eyes were blue. Did he know English? "Yes, I have a book." He thrust his hand into the satchel and drew out Eliot's translation.

"Book. God's book."

RED HAWK'S BELLY TIGHTENED. The strange white-haired man had a book. It was his dream. He stretched out his hand and touched the pages.

Nothing happened. "Buffalo Robe, what is he saying?"

"I am not sure, but I think this is their sacred book."

"I dreamt of this moment. His name is White Beaver."

His friends seemed to relax then.

Straight Arrow tucked away his tomahawk. "Why don't we find a place to camp? We can't bring a white man into the village."

True. They needed to keep him away from Laughing Wolf.

THROUGH PANTOMIME and bits and pieces of English—the darkest Indian, part Negro by the looks of him, knew the most—James understood what they wanted. They mounted their horses, and he followed them over a hill to another stream. Here they made camp.

James shared his food. One of the Indians spat out the piece of cheese he gave him, but Blue Eyes swallowed his sample, grimacing slightly. Perhaps being polite? Only the dark Indian actually seemed to like it.

He pulled out the miniature of Susanna.

"WHAT MEDICINE IS THIS?" Straight Arrow said.

Red Hawk stared. How could Su-anna's face be on the piece of wood? Even Buffalo Robe had no explanation.

White Beaver seemed to be asking a question. Was he looking for Su-anna?

Red Hawk touched the image. It was painted, he was sure of it, though he'd never seen anything so finely wrought. Sometimes when men went into battle they'd decorate themselves quite elaborately, but this was incredibly detailed.

"This is a sign," he said. "We are to bring Su-anna here. She knows the Shawnee tongue quite well and can translate for us."

SUSANNA WAS BECOMING IRRITATED. This was no simple expedition to gather herbs. Deep in the woods, Whiskey stood tethered beside the nearly invisible trail. Red Hawk mounted, then pulled her up in front of him.

Why hadn't he ridden the horse to the village? "Where are we going?"

"I have a task for you."

That was somewhat reassuring. But was it something he wanted to keep secret?

She ducked her head under low-hanging branches. Water dripped from the foliage above them, running cold down her neck and beneath her cape. How far were they going? She would need to feed the baby in a few hours.

Crazy man. She collected her thoughts. Over the months she'd had to discipline her mind to stay sane. Meditate on a verse of Scripture. Or mentally compose a letter to Anne Randolph. She decided to do that now.

Dearest Anne, there is no Canvas here. Nor Paper. But while the Shawnee may be Savages in some Ways, they understand Color and Pigments, which they obtain much as we do, from Clays and Plants. They prepare their Skin or Surface to be painted with Grease, then apply Red, White, Black, or Yellow. Green and Blue are less common, and I have not seen Purple. I am told the Colors have Meaning and even Power, which is why the Men paint themselves when they go to War. Women, too, decorate themselves, their Clothing, and their Pottery.

Finishing her imaginary letter, she was squeezed by homesickness. She dressed like a Shawnee, learned their crafts, and much of that was not a burden. But there was no refreshing gospel sermon on the Sabbath, no books to read, no one truly like-minded to speak to.

A thought struck her. They were not like-minded because they did not have the gospel. Could it be that any other differences were superficial? Red Hawk was a man like any other. He thought differently, but he was still a man.

Susanna had told Grandmother of the incarnation, but the older woman seemed unaffected, as if none of what Susanna believed applied to her.

She felt useless. She knew the Lord. There was even a Bible in the village. But they were all in bondage, and she felt helpless to do anything about it.

Lord, help.

Abruptly, they broke into a clearing. Buffalo Robe was there, and Straight Arrow, and a man—

"Jamie!"

~

SUSANNA—IT was Susanna. His heart seemed to stop. James called her name before he realized he'd spoken.

She almost fell in her haste to dismount. "Jamie!" Braids bouncing, she flung herself at him.

He found himself with his arms around her, murmuring. She seemed healthy enough. Sun-browned, and perhaps a little thinner. She was dressed like an Indian. He was aware of the eyes of the men on him. But their expressions were unreadable. He couldn't tell if they were angry or bored.

Her gaze took in the mules and their packs, then returned to him. "Why are you here?"

Susanna's face expressed all her questions bound up in that simple one—why and how and every other detail. He longed to explain it all, tell her of that day in the woods. But that was impossible right now, with the eyes of the Shawnee upon him.

"Mr. Craig recommended I equip myself as a trader." He showed her Eliot's translation. "Perhaps you can help me. How much of their language have you managed to learn?"

Blue Eyes said something, and Susanna answered in their language. She sounded fluent. But then, she'd been a quick study in French. He scanned her clothing again. The leather cape was beautifully painted—no, it wasn't mere decoration. Those red and white lacy markings were *words*. Scripture verses. His heart swelled. Despite her Shawnee garb, this was the Susanna he knew, the lass who loved color and wanted to paint. And the verses painted on her clothing meant she'd managed to cling to faith.

Her familiar brown eyes drew him. "Red Hawk explained that they want me to translate."

"Wonderful. I came to preach the gospel without knowing a word." He marveled. Susanna was here … and she was safe. On top of that, she could translate.

But would they ever release her?

JAMIE. Jamie Paxton was here. Susanna stumbled in her translation, her emotions in a whirl. She was glad for his presence, but fearful for his safety. If George Morgan had been turned away because he wore a white man's shirt, what would happen if Laughing Wolf discovered a white man here?

He was stocked as a trader, with no rifle that she could see. His white hair still startled her. Had he come to trade for her, to ransom her? Or had he come to preach? She remembered a letter in which he'd described speaking to a Catawba woman, and she recalled her reaction, disliking the idea of ministering to Indians. But that was long ago, in another world. Perhaps Jamie had traveled a long path to get here, too.

They all sat and Jamie opened his Bible. He began in Genesis, and Susanna translated the account of Creation.

"And He-Who-Creates-By Thinking said, 'It is not good for the man to be alone; I will make a suitable helper for him.'"

Red Hawk nodded.

"These are the tales of the white men," Buffalo Robe said. "Not fit for the Shawnee."

Susanna translated this into English.

Jamie didn't hesitate. He turned the Bible around so they could see it.

"He says the book is in two languages. The white language and Massachusetts."

"Who are they?" Straight Arrow asked.

"North of the Lenni Lenape," Buffalo Robe said. "I have heard of this people from my mother."

"So the book is written in two languages?"

"Yes," Jamie explained. "God speaks through His Word to all men everywhere, of every tongue. Including the Red Man."

He bolstered his argument from the Scriptures. " ... bought back to God ... by your blood out of every family and language and people and nation."

The shadows had shifted by the time the Indians were satisfied, understanding that the Bible was a single book, for all peoples of the earth.

She turned to Red Hawk. "I need to feed the baby."

"Yes, let's go."

~

JAMES WOKE to the chirps and peeps of songbirds. Above him dogwood blossoms floated white in the gray of daybreak.

He stretched under his buffalo robe. The huge pile of leaves and detritus the Indians helped him gather had cushioned his sleep and, amazingly, kept him warm through the chilly spring night without a fire. Even better, his leg had stopped aching.

He pushed aside the hide and sat up. *Thank you, Lord.*

His first contact had gone well. For one thing, he was alive. That in itself was a miracle. Red Hawk and the smooth-skinned man hung on his every word. Only the part-Negro Indian seemed to hold doubts. But even that man's questions had proved helpful.

Susanna was the greatest blessing. Susanna, safe and sound. He remembered thinking her a good wife for a minister. How wrong he had been at the time. And yet, in the providence of God, here she was, translating the Scriptures into Shawnee. God had gifted her to be able to learn their language in a short span of time. It would have taken him years to achieve her fluency.

Would they ever have a life together? It seemed impossible. Did she even care for him in that way? Her letters had encouraged him to think so. Well, one thing at a time.

He grabbed his water bottle and drank. Susanna had translated Red

Hawk's message that James would need to stay here for his own safety. They wouldn't be bringing him to their village.

James got to his feet and watered the mules at the stream. There was a good amount of grass in the area, and he had a large piece of canvas to use for shelter. He'd manage.

Susanna seemed well enough, but they hadn't been able to speak privately. He'd managed to tell her that her family was well and her mother safely delivered of a son before she mounted the horse to depart, and her face lit with gratitude. He saw how the blue-eyed Indian—he couldn't think of the man as white, even if he was—treated her with a certain carefulness. It worried him. Were they married?

He tried to shove these thoughts aside and focus on his reason for being there. *Lord, let not Thy Word return void, but cause it to accomplish Thy purpose. Deliver these men from darkness.*

James was still praying when the snap of a twig alerted him to the Shawnees' approach. They entered the clearing single file; Susanna rode the chestnut, a handsome mare with a wide blaze.

She dismounted, and he saw a burden upon her back. Sounds came from it. Baby sounds.

Susanna slid the contraption off her back and removed the child. She spoke to it in Shawnee. Then she looked at him.

"Jamie, meet Living Water. That's what her name means in Shawnee."

A baby? His heart plummeted.

40

Sundry persons... were now deeply wounded with a sense of
their sin and misery.

—David Brainerd, *The Journal of David Brainerd*

The Creator's book was fascinating. Red Hawk barely noticed the stops and starts of the translation process as he absorbed the words. The tragic tale of the first man's disobedience echoed something Grandmother had once said. Then White Beaver spoke of a great deluge—Grandmother had described an event almost identical to this. But the next story was new and unfamiliar. A story about a man, Father-of-Many-Nations, who had received that special name after the Creator accepted him.

Su-anna said that Father-of-Many-Nations had placed his full weight on the promises of the Creator. That the true sons of this man were those who did the same. True sons. Sons of the heart. Red Hawk understood this. His heart was Shawnee despite the color of his eyes.

White Beaver turned the leaves in the book. "Many years later," Su-anna translated, "according to the promises given before, a baby was born. His name was called Jesus, which means, Creator-Who-Saves."

The words of the man followed, as well as his deeds. Some of the words resonated with Red Hawk, but some were strange.

His stomach rumbled. He'd lost track of time.

Straight Arrow dug in his bag and passed out dried venison. They all began to eat. Buffalo Robe paced the clearing as he chewed. Red Hawk couldn't read his friend. He listened, but his face revealed nothing. A few times Buffalo Robe had asked questions, as they all did.

"Who was this man, Creator-Who-Saves? A sachem?" Red Hawk grabbed another piece of the jerky.

Su-anna was nursing the baby but relayed the question.

White Beaver tilted his gourd to retrieve the last few drops. Straight Arrow handed him his own drinking vessel. White Beaver sipped it and thanked him.

"Creator-Who-Saves had no human father. The breath of the Creator gave life to the woman's seed. This was foretold at the time of the disobedience. The woman's seed would defeat the evil one."

White Beaver described the nature of Creator-Who-Saves, that he was the Creator himself come to earth. Pure, without any fault.

Red Hawk stood. "How can this be?"

"The Creator is greater than any man. No man has fully understood how He-Who-Saves can be the Creator as well as a man at the same time. He is Creator-the-Son, but he also calls himself Son-of-Man."

It was difficult to grasp, and yet for the Creator to become man had powerful implications. His heart leaped at the notion.

Red Hawk studied the shadows and sighed. They needed to return to the village soon. And they would need to justify any future absence. "Straight Arrow, we need to make a better plan. A formal hunting trip?"

"It would take a day's preparation."

Buffalo Robe nodded in agreement.

Red Hawk hesitated to leave White Beaver unguarded. He also

yearned to hear more of this Son-of-Man, but it couldn't be helped. "White Beaver, we will return in two days."

SUSANNA RELAYED THE INDIANS' plans to Jamie. He nodded. The awkwardness returned—the awkwardness that had settled between them ever since he'd seen the baby.

"She's not mine." Susanna wished they had time to talk; there was so much to say.

His eyebrows lifted.

"An orphan." She had only a moment; they were leaving. "I couldn't let her die."

His gray-blue eyes regarded her. A wealth of unspoken emotion flowed over his face and settled into a soft smile. "I'm that glad to see ye safe."

Those simple words conveyed a wealth of meaning. By now it was clear her ransom was not the reason for his arrival. But it was obvious he rejoiced to see her, and not just for translation. She busied herself with Living Water, getting her fastened into her cradleboard. Inexplicably, her eyes filled with tears. "I'm that glad to see you too."

She mounted Whiskey and directed the mare after the others. Her heart yearned for the man known to the Shawnee as White Beaver, but she saw no clear path forward for them. She was a captive, despite her adoption.

The next day Dark Water was short with her. "We've planting to do." She thrust a sack of seed corn into her hands.

Susanna went to their field and hung Living Water's cradleboard on a nearby tree. The crumbly brown loam comforted her as she turned over the events of the past two days in her mind. Translating the Scriptures into Shawnee flooded her with joy. Even Buffalo Robe, despite his initial scowls, was listening.

Four ... five ... six ... She smoothed soil over the seeds and moved on to the next hillock. And the next.

Jamie ... The thought of him wearing the satchel she'd made, with the purple hemp strap, caused her chest and throat to ache. His features were so familiar, so dear—but different, too. He was a man full grown. It wasn't just the muscular roll of his shoulders under his linen shirt. The letters they'd exchanged had given her glimpses of his heart. A great heart. A tender heart.

Living Water hummed and fussed. Susanna stood, wishing she'd brought water. She decided to take the baby back to the wigwam and nurse her, then fill a gourd before returning to finish the planting.

Red Hawk and Straight Arrow emerged from the foliage cloaking the river. Susanna didn't understand all the Shawnee purification rituals, but often a sweat lodge and running water were involved. Major hunting trips required spiritual preparation.

She headed for the wigwam and halted. There was a man standing next to it. Dark Water approached him and said something, but the man ignored her.

Susanna recognized him. *Laughing Wolf.* What did he want?

He disappeared inside. Red Hawk and Straight Arrow were making their way back; they still hadn't noticed the man.

She circled and headed toward She-Who-Sing's dwelling to stay out of Laughing Wolf's line of sight.

Laughing Wolf emerged from the wigwam with an object in his hand. Red Hawk and Straight Arrow strolled up to him.

"More trouble," said Buffalo Robe, from over her shoulder.

She glanced at him. His skin fairly steamed from the sweat lodge.

"What is this?" Laughing Wolf's words were clearly audible. "White man's medicine?"

Now Susanna could see the object he held. *The Bible.* The Bible Red Hawk had showed her. She swallowed.

Wetness gleamed from his bare chest as Red Hawk stood silently, rigid. Straight Arrow muttered something in his ear.

Laughing Wolf chuckled as he tore out a page from the Bible and tossed it aside. "Why trouble yourself? Look! White man's medicine is weak."

Rip. Rip. Rip.

A naked child ran up and grabbed for the papers, hooting.

"Children's toys." Finished, Laughing Wolf flung the leather cover at Red Hawk, who caught it reflexively.

Susanna tensed. Still Red Hawk did nothing. A white man wouldn't have taken such abuse. But aside from the rippling of his jaw, she could discern no reaction on his part.

Behind her, Buffalo Robe spat on the ground and uttered a soft imprecation she couldn't translate.

What would happen now?

~

RED HAWK CLENCHED his jaw and strode ahead of Straight Arrow. A black birch sapling smote his face and neck with its branches. Irritated, he wheeled on one foot and halted, waiting for the others. Su-anna brought up the rear on the mare.

"I have an idea," Straight Arrow said. "We can capture White Beaver and adopt him."

Capture? "He is here of his own free will," Red Hawk said.

"Just so. He might be agreeable. Then Laughing Wolf would have no choice."

"If the rest accept him."

Buffalo Robe said, "Many still remember the treachery in Penn's Village."

They all did. "There is more at stake here than just White Beaver," Red Hawk said. Laughing Wolf's actions had troubled even Grandmother, who was normally imperturbable. "We must consult Big Turtle."

"What do you mean, treachery?" Su-anna asked.

Red Hawk told her about Grayfeather's murder. She paled and was silent the rest of the trek to the meeting place.

As soon as they arrived, Su-anna translated their plan to find another place a few miles away.

"We are too close to the village," Red Hawk said.

White Beaver made no comment but merely packed the mules and followed them south. The country was hilly, but pleasant, and soon they found a clearing next to a broad stream that seemed suitable for their purposes.

After some consultation, they decided to set out snares. Su-anna must have translated their discussion, for White Beaver approached them with iron objects in his arms.

"Traps," Su-anna translated.

Red Hawk fingered the metal devices. Yes, these would be easier—and quicker—to set up than their own versions. He wanted to return quickly and hear more about Creator-Who-Saves. "Thank you."

JAMES LED Gunner to a grassy patch, hobbled him, and scrounged up twigs for a fire. The Indians had left them alone here as they set up their snares, and they didn't seem to worry about Susanna escaping. Maybe it was because she'd be hampered by the baby.

"Red Hawk's grandfather, their sachem, was murdered," Susanna said.

He turned. "Murdered?"

"If I understand correctly, a delegation of Shawnee went to Philadelphia. They were killed." A line appeared between her brows. "I am not sure when."

"The first big Shawnee raid was when—just after Braddock's defeat?"

"Yes." She moved to the mare and stroked her neck. "This is Colonel Patton's horse."

He stared at the animal. "Are you sure?" Of course she was sure. She was John Russell's daughter and knew her way around horses.

"This is Whiskey, out of Cricket."

"Red Hawk killed James Patton?"

"No." She told him the details.

Squatting over his small pile of twigs and tinder, he struck sparks from his flint and steel and chewed over the information. A tiny wisp of smoke rose. "I see they have more motives than just some alliance with the French."

"Have you a skillet? I can bake some cornbread."

He handed her the cookware and a bag of meal.

"I'm not excusing them. Some of—"

"No, I understand. It makes me want to weep to hear it. They live in darkness without the gospel, and then white men, who live with the privileges of gospel preaching, treat them in such a manner ... why ..." His throat tightened.

Susanna placed the trivet over the fire. "Some men walk perversely even having heard gospel preaching. Like Simon McKee. The Shawnee ..." She paused in her work, shoulders slumping. "They are in bondage to spirits, like the wolf. It makes my heart ache."

As she scooped out the cornmeal, she told a strange story about a wolf attack. "And that's how I came to be Living Water's mother."

Oh Lord, help me to minister to these people.

"THE FIFTH WORD-TO-BE-OBEYED is to honor your father and mother," Susanna translated, wondering how the Ten Commandments compared to Shawnee customs.

"I want to hear more about Creator-Who-Saves," Red Hawk interrupted.

Jamie nodded. Holding his place, he flipped to the New Testament, and Susanna struggled to translate the verse from Galatians. "The Words-to-be-Obeyed are a guardian to bring us to the Anointed One, Creator-Who-Saves."

Red Hawk frowned but said nothing.

Jamie returned to the Old Testament. When she translated the injunction against murder, Straight Arrow raised his brows. "It is an honorable thing to kill in battle."

"Yes," Jamie replied. "I have carried a weapon into battle."

The Indians straightened.

"To defend one's family is not murder. There is no malice."

Susanna had to consult with Red Hawk to translate malice. Jamie was beginning to make things easier for her, using words with concrete meanings, but it wasn't always possible. They continued the discussion, and finally Straight Arrow was satisfied, though he remained thoughtful.

When they reached the tenth commandment, the baby fussed, and she lifted her out of the cradleboard.

"If I desire a white man's horse, it is wrong, even if I do not steal it?" Buffalo Robe asked.

"You may admire Red Hawk's mare. That is different from a strong desire to possess it yourself. Covetousness is at the heart of stealing."

Susanna translated the discussion while replacing the moss in Living Water's clout.

"How does this bring us to Creator-Who-Saves?" Red Hawk asked.

Jamie looked at each of them in turn. "These are the Creator's words. If we have broken them, we need one to save, to give an offering. My question to you is, have you broken these words? Do you need Creator-Who-Saves to step in the middle between you and an angry Creator?"

Silence fell in the clearing. Straight Arrow was the first to speak. "I have not obeyed the words. I killed a man who was not my enemy."

He untied something from his belt and held it out for everyone to see.

A scalp. Arch May's scalp.

41

> Visited the Indians for the past four days. The weather was cold and snowy. Was wet for the entire time but that is a small price to pay for the privilege of taking the Gospel to them.
>
> —John Eliot (1604-1690)

Buffalo Robe jumped to his feet. "But that is a mark of his courage!"

Red Hawk glanced at Su-anna. She was comforting the baby, who'd chosen this moment to fuss. Su-anna's face was drawn. The man Straight Arrow had killed was a friend or relative.

White Beaver, on the other hand, seemed unperturbed as he stared at the scalp, a flap of skin covered with gray hair. It was an old man's scalp. It didn't take much courage to kill an old man.

"I attacked this man." Straight Arrow ran his hand over his own thick hair. "I endangered his soul for the sake of a prize."

Su-anna blinked rapidly, then translated the comment. There followed a discussion between Su-anna and White Beaver.

White Beaver addressed Red Hawk. "What does he mean? The scalp has power?"

"Yes. A person's hair is sacred. To scalp a person is an indignity that reaches beyond this world."

White Beaver turned to Straight Arrow. "Do not be troubled on this account. The man you killed was a follower of Creator-Who-Saves. Scalping did not harm his soul. His life is safe with the Anointed One."

Even Buffalo Robe stilled at this pronouncement. White Beaver's words were radical. Could the people of the village accept them?

"How can we be sure of the Creator's words? Can we have a book made in our tongue?" Red Hawk asked.

To his surprise, White Beaver smiled. He wiped one eye before he spoke.

"It will take many days," Su-anna translated, her face shining. "But we can begin such a thing soon."

Straight Arrow toyed with a twig. "But my heart is disturbed. What offering can I make to the family, and what do I do with the man's scalp?"

White Beaver flipped through the book. "Stealing is easy to repay. Killing is another matter. And there are different kinds of killing."

Red Hawk easily followed the discussion. Malice marked true murder.

"Did you consider yourself to be at war with the men of this place?"

"Yes."

"If your heart is troubled, I recommend you arrange to have the scalp returned for burial."

Straight Arrow hung on White Beaver's words. "And I will give tobacco."

"Let me tell you the story of a mighty warrior who followed the Creator and was guilty of a worse crime."

In the fading light of sunset, White Beaver read to them, and when it was dark, he continued the story from memory.

~

Over the next few days, Susanna struggled to cook and keep the baby happy while translating almost nonstop. The only respite was in the early morning, when the Indians went out to check the traps and hunt. Every day they brought back something—a raccoon from the traps, or a turkey brought down by an arrow.

On the third morning of the supposed hunting trip Susanna toyed with the idea of baking bridies, but a simple meat pie in the iron skillet would be easier. It seemed odd at first to bake familiar valley food dressed in her Shawnee garb. But this jarring strangeness soon resolved into harmony, she and Jamie sharing a world of their own, neither Indian nor white, only Christian. She treasured these moments with him.

Jamie approached with an armful of branches for the fire. "D'ye think they'd understand penal substitution?"

"Penal—paying the penalty?"

He nodded, and Susanna's mind flashed back to a day when she'd resolved never to marry a minister. The reasons escaped her. Sitting here discussing theology with Jamie seemed as natural as breathing. With his warm gaze upon her, she marveled that a man, educated as he was, cared what she thought.

"Probably. Turning away wrath—propitiation—is an easier concept for them. But I think they have consequences for wrongdoing, too, though not on the scale or to the degree we do. Nothing is written down, and they don't have magistrates in the sense we do, only a sachem—a spiritual leader or wise man—to guide them."

"How about murder?"

"Remember Silas Sloan? Da always said the killing was not random, that it was their form of justice, a life for a life."

"The Scriptures mention the avenger of blood. It is an old custom."

Jamie helped her build up the fire and went for more water. He filled the kettle and set it on the trivet. "Would you like tea?"

"You have tea? Real tea?"

An awkward smile lit his face. "Bohea."

Susanna mixed dough for the meat pie while they waited for the water to heat. Jamie seemed restless.

Finally, he spoke. "Susanna ..." He didn't meet her gaze. "I dinna ken how to ask this. Maybe 'tis not the time or place." He looked up. "I think I have your father's blessing."

"Jamie." Her heart filled with emotion. *Her father's blessing* ... she wished her parents were here. "The only obstacle is that I am Shawnee in their eyes and you are not."

"Obstacle ... to marriage?"

It was her turn to look away. "Yes."

The kettle began to whistle.

Somehow they'd find a way. "Yes, Jamie, I will marry you."

COLD WATER STRUCK Red Hawk's ankles, but his feet were slower to feel it, reminding him he should have taken off his moccasins before stepping into the stream. Dark Water pestered him every time he came home with moccasins or jacket half-ruined. The special pair Grandmother had made him, painstakingly decorated with wampum and porcupine quills, he reserved for the festivals.

The mare followed him willingly, and the sound of tiny splashes marked the progress of the others behind her. Cloaking their trail by entering a stream or river came naturally, almost as a habit, but this time a dark cloud hovered at the edge of Red Hawk's consciousness. Laughing Wolf.

The water gambit would not fool a good tracker. Not if he were determined. And they were not going far, just to the old beaver dam they'd discovered the morning after their arrival. The beaver were long dead, but the remnants of their diligence sufficed to slow the flow of water and form an eddying pool.

Straight Arrow was going to be immersed. When White Beaver had described the ritual, Red Hawk had seen the significance instantly.

What he was slower to grapple with was the death and coming-to-life-again of Creator-Who-Saves.

It seemed obvious that He-Who-Creates-By-Thinking could not be held by death. And the meaning of the death itself he could grasp. But the implications were shattering.

White Beaver had said, "His death cuts a trail to the Creator. The perfection of the Son is given to His people. Our Creator becomes our Father."

Our Father. A knowable being. This shook Red Hawk to the core.

He led the mare up onto the bank.

Buffalo Robe was the first to join him. "This ritual could be a problem."

"White Beaver does not ask us to give up our ways."

"But consider. To follow Creator-Who-Saves means we will not follow what the medicine bundle speaks. It will cause division."

Red Hawk turned. "You speak truth. But we have known this all along. Laughing Wolf will be the first to condemn us, just for listening to this man. And he will not be the only one."

It was a serious decision to follow Creator-Who-Saves. And that was another reason he would not go into the water—not just yet. What would happen to Dark Water? And Grandmother?

They skirted several silver maples, and the trees thinned out. Between the narrow trunks of saplings they could see the old beaver dam; the animals' industry had thinned the woods nearby and created a modest clearing, where grasses grew lush beyond the cattails lining the bank. Shafts of sunlight invited them.

Red Hawk led the mare to a good patch of grass and tied her. The others did likewise. On the opposite bank White Beaver spoke to Straight Arrow; Su-anna translated nearby, but from this distance, the two men merely appeared to be engrossed in each other's words.

White Beaver placed a hand on Straight Arrow's shoulder and glanced up at the others. "Let us pray."

Red Hawk's heart joined in the prayer, marveling once again that the Creator would hear a man.

The ceremony was surprisingly short. White Beaver and Straight Arrow entered the pool.

"Buried with him ... rise to walk in newness of life."

White Beaver plunged Straight Arrow under the surface; he came up again, water sluicing off his body. Straight Arrow climbed the bank, face radiant.

Newness of life. Life from death, just as Creator-Who-Saves rose again. Yes, he wanted this life. The conviction rushed through him. He would—

A whisper of rustling foliage interrupted his thoughts. Red Hawk turned.

Partially hidden by the silver maples, Laughing Wolf's form loomed like a specter. He slipped around the low-hanging boughs and advanced into the clearing, his greased limbs gleaming in the dappled sunlight. The curve of his bow rose over one shoulder.

Laughing Wolf surveyed the scene and then settled his gaze on White Beaver. "A white man?" One finger touched the shaft of his tomahawk.

Red Hawk's throat felt dry. "He brings truth from the Creator."

"White man's truth. White man's religion. Or, perhaps that is what you want, to become one of them?"

Red Hawk was conscious of the soft murmur of Su-anna's translation. White Beaver's expression was still, his gaze fixed on Laughing Wolf. Still dripping from the ritual, Straight Arrow frowned.

Red Hawk fisted his hands. "The man is our captive." How long had Laughing Wolf been watching?

"I doubt that. Is Straight Arrow now a white man?"

So he had seen.

Buffalo Robe growled in his throat.

Laughing Wolf took the bow off his shoulder and plucked several arrows from his quiver.

~

WHAT HAPPENED NEXT HAPPENED QUICKLY, but later, when Susanna turned the event over in her mind, everything seemed to occur slowly, as if the participants were underwater.

She'd never been on a hunting trip, never seen the speed and ease with which an Indian could loose arrows from a bow. Laughing Wolf's motions flowed together, faster than her eye could follow. He grasped the bow, and then—

At her side, Straight Arrow lunged in front of Jamie.

Thwang! Thwang!

Grunting, Straight Arrow fell across Jamie. Crimson welled from the shafts of several arrows buried in the Indian's chest.

She wished to kneel and help him, but Laughing Wolf was wading across the stream, tomahawk in hand. Her limbs were locked in place.

Thwang!

Laughing Wolf gained the bank and halted, surprise and dismay on his face. The expression remained frozen as he tumbled to the ground, limbs at all angles, an arrow protruding from his neck.

Buffalo Robe stood unmoving, bow in hand, staring at Laughing Wolf, whose life quickly faded. Soon the limbs ceased their twitching.

Red Hawk squatted beside Straight Arrow, whose head was in Jamie's lap. Blood welled over Red Hawk's hands as he sought to explore the wounds and remove the arrows. Straight Arrow's eyes were glassy, and his lips moved. Susanna knelt at his other side.

Tears poured down Jamie's face.

"Don't weep ... for me." Straight Arrow's face brightened. His body shuddered once, and he lay still.

The forest seemed to hold its breath. A pale blue butterfly flitted nearby as Jamie closed Straight Arrow's eyes.

Then time resumed its course, and grief flooded her. With a sob, she knelt and curled over the body. After a few moments Jamie eased her up and placed his arm around her.

Red Hawk and Buffalo Robe were conversing. She blinked. She needed to translate.

"Elk Tooth will wish to avenge himself," Buffalo Robe said.

"That is for the elders to decide," Red Hawk said. "We will bring back the body of Straight Arrow as evidence. Those are Laughing Wolf's arrows."

Red Hawk sounded confident. But Buffalo Robe simply stared at Laughing Wolf's still form.

"Look," Red Hawk said, "the worst that can happen is they will exile you. We will travel west. As far as the meadow lands, if necessary."

Jamie rose and helped Susanna to her feet. "I am willing to face the elders. To run the gauntlet. And I will hunt for Straight Arrow's widow."

Buffalo Robe's expression lightened. "The elders will approve. And if Elk Tooth troubles you, I pledge my life for yours."

Living Water cried, and Susanna pulled herself out of her shock. She tended the baby as the men talked.

She took a deep breath. Laughing Wolf was dead. How could she take joy in death? And yet, it all seemed right somehow.

A bird twittered from the silver maples, and a deep sense of calm comforted her heart. *Thank you, Lord. Thank you for Jamie's life.*

EPILOGUE

They were yet hungry and thirsty for the Word of God, and appeared unwearied in their attendance upon it.

—*The Journal of David Brainerd*

Kanawha River, April 1760

Red Hawk tasted the rock he'd chiseled from the outcrop. The salt was good and would be easy to boil down. He thrust the chunk into his bag and slung it over his shoulder. The salt lick drew a plethora of game, judging by the tracks—deer, elk, and buffalo. Salt for trading and food for his family. A blessing from heaven.

He wended his way back, hopping from stone to stone along the riverbank. The day was bright, the spring chill refreshing. He paused on a stone and drank in the beauty of the land. Color throbbed from the hills, and his heart ached with joy. The whole world seemed new, and it wasn't just the turn of the seasons.

There was only one thing that troubled his nights. But maybe the Creator would answer his prayers even in that.

The previous day Red Hawk had spoken to White Beaver of this and that. "Should Shawnee men work in the fields like women?" White men did, but Red Hawk thought it unmanly. Inappropriate, somehow.

"What do you think?" White Beaver would never be as fluent in Shawnee as Su-sanna, but after three years, the man could make himself understood.

"I certainly would, if Dark Water was sick, and the corn would spoil otherwise." Red Hawk pulled out his pipe from his satchel.

"When the Scriptures are silent, love is our guide. And our conscience."

He grunted agreement, filling the pipe bowl with his father's favorite tobacco blend. These questions were easy compared to the greater question in Red Hawk's heart.

"You have spoken of your desire for a wife." White Beaver's hands turned the wood about. A deep hollow marked it as a cup. "Before I came here, I met a man with a Catawba wife. His daughter is of an age to marry."

"But the Catawba—"

"Are your enemies, I know." The knife worked to enlarge the cup's interior. "Think about it. This woman will not be accepted by the Catawba. She is half white, and she follows Creator-Who-Saves. But right now, the situation is even worse among white men. According to the letters we've received, your people are shot on sight. Despised."

"Does this woman know of me? Would she marry a Shawnee?" He frowned. "Does she know our ways?"

"Her mother plants corn and tans hides in the way of her people. I have written her father."

"What has he said?" Writing had turned out to be even more powerful than he'd hoped. Already short excerpts of the Creator's book had been written down on finely scraped doeskin, in his own language. "She speaks your tongue?"

"Yes. She is coming. With the Uchee trader."

Red Hawk's mouth fell open. They were expecting the trader any day now. "But what if—"

White Beaver chuckled. "She can help my wife until you have proved your worth as a husband."

He took a firm pull of his pipe and choked. "I-I do not know what to say."

Smiling at the memory, Red Hawk stepped around the mountain laurel marking the last landmark before the village.

If you could call it a village. Five structures nestled together in the narrow clearing along the river; the women's cornfields lay downstream, ready for spring planting. The hills on either side were full of game. They hadn't had to move to the western meadowlands after all. Even Elk Tooth hadn't caused any problems, claiming to bow to the will of the Creator.

Ironically, it was Big Turtle who'd forced their departure after consulting with the medicine bundle. They hadn't gone alone—even Dark Water had huffed at Big Turtle's pronouncement, saying she wouldn't allow her nephew to go without corn. Grandmother listened to White Beaver's words but kept her thoughts to herself.

A few others had joined them. The biggest surprise was She-Who-Sings, who not only joined Buffalo Robe in his exile but also attended to the words of the book. She threw many objections at White Beaver, even more than Buffalo Robe had, but in the end she grew silent. After many moons she began to smile. She still had not gone into the water, but something was happening, perhaps the same thing that had happened to Red Hawk's heart.

But there was no one for him to marry. He was Shawnee, and had never stopped being Shawnee, but some did not see it that way. To some—no, to many—to follow Creator-Who-Saves was to become a white man. Except for the members of this tiny settlement, he walked alone.

Could it be Creator-Who-Saves would bless him with a wife?

AT THE EDGE of the field, Susanna took a deep breath. The trees were beginning to leaf out, and the air smelled of new life.

"How do we know it's time to plant?" Living Water asked.

"When the hickory leaves are as big as a squirrel's ear." Her daughter was too young to be of any true help, but it was never too early to learn. She remembered herself at that age, sitting next to Mother and stabbing a needle into cloth. Her stitches had been preserved in one of the cabin's curtains. Horrendous.

She knelt beside the first of the mounds, prepared for the seeds. "We plant the corn here on top. It is the first of the three sisters."

Living Water thrust her hands cheerfully into the dirt. Susanna's father had tried the Indian method, as did some others, but he'd finally settled on crop rotation. Barley, peas, corn. And now hemp, of course. A few letters had made their way here, full of good news. The raids had diminished. Her new brother Willie was a healthy toddler. And Ian MacLeod had made a profession of faith in Christ. Thinking of the worn, well-read missives, an unexpected wave of homesickness rolled over her heart.

Susanna stood and shook off her malaise. There was so much to be thankful for. She ran her hand over her belly. She would tell Jamie soon. She was sure now. If only Mother could be here. But Clara King would be coming, and perhaps she'd be able to help, at least in the field and herb garden. In another five months, Susanna would not be able to do much.

The Uchee trader was due any day. Would her father be coming? He hadn't made any promises. In fact, she almost wished he wouldn't. It was dangerous. True, the French had been pushed back and Fort Duquesne taken by General Forbes, but the Indians were less predictable. The raids had stirred a lingering hatred on both sides.

"Time to fix dinner." She held out her hand to the child and they returned to the wigwam to finish assembling a stew. Dark Water had helped her to build the rectangular structure, as big as many of the cabins in the valley but not quite as high. Jamie had provided trimmed saplings for the poles, but the Indians regarded the actual construction as a female activity. Her shoulders had ached for days.

She paused in front of the bark-and-thatch-covered house. Beyond the other wigwams, the dark green of a hemlock stood sentinel next to the path to the old village. A low-hanging branch shuddered.

Someone was there. The Uchee trader. His mules emerged into view, laden as they always were. Then behind him, a familiar steel-gray pony.

"Living Water, come." Susanna said in English. "'Tis George, the trader."

A woman rode the pony. Behind her was a man on horseback.

Susanna's stomach dropped. *Da?*

John Russell dismounted and assisted the young woman down from the pony.

Then he turned.

"Da!" Susanna released Living Water's hand and ran to meet him.

"Susanna?" Her father's voice cracked.

He held out his arms and she rushed into his embrace.

"Oh, Da, I hoped you would come, but I was afraid ..." She buried her face against his leather hunting jacket. He smelled of sweat, pennyroyal, and horse.

He hummed in his throat, then cleared it. "Aye, it's dangerous, I'll grant ye that. But the raids have stopped."

"Truly?"

He nodded. "I've brought ye Rosemary. She'll foal in six weeks or so."

She released him. "Thank you." Behind her pony a mule stood heavy-laden. With wheat flour she could make bridies and scones—not that it was important, but it cheered her immensely to see the supplies.

"Who's that man?" Living Water asked in Shawnee.

"My father."

Jamie joined them and scooped up the little girl in his arms. "Mr. Russell, this is our adopted daughter. Her Shawnee name means Living Water."

Her father's eyes shone. "I'm that pleased to meet you. Ye may call me Grandda."

Susanna blinked several times, her throat tight.

"May I introduce Miss Clara King?" Her father said.

The woman—girl, really—stood to one side, her hands clasped. She wore Indian garb, but her appearance was ordinary, with dark eyes and hair like her own. The Kings' daughter was half Catawba, but she wouldn't have drawn comment dressed like a white woman. Not in the valley. But here, among strangers, she must feel awkward.

"Miss King? I am Susanna Paxton." *Paxton.* Even after all this time, the name felt strange. Da's eyebrow jerked at the sound of it. "You may call me Susanna."

"Thank you."

Wearing a red trade shirt, Red Hawk stood several yards away. His gaze was fastened on the young woman, his lips parted slightly.

Susanna smiled to herself. Red Hawk never wore shirts.

THE GLOW of sunset painted the sky above the hills gold and orange as the inhabitants of the village talked with George Morgan and John Russell around the fire. James straightened his leg to ease it. He rarely sat Indian-style; his leg didn't forgive him when he did. At his side, Susanna translated.

"Silas Sloan's belongings." Susanna's father handed a canvas parcel to Red Hawk.

Red Hawk's gaze had never left Russell's face as he described Silas Sloan, his conversion, and his death. Now his son turned over in his hands the few relics left behind: a shaving razor, flint and steel, and a corncob pipe.

"Thank you. I will smoke with this pipe and honor my white father." A line appeared between his brows. "I have a favor to ask."

Red Hawk rose easily to his feet and strode to a patch of grass where the animals were tethered. He led out Whiskey from the others. "I stole this animal and must restore."

Russell was on his feet, staring. "I ken this horse." He glanced Susanna's way. "Ye wrote me about Patton's mare."

James had known of Red Hawk's intention, but his heart seized up anyway. Some Shawnee customs were good and right—they always shared whatever food they had. But other ideas, harmful ones, were entrenched in their minds, so much so that sometimes he despaired of seeing true repentance. Yet here it was. *Thank you, Lord.*

"Wolf Killer—" the Shawnee couldn't pronounce the first letter of Russell's name—"will you honor me by returning this animal to Silver Beard's family?"

Susanna translated, including their name for him.

A sober smile crept across Russell's face. "Aye, it would be my honor to do so."

John Russell would also be returning Arch May's scalp to his widow. Superstitions regarding the spirit realm had been harder to deal with. Red Hawk and Buffalo Robe acknowledged the preeminence of Christ over the spirit realm, but only last year had they killed wolves without fear. At least, they had acted unafraid.

Russell sat down again, and James studied the man's face in the firelight. Susanna had been so glad to see him. It shouldn't be alarming—he was her father, after all. How long had it been?

And yet, a thread of worry tugged at him. Would she want to return? No, surely not. Their marriage was irregular, but then, many marriages in the valley were not sanctioned by the Church of England.

A voice piped up from beyond the circle of the men. "I don't want to go." Sammy Wilkins spoke in Shawnee, protesting his return to his white family. Captives in the Ohio territory were being returned as well; James wondered how many scenes there were like this. It had taken months for the lad to even consider going back, and still he fought.

"You will go and learn the book," She-Who-Sings said from the shadows. She couldn't be looking forward to the lad's departure, but she was insistent on a white man's education. Perhaps it was just an excuse to hide her grief.

"Ho, lad, I'll need ye to help me with the horses," Russell said.

A beat of silence followed.

"Can I ride one?" Sammy asked in English, finally.

"Ye surely may."

With that, the conversation turned to the war.

"Quebec fell last year to the forces under General Wolfe, who lost his life, sadly." Russell crossed his arms over his knees. "There's still fighting overseas, but the battle here has been won. Only a matter of time before a treaty is signed."

James thought back to that day in Russell's home when they'd looked at the geography book and seen the long arm of the French. But now their strongholds were taken.

Red Hawk spoke. "If the French leave, will the Long Knives come here?"

The fire popped and sparks flew upward.

Russell sighed. "The Crown has always tried to keep the peace with treaties." He paused. "But I would not put my faith in their words." His gaze tracked the hills, shadowed beneath the faint gray of twilight. "White men have already surveyed land past the Alleghenies."

Susanna translated, and the Indians grew still.

"I saw the chain-men in my youth," Red Hawk said.

Buffalo Robe gestured with his pipe. "If we follow Creator-Who-Saves, does that mean we cannot go on the warpath against them? Are we to allow them to slaughter us?"

The discussion that followed reminded James of a theological conversation with Mr. Craig. But the atmosphere was tense.

"I canna tell ye what ye must do in every case," Russell concluded. "But peace is to be treasured and esteemed over war. If ye can find a way to live in peace, ye must do so."

"Those were Grayfeather's words," Red Hawk said, and the rest murmured agreement.

Later, after the men dispersed, Susanna fixed a pallet for Miss King in the rear of their wigwam, near Living Water's sleeping place, and soon her soft snores revealed the young woman's fatigue. James banked the fire.

"Thank you, Susanna. I appreciate the labor of translation." Why did he feel so awkward?

She shrugged. "I'm especially proud of Buffalo Robe's achievement."

"Aye." The man had written a simple letter that would go with Russell on his departure, on its long journey to the man's father in Richmond. Most of the Indians now knew at least a few words of English, and Red Hawk was learning to write Shawnee. Buffalo Robe could write a little in both languages.

"You're quite fluent yourself, you know." She shifted closer. "I gave Da our marriage contract to take to Mr. Craig."

His doubts fled. "'Tis no' necessary, we are married before God and the Shawnee. But I would love to see the minister's face when he sees a contract on doeskin."

Susanna chuckled, but then she quieted. "Jamie. I have something to tell you."

"Oh?"

"When the chestnuts are ripe, you will be a father."

His throat tightened and for a moment he could not speak. "Oh, *dautie*. I do so love you."

He breathed a prayer of thanksgiving. *Oh, Lord, thou hast done all things well.*

AFTERWORD

Thank you! If you enjoyed my story, please write a review on Goodreads, Bookbub, or wherever you purchased this book. Reviews are the lifeblood of a writer, and we appreciate every single one!

For writing updates or to contact me, go to my website.

David Brainerd's converts among the Lenni Lenape (Delaware) remained steadfast, so much so that a traveler to some of their villages a century later found grandchildren of the original believers continuing strong in the faith. However, early missionaries to the Shawnee were typically rebuffed. It wasn't until many years after the time of my story, in 1836, that a Shawnee translation of the Gospel of Matthew was printed. My character James Paxton is totally fictional, and yet, who knows? Did the numerous captives taken during the mid 1700s, some of whom must have been Christians, have an impact on their captors? Only the Lord knows.

Bringing 18th century Shawnee characters to life was a challenge. I chose to simplify their theology, omitting the "Grandmother" tribal deity in favor of a flesh-and-blood wise woman. Typically they ignored the "Good God" or "Creator" in favor of personal or tribal spirits. One captive account gives great detail about a Wyandot individual who possessed great faith in the Creator's care, seeming to trust every aspect of his life to God, and it's conceivable that some Shawnee felt this way too. The heavenly bodies were acknowledged, though this may have varied from person to person and from tribe to tribe. There is archeological evidence of sun worship among the Muskogee Creeks.

Laughing Wolf's experience that resulted in his challenge to reject anything to do with the white man is based on the real-life event in the life of Tecumseh's brother, known as the "Prophet."

Braddock's Defeat, the slaughter of the Shawnee chiefs, and Draper's Meadow Massacre, in which Colonel Patton was killed, were real-life events. The raid at Woodstock really happened as described, and it was that event that spurred me to create a Shawnee character. I was frankly horrified at the description of torture, and knew that any story set during this time period would cause Native Americans to look positively inhuman unless I could craft their story, their point-of-view.

The discovery of the killing of the Shawnee emissaries brought a number of things into focus for me. There were very real, very human motives for the attacks on the settlers, and without excusing evil, we may at least better understand the wrongs on both sides.

I apologize in advance for any unintentional errors or shortcomings regarding the Shawnee or any other topic touched upon in the story (let me know about them, please). Students of all things Jeffersonian may have noticed that he's a tad older than he ought to be. This was on purpose. In *The Shenandoah Road,* the first book in the series, I established that John Russell was acquainted with Peter Jefferson. Susanna and Tom were playmates. But I realized that he would have been too young to escort her to the governor's gala if I didn't tweak things a bit. Please forgive my cheating! The green velvet coat was real, however.

The Great Awakening revived existing churches and multiplied the numbers of Baptists and "Methodists," those who were converted under George Whitefield's preaching and retained the basic doctrine of the Church of England. Baptists were classified as dissenters in the colonies, and often met with persecution of various types. In New

England they were fined. In Virginia Baptist preachers were beaten, fined, and occasionally jailed. In his old age, Thomas Jefferson viewed his greatest lifetime achievement as the crafting of the Statute of Virginia for Religious Freedom, written in 1777 and passed in 1786. The freedoms we take for granted today were slow in coming, even in colonial America. May we give thanks for them, remembering the pioneers who suffered.

Excerpt from Book three of the Russells series, *A Fallen Sparrow: A Novel of the American Revolution.*

> Let me observe, how fatal are the effects, of posting a standing army among a free people!
>
> —Samuel Adams, December 10, 1770

July 1771

The sun beat down on the back of his regimental uniform as Lieutenant Robert Shirley approached Ashby Castle, his mare trotting smoothly beneath him despite the long hours on the road. She had proven to be a good mount, worth every penny he'd paid Richard Tattersall.

Leicestershire was square in the middle of nowhere, but it was a beautiful nowhere. Lambs gamboled near their dams on green rolling hills; stands of oak and beech marked gurgling streams. It was the place of his youth. And it was the Shirley family seat, and no matter how the Shirleys might be whispered about in London, this place was still home.

His godmother had summoned him, and he had no idea why. Especially since his commanding officer had given him extended leave as a result. It was unheard of. The Countess of Huntingdon had a certain fame, but only in religious circles. How she could influence a colonel he had no clue.

The castle ruins loomed before him, and Robert guided his horse around the skeleton of the tower, slowing her to a walk. Beside his commission, the mare was the only property he had left; he would not push her past her limits.

Ashby Place came into view, a picturesque manor, the only part of the estate that had been maintained—and that just barely. Ivy crawled over weathered gray stone, and several rose bushes extended unpruned branches in riotous color.

A groom emerged from the stable. Robert dismounted and entrusted the mare to the young man before climbing the steps. Almost before he'd finished knocking, Grayson opened the door.

The butler looked the same every time he came, though today, as Robert followed the man through the hall, the butler's gait seemed slower than before, his stride more halting.

Robert glanced to the left, where a double door opened upon a large drawing room.

It was empty, which seemed strangely incongruous. The last time he'd been there, three years before, Mr. Whitefield had preached to a packed room.

The preacher's strange squinty eyes and humble dress had faded away before the dramatic force of his words. Standing against the wall listening, Robert began to understand the drawing power of the minister. And he believed the stories of huge crowds gathering in open fields to hear him speak.

But the magnetic voice left no lasting impression on him. Robert had been baptized in the Church of England and attended services occasionally, as all gentlemen did. That was certainly sufficient for his soul, though if others were benefited by this man's preaching, he welcomed it.

Grayson led him to the back parlor. Sunlight filtered in from a large window framed by aging green drapes; the familiar furnishings were worn but tasteful. A man sat with the countess, a tea table between them. The man wore no wig, but his cravat was fine and edged with lace. Robert stiffened to attention as the butler announced him.

"Come join us, Robert." His godmother's angular face retained a mature beauty, like the charm of the manor itself, ancient and settled. She addressed her companion. "Lord Dartmouth, may I present my godson, who is also a relation on my mother's side. Lieutenant Robert Shirley, the Earl of Dartmouth."

The man's dress, subdued in color but expensive, had already signaled his rank. Robert bowed. "I am honored."

The Earl of Dartmouth possessed warm hazel eyes and a lively mouth. "The biscuits are quite good."

He'd heard of this man, a devout "Methodist," a follower of Whitefield and the other new preachers. Once he'd heard the moniker Psalm Singer applied to him in mockery.

"Sit, Robert," his godmother commanded.

He perched on a faded settee and waited while the countess poured him tea, wondering again why he'd been summoned. His neck was abominably hot underneath his military stock.

She handed him a cup and he took it carefully.

"Countess, what news from Georgia?" The earl asked.

They ignored Robert as he sipped his tea, a strong Bohea. They seemed to be discussing George Whitefield's orphanage.

"The new caretakers have arrived," the countess said.

Listening, Robert gathered that Whitefield's orphanage had been left in his godmother's care. Not a surprise—she'd supported the minister financially while he lived. It seemed her religious work continued after the man's death, both across the Atlantic and in various other places, including a college for ministers. He focused on the tea tray, where biscuits crowded pastries and scones.

His stomach rumbled.

His godmother's dark gaze shifted to him. "Eat, Robert."

"My lady." He snagged a scone and nibbled at it. The house might look neglected, but his godmother had a fine cook. The flaky treat melted in his mouth, a far cry from anything the army had to offer.

He was on a second cup of tea when the conversation turned to him.

"Robert, Lord Dartmouth has a proposal for you."

"My lord?" He hoped he had no crumbs on his face.

Dartmouth put down his cup with a clink. "You have no doubt heard of the unrest in the colonies. And most recently, the unfortunate incident in Boston."

Robert replaced his cup. "The officers of my regiment took note of Captain Preston's situation." The earl's open expression encouraged him to continue. "Of course, there was great sympathy, and some confusion over the legalities."

"Oh?"

"The colonel of my regiment said the man ought to have been tried by a military court," Robert said.

"The colonel is right. But there were political realities to consider," the earl said.

Robert wasn't sure why this was important. In London, unrest was periodically put down, a few lives always lost in the process. Regrettable, but it was life. Peace and order must be maintained. In any case, no harm was done—the Boston court had cleared Preston of murder.

Robert studied the earl's face, remembering that he was Lord North's stepbrother. And a very important man in his own right—he held some kind of ministry post. Why would he take note of a mere lieutenant?

"Political realities are important," the earl continued. "We erred by passing the Stamp Act when we had no idea of how it would affect the common man."

Robert frowned. The citizens of Great Britain were routinely taxed; why the colonies refused a small contribution was beyond him. "My lord."

"I began to cultivate sources of information beside the usual channels. A sea captain, for instance, has regularly supplied me with intelligence."

Intelligence. Belly tensing, Robert nodded in response.

"Your godmother trusts you, and that is why we have summoned you today. You would report only to me."

"My lord—but—"

“”I have contacted your commanding officer. Your commission is now inactive. You are no longer under oath until such time as we deem it best to reinstate you.”

We deem it best ... He had no choice. “A spy? I will spy for you?” It was horrifying. Spying was dirty work. He was a gentleman. Granted, he had no title, but still.

The man’s hazel gaze turned no-nonsense and penetrating. “We are not at war with a foreign power. Our troops merely keep the King’s peace.” The earl reached for a pastry. “Therefore, you will not be a spy, only an observer. Still, there are several reasons for removing you from active duty.” He took a bite, chewed, and swallowed. “For one thing, you will be able to move about without suspicion. We may ask for information leading to the arrest of a ringleader. If you are able to insert yourself into their number, all the better.”

Robert’s mind whirled. He was being ripped from his duty here with the Fifth Regiment and inserted into the melee of Boston political intrigue, a totally unknown world. The parlor itself seemed to waver. “But General Gage? Does he have his own sp—sources?”

Dartmouth paused while the countess handed him another cup of tea. “General Gage uses his own judgment. We have given him considerable leeway in his command. After all, we are three thousand miles away. But consider this, lieutenant. It is clear the inhabitants of Boston hate the soldiers stationed there. How is Gage to gather intelligence? How is he to discover the thinking of the ordinary man? Worse, he will have difficulties discovering the plots of the rebels.”

Discovering the plots of the rebels. This was a serious task. He had only one more card to play, a weak one. “I have a cousin who might be willing to serve in this capacity.”

Lord Dartmouth studied him.

His godmother arched an eyebrow. “Nonsense. Lord Rawdon is too young.” Her voice dripped with what she would not say, that her grandson’s character was deficient. Robert’s cousin was a scapegrace and a follower of the rakehell Banastre Tarleton. Both had been behind him several years at both Harrow and Oxford, and they were notorious for bullying the youngest students. Rawdon's father had washed his hands of him, and his uncle had purchased him a commission.

She was right. There was no escape. "My lord, I am honored to serve King and country."

"Your country thanks you," the earl said dryly, "even if the King remains ignorant of your service. Your godmother brings a quiet honor to the Shirley name—"

Of course, the Earl of Dartmouth knew the ignominious elements of the family history. He'd been at the trial.

"—and you will receive a reward. You will receive your officer's half pay plus a generous stipend. And,"—his face turned friendly again—"I hear you have a mare with good bloodlines."

Robert wrinkled his brow. Horses didn't do well on Atlantic crossings. "Yes, she is a sweet goer. Good disposition."

"Statecraft stands at stud in my stables. I'll house her, and if you wish, breed her while you're away."

Despite Dartmouth's religious interests and modest clothing, he was a wealthy man, and it would not surprise Robert if he bred blooded horses.

"I'd be honored, my lord. I won't need a mount?"

The earl's mouth twitched. "Perhaps, but men are judged by their horses, and your mare will shout that you are not a humble bookbinder."

Robert's mouth fell open. "Bookbinder?" Gentlemen did not labor with their hands.

His godmother had a twinkle in her eye. *She knew?*

"I have arranged it. A discreet master bookbinder at Longman and Sons will teach you the trade, and you'll be ready to depart for Boston early next year."

Robert blinked. "Yes, my lord." What else could he say?

ACKNOWLEDGMENTS

This book would have never seen the light of day without the help and support of many people. I'm blessed to be a part of American Christian Fiction Writers and one of their critique groups. Thanks to Laura Hilton, Linda Strawn, Bob Kaku, Linda Quinn, and Diane Tatum whose critiques helped me greatly. A big thank you to John "Jack" Cunningham, Jr. whose encouraging feedback helped keep me going. I'd also like to mention my sister Susan B. Weir, for helpful comments, as well as Sydney Betts, Karen Bumpus Johnson, Patricia Clark Blake, Douglas Bond, and Tisha Martin.

Aaron "Casey" Walker is my biggest fan, and I asked him if I might name a Baptist minister after him. Christie Jensen gave me archery tips. Thanks to Gail Ostheller and Trudie Cordie, who catch my typos, and I'm grateful for Susan Caruthers Brown, who volunteered to help me with marketing.

I'd also like to remember the ministry of Particular Baptist Press and Terry Wolever, editor. I have in my possession a fine volume of the journal and writings of David Jones, 18th century Baptist minister, one of a number of publications produced as a way of remembering these saints of old. Not long ago I received word that Terry Wolever had gone to be with the Lord. Editing is a lonely, seemingly thankless task, yet the Lord will remember and honor all such as are faithful to what they are called to do.

Finally, I'm thankful for the support of my husband, who tolerates cobwebs in the ceiling longer than he should, because his wife is at the computer. Most of all, I'm thankful to God, whose great grace makes all things possible.

Soli Deo Gloria.

ALSO BY LYNNE BASHAM TAGAWA

Sam Houston's Republic

A Twisted Strand

The Shenandoah Road

Made in United States
Orlando, FL
19 May 2023

33279587R00232